The Hearthstone Mischief

Scott Gesinger

Contents

Chapter 1: Beating Day...1

Chapter 2: Nightmare in Stonecorn Field 17

Chapter 3: Snick and the Copper Coin................................71

Chapter 4: A New Partnership 103

Chapter 5: The Incredible Weapon 129

Chapter 6: Return to the Kingdom of Flamingo 183

Chapter 7: Attack of the Rats..235

Chapter 8: Joseph, Revealed 273

Chapter 9: Death from a Thousand Bites and Other Visions
....301

Chapter 10: The Offer...327

For Melissa, who has always believed in me.

For my Father, who has been my rock.

Please visit www.blackfootedferret.org to learn about the Black-footed Ferret, an endangered species. This unique and wonderful animal needs our help.

Author's Note

This is a fantasy story that doesn't follow many "rules" of fantasy. I avoided many conventions of typical fantasy, and used modern language that fantasy readers are not used to. Staged fights take place in a city park, not a jousting arena, and much of the slang the characters use will sound more twenty-first century than fifteenth. I based the story off a dream, but it evolved into a tale with deep meaning.

I mixed the joy and excitement of youth fantasy stories with harsh realities of war. There are consequences to violence, there is pain, and the heroes are truly afraid of what they must face. This story is both physically and emotionally graphic. It is for people mature enough to appreciate this terrible fact: there are times, no matter how much we hate it, that we must fight and bleed, both as individuals and as a people. As in reality, victory is far from certain and always comes at a cost.

I was in a hotel in Pasco, Washington, when I dreamt the basic storyline for *The Hearthstone Mischief*. I woke up the next morning, called my wife, Melissa, and told her about the dream I had about a ferret and a warrior fighting legions of rats. She said I really needed to write it down; it would make a great story. That day, during breaks from meetings I was hosting, I scribbled down notes and a basic outline. I was travelling a lot for work at the time, and I'd occasionally have a full day of travel, sitting in chairs at airports, restaurants, and planes. I would write for hours at a time, lost in my own world.

As a general rule, I don't show my wife anything I am writing until a solid draft is completed. This was my first novel, and I was nervous. I gave her a printed copy, clamped safely into a three ring binder, and a red pen so she could make notes. When I came home from work she was in class, and I saw she had placed a sticky note in the binder as a book mark. It was pretty far into the book. She had left me a note reading, "Scotty-I am love, love, loving the story so far!" As the wife of an author, she's contractually obligated to love, love, love everything I write. I had that clause added to our wedding vows.

I hope that you enjoy the story and come to love the characters as much as I have. The world you are about to enter has been a pleasure to create.
SG

Chapter 1: Beating Day

1

Gurril Lavoy could feel nervous excitement pulsing through him. His steel and wood war hammer felt warm in his hands, almost like a living creature. Every sound was alive with color, and every color stood brighter than on any other day Gurril could remember. It occurred to Gurril that the red of blood would stand out keenly against the green of the grass. He walked with his fighting hammer (bought for a silver and three coppers from a traveling second-hand weapons dealer) slung over one shoulder into the town park, where a banner reading "Beating Day Competition" hung between two tall oak trees.

He took in a large breath through his nose and pushed it out of his mouth while holding his eyes closed for a moment. When he opened them, he noticed the first of the spectators arriving. He felt his face flush, realizing that there was no going back; people had seen him, and if he retreated now, he might as well resign himself to a life of being taunted, held out of the group, and labeled a coward.

As the first spectators took their seats in the bleachers, they seemed to whisper to each other. He imagined that they whispered about him, what each one of them said, and what they would laugh about when he wasn't looking. They would push him away from anything that would make him fit with any group of them.

Gurril's walk to the park had been like a walk through a deserted land. He felt somehow as if the walk was an act of felony and at any moment people would come out of their homes, point to him, and hiss insults to chase him back home. To admit to anyone that he wanted to be the town warrior would have horridly embarrassed him, yet here he was, waiting to fight. He never had the bravery to admit to another soul that this was what he wanted, and Gurril wondered if he would have the bravery to actually swing his hammer at another human being.

His bowels tied themselves in knots, and he had to keep wiping his hands on his cotton pants to keep them dry from sweat. Each heart beat thumped so hard that the blood pulsing through his arms almost made them flap like the useless wings of a farm chicken. Gurril had to swallow away his fear over and over again, past the hard lump in his throat that seemed to be the center of his physical doubt. Today he faced his dream, his nightmare, and his fate. Everything he wanted, but was afraid to admit to stood before him in time, waiting. He forced himself to stand firm above the grass and below the trees, reminding himself over and over again why he was there.

Beating Day was a very special day in Hearthstone. The village was small and unimportant to everyone else in the world. As a result, only one warrior was needed. To be the town warrior was quite an honor. A portion of the taxes of the village paid for the upkeep of a villa the warrior would live and train in, as well as to provide a handsome salary of ten copper coins a day, two silver coins every two weeks, and a gold coin each month.

To Gurril, however, being the town warrior meant much more: respect. Gurril hoped that this would be the last day anyone teased him for his name, and the last day his mother complained that he could never be as successful as his brother Angus, a rich grain grower with a pretty wife.

Behind Gurril, the village stood quiet in the morning sun, not much more than a huddled group of houses and apartments, a large governing chamber, and a few shops. Beyond the buildings lay the winding river, its docks bustling early with the fishers (both men and women owned boats and ran crews) and a few short wooden grain barges.

In most places, Gurril would have been considered a great prize for any maiden. He was only twenty, his body was solid with muscle, and his handsome face framed light brown eyes that not only matched his hair, but looked as if they were made of lily petals when seen up close. Gurril, however, lived in a village known only for growing wonderful bread grains, and he had a name that lent itself to teasing. His mother had meant his name to be short for "gorilla" but she couldn't spell well, and from his first moments at the village school Gurril was teased for being "Gurril the girl."

Ah, but that was then. Gurril smiled as he thought about what life would be like tomorrow, after the competition. This was, of course, assuming that he lived through the competition.

2

Gurril sized up the other competitors as they paced around the park with him. There was a red-haired fellow named Peter who brought a small sword, an extra-short fat boy of about fifteen who Gurril didn't know, gripping plump paper sack that hid his weapon, a girl named Sheila who brought her hawk named David, and Gurril's best (and only) friend, Coska. Gurril began to plan out his battle strategy for each foe as Coska smiled at Gurril, and Gurril smiled back.

Sheila absolutely strutted, her long, muscular legs brimming with confidence. Her gray eyes and very long blond hair held Gurril's vision. He watched as she moved, her thick, red lips held together as her jaw tensed and relaxed over and over again. Gurril didn't know it, but Sheila had been thrown out of her parents' home when they found out that she planned to compete at Beating Day.

Peter would be tricky to beat, but Gurril thought if he could get up close, he'd be able to womp him with his hammer before Peter could slice at him with his short sword. The fat boy would probably be easy; he looked slow in the head. It would be a shame to beat someone slow-witted, but Gurril knew the rules dictated that each competitor must fight and face a beating.

Sheila and her hawk would be challenging. The large brown bird with yellow eyes looked over each competitor as if planning strategies, and Gurril wondered how much of the situation the hawk understood. Gurril couldn't predict how she would use the animal, and he always had a soft spot in his heart for pets. He hoped he could spare the bird; it was a beautiful specimen, dark brown and handsome. Sheila would also be tricky because he fancied her a bit, and didn't like the thought of fighting her. His eyes kept returning to her full chest, covered by a thin leather top, and he tried to steel himself against any attraction to her.

Finally was Coska. It broke Gurril's heart to see Coska here for Beating Day. First, he didn't want to fight his best friend. Second, Coska couldn't win. Even if he beat the others, once the town discovered that he—

"I hope your head's as hard as Mom always says it is!"

The mocking voice that yelled was Gurril's brother, Angus (she actually spelled *that* one right, thank heavens). He was in the first small crowd of spectators, just taking seats on a bleacher that faced the park. Angus wore his blond hair in a crazy sort of up-do, so that it rose a full eight inches over his skull. To Gurril, the skinny man and his tall yellow head looked like a stalk of wheat. His Adam's apple projected out from his thin neck like an acorn hanging onto an impossibly weak branch.

As Gurril turned away from Angus, he could hear the human wheat stalk say in a quieter tone, "If Dad were alive, he'd be laughing at you, too."

Coska approached Gurril and sighed. "Today…" he said, quietly.

"Today," Gurril replied, mixing his pronunciation of the word with a grunt. They stared at each other for what seemed like an hour. In reality, it was only seconds. "Coska, you shouldn't be doing this. To fight, you'll have to use your… talents."

Coska smiled, making his dark green eyes shine. His medium-length black hair was its usual bird's nest mess atop his head. "Either that or get my head bashed in by your damned hammer. That thing is so brutal, why didn't you bring a whip, or maybe a cat to eat Sheila's stupid bird?"

"Leave my cats out of this," Gurril replied, indignantly.

Coska had always teased Gurril about having cats. He used to say that a single man of Gurril's age who kept two cats was likely to be called gay and run out of town. He stopped after Gurril admitted to him one night over beers that when they were kids, the worst teasing he endured was when people said that because his named sounded like "girl" he must kiss boys like one.

Gurril and Coska loitered on the grass together, stretching their legs, shadow boxing, and warming up by doing a few simple exercises while waiting for the elders, the rest of the spectators, and the wizard. As the sun rose higher into the morning sky, it warmed Gurril's leather shirt and cotton pants, helping loosen his muscles further.

2

Three miles away, in a clover field that was currently being rained down upon by hungry bees, a ferret was born. His mother looked over him and her other six kits, tired yet doting. She licked their fur and slid her belly close to them, and one by one they found a nipple and began to feed. One of the kits, a male, sneezed lightly. She smiled at him, and in the way animals do, with shakes of tails and twitches of whiskers, she named him Pepper. In the clover field above her and the kits, bees continued buzzing to and fro, collecting pollen and making honey.

A strange vision came to the mother of the kits as she dozed off. She saw Pepper running through a field, very much like this one. A bright light shone, and he turned into a man. As she fell asleep, her final conscious thought was "I hope my little kit never sees that light."

3

In the kingdom of Flamingo (which sits about thirty miles off the west coast of the mainland), most Flamingoans had left their huts, raised about five feet high over the flat surface of the island, and were preparing their boats for high tide. Snick, having just turned eighteen and being the oldest daughter of the king, had begun her countdown to marriage. She now had three weeks to determine who she would wed. Everyone else on the island was either a fisher or a seacorn farmer.

Snick, however, was a princess. Her lucky suitor would become the King of Flamingo. All of her friends would wait until they were well into their sixties or seventies to worry about marriage and children, but she would have to start at the age of eighteen. It didn't seem fair to have to take a husband with at least another hundred and twenty years left of life, but Snick knew she was a slave to traditions. She sighed heavily at the thought of marriage. The Flamingoans lived extraordinarily long lifetimes, and could easily reach one hundred and fifty years old. It seemed to be a long time to stay married.

She thought of her parents. Her father had been the prince, and chose his wife based on beauty. Her mother, only forty years old now, had already birthed three children. Most of her mother's friends were still single, and had taken multiple lovers over the years. Snick's younger siblings, according to tradition, were adopted by various families of commoners and mixed into the general population of children; they might never know they were royalty. In the event that she died, the oldest of them would be pulled into the life of a prince or princess without more than a few minutes warning.

Snick looked just like the other Flamingoans. Her skin was a light brown, darker than the people on the mainland, but lighter than those who lived in the far south. Had Gurril described her, he would have said that her skin was the color of a perfectly baked loaf of wheat bread. Her long, straight hair was nearly a pure white, and her eyes were large and green. She wore the same brightly colored clothing as everyone else, fashioned to be practical for swimming and sunning. The small top and panty-like bottom barely covered her body, which was sleek and long. She stretched out her legs, watching how the curve of them shone in the sun.

She stared out into the open horizon, watching the tide come in and cover the island. Soon the shrimp would come and feed off what had been land just hours earlier. Then the flamingoes would come and feed on the shrimp. Flamingo. Why couldn't her island kingdom be known for something interesting, like sharks? As the rest of the island rowed off to fish and tend to sea corn, Snick began mixing up a new cream she was working on in a small wooden bowl her father had brought her from one of his diplomatic trips to the mainland. As she mixed the ingredients, she began saying the magic words she knew would turn the ingredients into a cream that would transform dried cod flesh into fresh fillets. This had to be done in secret, for in the kingdom of Flamingo (as in most places), witches were doled a horrible fate.

A few minutes later the cream was finished, and Snick pulled a piece of cod—dried to be a sort of fish jerky—out of a basket under her bed. She applied the cream and hummed a bit, smiling as she began to smell fresh meat. Snick didn't know where the ideas for the creams she made came from, or the words she needed to say to make them magic, but when the idea came to her, she had no choice but to make the cream and say the words. Not to do so would be like an artist refusing to paint, or the best fisherman in the village becoming a sea corn farmer.

Snick gobbled up the cod and turned to open her book of reading studies. As she opened it, she felt the sun sting at her

6

eyes, so she rotated her body a bit so the light would come over her shoulder. As she did so she looked up, and saw a sea corn farmer (she didn't know his name) standing in waist-deep water, staring at her. Hoping that her incantation hadn't been witnessed, she smiled politely and waved. The farmer ducked away, as if she had thrown a man 'o war at him, and Snick knew that she was caught. The farmer dove into the water and swam toward the central hut of the island, where her father, the king, was meeting with his council.

Fast as she could and completely panicked, Snick threw her favorite few items into two large, woven reed baskets. Simple things, like a warm blanket her mother made her, a few pieces of jewelry, her favorite book, as many ingredients for as many creams as she knew how to make, and the few clothes she owned all were tossed together by her shaking hands as she tried to stay as calm as possible. She threw the baskets into her small wooden boat below, her mind racing. Would she be caught? Which way was the nearest shore of the mainland? Where would she go when she got there? Should she plead with the people of the island for mercy? If she tried to run and was caught, would she be burned or drowned? Neither sounded like a pleasant way to die, and Snick began to cry as she leapt from her hut down to her boat and began rowing. She thought of her father and mother hearing the news that she was a witch, and pictured them weeping, knowing that even the king and queen could not prevent the punishment.

Snick wasn't a good rower. She was no more than a mile from the village when she heard the conch blow that meant the fishermen and farmers were being called in for an emergency. She stopped rowing, bent over until her head was on her knees, and began sobbing. As Snick contemplated the differences between dying by fire and dying by water, she felt her tears run down her shins and tickle at the tops of her feet, little pools forming in the webbing between her toes. She sniffed, and looked at her feet. They were, for Flamingoans, beautiful feet. Long, wide, and with webbing that stretched all the way back from the tip of each toe. Her tears shined in tiny pools there, and inspired her to a thought. If she mixed the oil of a shark's eye just right with the powder of a certain shell and a bit of sea water…

Ten minutes later, as the first fishermen's boats were coming into sight, Snick's rowboat shot through the water faster than any fish could swim. Instead of rowing, Snick was in the water, kicking with her legs to power the boat, her hair clumped together with a yellowish cream that soaked into her scalp and gave her legs incredible newfound power.

4

The crowd of spectators at Hearthstone waited anxiously. Gurril and Coska were telling each other nervous jokes, Peter was sharpening his sword (for the fifth time since he had gotten to the park), Sheila was petting her hawk's head, and the fat boy had fallen asleep under an ash tree, his puffy paper sack tied shut tightly with a bit of bright yellow yarn. A rumble in the crowd began as a small group walked into the park.

Coska perked up immediately. "Hey, Gurril," he said, elbowing his friend, "I think that's Martin, the wizard from Girand."

Along with Martin were the elders (six women and a man, who were old and wise), and Bruno, the retiring village warrior.

David the hawk let out a piercing screech as the crowd fell silent. Indeed, the wizard Martin had arrived. He stood tall and looked friendly, his black hair and eyes a contrast to his pale face. His thin lips smiled easily, and he had an air of kindness about him. In all places, performing wizardry was illegal except with a permit, which was a joke, because to get the permit you had to provide an example of wizardry. Most people who tried to get a permit were almost immediately tied to a stake and burned. Nobody really knew how Martin had done it, but now that he had his permit, he was sought out for small jobs like judging Beating Day and protecting the competitors. He would place a spell on each of them to help them heal very quickly. The spell could not prevent death from a very serious injury that would kill instantly, but it would put the body's healing mechanisms into an extreme state of hyperactivity.

At sixty-three, Bruno was old, even for a retiree. His long, gray hair hung in clumps in front of his eyes, and he shuffled forward quietly. He had been the town warrior for over thirty years, and everyone agreed that they were lucky to not have been attacked for the last fifteen of those. Bruno was already old for a competitor when he won his Beating Day, but he had been the best damned knife thrower anyone had ever seen. On Bruno's Beating Day victory, he had killed three other competitors. There had been no wizard to offer protection that day.

After today's competition, Bruno would leave for Girand with Martin, to live the simple life of a retiree on a vineyard. Coska and Gurril both smiled, dreaming of retirement. Town warriors from various regions had pooled their money together years ago to build a retirement villa in Girand, chosen because of its ability to remain neutral. The retirement villa was a huge vineyard, and the retired warriors settled in the acres of lush red, blue, and green grapes for their final days. Most of the work on the farm was done by beautiful maidens, each trained in ancient ways to be a sort of concubine-priestess to keep the retired warriors well-serviced with female companionship. Now and then, two warriors who had fought before retirement would get into a brawl, but the old men could almost always be settled down by the pleasures their favorite maidens could provide.

The wizard, elders, and Bruno would be judges today, but only in name. The main goal of each competitor at Beating Day was to kill or maim the competition. Before taking his seat, Martin motioned for all of the competitors to come to him and line up. Peter kicked the fat boy awake, and the five competitors took their places in front of the wizard.

Martin started at the end of the line where Gurril stood. He said some magic words that sounded like nonsense to Gurril, and slapped the hopeful warrior across the face, hard. He repeated this with Coska. Nobody noticed that when Martin faced Coska, the wizard's eyes widened and his face slightly drained of color. The words he muttered were also a bit different, but close enough that to everyone but Coska and Martin, they sounded the same.

9

The slap of Sheila's face echoed in the park. Where the hard slap had nearly brought tears to Gurril's and Coska's eyes, her eyes narrowed after the slap, brought into a cold focus. As Martin turned to Peter, Sheila cleared her throat and said "Sir?"

Martin turned to her, smiled politely, and said, "Yes, Child?"

"May you protect my bird, please, Sir? He is not only my weapon, but my truest companion, and the tool I use for my livelihood."

"What is your livelihood, Dear?"

"I am a huntress."

Martin's smile faded. "I don't mean to be cruel, Dear. But if I were to try and bless your bird, it would kill him. I hope for your sake and his that he lives through Beating Day."

The cold focus left her face, and a tear slipped from Sheila's eye while her chin quivered. David the hawk leaned his head over and dried her cheek with the finest feathers he had, just above his eyes.

Next was Peter. After Martin slapped Peter's face, he stepped up to the fat boy. "Jason," he began in a lecturing tone, "I know what you are up to. If you do not turn around and go home, you will be punished for your plan."

The fat boy, now known to Gurril as Jason, smiled the smile of a boy who would have lit his own mother on fire. "Just do your thing," he snarled.

Martin said magic words, but instead of slapping the boy's face, punched him in the stomach and loudly incanted "Penetrable!" The punch to the stomach was so hard that Jason threw up onto the ground in front of his feet.

Martin turned to go back to his seat, his long red robes swinging behind, slightly out of sync with his body as if they had a mind of their own. For all anyone knew, those robes may really *have* had a mind of their own. He took his seat with the elders, who all looked as kindly as grandparents. Bruno yawned, and a lump rose in his pants as he began dreaming of the maidens that awaited him at the retirement villa.

Each competitor now walked to a special holding area, where they would wait to see who fought whom. The area was just large enough for the five of them, and was constructed of wooden fencing about three feet high.

The elders had a brief discussion, and the lead elder, Trina, rose from her seat. "Jason, you will fight –"

There was a loud *pop* as Jason smashed the paper bag in his hands. Immediately, a drove of wasps flew from the now smashed open bag. The wasps were angry, having been first captured, then confined, and now smashed in this bag. They immediately swarmed only Jason, who had planned on them attacking everyone equally. The other competitors made room as the wasps stung Jason over and over again as he collapsed and writhed on the ground, screaming in pain. The wasps continued stinging until his writhing stopped, and then they flew as a squadron out of the park.

Martin stood from his seat as Jason convulsed one last time. "Wasp use," Martin announced, "Is cheating."

He sat back down as the remaining competitors watched Jason die before them, his puffy, stung eyes staring wide open into the grass as his body lay on its side. It was not unheard of for a wizard or other judge to execute a cruel punishment to a cheater on Beating Day, and as Gurril's stomach turned, he tried not to lose focus. Martin hid a smile, secretly pleased at how well his incantation had worked.

Trina, who had sat down for the commotion, rose again. "Coska, you will fight Sheila."

Gurril gave Coska a pat on the back as he and Sheila left the waiting area and walked into the center of the park. They circled each other a few times, David the hawk on Sheila's shoulder. She made the first move, screaming "Tora!" The hawk lifted off and flew high. It turned, and as it began diving toward Coska, Coska pulled out a wand from his pocket. The crowd gasped, and a few even were brave enough to shout "Wizard!"

Coska pointed his wand at the charging hawk and yelled out "Dove!"

David the hawk immediately transformed into a dove, a *poof* of feathers falling from its body as it changed from dark brown to white. He broke off his attack (he was a bird, not an idiot), and flew to the branch of an oak tree.

Shelia's eyes became huge and angry. "You bastard, you nasty *magician*!" She spit out the last word the way she would have spit out an insult.

"He'll turn back into a hawk in a day, I promise." Coska replied.

Sheila shrieked a battle cry, and came at Coska with hands out like claws. Coska simply side-stepped her, smacking the back of her head with his wand. Sheila fell onto the ground, unconscious. As she lay oblivious to the world around her, a strange vision emerged in her mind: she would be thrown in front of charging horses by one who loves her. Her lover would kill her in this way. The vision was really more of a thought than a picture. There was no visual cue to the action, only the knowing that this is how her death would unfold.

Sheila would lay asleep for three days after her Beating Day loss. When she awoke, the vision of being trampled to death under the hooves of charging horses would lay in the back of her mind, like a mostly forgotten dream.

While the crowd chattered, the elders, Bruno, and Martin had a short discussion. Willa, one of the elders, stood and addressed Coska in a demanding tone. "Boy, what kind of spell did you use on this young woman?" When she spoke, the crowd chatter faded to almost silence.

"Just something to put her to sleep for a time, Ma'am."

"If you had wanted, could you have killed her? Don't lie, or Martin will send those wasps back for you."

Coska swallowed hard and nodded. "Yes, Ma'am."

He hoped that the elders would see his action as mercy, or kindness. He hadn't wanted to kill the woman, and hoped that his action would show them that although he had great power, he was careful with its use. Behind him, a litter crew and the town nurse rolled Sheila onto a stretcher, and removed her from the park. The temporary dove David perched on the stretcher next to her, cooing at his master.

Willa sat down again, and the group of judges began a discussion. As they talked, and the crowd murmured, Coska took his place in the holding area with Gurril and Peter. Gurril scruffed Coska's hair a bit and tried to give him a reassuring smile. Peter stepped away, afraid to be close to the newly outted wizard.

Almost fifteen minutes later, Trina stood back up, announcing, "Coska wins round one. He also is given a permit to perform wizardry."

The crowd fell into a stunned silence. Angus quietly (but still loud enough to be heard by everyone around him) said "Burn the son of a bitch."

Trina turned to Gurril and Peter. "Gurril, Peter, you two are next. The winner fights Coska."

The two new fighters entered the center of the park, leaving Coska alone in the waiting area. The wizard sighed and sat on the grass, pulling his knees up to his chest.

Gurril looked down the town's main street where the litter crew and nurse were carrying Sheila. The distraction allowed enough time for Peter to start his attack on Gurril. Before Gurril knew what was happening, Peter's sword swung heavily downward, slicing deeply into Gurril's left shoulder, pectoral muscle, and down his left ribs. Gurril screamed in pain and backed away. Blood gushed from his wounds. Gurril could hear Angus laughing and cheering wildly in the crowd.

The two fighters stared at each other, Gurril now trying to handle his hammer with one arm, Peter in amazement that Gurril wasn't out of the fight. Peter swung his sword up high over his head and came at Gurril, screaming a battle cry. He had figured that Gurril wouldn't be able to use his hammer with one arm, and that it was safe to go for a kill shot. Peter was right that Gurril wouldn't be able to handle his hammer the way he normally would, but Gurril could manipulate it just enough. Stepping forward, Gurril drove his bloody left shoulder into Peter's chest before Peter could bring his sword down. Gurril brought his right arm, holding his war hammer, around Peter's left leg. This move also positioned Gurril's shoulders in a way that pinned Peter's arms straight over his head. As Peter and Gurril grappled, Gurril maneuvered the head of his hammer to the front of Peter's left foot, and the handle to the back of Peter's left leg. Gurril stepped to the side and yanked upward on the hammer as hard as he could. As Gurril hoped, Peter tripped, landing face down. Still holding his hammer by the butt of the handle, with the striking end straight down, Gurril lifted the weapon straight up, then pounded it down on the back of Peter's neck. Blood exploded everywhere as Peter's neck was crushed into mush. Gurril used his foot to roll Peter over, almost vomiting as he watched the young man's head twist around on a completely different axis than the rest of his body. The now blood-red globes of his eyes stared up to Gurril as his dying, shaking fingers gripped and relaxed at blank air a few times. Gurril stepped back from Peter and watched him die, his blood-filled mouth garping like a fish starved for oxygen.

Gurril knew when he came to the park that death could be a part of Beating Day, and that he may be the cause of that death. The fact that Peter would surely have killed him also came to mind. Neither of these things helped Gurril feel less pain in his heart, and he had to use every ounce of his might to hold back the tears that stung his eyes and the shuddering that wanted to overtake his body.

Martin stepped quickly from the crowd and knelt over Peter, saying more magical words in a desperate attempt to make the young man's body recover. After a few tense seconds, Martin looked up to the crowd and said loudly, "This boy cannot heal. We have our second fatality of Beating Day."

The crowd offered a mixture of cheers, boos, and other assorted chatter as Martin stood and turned to Gurril. He ran his hand across the wound Peter had given him and told Gurril, "This should heal in about two hours. Go to the waiting area."

Gurril returned, bleeding, to the waiting area with Coska. Coska looked at the wound and asked, "What did Martin say to you?"

"This should heal in about two hours." Indeed, the blood was already thick and Gurril could lift his left arm slightly.

"Do you want to wait to fight me, or just get it over with?"

"I don't know."

The only male elder, Roy, stood to address Gurril and Coska. The old man's voice was on the verge of cracking as he yelled at them, unable to hide his anger and frustration. "You two will fight now! No healing! We're now given the choice between a rotten magician or a loner. We had a great huntress and a well-respected young man but they're gone. You two fight, *now!*"

Neither Coska nor Gurril knew it, but Roy was Peter's great-grandfather. He had talked Peter into competing with promises of an early victory, followed by an easy life on the town payroll. Tears pooled in the old man's eyes and hung there, defying gravity. His thin white mustache twitched back and forth as he held himself together. The thin old man thought he might favor dying over the feeling he fought against now, having led his great-grandson to his violent and painful death.

The two friends walked to the center of the park and faced each other. Coska pulled out his wand, a gnarled stick of elm. Gurril was already feeling well enough to properly swing his hammer, although blood spurted everywhere when he flexed the muscles on his left side.

Gurril had to strike first. He knew that Coska had watched him train, so he had to use a fighting style he had not practiced for some time. He quickly flipped his hammer, catching it by the head so that he was holding the striking end, with the butt of the handle pointed toward Coska. Gurril jabbed Coska in the mid-section, knocking the wind out of him. He beat Coska about the head and neck with the handle of the hammer, feeling a definite crunch as he broke the orbital bone of Coska's left eye.

Coska fell to the ground and rolled away from the attack, using one hand to hold his eye in its shattered socket while he flicked his wand at Gurril. Gurril's war hammer turned into a rattle snake, and Gurril was now holding not the striking head of a hammer, but the poisonous head of a snake. Gurril didn't miss a beat, though, and began whipping Coska with the writhing body of the venomous beast.

About the time that the snake finally worked its way through Gurril's hand enough to bite him, the final whip that was delivered to Coska knocked him unconscious. Gurril fell to the ground beside his friend, poisoned. The two young men lay next to each other, beaten, bloody, and dying. Martin stood and quickly made his way to them, staring at the snake as it slithered to the base of a nearby elm tree. The wizard put one of his palms on each competitor's head and uttering more incantations. Both men opened their eyes, and the snake stiffened and morphed back into a war hammer.

Martin smiled at the two men, faced the audience of townspeople, and announced in a loud voice, "I believe we have a tie."

Chapter 2: Nightmare in Stonecorn Field

1

In the two years that followed Beating Day, Gurril and Coska became even closer friends. The elders had decided to split the salary of the town warrior between them, and they were ordered to share the villa.

The villa was certainly spacious enough for two bachelors, with two bedrooms and a large courtyard of grass inside a high wall. Gurril spent his days in the courtyard training with one of his new war hammers, or taking vigorous runs to patrol the areas around the small town. His old war hammer was now retired, sitting quietly under his bed, the flecks of blood and bone from Peter's neck long since wiped away.

The front door to the villa opened to a large open living area with soft, cushioned chairs. The furniture was fine oak and leather, and the living room chairs were usually occupied by a sleeping cat on warm days, or two cats piled together asleep on colder ones. Gurril and Coska kept a large book case made from pine in one corner, full of books about history, famous battles, and fighting styles. A basket with a few blankets and pillows stood between Coska's favorite chair and the book case. A kitchen and small dining table were to the right of the front door. The kitchen was small, but open with a lot of cupboards and a large washing sink with a tap of running water. The dining room table was of moderate size, comfortable for four diners. It was made of beautiful pieces of assorted driftwood that some long-ago warrior had collected from the river banks. The finish of the dining chairs matched the cushy living room chairs, light brown leather stuffed with down.

A hall on the left led to the bedrooms and bath, a modified outhouse that fed into the rudimentary town sewer. Running water and a toilet that led to the sewer were great benefits, with most town residents only experiencing such luxury if they stayed for a night in one of the more expensive rental rooms over the ale house. The floors of the villa were polished ash, and the walls were white stucco with finished ash framing. A few paintings and small tapestries hung here and there. If a visitor walked straight from the front door through the living area, they would exit the villa through a large patio into the training courtyard, a grassy space of about thirty by thirty-five feet.

Gurril was, on this day, learning some new battle methods with his smallest hammer. He alternated between reading through a book and examining the diagrams in it, and walking through the new moves. Coska sat against the frame of the patio door, babbling a bit and trying to change spiders from a jar into flies.

Coska stopped for a bit, and closed his eyes hard to squeeze some moisture into them. With a stretch and yawn, he asked "Hey, Gurril, how's it going?"

Gurril looked up from his book. "This one," he pointed to the book, "Is hard to follow. A town warrior called 'Melvin' wrote it. He isn't very descriptive."

"Hmm. My mother always said, 'Never trust a guy named Melvin.' I think somebody named that sold her some dull steak knives or something."

Gurril smirked a smiled and grunted a short laugh. "Hear anything from Martin lately? He hasn't visited you in a long while."

"Got a letter from him yesterday. He's been dealing with an outbreak of grabbing vines in the Girand grape fields."

Gurril came and sat in the doorway, facing Coska. "What's with the jar of toads?"

"Toads?" Coska looked down to his jar of what formerly were spiders. Where there had been about a half dozen arachnids, there now were two toads. "Huh. Guess I need to work a bit more on that one."

Gurril smiled. "Just don't turn any of our dishes into birds again. It took forever to get them out of the house and they crapped everywhere. I'm saving up for a book about fighting in swamps, and I don't want to spend the money on dishes again."

"I'll do my best. Did I tell you that I finally got the spell right to stop dogs from barking?"

Gurril grunted approval. "I thought that mutt next door has been quiet lately. I thought maybe you accidentally turned it into a rocking chair or something."

Coska laughed. "No, but I thought about it." He looked down to the jar of toads and added, "Well, I suppose he could have accidentally… You don't want to walk through anything with me facing you, do you?"

Gurril grunted a "No" back to him, and returned to the courtyard for more training. On many days when Gurril was learning new fighting methods, Coska would pick up an old sword they kept, and walk through as an enemy. When Gurril was ready to move to full speed, Coska would watch him from the doorway and critique his moves.

Coska spent the rest of the afternoon in his room, learning incantations that he either invented himself or received in letters from Martin. That evening, like many others, was spent listening to the concerns of the elders (mostly regarding what to do if the unseen mischief of rats that supposedly scurried about through the fields around the village decided to raid the grain stores). The later portion of the evening was spent sitting around a small bonfire in the courtyard, quietly talking. There were times when Gurril wanted to become a hermit, relishing his time alone. That night in the courtyard was not one of them, and he soaked in the company of his best friend as they joked and told each other about the dreams that young men have for themselves.

A small bit of excitement came about the next morning, as Coska was attempting to turn a small iron pot into a large pitcher of water. There was a knock at the front door of the cottage. Coska, not wanting to be disturbed, waited for Gurril to go to the door. The knock repeated, and Coska, now irritated, stood from his cross-legged position on the floor of the living room and went to see who had come to visit. He absently flicked his wand at the pot and said "Melvin," not knowing what to expect when he returned to it. As he walked to the door, the pot grew stubby lizard legs and trotted off toward the bedrooms.

In the courtyard, Gurril was happily pummeling a large wooden stump brought to him for training by a local lumber jack. He had four war hammers. His original, which he could now barely stand to look at, sat alone and unused under his bed, its oak handle brittle from not being oiled properly. He used his salary to commission new hammers from time to time. He currently practiced with his newest (and lightest) one: a two pounder with a long, thin iron handle. It was meant for throwing, and he repeatedly lined up and threw the hammer at the stump. His aim was perfect, but he wasn't happy with his throwing style; he needed to shorten his swing to cut down on the amount of time he was exposing his chest and midsection to an attack. He remembered well the way Peter had exposed himself during Beating Day by raising his sword so high over his head, and Gurril knew that was a fatal mistake to avoid.

His other two hammers were an iron six pound monster, with a thick iron handle, and a four pound hammer that had a long, thin head on it. The four pounder would work well as a shielding weapon. Gurril had heard the first, then second knock at the door and ignored them. He stretched his arms, looked to the stump with squinted eyes, and whipped his light hammer at it. It struck with a loud *thud* that tipped the battered stump over.

To himself, Gurril mumbled "If I use more wrist, I can throw it without lifting my arm so high. Good way to keep my body covered so I don't become a target for a throwing knife."

At the front door, a curious drama played itself out. Coska swung the door open to discover Sheila standing there, about to knock again. She had avoided Coska since Beating Day, but had recently been trying to approach Gurril during his frequent patrols outside of town. Coska noticed that she wore eye shadow and lip coloring. She looked not at all like a wicked blond bear, clenching her jaw wildly, the way Coska had seen her on Beating Day.

Coska couldn't hide his shock. Sheila watched as his mouth dropped open under his green eyes. His black hair, which he wore short, like Gurril, nearly stood up like a frightened cat's tail, and although she loathed the man with every part of her being, she was nearly brought to giggles by him. As she softened a bit, his shock faded a bit, and the two were able to look at one another now, rather than stare wildly.

"Coska," she said in a matter of fact tone, "I've come here for two reasons. First, I want to make peace. It's been two years, and I realize that you were just trying to win the contest. I want to tell you that I'm thankful you didn't harm David." She smiled. It was forced, but she knew she had to do it.

"Um, yeah. I, uh..." Never one for many words (unless they were being used in a spell or a joke), Coska stopped trying to talk, and motioned for Sheila to come in. "Your second reason?"

"I'd like to call on Gurril. Socially."

"You mean, like a..."

"Like a woman coming to ask a man to dinner, yes." She smiled, unforced this time. In Hearthstone, it was not uncommon for a woman to ask a man on a date, but it *was* uncommon for the town warrior to go on dates. Most warriors stayed single, except for the occasional meaningless fling. It was a generally accepted fact that warriors should avoid getting bogged down with a girlfriend (then wife), growing fat, and becoming of no value protecting the town.

Sheila had thought about dating Gurril for a very long time. She weighed the positives and negatives, and her mind twirled with the possibilities a future with Gurril could hold. Her decision to finally ask him out came to her while hunting rabbits with David in the woods north of the village one morning. She was strong, she was almost as good a fighter as any man she knew, and she would let no boyfriend (then husband) of hers EVER grow fat and lazy. With that thought, she smiled to herself, promised her hawk that he would always have a place in her heart, and came up with her plan to ensnare– or seduce– Gurril.

In the living area of the villa, she stood waiting, wearing a dress (a dress!) of all things. She had pulled her blond hair into a tight pony tail that hung to her left hip, and amazed herself by actually wearing makeup. Coska left to get Gurril from the courtyard, and Sheila's womanly nature took over. She noticed the lack of decoration on the wall, other than the limited number of paintings and small tapestries. Her eye wandered to the kitchen, where the pantry stood. She bet to herself that it was mostly empty, except for maybe a few hunks of jerky, a loaf of bread, and pieces of fruit. Men, those apish brutes, would sooner starve and die than have a proper store of food on hand.

In the courtyard, Gurril was moving in slow motion through his throwing style, thinking about learning an underhand throw to compliment his overhand power chuck. Coska stepped smiling into the grassy area, and said simply, "Take a bath—you're getting lucky tonight."

Sheila waited patiently in the living room, and was beginning to wonder if Gurril would ever come to greet her when she finally saw his shadow fill the double-wide patio doorway that lead to the house from the courtyard. He was sweaty, his nose was a bit runny, and he breathed very heavily. She knew it should have revolted her, but it turned certain parts of Sheila into burning embers. She smiled in spite of trying to keep her cool, squeezing her thighs together under her dress for a tiny, secret bit of thrill.

"Gurril…" she began, and looked at Coska, who had entered behind Gurril and was watching the show. She cleared her throat. Despite being a maiden, and here in a dress, she wouldn't have needed much prodding to drive Coska's head through the nearest wall if it meant being alone with Gurril. Coska sensed this, smiled lightly, then retreated to his bedroom.

Gurril spoke next, nervously. "Sheila. Hi." More of that heavy breathing that drove her mad.

"Hello. I was wondering, Gurril, if you'd like to take dinner with me tonight? At the ale house. They're serving fresh pike and stone corn." She blushed a bit when she asked, and Gurril now took notice. Her dress had a certain cut that was low on the top and high on the bottom. Years of walking, running, climbing trees, and other physical activity associated with her hunts had shaped her muscled legs well. Gurril imagined that under her dress, her tight stomach might show each muscle. He realized that he was staring, and turned away. The heat and electricity between them could have easily lit the room on fire.

"I should bathe first."

"Certainly." She was still trying to remain calm, despite her sudden urge to jump up and down (an action that Gurril would probably have enjoyed taking spectacle of). "I'll come back in an hour." With that, she turned and left. Gurril, still a bit in awe of what happened, went to the kitchen for the pitcher of water. Coska slunk out of his room and joined Gurril for a drink.

"So," Coska teased, "Pike and stone corn at the ale house tonight. Somebody's going to miss their morning training routine."

"I'll be home before midnight. Mom." The two men laughed. In their lives, neither had so much as kissed a woman, and as Gurril began to prepare his bath, he thought about an adage his late father had told him once: The smallest cat wishes for the biggest fish, but doesn't know what to do when it swims right up to him. Gurril had a big fish just swim up to him him, and he had no idea what to do. He silently prayed that she would figure it out for him.

2

A little over an hour later, Gurril and Sheila were walking down the hill to the Lucky Miller, a small ale house that served the village. The nightly dinner was always based on what the town's hunters and fishers had acquired that day, and because the town had such delightful bread, everything was always served as a sandwich. If the menu said "pike" it really meant "pike sandwich." If it said "venison" it meant "venison and cheese sandwiches" and so on. On good days, it was pike, venison, rabbit, or some other tasty fish or game. On bad days, it was nutria, raccoon, carp, or even loopo meat. Loopos were large lizards that roamed the countryside and were frequently easy hunting when other game was hard to find. Townsfolk sometimes called them "the worst tasting method of avoiding starvation."

For diners with the money, farm-raised chickens were always an option as well, but they were expensive and really didn't taste much better than the game around the area. The venison, rabbits, and other wild creatures all ate the wheat and stonecorn that made Hearthstone a relatively famous stop for grain buyers, and as such, instead of having a wild game taste, the meat of the creatures was more comparable to a domestic animal.

Tonight, however, was pike night. The town's fishers had a successful catch, and Sheila's hawk had even caught two pike himself, along with a rabbit and three grouse. All in all, it was a good hunting day. Meat that wasn't used would be salted

23

and hung to dry in the cellar. Three of the four tables in the pub were taken with quiet groups of diners. The five seats at the bar stood empty. Donatello, who served triple duty as the bartender, waiter, and pub owner, grunted a hello as Gurril and Sheila entered.

From the outside, the ale house looked like every other building in Hearthstone. It was a two-story structure with a lot of windows that usually stood open, allowing the smells, sounds, and moods of the people who lived in the upstairs apartments to waft out into the streets. The beige stucco siding had a firm, strong look about it, and the thick wooden shingles were solid and red.

Inside, it was a warm and open space, with a large fireplace for cold nights. Rugs made of bear and cougar skins hung on walls, and the worn planks of the oak floors seemed to call out for the occasional peanut shell to be carelessly thrown over a shoulder. There were patrons in the ale house nearly every hour of every day, but few of them became drunk to the point of rowdiness. It was a place made for comfort and stories, warm meat and fresh bread, and beers and ales brewed from the finest grains. Happiness for the tongue and the soul lived in the walls like spirits live in haunted places.

"Hello, Donatello. We'll have a table, please," Gurril said politely. Donatello only pointed to the one free table, and the couple sat at it. From the bar, he loudly asked "Pike or rabbit? Rest is eaten."

Gurril looked expectantly at Sheila, who smiled and said "Pike." Gurril held up two fingers, and Donatello grunted an acknowledgement. Gurril and Sheila looked at each other quietly for a moment, then began making small talk about the weather, the condition of the local grain crops, and other meaningless things to break the ice until they noticed a shadow fall over the table. It was Trina, the town elder.

"Excuse me," Trina began, smiling through long, coffee-stained teeth, "I know you two are probably in the mood for a quiet dinner, but Gurril, I just heard that there was a report of three rats spotted on Goose Hill this afternoon. Do you think you could run up there after dinner and investigate?"

"Certainly, Trina. Thank you for letting me know."

Trina smiled, "Also, I was wondering if tomorrow at about one in the afternoon you could stop by the council chambers. We elders would like to discuss a matter with you."

"Sure. We'll see you then."

"Have a good night, you two."

"And you as well." Gurril looked at Sheila after Trina had left the pub.

Sheila had a quizzed look on her face, and asked "Do they always know where you are?"

Gurril shrugged and grunted. "Part of the job." There was a pause, and he asked "Want to head out to Goose Hill with me after dinner? It'll be dark by then, so I probably won't end up finding any rats to smash. We can look for falling stars. Both moons are full tonight, too."

Sheila smiled. "I'd love to." She smiled at the thought of both moons full on the same night. Brios, the blue moon that never turned, and Fibro, the red moon that turned in a fast, tight rotation; they danced around the night together, and legends told of good luck when both were full. Under their dim light, there would be shadows of red and blue.

They continued their dinner, the lightly spiced pike served with a heaping side dish of stonecorn. Gurril bit into his corn, feeling the kernels pop as he bit into them, releasing the sweet syrup they held. Sheila grimaced slightly as she took a mouthful from her dish of corn. Gurril looked to her unsmiling mouth as she chewed. "What is it, Sheila?"

She shook her head lightly. "Nothing, they just cooked my corn a bit long. I can hear yours popping when you chew it. All the nectar is gone from mine. No pop." She shrugged her shoulders in an *oh well* gesture.

Gurril reached to her, squeezed her left hand with his right, then switched the small dishes of corn.

"Have mine, Pretty Lady. I like your sweet smile more than the taste of sweet nectar."

3

It was only as they began to climb Goose Hill after dinner that the conversation turned to Gurril's work again. They had talked all through their meal, and now had that easy feeling that comes after a few hours of good chemistry and a few pints. On the way out of the pub, Sheila had picked up a bottle of wine for the two of them to share under the moons. It was the least she could do, she felt. After all, she had asked Gurril on the date, but he had insisted on picking up the cost of dinner. She carried the wine as they walked along, talking.

They had just begun to mount the hill when a thought occurred to Sheila, and she asked Gurril "If you find evidence of rats, could I hunt them out with you? David would be awesome at ratting."

"You've seen rats before?" Gurril stopped and turned. It was illegal to see a rat within a mile of the village and not report it, and he wanted to be sure he wasn't on a date with a felon. Not reporting a rat was punishable by whipping.

"Yes, but David didn't actually attack one. We did see it, though. We were nearly five miles away. Almost to McLeod Township."

Gurril grunted, then said, "I've never seen one. What was it like?"

"Well, it was a baby, which is why David could have handled it if he had really wanted to. I think it had wandered away from its mischief, because there were no other rats in sight. It was maybe a foot and a half long in body, with a tail that was another ten inches long or so."

"In the pictures I've seen in books, they look like they have sharp teeth."

"Oh, yes. And long, too."

Suddenly, the thought of rats being on this very hill seemed a bit frightening to them both.

In an effort to help soothe herself, Sheila added, "I don't think his venom glands had developed, though. It didn't look like his fangs were very long."

Not only did saying this not soothe her, but it scared the hell out of her. Here she was, climbing a hill that could be hiding the poisonous creatures.

Gurril, trying not to show the fear he was now feeling, gulped hard. He began rooting around through the tall grass to try and find any evidence of rats, and realized that he had brought no weapons. Not wanting to think too much about the negative possibilities of their situation, he tried changing the subject. "That pike was pretty good, huh?"

"Yes, it was. Thanks for sharing your stonecorn. That was very sweet." Sheila was about to whisper something into Gurril's ear, when she saw a moving shadow and screamed in surprise and fright, causing Gurril to look up quickly from his search through the knee-high grass of the hill. He saw Coska there, just behind him.

Coska smiled and said, "Hi, guys. Trina dropped by and said you were going to check out the hill for rats. Thought I'd beat you to it so you could enjoy your evening together."

Sheila slapped his face and pointed her finger at his chin. "You snuck up on us!"

"I'm sorry, Sheila. You two were talking, and I didn't want to interrupt until there was a break in the conversation." He swallowed back the feelings that her slap had brought, not wanting to ruin his friend's date.

Gurril sighed. A third wheel was the last thing he wanted under the lucky light of two full moons. "So did you find any rats?"

"None. But I did find a bit of chewed stonecorn stalk. They were here, all right. But I think they're gone now."

Sheila addressed him carefully, "And you know animals well, right? I mean, that's where your magic lies. With beasts?"

"Yes. If they were still here, I'd know it. And they aren't here. So, then, there's no reason for *me* to be here. You two enjoy your wine." Coska winked to Gurril, waved a good-bye and trod down the hill, back toward town.

Sheila narrowed her eyes at him and said, "He bothers me, that one."

"He's not dangerous."

"All wizarding types are dangerous." As Sheila glared down the hill at Coska, Gurril decided it was best not to argue. He was the little cat who had been wishing for the big fish (or maybe it was the other way around), and he had come up with some ideas of what he was supposed to do with his catch. He grunted, and took Sheila's hand.

27

"Sit with me, Sheila. Let's open that wine." He pulled her into the soft grass of Goose Hill, and found hours worth of ways to enjoy his catch for the evening.

In the cottage, Coska was practicing a new spell when distant sounds filtered in through his window. They sounded similar to when Gurril was training with his heaviest weights, but mixed with a woman's moans. Although he had never been anywhere close to making love with a woman, he knew what the sounds were, and that they came from Goose Hill. He was pleased for his friend, and also a bit embarrassed for him. If Coska could hear them from the warrior's villa that meant the whole town could probably hear them.

Coska looked from the window back to the three worms that lay on the floor in front of him. The first had turned from its normal pink to a bright purple color with a pinch of a powder he had mixed. He was now modifying the magic words that went with the powder and tapping the second worm with his wand, in hopes that he could master the coloration spell with no powder needed. Each worm was thick and long, almost snake-like. After all the worms were purple, he would practice turning them into mice.

4

The next morning when Coska awoke, Gurril was in the courtyard. He had his lightest war hammer out, and was whacking polo balls back and forth across the lawn with it. He hit one of them so enthusiastically that it split in two.

Gurril chuckled and took in a deep breath of morning air as Coska raised his eyebrows and walked out to his friend. "Did we have a good night last night?"

"We did." Gurril's voice was a bit hoarse.

"You're not coming down with something, are you? You sound like your throat…"

"Oh, uh… No. Just the cool air last night, I guess."

Coska bit his top lip, stifling the urge to laugh. "Mmmm hmm."

"Trina asked me to stop by the council chamber at one. You coming with?"

Coska grimaced. "We share the job, why do they always ask you to come to the chamber and check out for rats, but never me?"

"You know why."

"It isn't fair. I didn't choose to be a magician. Just like you didn't choose to have brown hair, or have a neck as big around as the tree in your brother's front yard."

"Well, you'll just have to wait until you have a chance to show them that they're wrong about you, now, won't you?"

"Damn right. And yes, I'm coming with you."

A few hours later they arrived to the dark, cold council chambers. Where most of the buildings in Hearthstone were made of wood and stucco, the council building was mostly gray stone. In some long-ago time it had been the first few rooms of a castle, held by a long-ago king who was killed in his sleep by a daughter of his and his sister's incest. There was no fireplace, and no windows. The only light sources were a few torches burning here and there along the walls of the round structure. The building consisted of the large council chambers, and a small records library behind it. The council could oftentimes be found gathered in the large meeting room, or reading quietly in one of the sectioned off areas of the records library. It seemed odd to Gurril that the elders, people of great wisdom and care for the town, would seclude themselves to such a dreary place.

The entire council of elders was there, sitting behind a long table made of the singularly largest piece of granite anyone had ever seen. As usual, Trina did most of the talking. As the pair of young men entered, she stood from her seat and said simply, "Welcome. Let's get to work."

Coska and Gurril sat in chairs that were at a short table facing the council. The council sat side by side in plush chairs behind the granite slab table on a raised platform, so that they looked down onto anyone who they met with.

From the far left, the elder named Julie asked "Any evidence of rats on Goose Hill?"

Coska answered, "I did find some chewed stonecorn stalks, but no trails, holes, or droppings. I think maybe they were just passing by—"

Trina spoke up, cutting him off. "Fine. We'll ask the two of you to keep an eye on the hill for the next week. We've had some reports from nearby towns that a group of raiders has been robbing travelers on Morgan Road. We'd like you two to be on guard out at Stonecorn Field tomorrow for the course of the day. There is a wealthy and important group of people who will be taking a coach through the area. Stonecorn Field is the best place for an ambush if the raiders are nearby."

Julie now piped in again, adding "And we've heard that they are nearby. Chances are, you'll be seeing them. Get to Stonecorn Field before sunrise and wait. If they arrive to set up for an ambush, take them. No worries about prisoners; if they live through the battle, they'll be cut into fish bait anyway."

Trina now spoke again. "Boys, we'll let you know if we get any more information. In the meantime, get a good night's sleep. You have what might be a big day ahead of you."

Back at the cottage later that day, Gurril sat in the sunny courtyard. He had a small vial of a mineral oil that he dabbed into a cloth and rubbed onto the iron head of his heaviest war hammer. He used the time to meditate, and visualize himself in battle. In the two years he and Coska had shared the town warrior duties, they had not had to fight anyone. Nerves were a thing to calm. Gurril polished, then stretched his legs and arms, polished again, and finally walked through some battle moves, knowing that now was a time to relax more than to train.

Coska stood across the courtyard from Gurril, flicking his wand at a mouse. One flick would cause the mouse to issue a loud chirp, while another flick caused its feet to shrink slightly, but its ears to grow quite large. He flicked his wand at the mouse and said "Mystified!" The mouse stared at him in a dumb way. He pulled a second mouse out of a jar at his feet, and set it beside the first. He pointed his wand at this second mouse and whispered a word under his breath, almost as if he was afraid to say it. The second mouse turned to the first, a mouse he had peacefully shared the jar with for a week now, and began chewing through the mystified victim's throat. Coska felt his stomach turn over on itself, and he flicked the wand in a hard downward motion. Both mice fell dead.

30

Later, over a bowl of soup that was served with a thick loaf of bread for dinner, Coska looked at Gurril intensely. "Gurril, I'm picking up a feeling from you. It isn't good."

Gurril simply grunted (his favorite form of speech, it seemed to Coska), and looked into his bowl of soup. Coska sighed. "It isn't Sheila. You've been thinking about her all day, but that's not what I'm picking up on." Coska had always had intuition. He thought maybe it came along with his magical powers. He hated it when the intuition blossomed into a full vision of the future, because Coska always knew that every vision had some condition; there was the vision that a large tree would fall over the fence behind the town park. Coska knew that if he touched the tree, this would happen three days later. His will had slipped one morning, and he intentionally brushed the tree with his fingers as he walked by it on his regular early-day walk. Three days after that, a wind gust brought the tree down, crushing the fence beneath it. Thankfully, most visions were simple things.

The condition most often associated with the visions regarded telling people about the vision. In some cases if he told them, the vision would be guaranteed to come true. Other times, it was *not* telling them that would make the vision come true. He hadn't learned to decipher which was which, and he always feared what would happen when the intuition became a vision, and if he should or shouldn't talk about it. One time he had a dream about snow, mentioned it to Gurril, and within an hour it was snowing. In Heartstone, it snowed about once every fifteen years.

Other visions had included Angus beating his wife in a drunken rage. Afraid to upset Gurril, Coska said nothing. He hadn't seen the woman around town with bruises, and he hoped that holding back was keeping her safe. A vision of a woman throwing an unwanted newborn into the river was another that kept Coska up at night. Nobody had found a baby in the river, and the vision was beginning to fade. Coska was thankful not to dream of those blue lips and blank, dark eyes anymore.

As Coska thought of the snow, the beaten wife, and the drowned newborn, the intuition about Gurril became an idea. He didn't know whether to share it or not. Doing the wrong thing

31

with this idea could mean danger. He decided to tell Gurril what he was feeling. "Gurril, I think that you won't be sad about Peter anymore after today."

Gurril looked up, surprised. "Who said anything about Peter?" His tone was defensive. Gurril's guilt over Peter's death still felt fresh and tender, more than a full two years after the act.

"I know it still bothers you. Doesn't it?"

Gurril's eyes welled up with tears. They rolled down his cheeks as his chin shivered. "I didn't have to kill him. And I'm afraid. I've only had one battle before."

"And you won that battle. Really, you won two of them that day."

"I don't know if I can fight again."

"You train fourteen hours a day. Yesterday you trained for nine hours and called it a vacation so you could have a date with Sheila."

"Peter didn't have to die. I shouldn't have hit him so hard. These raiders... what if there are too many of them..."

Coska focused, trying to read his friend. The warrior's mind flashed through innumerable thoughts and feelings, a mixed jumble of mentality that made Coska feel dizzy. "Gurril, you're over-excited. I can barely keep up with your thoughts. Just slow down. Let's look at this one thing at a time."

Gurril sniffed, wiped his eyes, and buried his head in his hands. "I'm no warrior. Have you ever seen a warrior cry? I'm too weak."

"Weak? For the love of God, man, you're the strongest beast I've ever seen!"

"You know what I mean. I don't have the heart for it." He looked back to Coska with red, swollen eyes.

"Heart is exactly what you have for it. And spine, too. You killed Peter because the warrior in you took over right when you needed it to the most. And you cry now, because the human in you wishes that the world didn't need warriors. Gurril, you may grunt out half the words you should speak, but never fool yourself. You are a wise man."

The kitchen fell silent as a cat padded by, patrolling the house for mice. Gurril sipped at his soup. He wanted to not be hungry, but his body demanded food. His hard training led him to eat nearly three times as much as Coska. His stomach grumbled a bit, and he ate more soup. The broth felt good in Gurril's stomach, calming him. Across the table, Coska smiled, happy that the small incantation he added to the herbs in the soup didn't just calm down cats. It also calmed down muscle-bound warriors, afraid to go into their first real battle.

5

When dinner was finished, Coska cleared his throat and gingerly approached Gurril. "Uh, Big Guy... I've got an idea. For tomorrow."

Gurril looked up at him from the book he had just sat down with. It was a text written by a former town warrior about strategies for facing mounted enemies. "What's that?"

"We should head down to the ale house and round up a posse." Coska looked uneasily to Gurril. With the warrior so nervous about the next day, he was a bit unsure what kind of reception the idea would receive.

Coska was relieved when Gurril grunted a positive sound and said, "Good idea. We might be in for a challenge tomorrow."

After a few minutes planning, the two walked through the cool dusk air to the ale house. They had agreed to offer each posse member three copper pieces for each enemy in the bandit group, and to divide the spoils of the battle between all posse members equally. They approached the ale house, its walls full of sound, fresh light spilling from its windows. Gurril smiled. "Cards tournament tonight. We should have a big audience." Coska smiled back and nodded.

Gurril swung the door open, and they stepped in. Barely anyone took notice, until Gurril stood on a table and pounded his foot on its surface, the banging sound loud over the crowd noise. The ale house population stopped and turned to see the warrior. The table, which Gurril had thought was empty, was actually being prepared for a card game. The five players-to-be gave each other looks of confusion as the final few sounds of the crowd died away.

"I need a few men," Gurril began. "I have a possible fight in the morning. I'll pay each posse member—" Gurril stopped at the sound of a glass pitcher smashing to the floor.

A voice, dry and piercing, reached up from the crowd watching the warrior. "You'll make no such offer!" Coska pulled out his wand, afraid that a fight might be starting. The same voice, still unidentified by either Coska or Gurril screeched out again. "Put that damned thing away!"

Gurril saw a spot of white hair hidden behind a few standing hunters. The white hair stepped closer, and he recognized the man it belonged to. The lone male elder, Roy, owned the protesting voice.

He stood and pointed at Gurril and Coska with a bent, arthritic finger as he hissed out a scolding. "No posse! What the hell is wrong with you two! Get outside! Now!"

The man was old, but he still was commanding in his speech and body tone. Gurril felt, for the slightest second, a wavering in his bladder. *If this man can make me think I might piss myself, how will I face a group of bandits.*

Coska slipped his wand back into his robe as Gurril stepped down from the table. Roy grabbed Coska by the scruff of his robe, then clamped another hand on Gurril's wrist, dragging them both outside and around the corner of the building into an alley. He practically threw them against the wall of the building.

"You idiots! What part of an ambush do you think should be public knowledge!" He looked at them both, his cloudy blue eyes bugging.

"I, we…" It was all Gurril could push past his tongue.

Roy slapped his face, hard, then pointed a finger directly into it. "You dirty shit! You have the gall to kill my great-grandson dead for this job, and you nearly fuck it away the first chance you get!" He slapped him in the face again. "The raiders are moving between Hearthstone and other towns. Don't you think they just might have ears in places like ale houses?"

Coska spoke quietly to the old man. "It's my fault. I thought of coming here."

Roy turned to the young wizard and snarled, "You would. You filthy, rotten, magic-maker." He stepped back and

34

looked at the two young men. "You boys wouldn't get a posse anyhow. You," he pointed back to Gurril, "are a loner who doesn't measure up to anyone else in your family or this village. And you," he pointed to Coska, "Every time your name comes up anywhere in the town, the next question is always 'When do we burn him at the stake?' Get the hell out of my face, and don't you dare pull a stunt like this again! With any luck, the bandits will kill you both in the morning, and we can have a respectable town defender again. Like Peter would have been!"

When they arrived home, they sat silently at the kitchen table for a few minutes. They still needed to make final plans for the next morning. With shaking, unsure voices, they started talking about strategies. The next two hours were spent like this, the confidence of the two men growing again bit by bit after being scolded away by an old man.

6

Coska shivered as he lay on his stomach watching the sun rise through the stalks of stonecorn. It always seemed that the night was coldest when the sun began to rise; maybe it's because of the way the darkness retreats in daily defeat, leaving behind frosted dew. He looked over at Gurril, who was the absolute picture of what a warrior should be. He had thought ahead enough to wear a thick shirt covered by a fur coat. Gurril stared intently out of the field at the road, listening as the sound of a carriage approaching. The stonecorn stalks stood about eight feet high, each light green plant topped with a bright blue flower that had a yellow center.

As the sun flared its full body above the horizon, the rattling, clunking sound of the horse-drawn wooden coach was joined by the cleaner sound of hooves from another direction. Coska couldn't tell, but he thought the hooves were coming from across the road— the north side of the field. The carriage was coming from the east, Coska and Gurril's right side. Gurril was sharing this same thought, only he added another portion to it: If the hooves to the north were the harriers, and the carriage was coming from the east, that meant that he and Coska could flank the bandits when they turned to face the carriage. An added advantage would be that the sun, huge and glaring behind the carriage, would make it a harder target if one of the bandits still tried to attack it while Gurril and Coska fought them.

As it was, Gurril didn't get a chance at a flanking attack. The harriers rode out from their side of the field to the northeast, between the carriage and Coska and Gurril. The two saw them emerge and turn toward the carriage, which was still just coming into view.

Gurril stood and turned to Coska. "Coska! Slow them down if you can!"

Gurril began sprinting toward the harriers' horses, which had about a twenty yard head start on him in the race to the carriage.

Coska pulled out his wand and waved it in a high arc over his head saying, "Glued hooves" over and over again in quick, quiet speech. The harriers' horses slowed from a fast trot to a walk, then stopped. The harriers, who spoke in a coded language that neither Coska nor Gurril recognized, were confused enough that they didn't hear Gurril running up behind them. The confusion was a lucky chance for Gurril. As he ran toward the fight, he had the element of surprise.

Running at full speed, Gurril made mental notes. Four bad guys on three horses, all with swords. Looks like they haven't eaten in days. Secured well into their saddles. As he made this last note he jumped into the air and swung his medium-weight hammer in a power arc over his head, bringing it down into the back of the head of one of the bandits. The man's head caved in so far that the back of his skull touched the back of his nose. He flopped off his horse and lay motionless on the ground. Behind him, Coska changed from arcs to tight circles with his wand pointed in front of him, and the now free horse began jumping and bucking around frantically.

The bucking horse only added to the general confusion the bandits were now victim to. Gurril spun his body around and swung his hammer upward into another bandit's face, smashing the man's jaw to bits and knocking him unconscious. Instead of falling from his horse, this man fell backward in his saddle, and the horse took off running back into the field it had come from. Its rider bounced like a ragdoll on the horse's rump, the jarring scrambling his brains further.

The last horse had two riders. The man up front was old, and looked battleworn. The younger man on the back looked afraid. He began searching around for a place to jump from the horse and run on foot. This told Gurril two things: First, the younger man was inexperienced and would be an easy kill. Second, the older man was going to stand and fight. With the advantage of surprise gone in the nine seconds it took to beat the first two harriers, this man was now prepared. He pulled his sword from its sheath as the younger man jumped from the horse and began running down the road to the west, toward Coska. The young man issued a battle cry as he ran, and Gurril hoped Coska could handle himself as he realized the young man was not retreating in fear but running to engage the wizard.

The old man still could hardly control his horse, but he had it under enough control that he could make it stand on its hind legs and kick its forelegs at Gurril. Gurril backed off, and considered his options. As long as Coska could concentrate on the horse, the old man had limited movement. It would take a few seconds for the younger man, running much slower than Gurril had, to reach Coska. Gurril dove to the left, rolling hard and popping back to his feet at the horse's hind quarter. The horse immediately kicked back at him. Now he was between two wildly bucking horses, one uncontrolled and the other with a rider.

The young man ran toward Coska, pulling out a short metal spear from his coat. While his right hand twisted the wand in a slighter wider circle, Coska flicked the fingers of his left hand at the spear. It curled into a snake, the same trick he had used on Gurril on Beating Day. The young man dropped the hissing beast, and then ran past Coska without a second look, a hissing asp in hot pursuit. Coska had seen the fear in his eyes, and knew that he was no longer a threat. Gurril was in trouble. As Coska watched, his friend was kicked by the riderless bucker hard in the back. It knocked him down under the old man's horse. Coska could offer no further help; if he stopped concentrating on either of the horses, he would lose control over both of them and Gurril would be trampled by the old man. The third horse, now free of its unconscious rider, rejoined the group from the field. It began kicking and stomping with the other two

horses. Coska watched, amazed the old man could maintain his
mounted position on the only horse that still had a rider.

Coska redoubled his efforts, and yelled out some magic
words; one horse stopped bucking but began wildly biting at
Gurril as he stood from his fall. Gurril had been rolling around
dodging horses and getting kicked for only about thirty seconds,
but to Coska, it seemed a lifetime. He kept waiting for the old
man to swing his sword.

Tad Gallagher was an old thief. He had harassed
carriages on this road before, but usually could sense when the
old town warrior was nearby. Either that, or his rat spy would
tell him. Gallagher's senses of magic were never very keen, but
he knew he had them. For him, the sword was his second
weapon. Gallagher had charmed the horses to go mad if one of
their riders fell, and gone mad they had. He watched as the
young warrior was now bit by a very loyal horse, and then
smashed in the head when Gallagher's mount whipped his
muzzle into the man. The old thief knew that he had to stay
mounted to have a chance of winning the fight, and he struggled
to have a small bit of control over his mount.

Gurril was momentarily stunned from the horse's head
butt. He staggered back, and tripped over his own feet. He
stood one more time, trying to regain his senses. Gallagher saw
his opportunity, and swung his sword in a sweeping motion at
the young warrior's head. Just as the sword was about to make
contact with his neck, Gurril fell over again, kicked in the side
by one of the wildly bucking horses.

Coska watched as Gurril crawled away from the horses.
This was bad. Coska raced through his mind, trying to come up
with a spell he could layer over the one he currently had the
horses under and not knowing that the riderless horses had gone
mad. Gurril had brought his medium and heavyweight hammers
to the fight, securing them both to his back with leather holding
straps he made especially for the task of carrying multiple
hammers into battle. The medium weight hammer was now
dropped to the ground a good seven feet away from Gurril. As
Coska thought about layering spells, he saw Gurril sit up and
remove his heavy war hammer from his back. From Coska's

perspective, it looked as if Gurril was still shaken up, but able to fight.

Gallagher, flexing his leg muscles as hard as he could to stay in his saddle, swung his sword again, and its blade glided high over Gurril's head, unable to reach its mark. Gurril scooted himself back on his butt, so that when he stood he would still be out of sword's reach. Gurril made it to his feet and swayed slightly. He felt a trickle of blood come from his ear, and his head still swam. He turned to the first bucking horse, and swung his heavy war hammer into the general direction of its legs. The horse screamed and fell to the ground. The war hammer had caught the first leg as it kicked out, and the hard landing after the strike had broken a second leg.

Gallagher swore. One horse was down with two broken legs. Suddenly, Gallagher's control over his own horse went from almost nothing to absolute zero as Coska focused his magic's power to the remaining two horses. Gallagher hadn't seen the mage behind him, but he knew one had to be there. He grinned at the young warrior, who was now circling around to the other bucking horse.

"Going to break her legs, too? You're some piece of work. That's a good horse!" Gallagher spoke through gritted teeth as his horse now stood dull-minded beneath him, bedazzled by Coska.

Gurril looked up at him. "First I break her legs, then I break your mount's legs. Your skull is last."

Gallagher watched closely, trying to scoot around enough in his saddle to keep the young warrior in front of his view. He fought the temptation to leave the horse and run. Any chance he had of surviving depended on fighting from a mounted position. He knew the warrior could easily defeat him if he left the saddle. The young man, who Gallagher was now sure had every advantage in the fight, had taken an incredible beating. He was bleeding from one of his ears, and by the way he wheezed it sounded as if he had a few broken ribs, as well. The young warrior dug a handle out of the gravel and dirt, and now held both of his war hammers, one in each hand. The smaller hammer looked big. The larger hammer looked like something out of a nightmare.

As one of the bucking horse's front legs kicked, Gurril swung his hammers together in front of him, striking both shoulders of the beast. He felt and heard a satisfying crunch when the bones broke deep in the sockets. The horse screamed in pain and fell to the ground as if made of misshapen bricks. Gurril turned to the old man on the frozen mount.

The old man growled. Gurril growled back. The carriage had finally met the location of the fight, and had stopped well out of harm's way. The coachman watched in wonder.

On the other side of the standoff, Coska now only had one horse to concentrate on. He shivered his wand at the horse in a fast, twitching motion, and the horse fell to the ground, dead. Gallagher was trapped with a leg pinned under it.

Coska lowered his wand and fell to the ground. The exertion from using his magical power for so long had weakened him to the point where ever muscle in his body felt torn. It was all he could do to maintain his bowels and bladder, let alone try to stand or walk. After a few breaths, he regained his composure enough to stand on shaky feet, and began slowly walking toward his friend.

The coachman was enthralled. "Stay inside, we're either being robbed or saved, folks," he cautioned his unseen passengers inside their wooden enclosure. He could see one man who was obviously a magic maker walking toward the horseman and the muscle bound ass-kicker. An old man trapped under a horse wildly swung a sword around, trying to fend off the beastly hammer holder.

Gurril was very hot under his now torn and tattered coat. He made a mental note, that next time he should wear leather and skip the fur. He watched the pathetic old man swing his sword back and forth in front of him, trying to keep Gurril at a distance. Gurril simply timed a swing of his hammer so that the head of his hammer struck the man's hands as they held the sword.

Gallagher cried out in pain as eight of his fingers were crushed, the bones broken to splinters. He looked up at the warrior as the warrior placed his foot on Gallagher's neck. The last site Gallagher saw was the man swinging the heavier of the two hammers like a golf club.

The golf swing, as the coachman saw, removed most of Gallagher's head in a spray of blood, brains, and bone. Just after dispatching the old man, the warrior was joined by the mage. Together, they approached the coach. The coachman had knives, but nothing that would fend off these two. He began to pray to himself that these were town warriors, and not harriers out for a brutal robbing. The two young men stopped about ten feet in front of the horses that pulled the carriage. The mage said in a tired and shaky voice, "Welcome to Hearthstone. You have safe passage here."

7

When the carriage arrived in the village proper, two miles down the road from where the battle had taken place, the sight was enough to turn everyone's heads. The wooden carriage, pulled by two horses, had two dead bodies stacked on top of it, their heads beaten to pulp (mostly knocked off in the case of the old man). Coska and Gurril walked behind, each pulling the gravely injured raider by a foot. He had fallen from his mount in the middle of the field, and they had found him after a brief search.

The injured raider, who had been smashed from below in the jaw with one of Gurril's war hammers, was near death. The only reason Gurril hadn't finished him off was that he began getting very dizzy from the blows he had taken to the head, and he was afraid he might not be able to stand if he tried swinging one of his hammers again. The group stopped on the dirt road that widened into the main street of the village. Gurril and Coska dropped the foot each of them was carrying, and the injured raider lay still as villagers approached.

The injured harrier's jaw was nothing but a mush of bone, teeth, and flesh. A pool of dark blood stood in the cavity where his mouth had been. The war hammer had nearly disintegrated the man's jaw bone, and had smashed his hard pallet to bits. As he lay dying, some children old enough to not be afraid of the sight, but young enough to be foolish began closely examining the man. Coska shooed them away.

Gurril lost his balance and fell. He regained a kneeling posture, and vomited down the front of his shirt.

A fat woman stepped forward. "Coska," she said quietly to the magician, "Should I fetch the town nurse?"

Coska nodded to her and knelt beside his friend, surveying the dried blood that had trickled from both ears on the walk back to town.

Coska spoke to Gurril in a matter-of-fact tone. "Gurril, you've got a pretty bad concussion. Stay kneeling. The town nurse is on her way."

Gurril nodded slowly and silently, then dry heaved. A few moments went by, where curious onlookers watched. Coska noticed an unconcerned Angus in the crowd. He stood and walked to Gurril's brother.

"Angus," he began, "I know he looks badly hurt, but he'll be okay, I think."

Angus smiled, "Stupid shit. I knew he'd get his!" He spun on his heel and began walking off. He stopped, turned back, and looked to Gurril, who was now struggling to stay awake in the center of the onlookers. "Mom's going to be right pissed at you! Dumbshit!"

As the scene behind the carriage went on, the passengers had been let out and were mingling with the crowd. Coska couldn't pick them out from the townspeople. They may have been important to the elders, but in the end, they simply blended with the villagers and disappeared. Gurril teetered back and forth, and Coska steadied him with a hand. He had considered trying a charm to help him heal, but Coska wasn't confident that it would work. Spells gone wrong often times made things worse.

The town elders arrived and began shooing the crowd away. The crowd only partly obliged, moving just far enough to stay out of any trouble, but close enough to hear the conversation. Gurril couldn't tell which elder was which as his head swam and his vision spun. One of the elders congratulated him in a cold, obligatory way. Another said not to worry about the injured raider, the town fishers would finish him off since Gurril was too weak, and would be making the raider into pike bait in a few minutes. Another unrecognizable face swam into Gurril's view. This one said she was Cami, the town nurse, and that it was time to go home.

As the elders directed different fishermen to cut up the still-living harrier who lay on the street, Coska and the nurse scooped up Gurril so that he had an arm over each one's shoulders. They walked him to the villa that the two town defenders shared, and lay him in his bed. Then Cami, a plump but pretty woman who smiled in a timid way when giving orders, gave Coska careful instructions on caring for Gurril: Don't let him sleep more than a half hour at a time, give him only water for the next two days, and when he is ready to eat, give him only crackers for a week. There was more, but Coska forgot most of it immediately. He figured he could always ask the nurse again later. Before she left, she told Coska that Gurril would need at least two months to heal.

"In the meantime," she instructed, "No fighting for him. You're on your own for a while. Do not leave him alone until he is to the point where he can eat solid food. If you know any spells to help him, go right ahead. He'll be lucky if he remembers his own name after the beating he took."

The day, which had still been early when Coska and Gurril arrived back in Hearthstone, spun its way into evening. As the sun faded, there was a knock at the door. Coska opened it to find the carriage driver. "Yes?" Coska asked.

"Dear sir. I just wanted to thank you and your friend. You surely saved my life and the lives of my passengers today. I spoke with them, and we put this together for you."

The man, who was short, fat, and had a mustache the size of a push broom, handed over a small purple fabric sack, tied closed with a pink silk band. "I know the town pays you, but we wanted to say thanks. I hope your friend is well soon."

Coska thanked the man and bid him a good evening. After closing the door, he poured out the contents of the sack. Five silvers and a gold. Not bad for a day's work, but not good for the price Gurril's body (and probably brain) had paid. Coska began mixing up a small dinner of rice, fish, and peas when there was another knock at the door.

This time the caller was Sheila. Her eyes were red, and she looked very worried. "Where is he?"

"His room. Come in." Sheila followed Coska to Gurril's room. Her spirits sank as she saw how badly injured he was. He was lying on his bed wearing only loose shorts. His entire head had swollen up badly, and his entire rib cage was black with bruises. Both of Gurril's cats were lying at his feet, out like lights. Carmel, a tortoise shell, and Felix, an orange tabby, were curled together at the foot of Gurril's bed in what looked like the yin-yang symbol of two fish jumping into a circle. Every now and again, one would wake up, lift a head, look around the room, then sink back into sleep. Knowing how fond Gurril was of his cats, Sheila smiled, hoping their presence would help him heal.

"Gurril, it's Sheila. Can you hear me?" She spoke in nearly a whisper. Gurril's eyes fluttered open.

He breathed in deeply, grimaced at the pain it caused in his ribs, and said quietly, "Thanks for coming."

"I was hunting all day. I just found out you were hurt."

"How was your hunt?" His voice was thick and it sounded as if he fought pain with every syllable.

"Two rabbits, and I found a pile of horse hooves over by Stonecorn Field. I caught some small fish that I was going to bring over for your cats. I forgot them, though, when I heard you got beaten up so badly."

"Nobody beat me up," Gurril hissed.

"I'm sorry, you're right. Poor choice of words."

Coska, who stood in the doorway, now piped in. "You should have seen him. He was like a berserker out there." The wizard spoke with pure admiration for his friend.

Gurril smiled, "I kicked a little ass today." He grunted, and closed his eyes again to sleep.

8

Time moves slowly when all one is able to do is rest and reflect. Gurril read a few books about different fighting methods, thought a bit about buying horses for himself and Coska, and spent hours each day talking with Sheila and listening to her describe her daily hunts. One of the books he read was about rats, written by a former town warrior who claimed to have slaughtered an entire mischief on his own.

Coska now had less time on his hands. He and Gurril had previously spilt up the time needed to patrol for rats; with

Gurril healing, Coska had to do all the patrols on his own. He kept telling himself that this was the way it had always gone with one town warrior, he shouldn't think it a burden. When he wasn't patrolling he found books for Gurril and trained on new spells he was thinking up. He found that more and more often, he had those funny dreams about the future, the ones where he could never determine if it was safe to tell anyone about them or not. The visions still always had rules to them; he had one vision that Gurril's cats would get into a fight. He decided not to tell Gurril, and the vision came true—the cats fought over a mouse one of them had hunted. Another time, he dreamed that Sheila had a bloody finger. He told her about it, and the next evening when she came over to spend time with Gurril, she told him that her hunting knife had slipped while cleaning a rabbit, but she did not get cut. Coska knew the reason she hadn't been cut was because he had told her about the vision. No books he found gave Coska any indication of why he had visions or why they all had conditions attached to them. It seemed that this was something new to the world of magic.

Coska began practicing more healing spells. When he felt confident in them, he tried them on Gurril. He might tap one broken rib with his wand, or chant a spell while placing his fingers on Gurril's swollen cheek. He had only made one injury worse, and that was quickly corrected with a second spell that Coska knew would work correctly. The healing that was supposed to take months was far ahead of schedule due to this. Cami agreed that not only was Gurril healing well enough, but that any long-term brain damage was probably not going to happen the way it would with anyone else.

After one nurse visit, as Sheila slipped into Gurril's room, Coska sat reading the book on rats that Gurril had recently finished. As he read, he began thinking less and less of rats, and more and more of having a few drinks of wine. He considered his company, and called out "Sheila!"

Sheila came from Gurril's room, adjusting her bodice's top string, and smiling. Gurril had began getting more and more feisty with her, and she felt that very soon he would be healthy enough for her to please him with more than just a hand or her mouth. She entered the room, and saw Coska smiling at her.

She had grown more accustomed to Coska, and even felt the first tiny kindle of friendship for the magician. She appreciated the healing spells and careful attentiveness he gave to Gurril. They had begun talking and sharing a few stories during the times when the warrior would sleep.

"Yes, Coska?" She asked.

"When Grunty the Injured Manbeast falls asleep, share a bit of wine with me."

She laughed. "Grunty. He'll like that." She waved a hand at him and returned to the bedroom. Coska stood and stretched. The friendship that had started between him and Sheila was completely absent of anything resembling romantic chemistry, and he was happy for that. He loved Gurril as his closest friend, and if he ever thought that he would compete with Gurril for Sheila, he would have run away alone in the middle of the night rather than do anything that could have hurt his friend.

As he uncorked the wine, he heard her footsteps come back into the living room. From behind him, she said, "He's asleep. It doesn't take much, and the man is out like a light." For the next two hours, Sheila told Coska tall tales about hunting.

Gurril awoke and sat up in his bed. He had been feeling more and more energetic as his body mended, and the spells that Coska was using were not only helping him heal, but preventing him from losing valuable muscle mass while ordered not to train. He also felt very much like bedding Sheila. She had given him a lot of sexual attention, but sex itself was limited to things she could do to him while he lay still. He was ready to move his body into hers again.

He stood and walked to the bathroom, and she waved a hello to him in the hallway as she walked from the living room to Gurril's bedroom. He could tell she was a bit tipsy, but he didn't mind. Maybe tonight he'd get lucky. He looked to her when he returned to the bedroom from taking what seemed like the world's longest pee and growled in a way that asked her to come to him. She smiled lightly. Sheila had long ago completely forgotten the vision that she had on Beating Day. Something about Gurril's grunt reminded her of it now, and she recalled it more as a nightmare than a real vision of the future.

"Beauty, either take off your top or take down my bottom. I'm healthy tonight." She smiled again, but the mood to be physical with Gurril had left her. How could she relax when she had just remembered such a horrible nightmare?

"I just remembered an odd dream I had when Coska knocked me out on Beating Day," she said, "It somehow involved me getting crushed by running horses. Do you think it could be a vision of my death?"

Gurril became serious in a flash. "What?" He was in disbelief.

"It wasn't like anything I'd ever dreamed before. It seemed so vivid. I could smell the horses as they trampled me, even though I couldn't really see what was going on." Suddenly, she remembered that she felt in the dream like she was not supposed to tell Gurril. Between the time, the wine, and her confusion about what the dream had been about, she had forgotten until that moment about the feeling that telling Gurril meant certain death. She put her hands to her mouth, trying to keep it from dropping open.

"I have the most horrible feeling that I wasn't supposed to tell you about that nightmare, Gurril." Tears began to roll down her cheeks, "I think I've just cursed myself!"

Gurril sat up and began exiting his bed, "No! You won't be crushed. From this point on, I'll go with you everywhere." They embraced, and Sheila shook her head.

"No... It was a vision about hooves, and the one I love throwing me under them. I think that's you. If you are with me... you'll throw me under them, Gurril. You'll kill me."

Sheila turned and ran from the room. Gurril, still slow to move from spending nearly every hour of the day in bed, could only stumble clumsily out of bed after her as she left the small house and ran home. Before he was to the door, Coska had intercepted him.

"Let her go. I heard what she said to you. Let her go." Coska instructed.

Gurril looked at him and grunted a question.

Coska, knowing Gurril well enough to understand the question implied by the grunt, replied, "When I tapped her with the spell to knock her out on Beating Day, I must have somehow given her a vision. I think that my powers of foresight are dependent on odd rules, Gurril. Sometimes, telling a person, or even only a *certain* person about a vision can make it come true. She told you what the vision was."

Gurril nodded and grunted. Coska nodded back. "Then... Gurril, I hate to say this. But if she was certain that she should not have told you, I think she may be doomed."

"Think of something." Gurril glared at Coska, suddenly aware of why magicians were burned in most towns.

Sheila arrived back to her apartment, a small one room living quarter situated above a bakery near the town center. Gurril had never been to her apartment, and as she realized this fact, she began to cry.

David the hawk, always keenly aware of her emotions, chirped and scraped a talon at his perch. Sheila looked over to his large teak wood cage, and saw him staring at her. "At least you'll go free." She smiled sweetly at the hawk. She wished to herself that after her death he would fly free again. "David, we have to think closely about this vision. It seemed to me if I told Gurril about it, it meant I would die. How could that be?"

Sheila wiped her eyes and stood at her window, looking in the direction of Gurril and Coska's house. "The vision seemed to say that the one I love would see me die, or something like that. Maybe what it meant was that Gurril is the one I love, and if he sees me again, I'll die. Not seeing him is my key to survival, then?"

She questioned her reflection in the glass of her window over and over, asking herself if the way to survive was to stay by Gurril's side every minute of every day, or to avoid him at all costs. She wept at the thought that they might never lie together in the same bed again. It hadn't been long since they had become a couple, and although she felt a deep sense of caring for the warrior, she also knew that it was probably only that intoxicating spice of new love, which in time would fade. Her mother had told her about this many times; mostly while watching her father stumble drunk through the house. At least she would never have to go through that herself.

Three weeks had passed since the discussion about the vision. Gurril, thanks mostly to Coska's healing spells, was back to a full training schedule. His speed had slowed only slightly, and as he trained, he felt his body renew itself. He would be back to his regular fighting speed and power within days. It was late in the afternoon, and Coska was running a message to Sheila for Gurril.

Gurril, Sheila, and Coska, had all come to the same conclusion: the best course of action was separation between Gurril and Sheila. Coska would bring Sheila the two town defenders' schedules for the next day, and Sheila would make sure that she avoided the two men when they were out of their house. All of them knew this could only work for so long, and they separately worked out various scenarios that would keep Gurril and Sheila apart for the longer term.

Sheila had no family outside of Hearthstone. Leaving the town was akin to banishment. She knew a single young woman as strong as she could find a home in another place, but everything she knew and loved was here. Leaving was not an option she would entertain.

As Gurril worked through a long set of pull-ups using a beam that he had mounted in one corner of the house, a town elder named Laura entered the home. She did not knock, as was usually custom, and watched Gurril do a few pull-ups, impressed with his muscular frame. She was old, but not dead yet. The sight of the young man sweating and grunting was pleasant for her. After a bit of entertainment, she lightly cleared her throat.

Gurril dropped from the beam and turned to her. He looked at her questioningly, and said simply, "Yes?"

"The rest of the elders and I would like to meet with you and Coska, now that you are healthy again. We'd like to discuss how it came that you were so grievously injured."

"Oh. When?"

"Tonight at seven. It may be a long meeting, so eat dinner first."

"Okay. Seven."

"Good day, Gurril." With that, the old lady turned and briskly left the house.

Hours later, Coska and Gurril were standing in front of the elders in the town chambers. They had been questioned about many things, including a description of the man who had jumped from the back of the old thief's horse and ran away. As Coska described him, the elders looked warily at each other.

"He had red hair, and was very tall," Coska said.

"Quite thin," Gurril added.

Coska continued, "He ran right by me. Once his weapon was disabled, he simply ran away."

In a loud, growling tone of anger, Roy shot back with, "Maybe you could have disabled the *man*, and not his weapon!"

Trina, the elder who usually did most of the talking for the group, spoke up. "Did he have a resemblance to the old man? To Gallagher?"

Gurril and Coska answered "Yes," quickly and simultaneously.

The town elders whispered to each other, murmuring about. They seemed to be in an almost silent state of buzzing excitement.

Gurril was tired of not being in on whatever it was that the elders were so interested in. In a tone harsher than he intended, he snapped, "Whatever it is, just tell us."

The murmuring excitement ceased in the blink of an eye. Gurril suddenly felt weak, like he had gotten himself into serious trouble. Coska involuntarily leaned away from him as the elders, in a single motion, turned from each other's ears, faced the two men, and glared.

"When you need to know, we'll tell you," Trina said in a kind yet firm way. "In the meantime, we feel that this may have been prevented if you two had horses. We pay you well. Buy two sturdy horses. That is ordered by the elders. Come back in one week and speak with us again. We'll have an assignment for you then. Are you two ready to fight soon?"

They answered in unison one more time. "Yes."

Gurril stepped forward and took a less aggressive tone than his last statement had carried. "Trina, you pay us well for one man. For two... it is only about the average for people in town. We can't afford horses, and neither of us knows how to ride. It would take us months to save for a horse. If we bought one, it would be months more before either of us was an effective rider, let alone able to fight from a mounted position. We'll begin saving for horses, but this won't be of any help for a year or more."

Roy scoffed, and said, "Excuses! I see them buying bread, cheese, and wine almost daily. And he's feeding that blond huntress, you know!"

Trina turned to Roy. "He's right, Roy. Horses are a practical need, but that won't change anything in the short term." She turned back to Gurril. "If we begin setting aside an extra copper or two when the town has extra money from traveler's taxes, that should help you save a bit quicker, shouldn't it?"

Gurril nodded, and said, "Yes, ma'am."

"Good. The man who ran away from the fight is named Seth. He's Tad Gallagher's son. And he's something on an engineer. Our intelligence indicates that he's gathered the rest of his father's gang—about six more men, and that they are building weapons. He means to attack the town for revenge. In the meantime, we'll find a way to attract him to a good ambush point for you two. When you come back to the chambers again, we'll have more instructions for you."

Coska furled his brow. "Excuse me, madam, but how—
"

"No more questions!" Roy's face was flushed as he shouted. Coska could see that Trina had already said more than the other elders had wanted the two men to know.

Back at the house, Coska and Gurril shared a bottle of wine. Gurril scratched at his chin. "I don't understand. What do they mean by 'intelligence'?"

"They mean spies," Coska answered. "Spies who know the bandits' names, and what their talents are."

"Bullshit. How could they find that out?"

"Maybe they've infiltrated the bandits' camp." Coska finished a glass of wine, and immediately poured more from the bottle. "How do you think they'll lure them into an ambush?"

Gurril smiled and growled lowly. "I know how I'd do it."

"Really? How?"

"Seth is an engineer. So he builds forges, wheels, and is good at blacksmithing. Iron is harder to come by than gold when you need a ton a time."

Coska smiled, "Especially when you're wanted in every town!"

"We order a load of iron, and then hit them when they try to steal it."

"You're right. But we got lucky last time. What if the spies in the camp give us the wrong ambush point next time?"

Gurril grunted, thinking. He refilled his wine glass and paced the room. There was a knock at the door. It was late, and neither men were expecting a visitor. Coska stepped to the door and opened it slowly, revealing Gurril's brother Angus, and the two brothers' mother. Without being asked, the two stomped into the house, muddy shoes and all.

Coska protested. "Hey, we just cleaned the floors!"

Angus lifted his lip in a slight snarl. "Bugger off, you bastard wizard. We're here for him."

Angus pointed at Gurril, whose shoulders slumped as soon as he saw who had arrived.

Gurril's mother put the backs of her hands on her fat hips. Her snarly blonde hair stood clumped on her head, and her brown eyes burned. "My son. My son, the weak town warrior who gets beaten up by a lowly group of bandits. You and your witching man. What the hell are you two, anyway? You can't fight. You sit around the house with cats like a couple of old men who'd rather lay with each other than with a woman."

Gurril tried to make his voice sound strong, instead of ashamed at the accusations his mother made. "Why are you here?"

"I wanted to make sure that you've seen the town recorder."

"Why?"

Angus piped up, saying, "So that when you get yourself killed, your remaining possessions go where they belong, and not to your man-wife magician!"

As he spoke, he jerked his head around like a chicken, making his tall tower of blonde hair bounce back and forth.

Gurril's jaw tightened, and his teeth ground together. Behind him, in the kitchen, Coska's hands tightened to fists. Gurril growled like an angry dog as he spoke the words, "Get out of my house" through clenched teeth.

Angus spied the sword the old man had brought to the fight, leaning up against a wall. Gurril and Coska had wanted to save it for a training aid. Angus picked it up, and pointed it at Coska. Angus laughed, and said to Coska, "You are the girl of the two of you, right? Oh, wait..." He spun on his heel and pointed the sword at Gurril, "*You're* the Gurril. Mom even named you so!"

Angus laughed, unaware that Coska now stood directly behind him. Coska, who normally fought with only his wand, was in the mood for fists at this point.

Gurril pointed his finger at his mother's forehead. "You!" He roared, his face now a red picture of fury. "Get out! I *will* see the town recorder tomorrow. I'll ensure that you two get NOTHING! If I die, you get NOTHING!"

Gurril's mother finally began to feel fear of the man who stood before her. He was fully a foot and half taller than her, had killed other men, and his eyes were bulging red flames of hate. She slowly walked backward toward the door.

Coska, still standing immediately behind Angus (who was watching the fury of Gurril with delight), tapped the human wheat stalk's shoulder. As Angus turned, Coska yoinked the sword from his hand and held it in a ready position with his right hand. With his left hand, Coska punched Angus square in the nose. Angus's head flew back and sprang forward again, but now with a look of horrible surprise on it.

Angus had blood flowing fast from his nose and onto his cotton shirt. It soaked there, making a bright red pattern that made Coska's war-sense bloom. Angus said in surprise, "You're a magician! You don't use your fist or a sword!"

Coska snarled in a warrior way, and replied, "Who the hell do you think the ape over there trains against?"

Tears of pain and surprise stood out in Angus's eyes. Coska roared a war grunt, and swung the sword sharply at Angus's scalp, mowing off his tall blond hair less than an inch from his skull. The blond man wailed in fear, and ran for the door as his mother chirped out a cry of anguish.

Gurril raised his hand as if to use the back of it against his mother's face, and she turned and followed Angus out the front door and into the street. Coska and Gurril were breathing in heavy huffs, as if they had just faced two seasoned warriors rather than a fat woman and a spoiled man. Coska began giggling. Gurril frowned and looked to him.

"What the hell are you laughing about?"

"It doesn't take a vision to tell me that you won't ever be seeing those two again. You overcame something big tonight, Gurril."

"Tomorrow I go to the town recorder, and write them out of my life. Tonight, I'm going to finish that bottle of wine, go to Sheila's apartment, and have sex until dawn."

"Great plan, but what about the vision?"

"There won't be any horses in her bed."

"Okay. No horses, but one stallion, I guess. I'll feed your cats breakfast in the morning, and see you for training at nine. Until then, I'll finish my book, go to my room, and dream of the maidens at the retirement village until about eleven thirty." He paused, becoming serious. "You're sure about the vision?"

Gurril shook his head. "It won't happen tonight, Coska."

10

Gurril and Coska worked out the details of their plan prior to the next visit with the elders. They had just finished explaining it, and were now waiting for the elders to finish their council together in another room. The chambers were dark and cold, and Coska's stomach growled noisily. Gurril looked over at him as they stood, waiting for the elders to return.

"I told you to eat before we came." Gurril said quietly. After his words, he grunted his disapproval grunt.

"Quit growling at me like that. I wasn't hungry then. I've got an odd feeling, Gurril."

"Odd? Like another vision?"

"Yes, but not really a vision. Just an odd feeling. I can't really explain it."

"Then why are you talking about it?"

"You told me I should have eaten."

Gurril furled his brow. "So?"

"So... If I didn't have to explain to you why my stomach is growling, I wouldn't have to talk—" Coska was cut off by the elders re-entering the chamber. They looked solemn. They sat in their seats, and stared ahead at the two young men for what seemed like an hour.

Trina, ever the spokeswoman, sighed heavily. "Do you two really think this plan will work?"

Coska spoke up. "As long as you trust that Seth and his men will find out about the coach in question, yes."

With authority, Trina said, "We'll see to that. Seth and his men will definitely attack."

Now Gurril knew for sure that the elders had a spy. To make the plan work, it had to seem as if the coach was taking every precaution not to be attacked. These extra measures to hide its real identity would work perfectly to lure in Seth's gang.

"When, then?" Gurril asked.

Trina looked over to Rona, the youngest looking of the elders. She scratched behind her gray-covered head.

"Nine days." Rona said simply, her voice light but firm.

Trina turned back to Gurril and Coska. "You two have nine days to get this plan ready." Trina scribbled a note on a bit of paper and held it out to Gurril. "Here is the name of the coachman to see. He'll help you set up the coach. But don't let him know the plan. As far as he's concerned, you're just offering a security consultation. In fact, mislead him if you have the chance. Just in case he's... Well, just in case."

11

Seth was in his camp, daydreaming about reclaiming his father's sword. The metal was nothing special, really. Tad had stolen it fair and square from a sleeping man. Seth was always proud of his father's capers, and had spent his nights listening to the old man yarn for hours. The bastard with the huge muscles and war hammer had stolen the sword after cheating by pinning

55

Seth's father under a horse. He stared into the night fire, dreaming up inventions to kill the warrior and the mage, when a pair of bright red eyes approached from the darkness.

Seth sat to attention. "Billy, is that you?"

The rat crept out of the darkness and into the light of the fire. He nodded, hunched up on his hind quarters, and spoke. "Me. Billy."

The rat, four feet long and stinking like a nightmare, shook with excitement. "News from town."

Seth hated speaking to the rat. As with all rats, his voice creaked like an old oak falling. Speaking like a human was, for rats, difficult. Billy was good at it compared to others, but it was still a struggle for him. His eyes were bright red and bulged out from their sockets like blood-filled fruits. When he smiled, his pin-sharp teeth gleamed. The exception was the set of four fangs, two in the upper jaw and two in the lower jaw, that were covered in a pink mucous. Those teeth didn't gleam; in fact, they seemed to suck the light away. The rat that stood before Seth was a mottled gray color, his fur short and dirty. His large round head had small ears, and his dark brown tail swooshed back and forth when he got excited. His breath reeked of rot, and it was not uncommon for his red tongue to hang from between his pin teeth.

"What news?" Seth asked. He had lately become bored with the rat, and his annoying lack of good information. Soon, he'd have Billy the rat killed and burned to ash. Usefulness, Seth had always found, was fleeting.

Billy flicked his tongue over his teeth. "Any meat first?"

Seth sighed. He pulled a hunk of rabbit jerky from his breast pocket and tossed it over the fire. Billy reached up with his hands—no, Seth reminded himself, those were *paws*—and gobbled up the jerky.

Billy smiled again. "You're so nice. Coach coming through in six mornings. Hearthstone to Domar. Full of iron."

Seth immediately perked up. His young face was barely old enough to shave, and his excitement made his look turn from that of a bored teenager into that of an excited little boy. "Iron? Are you sure?"

Billy nodded. "Coachman making coach look like it hauls empty barrels. But really iron. One ton."

"Will it be guarded?"

Billy shook his head to indicate a negative answer. "Using tricks, not muscle." Here, Billy the rat, spy for the elders of Hearthstone, strayed from his instructions. Trina had told him to say that the bad man with the muscles was still too hurt to fight after being kicked by Seth's father's horses. Instead, Billy said, "Bad man with muscles ready to fight horses."

This confused Seth. "What do you mean? They're using trickery, but the warrior is ready to fight horses?"

Billy nodded. The rat had a plan, and if all worked, it would end with the gang dead, and Hearthstone village defenseless. He concentrated hard, trying to say the words just right.

"He ambushes you in same place. All muscle, no creativity, this man. You should have beat him once. Now beat him right."

12

Anyone who has seen a great wizard be seriously injured or killed will tell tales of an awesome release of power at that moment. For instance, when Danforth the Wicked was burned at the stake in the town of Cold Water, the minute his skin began to melt a great wind blew straight upward from his body. Every bird for a mile around the town had fallen dead.

In another instance, in a small farming village with no name, a witch had been drowned in the river. When the bubbles coming from her submerged, pleading face stopped, the river began to boil. It boiled for eight days, killing every fish, and poisoning the water for a generation.

The darkened room of a hotel was witness to a wizard being stabbed in the back while having sex, causing the young woman he was with to utterly explode. The man who had stabbed the wizard was a jealous romantic rival, and upon seeing his love blown to bits, he turned the knife on himself. When he ran the knife across his throat, rather than kill him it set him on fire, and he burned to death over the dead bodies and spread out guts of the other two.

A final tale of this type is of a child. Nobody actually knew the child had magic in her, until one day when she was seven. A drunken patron at her father's ale house had reached his hand up her skirt and shoved a finger deep into her after stealing her away to a back room. Upon the pain of her hymen being violated and broken in such a manner, her fingernails uncontrollably shot out of her fingertips like missiles, flying with power and speed through the man over and over again, shredding him to ribbons. He lay there, dead in a pool of blood, the little girl's body regenerating and pushing out a new set of nails on her fingertips. When she told the town elders what had happened, they decided she was a threat, tied her to a tree, and poured boiling oil over her to kill her. The boiling oil froze when it touched her skin, formed into small ice pellets, and shot through the air, wiping out the entire village. She disappeared into the forest after that, a full three generations ago.

In time, one tale of this sort would be told in Hearthstone.

13

The morning of the attack, the young ferret named Pepper collected seeds from the dirt of Stonecorn field. He ran quickly back and forth to his den, happy to feel the dew brush against his whiskers. Every now and again, he'd roll in a bit of dirt, or spray some musk to make sure every creature knew this was his home space. As far as Pepper was concerned, the entire world consisted only of Stonecorn field. He had never left its borders, and felt as though he'd never have to. As he scurried along, under some low brush, he heard the sound of hooves on the road. The sound of hooves passing this time of day was normal, but something was different today. He listened closely, and determined that the horses today carried a heavier than usual load. He mentally noted the information, and went back to his scurrying.

Seth and his men quietly watched the road from a small escarpment of woods on the border of Stonecorn field. His mouth watered at the thought of a full ton of iron to work with. His weapon to rule every town in the region could be completed.

Seth and his men waited, hidden in the woods. If the warrior meant to wait in the same place and hope for a fight, that's what Seth would give him. Even if the rat was wrong about that part, this was still the best place for an ambush. Seth was excited. He wanted to see the warrior try to attack their horses again; he had some new trickery to try out. With any luck, his plan to counter-ambush would result in a ton of iron, a dead warrior, and a dead magician.

As the coach passed the first wooded area that marked the beginning of Stonecorn field, Sheila took notice. She and David had been tracking a deer through this area. The hawk couldn't take down the deer, of course, but he could track it from above while Sheila followed on the ground, waiting for a chance to launch a spear into it. She had only recently taken up spear throwing, but her skills were already enough that she had hit and killed a large fish in the creek. Now she wanted something with fur on it.

She enjoyed sunrise hunting. If she was lucky, she could kill early and have the rest of the day to herself. Her late-night encounter with Gurril over two weeks ago still lingered in her mind. She felt a warm, wet feeling begin to overtake her as she tracked the deer, and considered lying down in the field to touch the place that desired Gurril the most. It would be even more exciting, knowing that people were passing unaware on the road so close by. There was usually a coach passing by this time of morning, and Sheila took no special notice of it beyond her fantasy. She did, however, notice that David the hawk was now circling to indicate that the deer she tracked was at her eleven o'clock position, about sixty yards ahead. She turned slightly away from the road, and began walking as quietly as she could to the spot where the deer was resting.

Seth watched as the coach cleared the woods across the prairie and entered the way through Stonecorn field. He smiled as three riders came out of the woods behind the coach. These were his men, his rear attack on the coach, his great diversion. Soon, the magician and the muscled warrior would leave their hiding spots on the ground and begin an attack on the raiders following the coach. Seth watched, waited, and anticipated. The coach came closer, and closer still.

Seth began to worry. Soon, the coach would be approaching his position. He and his larger group of frontal attackers would have to expose themselves before the two town defenders tried their ambush.

Behind Seth, one of his gang members whispered, "We're going to have to take the coach now, Seth!"

Seth exhaled heavily, hoping that the rat was just wrong on the location of the ambush, and that Seth's men would have an easy time with the coach. "GO!" he shouted to his men in the trees.

As they started out, the last rider in line felt a jerk pulling him backwards, rather than the launch of an excited horse. He turned and looked behind him to see a grabbing vine twisted around the horse's right hind leg. The yellowish-green vine worked its way around the horse's legs and the rider jumped down, pulling his sword from its sheath. The vine had a series of pods on it that opened, revealing white flowers. The flowers' stigmas jutted straight out, and sprayed a dry poison in the direction of the man that irritated the skin and eyes. He worked through the irritant and began hacking away at the vine with his sword, searching for the base plant that it had come from. He listened for the distinctive hissing sound that grabbing plants emitted from their base when threatened and moved toward it, hoping not just to save his horse, but to get into the fight as soon as possible.

The coach driver hadn't noticed the three riders following him, but he did see the five that sprung out of the trees ahead of him. One of the riders had some sort of crazy wooden brace on the left side of his horse. The coachman pulled back on his horses' reins a bit, but then decided to charge through the group. He was sure they would kill him, so he might as well go down racing through them, rather than on his knees begging. He snapped his reins, and his four horses charged ahead, the lead one whinnying.

Sheila had heard Seth's shout, and knew something was going on. She pulled one of her short spears from the quiver of six on her back. A glance back to the sky over where she had been heading told her that David was far off from the fight, and would be focused on the deer. The hawk would be no help to her in a fight if there was going to be one.

The area where she had been walking was tall with corn stalks, and Seth hadn't seen her hunting. She could see the five riders coming toward the coach due to their height over the corn, and she knew instinctively that they were raiders. She gauged their speed, timed her mark, and threw her first spear.

From inside the coach, Gurril and Coska watched the riders approach from the front and rear. Gurril was baffled at why they would have attacked in the same place as they had before. His entire reasoning for hiding in the coach (not even the coachmen knew they were there, stolen aboard inside of large wooden barrels) was that the raiders would be fools to pick the same ambush point twice.

Coska watched the rear group through a peep hole. "They're staying back a bit. Maybe hoping to surprise the driver once he gets stopped by the front group."

Gurril grunted with pleasure. A delay would allow him and Coska to take out some of the frontal assault first. He watched the lead group through his peep hole. He shouted a surprised "Whoa!" when he saw a spear about thirty inches long come out of the air to the right of the lead horseman, striking the raider in the space where his neck met his shoulder. The struck man fell dead off his horse.

Gurril wasn't the only one surprised by the spear. Seth had seen it only a split second before it struck the man in front of him dead. Seth immediately pulled back on his horse, and made a quick loop around to the side of his bandits that was opposite from the side the spear had come. He had taken a strong horse in order to handle the killing machine he had designed to ride on the mount, and was pleased that the animal could still keep up and maneuver. He looked into the corn field franticly, hoping to find Gurril there. Instead, he saw nothing, and watched another spear fly from seemingly nowhere and take out another of his men. The coach slowed and halted. Seth's men, ever disciplined, took out the driver with throwing knives while Seth was searching for the spearman. They rode to the side of the coach that would block them from more spears as the coachman's body rolled off the bench seat and fell in a pile under the carriage. Seth looked to his two groups, now a total of himself and five other men, hiding behind the coach.

"They're out there, somewhere!"

Seth punched the wooden coach, cutting open his knuckles.

Sheila was now in the heat of battle passion, thirsting to kill more gang members. She knew the raiders were on the opposite side of the coach as her. She crept closer to them through the corn, and threw a spear at a high angle in the direction of the coach.

The man next to Seth spoke up. "Seth, we can break up into—guh!" A spear seemed to come from straight above, graze the man's face and chest, then drive itself into his lower abdomen. It also pierced his horse's spine. The rider and animal fell dead in front of Seth. He was on the verge of panic.

"Spread out! Get into that field and *kill that spearman!*"

Gurril's eyes were as wide as saucers. The group of eight bandits was down to five, and he and Coska still hadn't given away their positions. The mounts circled around both sides of the coach and began entering the corn field. This was perfect. He and Coska would now be able to attack from behind. Gurril looked to the young wizard. Quietly, he motioned to the coach's side door that the raiders had just been near. The two town defenders, as quiet as could be, opened the door and slipped out. Coska stood on the coach's rear side, watching three riders enter the field. Gurril stood near the coach's horses, watching Seth and one other man enter the field from the front side of the coach. Gurril instantly recognized Seth as the young man who had run away from the last fight.

Gurril heard Coska mumbling magic words. Two of the horses nearest Coska in the field buckled and fell, leaving their riders on the ground. Gurril issued a loud battle cry, and ran toward the horse Seth rode, a war hammer in each hand. Seth heard the battle cry and turned. Because of the angle of his turn, it wasn't Gurril he saw, but Coska. Seth smiled at the thought of killing the filthy magician, and spurred his horse toward the man. In the field, another spear shot through one of the rider's chests.

Coska watched as Seth's horse closed the short distance between them quickly. Neither he nor Gurril had noticed before, but now Coska saw an odd contraption on the left side of the animal. To Coska, it looked like the horse had some sort of wooden beam running along its side. Seth drew a sword and swung, striking the coach as he passed Coska. The swing looked to Coska like a near miss. It had struck, however, exactly where Seth had aimed. His goal was not to wound Coska, but to send the young wizard running.

In the field, Gurril was swinging his hammers in the center of the remaining three thieves, only one of which was still mounted. Each of his opponents was armed, but all of them had trained so heavily in mounted combat that this mixture of mounted and unmounted fighting had become confusing to them. Gurril was doing well blocking most blows, but he had counted on Coska helping him with the group fight. Now that Coska had turned to run for cover from Seth, Gurril was on his own.

Only, he wasn't quite on his own. From somewhere in the field, another spear came down, impaling the last of the riders. As the man fell, Gurril was able to attack a foot-bound enemy who was surprised to see his comrade fall dead. Gurril struck the side of the man's face with a medium weight war hammer, caving it in and killing the man. The fight was now Gurril and an unseen spear thrower against one man in the field and Seth on the road.

The final mounted raider finally joined the fight late, having freed his horse from the grabbing vine after delivering a vicious chopping to the plant. He still had some of the powdery poison from the vine's flowers stuck to his clothes. The mounted man guided his horse to the dirt road, joining Seth in his chase of Coska. A spear spliced the air where the man had been just a second earlier, but missed him entirely. Just as Gurril was about to take a low swing at the knees of his remaining opponent, a spear burst through the raider's chest from an angle below the man's sternum. As the gang member fell dead, Gurril saw Sheila standing behind the man, her quiver empty. He was stunned. "Sheila... You fight like a helldog!"

She smiled, pulled the spear from the dead man's body, and said "Let's go save Coska."

Coska's run for cover had become a run for his life. Seth had swung a sword over his head a few times, then rode past him, and was now charging toward the magician. "Cast a spell now, demon!" Seth yelled as he approached Coska. Coska skidded to a stop, and turned one hundred and eighty degrees, running straight away from Seth.

Gurril and Sheila watched as the scene before them seemed to unfold in slow motion. Seth's horse was easily going to overtake Coska before they could get to their friend. When the horse was galloping just short of alongside Coska, there was a loud *sproing!* sound as the beam attached to the side of the horse swung out toward Coska with lightning speed and force.

Coska heard the sound, too. In his rush of fear, it caused him to unconsciously jump into the air as he ran. The heavy wooden beam would have struck his head, shattering his skull to bits had this not happened. As it was, Coska's jump saved his life, and the heavy wooden beam struck the magician at the point where his neck met his body. Instead of his skull shattering, it was his spine, both shoulders, and both collar bones.

When the beam struck Coska, a great white light shot straight out of his body and into a corner of Stonecorn field. As the light burst out, Coska's body somersaulted through the air, landing in a heap on the side of the road. The area where the light had landed was smoldering, and Seth looked to it in amazement, his jaw hanging open. The beam attached to the spring mechanism on his horse glowed slightly, and his leg on that side had begun to tingle a bit. He heard footsteps on the road, many yards behind him. Seth turned to see Gurril and Sheila sprinting toward them, just as the last man, stained with grabbing vine poison, joined him on the road.

Seth saw the muscle man holding one of his damned hammers. The spear throwing bitch had a bowie knife the size a trophy perch in her hand. He pulled a cord to wind his beam back up, and told his last remaining gang member, "We'll charge at them. Now!"

Gurril felt like he was burning with a fire from hell. He had just seen Coska get struck, and thought for sure that his friend was dead. Gurril was instantly flung into blind battle rage, ready to not just kill, but to utterly erase the man called Seth. He and Sheila ran toward the two horses, who galloped toward them in a counter charge. As the two sets of fighters approached each other, Gurril remembered the vision that Coska had about Sheila dying. Hooves. This was it! As the horses approached, Gurril flung out his arm and planted his feet, stopping Sheila. She just had time to utter a confused, "Hu?"

Gurril timed it perfectly. The two horses were on a path to trample him and Sheila, so at the last moment before they were going to be hit, he grabbed her shoulders and flung her as hard as he could to the side, hoping he would survive the trampling and that she would hide in the field and use the cover of the tall, green stalks of stonecorn to escape. As Gurril watched, time became so slow it was almost immobile. Both riders broke off to the side, afraid their horses would be smashed in the head by the warrior's hammer. Gurril had inadvertently thrown Sheila directly into their paths. He watched in horror as Sheila was struck by the chest of the first horse and thrown downward and forward into the path of eight hooves. The hooves did their terrible work, crushing first her waist, then her chest, and finally, smashing into her skull.

Her shattered face was contorted in pain and confusion as she lay dead on the road. Gurril stood stunned. Every inch of her above the waist was a sickening color of black and blue, and part of her head behind her right ear was caved in. Her dear eyes stared straight ahead at the dirt of the road, and blood leaked out from her mouth, ears, and nose. Gurril had killed his love, only seconds after believing he had watched his best friend die. Sadness and rage welled up inside of him, and Gurril shrieked a war cry so great, that no other cry in any warrior's life could match it. The very trees shook in fright of him.

Seth and his companion rider pulled up and around to face the warrior again. They had heard his shriek, and could feel each other's fright.

"Ride toward him, then break off just before you hit him. Like our last pass." Seth instructed in a voice shaky with fear. "I'll be behind you to hit him with the beam when he's swinging his hammer at you."

Without a word, Seth's last man took off toward Gurril, and Seth followed behind him. As Seth rode, he evaluated his situation, and determined that with no more men, a ton of iron would not do him much good. As Gurril leapt straight into the air and turned the first rider's head to a mist of blood and brains with his largest war hammer (neither the rider nor Seth had thought any human possible of such a thing; indeed, the rider had no inkling that he was on a very short suicide mission), Seth decided to retreat. He rode far clear of Gurril, then jammed his spurs deep into the horse's side, racing the animal down the road as fast as possible away from the blood-covered demon who roared battle cries at him. Gurril watched Seth trying to ride away from him, growled, and threw his small hammer in a high, fast arc.

Gurril watched the hammer spin end-over-end through the sky as it rose to a peak height, then came down and struck the top of the man's head. It took nearly a second for the sound of the thump to reach him. The scene around him, which had been so loud with battle cries, screams of pain, and whinnies of horses, now fell to complete silence. Gurril looked to Coska down the road, and to Sheila very near to him on the gravel. He decided to go to Sheila first since she was closer.

He kneeled beside her body, in wonder at how she had gone from being so beautiful in life to so wretched in death. Although she had died only moments before, her tongue was already swelling out of her mouth. Her eyes stared blankly ahead, the right one losing its shape as thick goo ran from it. Most of her face and head was crushed and discolored, and instead of her usual vanilla scent, she reeked of blood and foul air that escaped from internal cavities. Gurril used his fingers to pull her eyes closed. He wanted to kiss her goodbye, but the sight of her was making his stomach turn in a bad way. He decided he would have to wait until she was cleaned for her funeral for the final touch of his lips to hers.

The warrior stood and began jogging to the site where Coska lay. He stopped when he reached his friend, whose body was piled in an unnatural way on the roadside. Coska's body was crumpled so badly that Gurril wasn't sure if it was even one piece anymore. The magician's face was turned up, and Gurril looked to his friend's face. The death he saw in Sheila's eyes was not present on Coska. The magician was alive!

"Coska! Coska, can you hear me?"

No response. Gurril looked to Coska's chest, and saw it rising and falling slightly. Coska blinked.

"Can you blink again, Coska?"

Nothing. Gurril reeled. Was his friend now an empty shell? What was the light? Gurril rubbed his forehead, and remembered that he still needed to confirm that Seth was dead. He stood and looked down the road another forty yards, to where Seth had gone down from his horse. The horse was still there, as was Seth. The evil leader of the raiders lay in a pool of blood. Gurril could see from where he stood that the man was not moving, but was alive.

Perhaps, Gurril thought, Seth was now as empty a body as Coska seemed to be. He decided that if this was not the case, he would do anything he could to make the man's suffering so severe that hell would be a relief when he reached it. If Seth was an empty shell of a body, Gurril would simply smash his head to bits and end it now. Gurril moved his head to the left and right to crack the joints in his neck, then he walked to where Seth lay.

The young man who had engineered the wooden spring-loaded beam was just conscious enough to know that the tingling in his leg had spread to the rest of his body as he lay on the rough gravel road. He could also feel the future within him in a funny sort of vision. If he were to survive here today, he somehow knew he would never harm another person. If he were to die here today, he would go on to kill many. Seth waited for the warrior to come to him, wondering how it was that by surviving he would harm none, yet by dying harm many. He was pondering this over when he realized that he could not see.

Gurril's hammer had caved in Seth's skull directly over the portion of his brain that controlled his sight. Blood pumped from the wound in gushes that became smaller and smaller as the man bled and weakened. Gurril approached, and instantly recognized the wound for what it was: a mortal injury if no healing aid was given quickly. Seth wasn't an empty sack of human flesh like Coska now was, but without serious medical attention he would be dead in minutes. Gurril placed his boot over Seth's throat, choking him. Just before Seth could lose consciousness, Gurril removed his boot. The warrior did this over and over to the man, until the blood pumping out of his

67

head wound only trickled. Gurril gave one final stomp, hard and fast, to the man's face. The stomp crushed his dying bones, and Seth breathed no more. To Gurril, it made Seth look similar to Sheila after death. The warrior, facing this realization, fell to the ground and wept.

14

After Gurril regained his composure, he realized that he needed to come up with a plan to clean the area. There were several bodies that needed to be policed up before rats got wind of the smell. The idea of Sheila's corpse becoming rat food turned his stomach, and the idea of Coska being eaten alive, even if he was brain dead, was even worse. Gurril thought about plans to transport bodies, but was distracted by the sound of someone stumbling around in the charred area where the beam of light had struck the field.

Gurril trotted over to investigate, ready to brawl again if a raider had survived and was trying to escape. When he arrived, he found the strangest sight he had ever seen: A patch of burned ground, with what looked like a half-man, half-ferret in the center of it. The creature was trying to stand on his feet, but kept falling over. It looked to Gurril with pleading eyes, and tried to speak. Struggling to form words, his mouth silently opened, seeming to add to the animal's confusion and fright.

Gurril could see that the creature was naked, except for his thick coat of fur, and as afraid as anything in life had ever been. His black nose was followed by a ring of white, then another ring of black. These concentric rings continued down to the tip of his tail, which ended in a bit of red tufted fur. There was another tiny red tuft of fur, Gurril noticed, at the tip of each ear. The warrior grunted, and held out his hand. The creature took it, and Gurril felt a combination of muscular power and graceful gentleness that he hadn't suspected. The ferret stood, swaying a bit. Gurril was surprised to see that its height was at least a full seven feet and change; maybe eight feet.

Amazed, Gurril looked it in the eyes as its black nose twitched. "Did the beam of light do this to you?"

The creature nodded.

"Were you just a normal animal before this?"

The creature tried to speak. "Ah…" was all that came out.

"Okay. You can't talk, at least not right now. You're an animal. What do I do with you?"

Gurril was confused; he was also beginning to become angry with this huge, useless thing before him. He had bodies to move.

The ferret-man pointed toward where Coska lay, then back to himself. In his deep voice, he formed his first words as he pointed to Coska one more time. "From him…" He struggled again with other sounds as he pointed back to himself.

"Yes, something from him did this."

The ferret stood there, shaking with fear, staring at Gurril. He pointed to himself one more time, and said, "Pepper." He stuck his powerful finger into Gurril's chest, and said, "You are Gurril."

"Yeah, I'm Gurril. I don't like that you know that."

Pepper shrugged, as if to say that he had no control over it.

Gurril asked "How do you feel about rats?"

Before answering, Pepper worked his jaw a bit, opening it wide and closing it again, then wiggling it back and forth with his hands as he stood there. To Gurril, he looked like a boxer who had stayed on his feet after a vicious uppercut, checking that his jaw wasn't broken. "I hate rats. The damned things ate my mother."

"I'm sorry to hear that, but if we don't move these bodies, they will attract rats. I need your help loading them onto the coach so we can bring them to town. We have to be very careful with Coska, or we might injure him worse. The way he is now, he's either a body with a dead brain or he's in a sort of deep sleep. I think I read about it once; it's called a 'coma.'"

The two walked together silently to begin their task of loading bodies. As they approached the road, Gurril saw a giant crow standing on Sheila's chest, pecking at her face.

"Hey!" he shouted as he began to run toward her body, "Get away from her!"

As Gurril came closer, he realized that the bird was not a crow, but was instead Sheila's ever-loyal hawk, David. With the still-rising sun on the other side of him, the silhouette of the dark brown bird had only looked like a crow. He hadn't been pecking at her, but was instead pulling hair out of drying blood and away from her face. As Gurril watched, David the hawk wept silently and rubbed his forehead tenderly on Sheila's battered cheek.

Chapter 3: Snick and the Copper Coin

1

With the dirt and gravel of the road crunching under her feet, Snick remembered her escape from Flamingo. As she had approached the mainland, she had no plan of what to do. All Snick had was a collection of bottles, some clothes, and her small boat. She knew that there would be people coming for her. The pier ahead would be the entryway into her new life, and she cursed herself for never coming up with a plan if she was discovered and forced to leave her island kingdom.

Her first order of business was to separate herself from the boat and to find a way to safe passage. She had no money, but a prompt sale of the vessel to a local gave her a few coins. She washed out the cream from her hair in the shallows and hoped the sale of the boat had provided enough money to get her to a new location as fast as possible. As she walked to the ticket booth at the coach station, she passed a handful of sailors and fishermen who eyed her exotic beauty the way a gull eyes a fresh piece of scrap on the fillet table. Snick knew that if she ever became desperate for a quick handful of coins, she would have no problem earning it from men who had never seen a woman like her before. The thought made her feel sick inside, but it was better (maybe) than being burned at the stake, drowned, or fed limb by limb to a shark.

Indeed, to the sailors who walked by, the young woman was something to behold. A bit taller than most women of the mainland, she had a full, perky bust. Her waist pulled in tightly, and years of swimming had thinned her to the point where her abdominal muscles showed through her skin. The smooth curve of her hips led to long, extremely muscular legs. After passing by her, the sailors all turned to look at her ass, which was round and tight with muscle, each cheek a perfect handful. Every one of the men would close their eyes and picture her when they lay with their whores that night.

As luck would have it, she had just enough money for coach fare. She bought a ticket on the next coach, not caring what the name of the destination was, and wished for good luck. She sat inside the coach and waited. It was scheduled to leave in

71

under an hour. Biting her bottom lip and tapping her feet, she hoped that was soon enough.

2

Snick awoke with a slight yelp of surprise. The stress and hard, magic-aided swimming had taken its toll on her, and she had fallen asleep. The coach left as she napped inside of it. When the coachman had cracked his whip a few miles down the road it jarred her back to reality. She sat in a seat that faced the front and couldn't resist the urge to look behind her to see if there were pursuers. She stuck her head out the window and surveyed the scene behind the coach, and saw no horses chasing it.

Across from her, an old woman with extremely thin hair smiled. Aside from a sleeping set of men dressed for business (probably in the fishing village to work out a trade deal, Snick thought), the princess and the old woman were alone.

The old woman asked her, "Are you one of those islanders I've heard about?"

"I'm a Flamingoan. Yes."

"Can I touch your skin? I heard that brown skin is good luck."

Snick smiled in spite of her predicament. "Sure."

She considered an alias for a few moments, then decided that her appearance alone would be enough for anyone to know that it was she who had ridden the coach. Most inlanders had never seen a Flamingoan. She was going to stick out like a sore thumb.

"My name is Snick. What's yours?"

"Ellen." Ellen reached out and ran her fingertips up and down Snick's arm. "My, but you're lovely. I don't think I've ever seen a woman as pretty."

"Thank you."

"I used to be quite pretty myself. But, you know… age. Even as an old woman, I was handsome until I started losing my hair."

Snick smiled politely, unsure how to respond. Then, she had an idea. "You know," she began, "I have a few ingredients here that I could mix up that will help your hair grow again."

72

The old woman narrowed her eyes. "It isn't magic, is it? I'd kill a magic maker myself if I met one!"

Quickly, and trying to hide her nerves, Snick said "No. Of course not. Just special things from nature. Fish oils, herbs…"

The old woman was still a bit hesitant. "All right. I'll give you a few pieces from my purse for it. You wouldn't cheat an old woman with snake oil, would you?"

"Never one as kind as you, Madam." Snick smiled. The old woman smiled back, and Snick's career as a medicine maker was born. She mixed up a few of her creams (humming to herself to make the magic words seem like random sounds and music) into a batter, and rubbed it into the woman's head. The two business men awoke to this sight (they were bankers, indeed on a trade mission), and agreed to buy the same treatment after examining the way their scalps were balding. By the end of two hours riding, Snick had made a small amount of money that would help her start her new life on the mainland.

3

After giving everyone their hair treatments, Snick went back to napping. As she slept, she had a dreaming realization: the men from Flamingo would surely ask around until they found out that she had taken a coach to whatever town she was headed for. They would know where she was going before she did! She would have to throw them off her trail.

The coach came to a stop a few miles later at a small roadside rest. There was a park bench, outhouse, and well tap for fresh water. The four riders and the coachman stretched and strolled, talking in friendly ways to each other. The riders that Snick had treated all felt as if their skulls were tingling, and Snick told them that was the cream doing its work. She had to assure them again that it wasn't magic, just a recipe of healthy items from Flamingo mixed together in the right way.

The coachman approached, twisting his lower back to crack it. She looked at him and smiled as she heard his spine popping above his hips.

"Say," she began, "It sounds like your back gets pretty sore on these rides."

The bearded man in his early forties smiled and rubbed at his pot belly. "Yup. Ain't got a good seat, so I bounce a lot. Gonna be an old cripple by the time I reach a good age to retire, I guess. Workin' man's curse."

He smiled at her, his teeth stained brown from coffee, and his eyes red from road dust. A few dead bugs hung in his beard, smashed out of the air as the coach sped down the road.

"If you wait here a second, I've got a fish oil pill that people in my land take to help their backs feel better. First one is free, then three for a copper after that."

"Hmm." He rubbed his beard. "Won't make me stupid or anything, will it? I need to get you folks on your way without killing us all."

She giggled at him. "Not at all."

The coachman felt any hesitation melt at Snick's giggle, while at the same time the bounce in her chest caused a hardening in his shorts. "Okay, I'll try one. How long until it starts to work?"

"Right away. I'll just go fetch it, and be right back." She trotted to the coach, and the man watched her legs and bottom as she moved. His manhood hadn't raged like this in ages! She was every dirty dream he'd ever dreamed, come to life! He decided that when they got to their destination (a small town called Parkham), he'd offer her three gold pieces for one night in the hotel there.

A few moments later, she was back with a pill. It was a potion in a gel consistency that she had rolled between her fingers to make it a rough pill shape. She smiled and held it out to the man, who popped it in his mouth, then walked to the tap and ran water into his cupped hands. He sipped the water, smiled, and twisted his body back and forth.

"Wow," he said, truly surprised, "This really does work right away. You sure this isn't a magic thing?"

"Positive." She swallowed hard, trying not to show her fear. She would have to be very careful if she wanted to make a living this way.

"Okay. How many you got?"

She calculated her ingredients quickly in her head. "About thirty, I think."

"I'll take every one of them."

"I just need to count them out and make sure I don't accidentally give you any of my vitamins," she said as she trotted to the coach. He watched her again, this time stealing a small squeeze to his crotch.

A few minutes later, Snick sat on the park bench counting her new coins and wondering what to do. She had to get away from her pursuers. They would follow this route and head to the town where this coach was headed. She hastily mixed together a few oils, and quietly said the magic words needed to activate them. Then, one by one, she approached her companions.

"Here," she invited, holding out the small bottle of oils she had mixed, "Smell this perfume and tell me if you like it."

As each one smelled the perfume, they began to see her not as a beautiful woman with brown skin and white hair, but as one of the women from the north lands, with an unusually fat neck, pale skin, and nappy brown hair. Even through this haze, the coachman wanted to stain a bed sheet with her.

"I'm going now," she said. Each of them smiled lazily and waved goodbye. The coachman shed a tear, sad that he would never know how wonderful the woman's body (which he now found repulsively ugly) would feel as she rode him. Snick took her small collection of luggage and walked into the prairie grass, out of the other four people's lives. They boarded the coach behind her, and rode off to Parkham, no longer able to answer questions about the Flamingoan who had ridden with them.

Snick wandered and wandered into the prairie, fearful of being captured and hauled back to Flamingo. That night, as she slept in the grass under a small blanket, she woke several times from nightmares of being burned at the stake. Had she known what her pursuers had done when they arrived on the mainland, she would have slept easy. They had arrived at the pier and quickly identified her boat. The group began discussions on how to form a posse to find the witch, then decided that soon enough she would be discovered as a magic maker by someone on the mainland. The natural result would be a death sentence, and the king decided that the best course of action was to consider his daughter banished and as good as dead.

4

Years passed, and Snick became more and more adept at hiding her magic while still making a living from it. Her life was simple: find a town and make as much money as possible, then move on before being discovered as a witch. Everywhere she went, she was remembered for her beauty. It was impractical to try and do her perfume trick with entire villages of people, so she never said where she was going next, and always left unannounced in the middle of the night. Friends were a dream. She often cried to herself, hoping someday that she could find one place to stay and one person who she knew she would talk to for more than a few weeks.

She remembered the other girls on the island, and how she and her friends would all swim together and tell stories about boys. She used to watch the large flocks of flamingos feed when the tide was high, asking her mother questions about what it was like to be the queen. Now, here she was, alone on dirt roads, running for her life. The ground on the mainland was all sharp rocks, weeds, and dirt; her feet and webbed toes missed the soft sand and smooth rocks of the island. She had to buy shoes to walk here and missed the feeling of her bare feet on a volcanic beach with sand worn soft by waves. Men stared at her when she wore her traditional garments, so she usually wore a dress now. She missed the feeling of having the sun and wind on her skin, of lying down at night and being able to easily reach into the small bottoms of her outfit to touch herself while she dreamed of warriors making love to her.

Shaking the memories of escape out of her head, Snick walked along a dirt road that was a common route for coaches. She could tell that the road had been travelled earlier in the day by the fresh multiple imprints of coach wheels. She wore a loose, reddish dress that hung awkwardly around her and hid the curve of her waist. Snick was forced to keep her possessions few, and her entire wardrobe consisted of the dress she wore, two more packed into a tote bag, her Flamingo garments, and the shoes on her feet. Snick almost always wore her Flamingoan garb under her dresses to remind her of home. It was odd to her that she could be homesick for a place where they wanted to kill her, but it was the only place in life where she had friends, family, and had felt as though she really belonged.

She pulled a small rickshaw with her, filled with bottles of oils, creams, batters, and the like. Her lifestyle of walking and eating the fresh greens of the country had been good to her beauty. Her eyes were still their dazzling green, and although many a man who looked into them (if they could pull their eyes up from her legs, then waist, and so on) fell instantly in love with her, she had not taken a lover on the mainland. She had well over a century of life ahead of her, and was in no rush for romance. Besides, she told herself as she stopped to collect some interesting looking flowers at the side of the road, a lover would be a distraction and only make her more likely to get caught and killed for being a witch.

Snick wandered back onto the road, intuitively knowing that the ground up petals of the flowers she just collected would make a nice addition to her ingredients. The field turned to forest as she walked, and as night fell, she set up camp at a spot where the forest transitioned into a field of odd-looking corn with blue flowers on top of each stalk.

As Snick lay on top of the thick blanket she had bought in the first village she ever set up shop in, she stared up at the stars, wondering if she would ever see the oceans again. Her life on land was fine, but her body was made for the sea. She had webbing between her toes, and her eyes were able to see through the glare of the sun reflecting on water. She could see far deeper into the water than any mainlander. Now and then, she would wander by a lake and spend hours watching all of the fish within it, almost as if she were watching an aquarium.

Snick slipped off her shoes and dress so she was in her lighter Flamingo clothes and pulled the blanket her mother had made over her body. She said a few magic words that were meant to help hide her from any wandering predators, and wished for a bed in a house. The protection spell was weak, and Snick feared that something hungry enough might still find her one night. She flexed her toes back and forth a few times under the warm blanket, allowing the webbing between them to finally feel free from the confinement of her shoes. She fell asleep and dreamed of watching a large lake full of fish, while in the field beside her, an owl screeched and dove onto a kangaroo mouse.

5

A scratching feeling at her head and the sound of loud sniffing woke Snick. She sat up quickly and heard an animal scrabble for safety behind her head. She looked over and saw a pair of glowing eyes staring at her. The first pair was joined by a second, then third pair. As Brios came clear of a cloud, pouring blue light out, she saw that three rats had joined her resting place. They stared at her greedily. The largest rat was about six feet long in body, and the other two were about two feet shorter but no less ferocious looking. They all had long, pointed teeth that glowed a dull whitish color in the moonlight. Except, that was, for their twin sets of fangs on the bottom and top jaw of each beast. Those, Snick could see, were covered with a thick pink mucous. At first she mistook the mucous for her own blood, and she felt the top of her head for a wound.

She found no blood there, and decided (correctly) that the thick pink fluid must be some type of venom. The lead rat snapped his teeth twice at her, hissed, and took a step forward. Snick quickly bent down and grabbed a knife from a pocket on the underside of her cot. "Come on then, you won't be eating me tonight." The knife was an empty threat; she had little idea how to fight with it, and used the short blade mostly for cutting up potion ingredients.

The lead rat hissed again and advanced another step. Snick hadn't known about the battle earlier in the day, or she would never have set up camp where she did. On the road beyond her the death had been great as it was dealt out by Gurril and Seth in their fight against each other. The bodies had been collected and brought into Hearthstone hours before Snick arrived on the scene. She hadn't been able to smell the death, but these rats had. They were hungry for human flesh, and Snick seemed the perfect way to forget their disappointment over the removal of the easy meals of carrion they had anticipated.

The lead rat stood up on his hind feet, and Snick could see long claws slide out of his finger-like front paws. The claws

78

were catlike, but longer and thicker. Snick had never seen a rat before, but she had heard stories that their claws were strong and sharp enough to dig two full inches into human flesh. She had never quite known whether to believe those stories or not until now. The smaller rats were not as tall as Snick, but were much thicker. The lead rat's mouth looked huge as it snapped at her, and it was close enough that Snick could smell the dirty beast's venomous breath.

Behind the lead rat, the other two took up positions on the left and right to create an echelon, and rose to their hind feet. Snick began to shake with fright. She had never been in a real fight. She hadn't even *seen* a real fight. The closest thing she could think of was the time a friend of hers, an older Flamingoan boy with very high cheek bones, had used throwing knives to kill an aggressive seal while out fishing with her. The lead rat was just over an arm's length away; too close for her to throw her knife.

Snick remembered what the boy had told her when he killed the seal. The swells had been high but calm, the boat slowly rising, then slowly returning to the trough before the next peak approached them. "Just hold the blade like this, and flick your wrist when you throw, so that the knife spins over and over. You have to practice to get it to hit blade-first." At the peak of the next swell, he had used a powerful overhand throw to sink the knife deep into the seal's neck.

Snick looked to the side of the lead rat. She flicked her wrist quickly, throwing with very good form, and the knife went toward the rat on the left side of the lead attacker. It struck the rat squarely between the eyes, sinking barely past the tip. The rat was a female Snick noted, watching her six large milk sacks bounce as she knocked the knife out of her head with an annoyed paw. The knife had struck perfect, and Snick was actually surprised she had hit her target. *The skulls of these beasts must be like iron*, she thought.

Snick wondered how fast her death by rats would be. If she was lucky, the venom would kill her quickly, and she wouldn't have to feel them feasting on her flesh. She watched as the lead rat ran his tongue down one of his upper fangs until its tip was full of the pink mucous. The rat then snapped his tongue at Snick like a whip, sending a pink ball of venom at her with incredible speed. Snick tried to dodge the venom, but it struck her on the left side, just below her collar bone and above her breast. The spot instantly began to burn like a branding iron and Snick cried out loudly in pain.

She crouched away from the rats and held out her right hand in a defensive posture. She felt more of the burning venom hit her palm and fingers, then her right side below her ribs. The pain there seemed to make her kidney burn, and she lost control of her bladder. This, Snick realized, must be what it felt like to be burned alive. What was worse, she suspected that the rats would start their feast while she was still conscious.

She squeezed her eyes closed as tightly as she could, pulled her right hand back to her body, and waited for the bites to come. The first bite sunk into her calf, pulling her from her crouched position all the way to the ground roughly. While the venom on her skin had felt like red-hot iron, the venom-covered teeth were like hell itself. She screamed in agony, watching as the rat she had thrown her knife at smiled, sinking its teeth deeper into her flesh.

6

Gurril, even in his agonizing grief, still had a job to do. Trina had pulled him aside after Cami had brought Coska to his bed to begin examining him. Trina told Gurril that Pepper would have to face questioning alone with the elders, and that the creature would likely be assigned to Gurril's care in the morning. Next, she reminded him that the smell of the dead would draw rats to the battle scene. The town would be safe— no rats would dare attempt to raid the village itself for corpses— but where there were rats to be found, Gurril had a duty to stamp them out.

It was this bit of feared duty that Gurril faced as he walked along the edge of Stonecorn Field. He was afraid of the yet unfaced threat of rats; fighting in the dark and alone the first time he ever faced one would be a challenge. Gurril hated being told to go on the patrol, because he only wanted to be home with Coska. He noted that David the hawk had remained perched on Sheila's body until the very end, when she was brought into the funeral parlor for burial preparation. At that time, the hawk took flight. Gurril now saw David circling above him in the moonlight. Ahead of him there was a scream of utter terror, and Gurril ran toward the sound.

The sight shocked him. Three rats were taking their first tastes of a shadowed figure (a woman, judging the pitch of the scream) in a roiling mound of fur and flesh. He was exhausted from the earlier battle, even after having eaten, bathed, and napped a bit. Through his exhaustion, he roared out a battle cry and ran to the scuffling group. The three rats were the first rats Gurril had ever seen outside of an illustration in a book. There was one huge rat and two smaller rats (if you could call a four-foot long beast with fangs and claws small). One of the smaller ones turned, stood on its hind legs, and screamed at Gurril. The scream was a horrible sound, something between a fighting cat and a wounded horse. Still in a run, Gurril swung his heavy war hammer into the thing's rib cage. There was a satisfying set of cracking sounds, and the rat squealed in pain. It fell to the ground, and the other two rats turned from their dinner and stood to face Gurril.

Like a shot of feathered lightning, David slammed into the largest rat's face. There was a sound of pained squeals by the rat and high pitched calls from the hawk. Feathers flew as the rat tried to grab at the bird, and with a loud *woosh* David was airborne again. The rat groped at his face, his eyes missing, and blood pumping out in jets from the empty sockets. The distraction was enough for Gurril to catch the final rat off guard, and he swung his hammer in an upper cut motion, crushing the beast's jaw and skull from the bottom up. It dropped dead before him, as the rat with the crushed ribs stepped behind Gurril to rejoin the fight. Gurril turned and swung the hammer around his body with him, this time catching the rat in the neck. There was a wet snapping sound, and the rat fell to the ground gargling blood from its mouth.

The lead rat was stumbling blind through the field, trying to get away. Gurril ran up behind it and swung his hammer in a large arc that began at his back, went over his head, and drove straight down onto the top of the large rat's skull. The rat fell dead instantly. Gurril looked at its body and huffed, tired of killing. An image of Peter flashed through his head as he turned and walked past the rat with the crushed neck, still in the throes of death as blood continued to bubble out of its mouth.

The woman who was being attacked never stopped screaming. Gurril stood near her, unsure what to do, but as sure as he could be that she must be in incredible pain. She had the poisonous rat mucous all over her body, and deep bites in her right calf, left shoulder, and the right side of her rib cage. She thrashed in pain, and Gurril cataloged his knowledge of rats that he had gained through reading several books about the furry devils.

As he tried to find a way to ease the woman's pain, she calmed herself enough to look at him with pleading eyes. "There," she begged, pointing to the rickshaw she parked on the side of the road, "Go there and get me the wooden case that says 'Set P' on it. Hurry!"

Gurril went to her cart and saw the box almost immediately. He brought it to her, and as tears streamed down her face she opened it and began franticly rummaging through the several glass vials in it with shaky fingers. She pulled out three vials and a bowl. She emptied the vials into the bowl and screamed in agony again.

She looked at Gurril, and he could see that blood was running out of her green eyes. The poison was deep inside her, and Gurril knew that no matter what it was she was trying to do, she was as good as dead. He held out hope only that she could relieve herself of some of the pain the next few hours would bring her.

He watched her as she mixed the two oils and one powder from the vials together. The muscles of her body where she had been bitten twitched viscously, causing her to scream out in terrible pain again. Then, an amazing thing happened: this woman, who was writhing with death and pain, began to use magic words as she mixed together the ingredients in the bowl. Gurril's eyes widened.

Snick finished mixing the cream-like potion and looked to the hulk beside her. Where her knife, thrown as hard as she could throw, had only caused a flesh wound, this man had crushed bone and fang and claw. She could only hope he wouldn't do the same to her after realizing she was a witch.

Then again, the strong never were very smart in her estimation. Maybe he wouldn't know what she was doing.

Through tears of pain and grit teeth, Snick could only point to the magic cream and say "Rub, rub." Then point to her wounds. The muscle man with the iron hammer the size of a shark's head nodded, and did as he was told. The relief in her calf was instant, but not total when he worked the healing potion into her wounds there. As it set in, she dipped her fingers into the cream and rubbed it into her ribs as he massaged it into her other wounds. "More! More!" She began to shiver and silently cry tears of thanks that the pain was fading.

Gurril rubbed the lotion into the woman, who he only now noticed was brown skinned with white hair. Had this been a different situation, had Sheila not just died, had it been in a soft bed, Gurril would have thought it a fantasy. The woman was beauty itself, and her skin and muscle under his hands felt firm and smooth. He rubbed the cream into her wounds, and she moaned in relief. When he was almost out of cream to rub into her now healing bites, her eyes rolled back and she passed out from shock.

7

The next thing Snick knew, it was morning. She lay in a bed inside of a house. There was an open window in the room, and a hawk was perched there, staring at her. She felt something firm and warm on her chest, and another similar feeling between her knees. She looked down at her body, and on top of the incredibly soft blanket covering her were two cats. They both snoozed lazily, one on her chest and the other between her knees. Snick took a deep breath and let it out, causing the cat on her chest to briefly open its eyes, purr for a second or two, and fall back asleep. She took this place to be heaven.

Snick pulled her right hand out from the blanket and looked at it. It was swollen from the poison last night, and she decided that rather than heaven, this was either the world's most luxurious prison or a hospital. The warrior from last night had either dropped her off at the prison to be tried for witchcraft, or had dropped her off at a place of healing. If he was as stupid as she suspected, this was a hospital, and he didn't realize that she was casting a spell to save herself last night. As she thought about this, the warrior himself came into the room. He looked at her with kind, sad eyes.

Snick wanted to sit up, but the cats seemed too comfortable for her to disturb. She also realized that she was completely naked under the blanket, and wanted to remain modest with this man (even though he had rubbed most of her body with a lotion the night before). He smiled shyly at her. "My name is Gurril."

"Girl?"

"No. Gurril. Grr-ill."

"Oh. Sorry. Why are you here? Are you taking me in to a constable when I'm healed and ready to leave the hospital?"

"This isn't a hospital, it's my house. I slept on the couch last night. You're in my bed."

A thousand reasons to be embarrassed entered Snick's mind, but foremost among them was the thought that this man had put her into his bed as she was naked and passed out in shock. She remembered that last night she had been bloody and lost control of her bladder. She felt clean now. He must have given her a sponge bath, as well. Then a horrible thought— had he... No. He hadn't raped her. Although she hadn't been with a man for over two years, she hadn't forgotten the feeling of soreness that lingered the morning after sex.

"This is your house?" she asked.

"Yes. Although this morning it may as well be a hospital. Or by the looks of this room, a zoo. You make fast friends with animals."

Gurril watched as the woman shrugged and smiled.

He continued, "I've made breakfast. Do you feel like you can get out of bed?"

"I think so."

Gurril grunted in approval. "What's your name?"

"Snick."

"All right, Snick. I'll leave you to get dressed. You can stay here until you feel well enough to leave. The town nurse, Cami, will come to visit you soon; she was busy with my friend last night and couldn't see to you then."

"I've been bathed. Did you do that?"

84

Gurril smiled and turned a bit red. "Um… I didn't want my bed to be a mess."

"Oh." Snick's subconscious took control of her right hand, and she brushed her hair away from her face with it, not realizing the flirtation the move conveyed. She noticed that when Gurril saw her do this, his eyes nearly pooled with tears and he looked away from her.

"One last thing. Don't tell anyone you're a magic maker. I don't know what they do where you're from, but most people here would probably kill you on sight for it."

8

By the time Trina arrived to deliver Pepper to Gurril, he and Snick had nearly finished breakfast. Gurril hadn't spoken to Snick much during the meal, only enough to tell her a few bits of information that she should know about the village; where she could get a room, the location of the ale house, and a few other small things. Trina knocked and then entered without being asked to do so. Seeing Snick at the breakfast table, her eyes grew large.

"Good morning, Gurril. I see you have a visitor." Unspoken in this was *A pretty girl in a pretty dress, no less!*

Gurril, realizing that it must look like he had gotten over his sorrow for Sheila by bedding this beauty the very night of the former's death, was quick to stand and begin his explanation. "Trina, this is Snick. I found her under attack by some rats last night over near where the fight took place."

"Rats?"

Snick replied, "Indeed, madam. Three big ones."

Trina looked incredulous. "Gurril, why didn't you report this to me last night?"

"I would have, but I wanted to get this young lady back to shelter. I also wanted to attend to Coska. I exterminated all three of the rats and knew that you and I would be speaking first thing this morning."

Snick made a mental note to herself that she had been wrong about this man. He was anything but stupid or even the slightest bit slow-headed. His mind was as sharp as his biceps were large.

85

She spoke up again. "Madam, now that I'm safe, is there a place in town I can rent a room for a few days? I'd like to stay in Hearthstone for a while."

Even though Gurril had already told her where she could rent a room, she wanted to immediately establish her desire to be in her own space. It was obvious that the old woman had wanted and expected the warrior to be alone.

"Of course. In fact, you can go there now and give me and Gurril a bit of time to speak. Just go left down this street, and you'll see an ale house. They rent rooms above, as does the apartment building next door to there. Do you have a trade? Young women of your build without a trade may not be as welcome as you think."

Snick was confused for a moment, then realized that the old, short woman before her was asking her if she had a real way of earning money, or if she sold her body to men. "I make creams and lotions."

"Really? Like what?"

"Well…" she turned to Gurril. "Gurril. Your skin looks like you shaved this morning. Is this correct?"

Gurril grunted a yes.

"Good. And does your skin feel nice and smooth?"

Gurril took his palm and rubbed his cheek, creating a sound like sandpaper on a rough stone.

She smiled, and said, "Doesn't sound smooth. Let me run outside and whip something up that will make the skin on your face feel five times better. I'll be back in just the shake of a tail. Wait, where's my rickshaw? Did you bring it back last night?"

Gurril pointed to the back door of the house, and said, "Courtyard."

"Okay!" Snick hopped up from the table and trotted out the back door.

Gurril turned to Trina. "Where's Pepper?"

Trina frowned. "In my pocket."

And with that, a tiny ferret head popped up from her pocket, and a regular-ferret-sized Pepper smiled at Gurril and said "Hello!"

The ferret, about sixteen inches from the tip of his nose to the tiny red tuft on his tail, jumped down to the floor and ran over to Gurril, climbed his leg, and sat on the table to look at him. He smiled again and said, "My speaking is coming along pretty well, don't you think?"

Gurril growled a displeased grunt. "You're tiny. You're tiny, and you talk."

Pepper stood on his hind feet and made a clumsy bow. "I also can walk like a person when I'm small like this. I think that I may have some talking to do with Coska, though. Is he up?"

"He's never going to wake up. He's in his room and braindead. You can't talk to him."

"Oh, but I can, and Gurril, he's anything but braindead! We've got a connection now, we two. Part of him was transferred to me and we can speak mentally. I could hear him all evening last night, but only faintly. I think we've got to get close and practice before we can talk over a distance."

In an irritated tone, Gurril asked, "Why the hell are you tiny again?"

"That's what I aim to find out." Pepper wrapped his two front paws around Gurril's pointer finger and shook as if he were shaking a hand. "Trina says we're roommates! Well, I'm off to see Coska."

The ferret jumped down off the table and bounded toward Coska's room in a loping run. When he ran by the door to the courtyard, Snick returned with a small jar that had a cream in it. As he passed her, Pepper realized that one of the things transferred to him was an appreciation for the human female form. He slammed on his brakes to look at her long legs and waist, shown well in the dress she wore that morning, with a high cut over the leg and a tighter fit around the waist than the dress she wore the previous night on the road.

Snick, surprised to see yet another animal in the house, let out a tiny yelp of surprise. "Oh! I didn't know there were more animals here. Hello, there."

Then her eyes grew to saucers as the ferret stood on his back feet, bowed to her, and said, "Good morning to you, too."

Then, with a wink and short whistle (she would have taken it for a cat call by any human male), he ran off to Coska's room.

Snick looked to Gurril. "That was…"

"I just found him yesterday, before I found you. I guess he and I are roommates." Gurril looked to Trina in a way that said the old woman had plenty of explaining to do.

"Well. I wonder how the other animals will feel about him," Snick said. She continued her walk into the kitchen, and sat down again next to Gurril. "This might feel a bit cool at first." She rubbed the cream into his cheeks, chin, under his jaw, and onto his neck. At first, he was annoyed to have a stranger rubbing at his face, and he fought the urge to slap her hands away. The cream did indeed feel cool to Gurril, but his skin almost immediately began to feel much less irritated than it usually did after shaving.

Gurril grunted pleasantly and smiled. "Nice."

"Give it an hour or two. You'll feel like a new man." Snick winked at him.

Trina cleared her throat. She was clearly bothered by Snick, who still didn't know that Gurril's lover had been killed the previous day. "Young lady, I really do need to speak with this man alone. Perhaps now would be a good time to make your room arrangements. You can return later for your rickshaw."

"Yes, Madam." She turned to Gurril and smiled. "Until later, then. And thank you for helping me last night. I owe you greatly." Snick turned and left, giving Trina a smile and slight nod as she exited the house.

9

Trina watched until Snick was down the street a bit, then closed the door and sat at the table with Gurril. She looked very seriously at the warrior. "You two didn't—"

"No. Not even in dreams. I thought she might be wounded when I took her in, and with the late hour doubted that she would be able to ring the innkeeper anyway."

"Good. That would have changed greatly my thoughts of you, Gurril. No man who could take in a one-night stand the same day his lover dies would have the moral character to be a good town defender.

"We have four things to discuss this morning. First, I've been in communication with the nurse on and off through the evening. It seems that Coska is a much more powerful wizard than anyone thought. Cami's books reference a phenomenon like yesterday as happening only to the most powerful ones. What she can tell us is that his grave injury caused a sort of power surge within him. Because his powers were aligned with the world of animals, it is natural that they would seek an animal when they left his body."

"Which is why I've got a new pet."

"Not a pet. A partner. That's the second thing I want to talk to you about. Pepper is a very unique animal. We think that there may be a way for him to temporarily turn into his human-sized self from time to time. You fight best with a partner. Find out how to make him change over, and then train him to fight. In his taller form, his muscle power alone should make him an impressive fighter."

Gurril began to protest. "Wait just a—"

"No. *You* wait just a minute." Trina pointed her finger at Gurril and narrowed her eyes. "You've fought in two battles. In each one, you would have died had it not been for your teamwork with others. You need a partner. If you killed three rats last night; that means that there's an angry mischief nearby. They've already done something that leads me to believe they are up to no good."

"What have they done?"

"They stole Seth's body from the undertaker's storage place. The only one they took was Seth, and there were other bodies there that they could have had."

"Why would they do that?"

"I don't know. Maybe there was something on him they wanted that we missed when we searched his remains. But that's the third thing to talk to you about. I need you to investigate the theft of that body."

"All right. The fourth item of business?"

"Take the day off, and start on the other things tomorrow. You have a young lady friend to bury, and I think that your sorrows will be great."

10

Gurril sat alone next to Coska. Pepper was in the living room. The ferret would close his eyes in concentration, nod a bit, then step a few feet further away. Gurril assumed that he and Coska were learning how to communicate at farther and farther distances. Gurril looked to his permanently sleeping friend, and gently touched his forehead. "I hope you speak to me someday."

Gurril didn't know it, but Coska could hear him. In fact, Coska was very aware of the world around him. He knew that he was home, he had felt the pain as Cami fitted him with a catheter for his bladder, and he knew he needed sunshine. He communicated this mentally to the nurse. She understood immediately, and he explained to her the way his body would change. She had left the room and ordered Gurril to cut the roof out over Coska's room.

"The roof?" he asked incredulously.

She nodded. "The roof. He tells me he needs sunshine."

Gurril scratched his head. "Okay, I'll cut out the roof. What do I feed him? *How* do I feed him?"

Cami smiled in a nervous way, her brown eyes widening a bit. "He tells me he only needs sunshine and rain, no food. Just cut him a hole in the roof."

Gurril hadn't cut out the roof yet. He was waiting at home for Snick to return so he could give her cart back to her. He sighed and stretched in his chair. Gurril glanced up at the roof, and wondered what the best way would be to remove it. He looked back at Coska. "You should tell me these things. Not another person who has to be a messenger."

Coska wished he could communicate with Gurril, but he had had a realization after being struck by the beam. The realization was a vision, but not a certain future event. It was just a sudden knowing of something. The realization he had was that if he ever communicated directly with Gurril, it would be the day that Gurril was killed. This realization could never be

90

shared with anyone, or Gurril's death would be slow and filled with pain.

This understanding about Gurril, and the rule that went with it, were new to Coska. Almost all of his previous visions depended only on one person being told (or not told) about the vision. Now, with Gurril, there could be no communication. Coska searched deep into himself, and could find no answer why.

Pepper, still small, padded back into the room on all fours. While he had been out, both cats had taken up residence on Coska's bed, near his feet. They heard Pepper come in, and Felix jumped down. Seeing the ferret, the orange cat hissed and growled. Felix was about to take a swipe at the ferret, when Pepper stood on his hind feet, made a fist, and punched Felix square in the nose. The cat backed up quickly, sneezed, and shook his head. He turned and looked again at Pepper, decided not to push the issue, and jumped back onto the bed.

Pepper smiled. "I guess I won't be having any more trouble with him, huh?"

Gurril grunted in agreement.

"Why do you grunt like that so often? You're a very smart man. Your dialect should reflect that."

Gurril shrugged and grunted something that sounded a bit like it would have been "I don't know," if he had spoken.

Pepper huffed at him, and said "Coska called me in. He said he's got a vision to share with me. He ever do that with you before?"

"Never. He had a vision that Sheila— the woman from yesterday— would be trampled by horses. She wasn't supposed to tell."

"Oh." An awkward pause. Then, "Well, let's hope mine is more along the lines of fortune and fame."

Gurril grunted, and stood to leave. He decided he would walk down to the inn next to the ale house to see if Snick was ready for her rickshaw yet. As he approached the ale house, the door to the building swung open, and Snick appeared. She smiled brightly at him. "Beautiful day, isn't it?"

"Well, the weather is nice. You can go over to my place and get your rickshaw whenever you want it."

He kept walking, meaning to make his way to the undertaker to say goodbye to Sheila and see her into the ground. Snick took up pace by his side.

"Are you mad at me?" she asked him.

"No."

"You seem a bit mad. I might have something to lighten your mood."

Gurril turned and stared down into her face, growling as he spoke. "I'm going to bury a loved one who died in battle. At my house, I've got a magical ferret that I have to try to turn into a seven-foot-tall warrior, and my best friend has been turned into a turnip. I'm not happy today. And no, I don't want a fucking cream to cure it!"

Gurril rarely used such language, and he immediately felt embarrassment over doing so in front of a lady.

Snick melted back from Gurril, tears of surprise and fear pooling but not dropping from her large eyes. Had she only known, she would have approached everything about this man differently. She placed a well-meaning hand on his shoulder. "I'm sorry, Gurril. Your loved one... A brother? Another warrior who you were comrades with?"

"A woman," he said softly. "A woman who I loved."

"I see." She looked at his face, so full of pain but so willing to bury and hide that pain. "Please wait to bury her. I have a special oil I can mix that will freshen her before burial. I think you must want to see her more as she was in life than as she is in death."

Gurril thought about how she had looked after being trampled, how she had smelled. It was warm out, and the funeral parlor could only do so much to make the smell of a body tolerable. He realized that Snick was right; he didn't want to see her and smell her like that. He wanted his last memory of Sheila to be beautiful.

"Thank you." He swallowed back the hard lump that seemed to have taken a permanent residence in his throat. "I'll wait in the ale house."

"You aren't planning on getting drunk, are you? I don't want to waste the oil for a blubbering drunk. It needs to be for someone who can truly appreciate the sentiment of saying goodbye properly."

"I won't be drunk. I need lunch."

11

It was close to an hour later when Snick retrieved Gurril from the ale house. She led him down to the undertaker, and watched as he approached the pine box that held Sheila. The shape of her face and head couldn't be changed, but with makeup and the proper hair dressing, they had at least been made to look closer to normal. Her skin was radiant and pink, and she smelled once again of vanilla.

Gurril turned and looked to Snick. "How did you know she perfumed herself with vanilla?"

"She's a lovely woman. She'd use a lovely scent."

"Can I have time alone with her, please?"

"Of course."

In that time, that few minutes of good-bye, Gurril wept. He kissed her undamaged cheek and her lips over and over again, wishing that each kiss could bring back a moment or two of life. He held her hand and spoke to her of things he had dreamed— a wedding, children, and retiring with her in the village rather than the vineyard with the maidens. She was all the maiden he needed. He slipped a feather from her hawk into her hand, and kissed each finger.

Later that night, after he had watched the box be nailed shut and buried near her favorite place to fish with David, he sat on his bed staring out the window. The hawk was perched there, and from time to time flew off to exercise or hunt. Maybe, Gurril thought, he was visiting Sheila. He promised himself to visit her burial place with the hawk in the morning. The bird was uncannily smart, and he knew that David would return to that spot the same way Gurril would from time to time to speak to the one they both adored.

12

The next evening, Gurril sat at the table while Pepper sat on it, their dinner between them. The two quietly stared at each other. Gurril had bought and prepared a rabbit for the two of

93

them, and between stares, they ate in silence. Gurril chewed as Pepper now spoke.

"I'm surprised you can eat. You've been upset all day."

"I'm always ready to eat. No matter what, I have to maintain my body for my duty to the town. If I don't eat, I can't stay fit and then can't fight. That's your first lesson: the defense of the town comes before your own needs."

"It's just that when a rat ate my mother, I didn't eat for three days. I couldn't handle even the smell of food."

"I'm not you. And speaking of smell, you reek. Take a bath or something." Gurril grunted and took another bite of rabbit. He really didn't feel hungry, and ate only out of a feeling of obligation to do so.

Pepper cleared his throat. "You don't like me very much, do you?"

"I don't know you."

"You resent me because Coska, your best friend, shares things with me but not with you."

"Wouldn't you be upset? What vision did he have for you today?"

Pepper visibly shivered at the mention of the vision. "I can't tell you about it or it'll come true."

"Not fame and fortune, then?"

"Definitely not." They ate in silence again for a bit, and there was a knock at the door. With a grunt, Gurril stood and opened it. In the doorway stood Snick, wearing a conservative blue dress.

Snick smiled at Gurril, and said "Hi. I didn't feel like sitting alone in my room any more, and I thought maybe you and... uh, the ferret..."

"Pepper."

"Yes! Pepper! I thought maybe the two of you would like some company."

Gurril sighed. He wanted his old life back, not this new, odd life, mirroring his old one in so many ways that were not comfortable to him. He motioned for Snick to enter, and she followed him to the table. Pepper smiled at her.

"Hello, Snick!" The small creature said brightly.

"Hello to you, Pepper. How's your evening?"

94

"Quite nice. It'll be good to have someone to talk to who doesn't grunt most of a conversation."

Gurril growled at Pepper.

Pepper quickly added, "Not that I mind. He's a lot bigger than I am for now."

Snick chuckled and asked, "What do you mean by 'for now'?"

"Well, you see, when he found me I was over a foot taller than he is. Probably stronger, too."

In a growling tone, Gurril said, "Don't push it, Stinky."

There was a moment of tense silence that made Snick begin regretting her call to the house. Then, she asked, "Is that rabbit?"

"Yes," Pepper replied.

"Would you like a bite?" Gurril asked.

"I'd love some." Snick said with a smile.

An hour later, the three were having a cup of coffee and playing a card game. Gurril still wasn't happy about these new people in his life, but he had to admit to himself that it was better than a night alone with Coska in the other room like a ghost whose body is still clinging to a wayward soul. Snick excused herself to use the bathroom, leaving Pepper and Gurril alone for a few minutes.

Pepper looked to Gurril with a challenge in his eye. "I'd call dibs on her," he said, "But I don't think the cross-species thing would work out well."

"I just buried my love yesterday. Don't tease about women right now." The two stared at each other, Pepper realizing that he would never find another of his kind to mate with, and Gurril feeling like he would never *want* another to love.

As Snick returned from the bathroom, she passed by Coska's room, and heard his voice inside her head. He said, "Hey. Come in here. I need to talk with you."

Snick stopped, startled at the feeling of having this other person in her head. She looked over to the dining room table, where Pepper and Gurril seemed to stare at each other curiously. Then, she pushed open Coska's door, and peered into the dark room. "Yes," the voice commanded, "Come in and sit. Just for a while. I have a vision I think you should see."

Pepper and Gurril were still staring at each other when she returned from her visit to Coska. Both of them noticed that as she approached the table and sat back down to the card game, she looked at Gurril in an almost frightened way. Neither of them could ignore it, and they both began to speak in unison. They stopped, stared back at each other again like rivals, and Gurril grunted for Pepper to speak.

"Thank you, Gurril." The ferret turned to Snick. "You've got a look on your face that seems quite odd. Is everything All right?"

She swallowed hard. "I spoke to Coska."

Gurril leaned forward, and asked, "Coska? What did he say to you?"

Snick looked first to Pepper and then to Gurril. She grimaced, took in a breath to speak, held it, and let it out. She took in another breath, and said, "I don't know if I should tell you. If I tell you, it will come true. That's what he said. And I don't know if I want that. I don't know if I ever will want that."

Gurril pounded his fist on the table, causing every dish and utensil to jump with surprise and fright. "Why won't he ever tell me anything!" He roared through grit teeth.

Pepper, who kept a cool head, said plainly, "We should finish our game. Snick, it sounds like if the vision comes true, that it isn't necessarily a bad thing. Right?"

"I guess not."

"And if it doesn't come true, that isn't necessarily a bad thing either?"

She nodded, then said, "Which means I have time to figure it out for myself." With that, she visibly relaxed and was able to enjoy herself again. From time to time, she would look over to Gurril in an odd way. Pepper was vexed, wondering if she feared or adored the man.

When the game was finished, Snick bid her new friends goodnight and walked back to her room on the second floor of the inn. As she walked, she felt that she was being watched. She stopped, turned to look behind her, and saw the same hawk that had been in the window of Gurril's cottage earlier perched on top of the sign outside of a shoe repair shop. She smiled. "I know you." She said.

Without being prompted, the hawk flew from the sign and toward Snick. She instinctively held out her arm, and the hawk landed there. She was surprised both by the gentleness of his talons, and how light his body was for its size. He was a large hawk, yet she could easily hold him as he perched on her arm. She took him to her room and fed him some scraps of meat she had tucked away, and from that night on she belonged to David the hawk, and the hawk belonged to her.

13

The next few days were spent by Pepper and Gurril going around town and introducing the ferret. They coupled this with an investigation of the rat break-in at the funeral parlor. The town, it seemed, had never grown less fearful of magic as they had gotten to know Coska. The fact that this new creature did not produce any magic, but that it carried some of the magician's personality, did nothing to help endear Pepper to the villagers. News of the ferret had travelled fast, and as he rode around on Gurril's shoulders, townsfolk would come up and introduce themselves in a nervous way, obviously full of curiosity. At one point, just as Pepper was beginning to think that people were saying hello because they liked him, Gurril whispered, "Be careful when you go out alone, Pepper. These people are already half ready to burn you for magic, whether you practice it or not."

Pepper wondered how a man like Gurril could put the town before himself. He made a mental note to ask him about it if the man ever started to like Pepper.

At the undertaker's office, they examined the broken window where the rats had entered. There were a few bloody paw prints that were easily identified as belonging to a rat.

"He's about four feet long. Be more like six if he stands on his hind feet. About the same size as the big boy in the group I fought. Maybe he did it to gain some status with the mischief." Gurril said as he examined the scene.

"If he wanted status," Pepper said, "He should have brought back more than one body."

Gurril grunted in agreement and said, "Why, then?"

"Is it possible that Seth had something the rat wanted?" Pepper asked.

"That's what Trina suggested. The undertaker hadn't gotten to stripping his body yet, but maybe there's a clue on one of the other bandits' equipment." Within minutes, they were rummaging through the materials gained off the other bandits. There was nothing much of note: A few throwing knives, a deck of tarot cards, and other such odds and ends.

Gurril huffed and said, "This is getting us nowhere."

Pepper nodded in agreement as he stood on a desk, looking through small objects like coins and a tin button. "You're right. When you told me about Seth and about the battle, you said that he was a good engineer, right?"

"I've never seen a mechanism like the one he built. It was complex."

"Maybe the rat wanted some plans he had on him." Pepper scratched at his chin. "Or," he added, "Maybe the rat is the elders' spy, and there is evidence that he needed to hide away."

"I don't understand. Why would he hide evidence of being a spy?"

"You *wouldn't* understand. Coming from the world of creatures, I can tell you that we know many things you wouldn't think we know. If the rats found out that one of their own was working for humans... Why, they'd peel his skin off for torture, then eat him alive."

"We can't ask the elders if their spy is a rat."

"Why not?"

"I have to hide my cards from them the way I've been hiding them from you when we play fish poker. If they think I know too much, they'll tell me even less than they do now. If the town ever found out that the elders allied with a rat, there would be a revolt that could only end after all seven old people were strung up together by their necks."

The two finished looking through the materials, and headed home. As they ate, Gurril finally spoke on the subject of training for battle. "Pepper," he said, "Along with figuring out how to make you large again, we'll need to determine your fighting style. The best way to do this is to train together. I'll teach you a few things, and observe you. We can try out a few weapons, and match a weapon to your style."

"I've been thinking about that, too. With my large size, if I ever get it back, I don't know which would be better, a heavy thing like your hammer, or a fast weapon. Maybe something with range."

"We'll see. The only way to really know is to train together."

Days were then spent training. It was odd to watch a creature less than two feet tall go through battle moves, but Gurril enjoyed teaching the ferret. The warrior found himself a natural at martial arts instruction. Gurril refused to take Pepper on his now increased patrols for rats through the surrounding area, even though Pepper begged. They finally came to the agreement that Pepper could join the patrols after he was turned large once more.

Gurril had finally gotten around to cutting the roof from over Coska's head. He had temporarily dragged his friend's bed out of the room and into the living area of the house to prevent any debris from falling on him. Pepper helped by standing just outside the room and looking into the doorway to guide Gurril's saw as the young man cut from the rooftop downward. Piece by piece the roof came out, until finally the former bedroom was now a sort of open courtyard space.

As Gurril dragged the bed (with Coska in it) back into the room, Pepper groaned. Gurril stopped dragging the bed. "Are you All right?" he asked.

"I feel ill."

"Maybe you've inhaled too much saw dust and plaster. Lie down, and I'll make you some soda water after I get Coska put back."

In no time, Gurril had placed Coska back where he belonged. He could still hear Pepper moaning from the basket that served as his bed in the outdoor training courtyard. Gurril was about to check in on the ferret when Snick knocked, then pushed open the door.

"Hi, Gurril," she greeted happily. "I was hoping you and Pepper were up for another game of cards tonight. I've been selling a lot of creams, so I bought dinner and a bottle of wine."

Gurril noticed the basket she carried with her was stuffed with bread, meat, and a bottle of red wine. It looked and smelled divine.

He grunted, and said, "Pepper isn't feeling well."

"Oh. Maybe I can whip something up for him."

"Come to the courtyard with me, we'll take a look."

In the courtyard, Pepper moaned in pain, and saw that his body was beginning to change. He began growing larger, and cracking sounds popped from his body. It was like every bone being broken and mending over and over again. The pain to his skin was like a tearing, burning sensation. Had he been human with an older brother or mean playmate, he would have compared the pain to an Indian burn, except instead of being confined to the wrist, the agony was covering his whole being. The pain even hurt his eyes, making it feel as if they were going to swell so much that they would simply burst, spraying the courtyard with their clear fluid.

By the time Gurril and Snick walked through the arched doorway into the courtyard, Pepper was over seven feet tall, lying on the ground. The wicker basket that had once been his bed was now crushed underneath him, and Pepper was huffing and puffing in pain. The creature moaned in agony, and reached out one of his hands (more human-like, now that he had grown) to Snick and Gurril.

"Coska," he moaned, "He can make me big now. It hurts, though."

Snick kneeled beside the large beast. "Is there anything I can get you?"

He shook his head. "Coska says that the more we do this— make me big, that is— the easier it will be. It hurts now, though."

Gurril touched the ferret's shoulder. "Can I do anything?"

"No." Pepper breathed heavily. "It just needs to take its course. Eat. You're good at that."

Snick laughed, trying but failing to stifle it with a set of curled fingers.

Gurril looked at her, a bit offended. "What are you laughing at?"

"You *are* a tremendous eater." Gurril grunted disapprovingly at being the butt of a joke, then decided that this teasing meant that there was no way out of the fellowship these three (four if Coska was included) now shared. He and Snick stood.

Before turning for the kitchen, he said to Pepper, "Call us if you need anything. We'll see you inside soon, I hope."

"You will," the ferret said and smiled. "It hurts a lot less already. Snick, whatever you brought in that basket smells wonderful. If I'm feeling better later, maybe I'll come in for a bite."

Snick smiled to him. "Of course. We'll save you some." She pet his furry head, gently rubbed one red tufted ear, then stood to go back into the house.

Gurril and Snick ate in silence, both worried about Pepper. Snick's basket had been filled with bread and spiced venison, which she had bought at the market earlier in the day. When dinner was finished, and Gurril had drunk a few glasses of wine, he asked Snick to stay at the house while he went on a short patrol for rats. He didn't want Pepper to be alone this soon after going through his painful transition to human size.

Snick obliged, and soon found herself in a silent house. Pepper had fallen asleep in the courtyard. Both cats were curled up on Coska, who had become their favorite napping place, and David the hawk watched her silently from a tree overlooking the courtyard.

Snick had to make a decision. She told herself that if she stayed in the village much longer, she was likely to become a permanent resident of Hearthstone. She had never had people she felt as close to as she did now. Even if she and Gurril didn't talk much about her magical powers, it was still nice to know that she could talk to somebody about them if she wanted to. And she found that she adored the friendship of her happy little ferret friend more and more each day. The vision that Coska had shared with her had troubled her sometimes, yet made her feel filled with hope at others.

She couldn't decide what to do. Snick told herself that she should leave it to fate. The best way to leave a thing to fate, she always believed, was with the throw of a coin. She reached into her purse as she stood in the living area of the cottage, and pulled out the copper coin the old lady on the coach had given her the day she escaped Flamingo, kept all this time for luck. On one side was the portrait of some long-forgotten but somehow still important man. On the other side was a fish. The man, she decided, would be the side that told her to stay. The fish would be the side that told her to go. If she left, she would do so this very night. She could always come back if she wanted to. If she stayed, she could always try to leave later if the tide turned poorly.

With a bit of hesitation, Snick flipped the coin into the air using her thumb. It rose and spun, then seemed to hang in the air. The coin finally fell, bouncing off the rug that covered the wood floor and rolled into the kitchen. She followed it, and watched as it finally tipped over and came to a rest. Part of her wanted to smile, and part of her wanted to cry. From the floor, an important but long forgotten man stared up at her from the coin.

Chapter 4: A New Partnership

1

Goose Hill stood at nearly the exact halfway point between the center square of Hearthstone and the place where the road led into Stonecorn Field. It was a tall, fat hill that had long, soft grass growing over it. Most of the villagers believed the hill was dirt mounded over some sort of subterranean rock formation. In reality, some of the first settlers to the area had constructed it as an ancient mound for the victims of a great plague. Had the villagers of Hearthstone known this, they probably wouldn't have thought the hill anything but a relic of their long-ago history. However, there were now over eighty rats that lived in tunnels burrowed within the hill. This fact was unknown to the village; knowledge of the mischief would have led to the hill being razed.

The mischief moved into the hill shortly after it had been formed by the ancient dwellers of the area. The rats had been the ones to bring the plague to the village by shitting into the water wells. The disease was an effort to wipe out the humans and use their carcasses for a feeding frenzy. When the plague victims had been piled, buried, and covered over with another set of victims again and again until a huge hill stood where there had once been a shallow ditch, it was natural that the rats would begin tunneling in, craving the rotting flesh as it turned bitter.

The village at that time had been a much larger place, and the surrounding area had been quite populated as well. What had remained after the plague were the few townsfolk who decided to stay. They were extremely wealthy, having collected the leftover monies the dead had left behind. This money, along with all the belongings of the dead, had been brought to the next large city in order to buy the labor needed to finish the hill.

When the ancient people of Hearthstone got to the next town, they discovered that the plague had reached there before them, spread by people escaping from the disease in Hearthstone weeks earlier. There were few survivors in the town, and they were quickly and unceremoniously beheaded by the new explorers. The Hearthstone group raided the now unguarded and unclaimed wealth of the place, and was on their way again— this time with two towns' worth of wealth in tow. By the time they reached a population center that had not been struck down by people trying to escape the fast-moving plague, the remaining Hearthstonians were incredibly wealthy. They ended up buying the poor and starving human detritus of the final city they reached as indentured servants, rather than paying transient skilled laborers to come back with them. It was this set of slaves and remaining townsfolk who made up the ancestors of the villagers that thought of Goose Hill as nothing more than a dirt-covered rock formation.

When the rats first forayed into the hill, they built a tunnel in search of rotting bodies. When a pocket of bodies was found, the rats would feast on the carrion until the pocket was hollowed out. One by one, pockets went from being filled with bodies to being individual den areas for the mischief. When the rats had finished their excavation and exploration, they met to decide if they should next raid the village and eat the remaining humans. It was decided that the rats should find other means of feeding themselves, and that the village nearby would provide dead flesh, bread, and other foods as the rats could steal it.

Religion came with food and a settlement, and from that point onward, the common rat prayer was:

> Oh, Great Giver of buried flesh,
> we rejoice in your cold touch.
> The bitter taste of your charity
> gives us hope in the deepest
> tunnel. Please deliver us into
> your kingdom as masters of all
> flesh, and may every village be
> wiped into our mouths by
> another plague.

The tunnels opened about a quarter of a mile away, near a part of the river bank that was secluded under a series of leaning willow trees. The lower hanging branches and partly exposed roots made good cover for the tunnel openings, and the fact that there were very few areas with good fishing on this portion of the river meant that the rats could generally come and go without much thought about staying hidden from people. If a villager were ever to have hid as a spy in the trees on the opposite side of the river, the typical movements of the mischief would be easily observed.

Just after sunset, the first few rats would emerge from roots and branches, or break the surface of the river if the water was high. They would stay within the shadows, hating sunlight almost as if it caused them pain. In reality sunlight did slightly pain them, because their eyes were designed so perfectly for the darkness of their tunnels. The rats, after emerging from their earthen home, would move out to the fields, where they would hunt for almost anything they could catch or bite. The pink mucous that dripped from their teeth was a harsh poison that caused pain, cramping, and put the victim into a state of twitching fits. Of course, the rats would usually rather take the easier route and steal their food from a fresh grave, a storage bin, or some other human-infested area.

The rats would be gone until just after daybreak, when they would return, some carrying remains to share with the group. The loose social order of the rats dictated that when a member of the group (or members who hunted in a pack) caught a meal, they ate as much as they could and would bring back any leftovers for the old, young, or weak. These rats, the ones too small or too old or too weak to hunt, would stay back and hope for a meal. The youngest would growl out cries until their mothers returned to feed them milk.

During a recent night when most of the mischief was hunting, four of the adolescent rats who were not quite old enough to go out and hunt, but were too old for mother's milk, gathered around a sick old warrior. They were tired of waiting for someone else to bring them a meal, and were tired of being treated like babies. They wanted to hunt, to kill, and to cause every terror a rat dreams of causing. The four of them stared at the old rat (who was grandfather to one of this group) intently as he slept, dreaming of a nice meal of rotting fish. He sensed them near and popped open his eyes to see the small band of young rats watching him; the old rat knew the look in their eyes, and he sprung to his feet as fast as he could, baring his claws and teeth. For the young rats, this was an easy challenge. Two went high and two went low, all of them clamping on with their teeth and tearing at the old rat's flesh. His screams of pain and fury added to the feeding-frenzied excitement as the four adolescents tore chunks of muscle from the old rat's living body, and into their chomping mouths. Within minutes, the old rat was reduced to a few scraps, a few chips of leftover bone, and a few echoes of screams running through the tunnels. Such was life in the mischief.

2

It was the morning of a rat funeral, still over an hour before sunrise. Three rats from the mischief had been killed on a hunting trip the night before, and a fourth was missing. The bodies of the three slaughtered rats lay at the feet of the five mischief leaders, who snapped and growled at the other nearby rats who had gathered for the funeral. The gathering crowd salivated and groaned for flesh, reaching out to try and snatch away a body.

"These three Dear Brethren are ours!" One of the leader rats hissed at a member of the crowd as he stood over the bodies of the three dead rats. This leader of the mischief stood at just under eight feet tall, and had a forked tongue that flicked out every now and then. The next leader closest to this one, a six-foot-tall rat with one broken fang, slashed out a claw at another intruding mischief member. The leaders knew that the funeral would have to be quick, or they would miss their meal.

One of the rats from the group intruding on the bodies stood on her hind feet and asked, "Did Billy do it? Where has he been? I'll kill him if you want me to."

The rat leader who stood at eight feet smiled. "Billy is too weak for this. He doesn't even hunt, only begs for food from the human, Seth. I think that when Billy comes back, we should all eat him!"

All the rats in the mischief howled approval at this, snapping their teeth in the air and shaking their furry backs. The leader smiled again, knowing he had just bought himself a bit of time to begin his given funeral right.

The group quieted, and the tall rat leader spoke again. "Here lie three weak, dead, corpses of rats, killed on a hunt. We leaders will consume their flesh as a gift to the mischief first, then all can join. Hope someday, my sons and daughters, that you may be consumed by your mischief, as well."

With that short eulogy, the group of leader rats squatted by the three bodies and began to tear into the dead and bloated flesh with sharp, ravenous teeth. When they had finished feeding, the rest of the mischief moved in and began gnawing the bodies down to nothing.

3

Billy crawled on the side of the river bed, his head aching and his body twisted with pain. He had been observing the battle in Stonecorn field; that much he remembered well enough. He had been watching as Seth rode in on his horse to kill an ugly magician, then everything went black. Billy normally wouldn't have been out at the hour of the battle, but he knew of Seth's plans and decided that the pain in his eyes from the bright sunlight would be well worth digging into whatever fresh carrion would be left over from the fight. He had heard that the flesh of magicians was extra bitter, and wanted to find out if this promise of a fine-tasting meal was true.

Whatever had happened to Billy, it had knocked him into a stupor that he didn't wake from for hours. When he did wake, he followed a scent trail of blood to the village, and broke into the funeral parlor. He knew it was risky, but he somehow just couldn't stop himself. It was a compulsion he had no resistance against. There was a thrumming in his head that drove him to it. That thrumming had led to a splitting headache, and when Billy found the body of Seth in the cool air of the parlor, he ate it in large gulps, leaving nothing behind. The meal (large even by rat standards) made the headache go away for a time.

The walk back along the river had started fine, but soon the headache returned. Billy thought that maybe he had been hit with a stray weapon during the battle, so he checked himself for wounds. Nothing. He walked again along the river toward his mischief's den, aware of the fact that soon the humans of the village would wake up, find Seth's body gone, and would likely begin a search for it. He walked faster, not relishing the thought of a horde of humans chasing him down. He could easily kill up to three humans by himself (any healthy rat could, really), but an entire village might be able to take down even the largest rat. And humans had tools. And chemicals. And trained animals. Billy had watched a time that a pack of seven stray dogs had taken down a rat. It was a fierce fight, ending with five dead dogs, two dogs alive, and one dead rat.

As Billy walked, trying to entertain himself with the memory of the epic battle between seven dogs and a rat, his body began to ache like his head. It grew worse and worse, and now, as he approached the tunnel into the mischief beneath Goose Hill, the pain grew to the point where Billy could only stop crawling and writhe slowly on the ground. At one point, it became so bad that he cursed and wished for death.

Billy lay on the ground near the river, listening to the water run by, his body gnarled in pain. He gasped and huffed, clawing at his face. He considered rolling into the river to try and drown himself in order to end the pain, but couldn't quite work up the will to do it. Finally, and all at once, the pain left him. Billy sat up, shook his head, and smiled. He didn't know how, but he *knew* things. Things that were going to happen in the future. He knew other things, too. Like, if he said the right words in the right way, and moved the third claw on his left forepaw just so, he could turn a regular rat into something else. Billy, who had always been as close to an outcast as a rat could be without getting eaten by the rest of the mischief, also knew that he could make rats (and humans) do the things he wanted them to do. He huffed out a big breath, and walked into one of the tunnels that led beneath Goose Hill, feeling reborn.

4

As Billy entered the main chamber, he could see that the funeral was almost over. He hadn't seen who had died, but could tell that there were three bodies that were almost completely eaten. Soon, the last few swallows would be made, and the rats would begin having an orgy. This was the way the rats celebrated death, by gorging themselves on flesh in so many ways.

Billy knew that the rat leaders had been waiting for a time to call him an outcast and sentence him to be eaten alive, so there was no surprise when the tallest rat leader saw him and immediately yelled "There's Billy! Eat the outcast!" Billy, in order to draw the mischief around him, put on a look of fright, and quivered.

As the mischief of eighty rats turned toward Billy, he said the magic words, waved his claw just so, and in one moment, every rat around Billy went from a solid being, to a bundle of flesh in the shape of a rat, made up of dozens of smaller animals that writhed in a pile. The things in the piles were just like the rats, except that they were a foot from nose to tail at the largest, and they squeaked instead of spoke. The bundles of smaller rat-shaped animals collapsed around Billy. This new mischief, these tiny rats that were merely pieces of larger ones, looked up at him in wonder and fear.

Every one of them was at the command of Billy. He grinned and roared in delight. There was a new plan now, not one that relied solely on Seth and his stupid engineering plans. No, this idea was much better.

5

Gurril had taken down not just the roof over Coska's room, but the exterior wall, as well. The magician's skin had taken on an odd green hue, and Gurril was worried. He was about to finish removing the last few boards from the base of the former wall when Pepper, back to his sixteen-inch tall form, tapped him on the lower back. Gurril turned and grunted. The ferret, it seemed, would grow and shrink at random times. When Gurril woke up in the morning, he never knew if he would have to prepare a huge breakfast for a behemoth, or a tiny bit of breakfast for a fuzzball.

"I've got an idea," the small animal said with a smile. "I'm ready to start training with weapons."

"Really? How? You're tiny. We still can't control your size; you were nearly eight feet tall just a couple of days ago." Gurril stared at the furry ferret. It was odd how the thing was almost always smiling, no matter what happened. He never thought that an animal could be happy like this, and he often wondered what it was that the creature was thinking about that made him walk around grinning like an idiot.

"For the last month now, we've been practicing making me big if I talk with Coska. It's gone faster each time, and it almost always works reliable when we attempt it."

Gurril grunted in agreement. "But it still hurts you."

The ferret smiled again. "I can take the pain, and he's got a plan to make it easier. I want to learn to fight now."

"All right." Gurril sighed. "Am I doing what he wants? What's his plan?" He motioned toward Coska.

"Oh, yes!" Pepper said with excitement. "He loves the fresh air. Have you seen his nice greenish color?"

"I thought he was getting sick. Why do you say it's nice?"

"He told me in a dream last night that he's turning himself into a tree. I'll bet the fruit will be amazing!" Pepper clapped his hands together excitedly, then looked from Coska back to Gurril. "I want to start with a bow staff. Can we do that?"

"A tree! What is he thinking?"

Pepper grinned larger, and said, "Don't know. But I can tell you that he's got a plan, and whatever it is, it'll be brilliant!"

Gurril scoffed, and said, "A tree. Brilliant. Hey, everyone, look at my best friend, the tree!"

Pepper playfully punched him in the thigh, and said, "You'd be amazed at what trees can do. Now, about my training. When do I get a bow staff?"

Gurril considered this for a bit, trying to picture the ferret with a long, staff-like piece of wood as a weapon. The bow staff was a light piece, best used by a slow or weak warrior, who could only handle the weight of what was, more or less, an overzealous curtain rod.

"I'll have to talk with a carpenter. We'll have him make you a few different types of weapons out of wood. If there's one or two you really like, we'll see about getting them forged. And I still don't understand how turning into a tree is a plan for anything."

"But if I like a bow staff, we won't need to get it forged. We'll just need strong wood. And I don't know what the plan is. We just have to trust Coska."

"You won't like a bow staff," Gurril grunted.

"Why not?"

Gurril just grunted instead of saying anything.

Pepper narrowed his eyes, "Hmm. Well, I want to try one anyway."

"Sure. But only if you promise to train just as hard with a heavy weapon or two."

"Sure thing, Gurril. And don't worry too much about Coska. He knows what he's doing."

6

Gary the carpenter stood at the business counter of his shop, talking with Snick. She had shown him a cream that she said would not only stain wood, but would protect it from being eaten by oak moths.

Gary nodded slyly, and told her, "I don't think that my customers would really want to pay much extra for this."

Snick, being just as sly with business matters as the carpenter, replied with ease, saying, "I sell hair creams to most of the town's gossipy women. I'd hate for them to hear that their husbands could have gotten a better piece of furniture from you, but you didn't think it was worth the price."

Gary's eyes grew large, and he stammered. "Well, now... Maybe we can work something out. I mean, I could always add it to furniture at a small upcharge that is..."

"Offer it to them as an additional option they can purchase?" Snick offered.

"Yes, yes! An option."

Gary smiled at Snick, and treated himself to one fast glance down from her eyes to her body. It was warm out, and she walked around town wearing her small top that showed more cleavage than most of the village men had ever seen a woman show, and ended high above her waist. Her shorts were only large enough to be legal. To Snick, this was the common dress of her home kingdom, and she still was most comfortable in these clothes on hot days, despite the types of looks the people on the mainland gave her. For most of the people in the village, her outfit looked more like underwear than anything a respectable woman would wear out of the house.

Snick and Gary were just finishing the details of their agreement when the door opened, and Gurril strode in, with Pepper riding on his shoulder. The dark-skinned woman smiled and approached Gurril. He smiled in return, although his was not as large and bright as hers.

"Snick," Pepper said from his perch, "How wonderful to see you! Coska has been asking when you'll come by for lunch again."

"I'd love to come by! What are you two gentlemen doing for lunch today?"

Gurril grunted something that sounded like a negative, then jerked a thumb up toward Pepper and said, "He starts learning weapons today. No distractions."

Pepper huffed in surprise, and told Gurril, "In that case, she's coming over for supper."

Gurril slumped his shoulders slightly, and said, "Fine. Now let's get you a few training weapons."

Snick smiled and winked, saying, "Boys, I'll see you for dinner at six."

Without turning to watch her leave the store, Gurril said "Make it seven. And you bring the food."

Gary watched Snick as she left, admiring her body through the window of his door long after she was in the street. He turned to Gurril, saying "You're a lucky man. I love to watch that woman walk."

"I'm not here to talk women. I need weapons to train the ferret."

As Gurril said this, Pepper stood up straight and smiled.

"Yes," Gary said slowly, "I've seen him riding your shoulder. And I've seen when he's the size of an elephant. Seems like a spear-thrower to me."

"He won't like spears."

Pepper leaped from Gurril's shoulder to the counter, then stood on his hind feet between the two men. "Why won't I like a spear?" he asked indignantly.

"You won't," was all the reply he was going to get out of Gurril.

Pepper turned toward Gary. "My good man," he began, "I think I'll take a training spear, *and* a bow staff."

112

Gurril grunted, holding back as much of an angry sound in his voice as he could, and added "Make sure short and stinky here gets a long sword, as well."

Gary nodded. "So we've got a bow staff, a spear, and a long sword. All for training, so I'll have to weight them the same as steel, or at least as close as possible."

"Oh," Gurril added, "Two sets. One for him at this size, the other for him at his large size."

Gary nodded again. "I see. Well, let's come back and get you measured, then. Gurril, this will cost seventeen copper."

Gurril grunted and flipped the man a silver. He took it, slipped it into his coin bag, and returned three coppers to Gurril.

The process of measuring Pepper in his smaller state was relatively simple. Gary would use a bit of twine to make the measurement, then compare the twine to a ruler. He sketched down the length of Pepper's arms and legs, as well as the length of his back and his standing height.

When he was finished, he said, "Fellows, we'll have to have you come back when this one is in his larger state. Any idea of when that will be?"

"I'll be ready this afternoon, before dinner." Pepper said with a smile.

Gurril shook his head. "No. Tomorrow."

Pepper looked at Gurril and shook his head the same way. "No, this afternoon."

Gurril sighed, not wanting to argue the point. "Fine. But if you're still in pain, don't be surprised if his measurements are off."

Pepper smiled wider, knowing he'd been lucky to get his way. He bounded up Gurril's muscled arm and perched on his shoulder.

"Gurril," he said confidently, "I'll feel fine!"

7

The rest of the morning and mid-day was spent on battle theory. Gurril found that Pepper had acquired the ability to read along with his other human-like traits. As Gurril cooked lunch, Pepper read an ancient tome about ways to battle multiple opponents on a hill.

113

They talked about ways to swing a weapon and various martial arts moves. Pepper learned ways to psychologically gain an advantage over a physically stronger enemy. Finally, it was time to head back to the carpenter's shop.

Gurril looked softly at the ferret. "If you want to wait to become your larger form, I understand."

Pepper's smile faded, and he breathed in deeply. "No. I just have to learn to take the pain, and Coska's been telling me that he's ready for me to grow large again. The pain really will go away when Coska's plan is done."

Gurril grumbled something under his breath about not knowing what the plan was, and grunted toward Pepper.

"Do it, then." As he watched the ferret drop to the floor in pain, he couldn't help but feel sympathy for the little fuzz ball. The past few weeks, he had been happy for the company. For that matter, although he put on that he didn't like Snick coming around, he enjoyed her company, too. If Pepper could be trained to handle a weapon, Gurril thought, he might just make a good fighting partner. Gurril had always fought best in tandem with Coska; maybe he could fight well with this one, too.

Pepper writhed in pain on the floor, tears running from his eyes, his bones and joints crunching as he grew. Every fiber of every muscle screamed in agony as it tore and repaired over and over again, trying to keep up with bones that were at times nearly poking through the flesh that covered them. Finally, it was over. He lay on the floor, panting in pain. Pepper looked up at Gurril, who kneeled beside him and gently scratched behind one of his ears.

Gurril smiled and said, "It's okay, big guy. You know the pain goes away quicker each time."

Pepper nodded and lay on the floor, gathering his strength. Gurril looked to Pepper and saw a creature that became only a little less annoying each day, a creature that he was forced to share his home with because of his job. Pepper looked back and saw one of his two only friends in life.

Gurril smiled in a sly and teasing way, and said, "You know, you don't smell as bad when you're so tall."

Pepper smiled back through the pain, and told him, "I think my musk glands go away in this form. But I get hungrier for beans, so in the end it's a wash."

Within minutes, they were both back to their feet. Pepper immediately headed for the door, excited to be measured again for weapons. Gurril cleared his throat. "Uh, Pepper…"

Pepper turned, "Yes?"

"Don't forget your pants." Gurril laughed under his breath as Pepper looked down and realized that he was naked. Being naked in his ferret size was no problem, but when he turned into the giant human-ferret cross, he had to cover himself to avoid embarrassment. Pepper placed his hands over his crotch and left for the courtyard, where his short pants hung on a drying line. They were loose and made of cotton dyed dull green, buckling together just below where his belly button should be (the absence of this physical feature disturbed Gurril somehow, like the ferret had never really been born), and extended to just over his knees. Gurril had designed them for Pepper, meaning for the shorts to be giving enough for free movement in battle, but close enough in style to the jeans and other cotton clothes of the townsfolk to help the animal fit in better without getting too warm.

They made their way to the carpenter's shop, and Gary measured Pepper. He already had the small version of the bow staff ready, and he sent it back with the two warriors. Pepper curiously held it in his hand. It looked so tiny now, and it amazed the ferret to think that sometime in the next day or two, he might uncontrollably shrink down to a size that would make this tiny weapon just right for him. He looked forward to Coska being able to control the size changes better; to having more predictability of when the horrible pain would overtake him.

Gurril and Pepper were sparring, trying out some hand-to-hand combat moves that Pepper had read about. Gurril was amazed at the size and bulk of the ferret in his human form. He realized that the term "human form" really wasn't right. The ferret stood over seven feet— maybe even close to eight feet, and he had muscular development beyond anything a human could ever hope to achieve. This thought ran through his mind as Snick arrived for dinner, and Gurril suddenly found he was a bit happier that the ferret would someday fight beside him.

She had a basket of cooked fish with her. To Pepper, the fish smelled like heaven, and as soon as the group sat at the table, he began gobbling them up. He crunched and chewed loudly, while Gurril and Snick tried to talk. Eventually, the two humans left the ferret to his fish, and retired to the living room with some wine so they could speak without having to raise their voices over the nom-nom-nom in the kitchen.

"Gurril," Snick said after she had become relaxed from wine, "It's been over a month. Are you still in mourning?"

Gurril set his jaw. "Why?"

Snick reached out and touched her fingertips to his bulging forearm. "I only ask as your friend. I see that you seem less pained every day. I just thought that maybe you'd like to talk about Sheila. About your feelings now that some time has passed."

Gurril thought for a moment. "No." It was a quiet response, just more than a half grunt.

"Have I told you that David has taken to hunting with me? Just this morning, we took three squirrels down by—"

Gurril pounded his fist against his leg and almost roared, "Enough! I don't want to hear anything else about the hawk, or my mourning, or anything! Enough!" He looked to her, his eyes bulging with anger.

Snick stood, and began to pack her things into the basket she had brought, tears streaming from her eyes. Quietly, she said, "I only wanted to tell you about my day. David's a part of *my* life, too."

Pepper stood from his chair in the kitchen and went to Snick, giving her a hug, and whispering, "It's okay. He didn't mean to be hurtful, Snick."

"I should just go." She looked over to Gurril, his forehead pressed down into his palms.

Pepper had pleading eyes. While his voice nonchalantly asked, "Can you just sit for a while," those eyes begged her to stay.

She sighed heavily, nodded, then sat back down in the living room, facing Gurril.

Quietly, but firmly, she said, "Gurril, I'm sorry I upset you. Could we talk about the farms here? I don't think I've ever seen so much wheat."

In a pouting, quiet voice, he said, "Makes the bread good. We trade it with Newlesser for wine."

"That's why this town is all about sandwiches, then."

He nodded in response, and sighed, looking out the window.

Snick sighed in return, and said, "Okay."

They shared a silence that was about to become uncomfortable, when, after returning to the dinner table, Pepper emitted a huge burp, and smacked his lips.

From the kitchen he called out, "Do you have any wine left? That burp was really fishy."

Snick laughed first, and was joined in short order by Gurril. In that laugh, he found himself incapable of holding onto the sadness that had gripped him so in the days after watching Sheila die. He also knew then that at some point the memories of Sheila would become less haunting and more a source of joy and warmth. When he remembered her now, a bitter feeling overcame him. He wanted the bitterness to leave, and to remember her with a smile instead of tears.

He felt horrible for yelling at Snick, and promised himself that he would be more understanding next time she brought up something that reminded him of Sheila. After all, Snick had never known the woman who previously had hunted with the hawk and loved with the man.

Snick stayed late that night, and the three of them played card games. When she said goodbye, she kissed Pepper on the cheek, and gave Gurril a hug. Before turning to leave, she squeezed both of his hands with hers.

8

Gurril stood in a familiar place. The road through Stonecorn Field. It was the middle of the night, and a cold breeze made the tall stalks of stonecorn rattle together, like the tails of a hundred angry snakes. Gurril shivered, and looked down at himself, wondering how it was that he had forgotten his insulated tunic. Behind him, the gravel of the road made a scratching sound that announced the approaching steps of a person who dragged their heels over the gravel and dirt of the road. Gurril whirled, pulling his small hammer from his belt and into his right hand.

Sheila approached him in the moonlight, her face pale of color but missing the wounds that were present when she died. She was naked, and stared straight into Gurril's face as she walked up to him. Her body was unbruised, her bones uncrushed. He dropped his hammer to the ground, and a tear slipped out from his left eye. Sheila came closer, and he could see a glint of silvery moonlight shine on her inner thigh as a drop of wetness dripped and ran down her leg from the place she liked to call her honey pot.

Gurril swallowed and held out his arms. Sheila's pace did not quicken, and he watched her approach, waiting. Finally, she was there, in his arms. Her body was cold, and he knew that although she walked, she was dead. He pressed his lips to hers and felt himself become engorged with excitement as he pressed his hips against her naked body.

She whispered "Take off your clothes, My Love" into his ear. Without knowing how it had happened, Gurril's clothes were in a pile on the road next to him.

Sheila led Gurril to a grassy area beside the road, and pulled him to the ground. They kissed as he entered her body, feeling her wetness but not her heat. Inside she was just as cold as she was on the outside, and Gurril knew again that he was loving a body with no life. He closed his eyes and worked into and back out of her again and again, breathing heavy and fast as his climax approached. As he came, he opened eyes to look down at her moaning, writhing body. What stared back up at him was a dead rat, the female he had killed the night he rescued Snick.

Gurril screamed in horror and rolled off the rat, too late to stop from discharging his passion into it. The night swirled into a million hues and gray and black, and Gurril screamed again. He thrashed about, and a realization came to him: this was his nightmare, returning to haunt him one more time. He awoke, and sat up in his bed. He was horrified to see that his sheets made the shape of a tent just below his waist.

Gurril huffed out breaths of terror, and looked to his doorway, hoping he hadn't awakened Pepper. He was embarrassed and ashamed to see the seven-foot-tall creature standing in the doorway.

Pepper quietly said, "I heard you having a bad dream. Are you all right, Gurril?"

Gurril grunted a positive, and lay back down. As Pepper left to go back outside to the courtyard to sleep, Gurril said, "Thanks, Pepper."

The ferret turned back, and smiled at his friend. "You're welcome, Strong One."

"Why don't we see about expanding this place a bit, so that you can sleep inside."

Pepper nodded. "Sounds good. We'll talk it over in the morning." Pepper knew why Gurril had kept him outside, instead of moving Coska into the courtyard and giving the ferret the magician's room. Keeping Coska in his old room was healing for the warrior. It was a feeling that there was at least one part of life that hadn't changed. As he curled up under a blanket in the cold courtyard, Pepper smiled to himself, knowing that his own room inside the house meant acceptance. He fell back asleep, feeling far less alone in the world than he had in a very long time.

9

Gurril woke late the next morning. His sleep did not refresh him, and he looked old and haggard in the bathroom mirror. He went to the kitchen to make himself breakfast, and saw a note from Pepper:

> "Went to the carpenter to check on my weapons. See you around lunch time. P."

Gurril grunted to himself, wondering how it was that the ferret could write. He rubbed at the scruff covering his chin, and pulled a few pieces of bread and some strawberry jelly out of the cupboard. After eating he sat alone in the kitchen, the faces of everyone he'd killed flashing before him. The faces said and did things they had never done in Gurril's real memories: Peter begged for life, Sheila told him she would marry him, and Seth smiled.

119

Coska lay in his room, sensing that Gurril was in pain. He had secreted into the warrior's mind in the night and lay down the seeds for pleasant dreams after sensing that something very disturbing had gone on inside the man's head. There wasn't much Coska could do anymore as a human; he was nearly halfway through his conversion into a tree. He lay silently in his tiny courtyard-room, his skin green and knobby. The morning sun baked down on him, and he thought about the visions he'd had since being crushed by Seth's machine, and transformed into this new being.

Most visions still had what Coska liked to think of as "rules of knowing." These were the rules that said that some visions had to be shared to come true, while others had to be shared in order *not* to come true. The vision Coska had about Gurril had its own special rule. In the vision, which had become more and more clear as time passed, Gurril was killed by a chunk of red-hot iron thrown through the air. Coska knew that if he were to ever have direct communication with Gurril, or to pass a message on to the warrior through an intermediate, this vision would come true the very same day. Just as dangerous, if he shared the vision with anyone, and that person told Gurril, the vision would come true. Coska wished he knew why the vision about Gurril was so different from every other vision.

The vision he saw for Snick would come true only if she told Gurril. Coska, being a naturally curious person, wondered if she would tell Gurril about the vision or not. She controlled her own future, and her future was hinged on what could boil down to one simple sentence.

Pepper, on the other hand, was another situation all together. The vision he had of Pepper all depended on when the ferret told someone about it. There would be a window of time, a sort of sweet spot between the event Coska had seen, and the survival or death of Pepper. In that window of time, the ferret had to tell someone about the vision, or death was certain. Coska sighed in a way that only a magician transforming into a tree can do, creaking and rustling his growing trunk, branches, and leaves a bit, and enjoyed the sunlight in an attempt to let his worries go.

Gurril, having finished his breakfast, stepped into the courtyard that had been a room only a few days earlier. He sat beside his old friend, and ran his fingertips over the green skin of Coska's forehead, noting that it looked almost green enough to be the color of a leaf, but felt knobby like bark.

Gurril smiled. "So what kind of tree will you be? Hmm?" He leaned back in his chair and crossed his arms. "I'll bet you become some sort of goofy tree with big fruit. Yeah..." He rubbed his scruffy chin in thought. "Big fruit that makes people feel funny. Not drunk, but kind of happy and like they can't stop smiling."

Gurril leaned his chair forward and peered under the bed. One thin, twisting tap root hung from the bed, reaching desperately for the floor. It looked vaguely as though it had once been a spinal column.

Gurril grunted. "Maybe I should take out the floor, huh, old friend? I'll bet you'd like to get into the dirt with that root." The warrior leaned forward, and poked Coska's arm. "Green bark. You always were kind of weird."

A tear rolled down Gurril's cheek and he sniffed. "I miss you. I miss Sheila. One day, I have the two of you in my life, and the next, you've been replaced by a ferret and a brown-skinned beauty-goddess come to earth. It's confusing, Coska. I feel a natural kinship with Pepper, like I did with you. I'm convinced that a part of you has become engrained into him. I think it happened when you got hit with that beam. You didn't just send out magic to the animal, you sent out some of your*self*, too. It isn't just the reading and writing and talking. It's his personality. So much like yours..."

Gurril sniffed again and wiped a tear away, and began again. "Part of me wants to hate him for replacing you. But I can't help but adore his friendship. He's helping me through this all at the same time that he's making it harder to mourn. I think we'll get along well as time goes. We're already better at living together. I've agreed to make him his own room. I don't know quite where I'll put it yet. Maybe I'll remodel the whole damn place, buy a couple of horses and stable them out back like the elders want. Guess I'd have to learn to ride, though. Who knows." Gurril grunted. "And Snick. My god, every time I see

121

her walking around in that little swim suit she wears when it's warm out... Part of me wants to rip it off of her and love her until both our bodies are raw. And part of me hates her, because I feel like I am being untrue to Sheila for thinking those things. How can you be true to a dead love, Coska? How can you be true to a friend who is turning into a tree?" Gurril laughed, "And what in the hell are you doing? You must be an incredibly powerful wizard, Coska. I've never heard any stories of this happening. Wizards turning themselves into deer and running away, now *that* makes more sense. But never a tree."

Gurril sighed, touched his friend's forehead again, and stood. "Coska, when you want to talk to me, I'll be waiting. I know you've talked in your way to the others. I hope someday that you'll talk to me, too." With that, Gurril turned and left the room to get ready for the day.

Sensing that Gurril had left, absorbing the words that he had said, Coska wept inside. He wanted to be the friend he had always been, wanted to tell Gurril a joke and then tease him for being the most emotionally sensitive warrior the town had ever seen. Coska sighed again, in his way, and resolved himself to be a tree that would bear fruit, the way Gurril had joked to him.

10

Pepper's visit to the carpenter had gone well, and the ferret decided to stop by the pub for a pint and a piece of whatever meat a few coppers could buy him. Pepper had arranged to pick up all of his weapons in an hour, and felt hungry while killing time around town. He sat alone at the bar, but amiably said hello to everyone who passed. As he was finishing up the day-old prairie chicken that the cook had baked him, a drunken fisherman sat next to the ferret.

"So..." the slobbering oaf of a man began, "You're some kind of *rat*, aren't you?"

Pepper swallowed his piece of chicken and offered his large smile to the man. "Oh, no sir. Not a rat. A ferret. I hate rats... In fact, it was a rat who—"

To the drunken man's eyes, Pepper's mouth wasn't a smile, but a glaring wall of razor sharp teeth. To his ears, this wasn't a story about hating rats, but being kin to them.

The fisherman cut the ferret off with a loud "Screw you! Worthless rat."

The fisherman stood up, knocking over his stool, and grabbed the fur under Pepper's neck as if it was the collar of a shirt. The man's drunken state seemed to convince him that the animal he was picking a fight with wasn't two and a half feet taller than him (even with his tall straw hat on his head). He shook the ferret with all of his might, but the animal didn't move; instead, it was the man who shook himself, raising a laugh from the other lunch-goers.

From the other side of the room, a person hollered, "Sit back down, Jones! You're being an ass."

The laughter infuriated the man, now known to Pepper as Jones, and he reached out with his left hand in a long arc over his head, slapping Pepper across the chin.

"Take that, you nasty, filthy rat!" He let go of the ferret's fur, and stood with his fists at his side.

Pepper sighed in a worried way. He had never been in a real fight in his life, and he didn't intend to start like this. The fact that he was training with the town warrior and was waiting here to pick up weapons hadn't really been connected with the reality that would inevitably follow: fights upon fights.

"Sir," the ferret said, holding back only slight tinges of anger and fear, "I believe you should sit down and enjoy a large glass of water to help you sober up a bit."

"Fuck you!" Such language was so extremely rare in the town that people in the bar instantly went from laughing at Jones to disgusted silence at his behavior. Pepper saw the shine of metal in the man's right hand, and realized that he had drawn a long and very sharp looking fillet knife from his belt. The sharp metal gleamed in a beam of sunlight that shone through the window.

The limited training that Pepper had taken up to this point kicked in, and he pushed straight out with his left hand to block the fisherman's right. With his right hand, he issued a powerful open-handed blow to the man's diaphragm and backed away quickly as the man, still holding his fillet knife, doubled over, coughing.

Without taking his eyes off of the fisherman, Pepper calmly said, "I'd appreciate it if someone would please go get Gurril. He should be at home."

The fisherman stood back upright and held the knife out in front of his face, as two strangers left the bar and ran toward Gurril's villa. "I'm going to cut you," he threatened.

The thrill of an oncoming fight suddenly hit Pepper, and he knew now what his training was for. His heart raced and every one of his senses immediately became much sharper than the knife that threatened him. Pepper knew in some place deep inside him that his body was a thousand times more dangerous than that knife, even with only a limited level of training. Pepper smiled a different kind of smile, and it made the man's drunken blood run ice cold.

"Trying to cut me," Pepper said evenly, "Would be a bad idea."

The man swallowed hard, and Pepper could sense the fear that now radiated off him. The wobble of the man's knife-wielding hand was imperceptible to everyone in the bar except for Pepper. The smell of new fear pheromones was picked up by no one but the ferret. Pepper stomped his right foot, and the man turned his body toward the stomp, ready to attack the ferret as it came from that direction. Instead, Pepper shot his left hand forward, grabbing the man's wrist and forcing it straight into the air. He hooked the man's left foot with his right foot, and pulled the man's foot forward, so that the man fell flat onto his back, with the knife in Pepper's full control pointing up at the ceiling. Pepper squeezed as hard as he could with his left hand, and crushed both of the bones in the Jones's right wrist. The knife fell to the floor and stuck into the wood with a *boing* sound; it teetered back and forth like that as the hushed crowd watched. The drunken man named Jones whimpered, and tears rolled from his eyes.

"I'll let go of you now, but you must promise me you'll behave while you and I walk to the town nurse to get you started on mending. Okay?"

Pepper smiled at Jones. The man nodded, and Pepper helped him to his feet.

Behind him, Pepper heard Gurril's voice. "Can someone explain to me what just happened here?"

A wrinkled old man with a mustache stood up in the back of the bar. To Pepper he was a stranger. To Gurril, he was recognized as the only male elder, Roy.

"Gurril, Pepper, you will meet with the elders this evening. It's time that you go back to full duty, Gurril. And Pepper is ready to join you on patrols. We'll see you at seven." With that, the old man shuffled out.

Pepper sensed that he was in trouble as he and Gurril escorted the drunken fisherman to the town nurse. Gurril wasn't saying a word.

They arrived at the nurse's cottage, and Gurril turned to Pepper. "Go ahead and bring him in. Tell Cami what happened, and she'll take care of him from here."

Gurril turned to the fisherman, and said "Jones, if you ever threaten a town warrior again, I'll make sure you're cut into bait with your own knife." With that, he was silent again.

Pepper walked the man into the nurse's cottage, knocking on the door as he opened it. Cami smiled at Pepper. "Why, you're looking well, Pepper. What happened to Jones?"

"Um, well." Pepper was embarrassed by what he had done. "I, uh…"

Jones spoke up. "I threatened him with my fillet knife. I was pretty drunk, but a crushed wrist seems to have worked to sober me up a bit."

Cami looked sternly at Pepper. "Pepper, you broke this man's wrist?" She asked the question in the way an angry mother would have.

Pepper nodded sheepishly.

"And I'm to take care of him now?"

Again, Pepper nodded.

The nurse looked at Jones, and said sharply, "Any other town warrior would have already put you into fifty pieces and sold your children as slaves. Your lucky day."

She looked back at the ferret. "Pepper, if he ever threatens you again, I don't expect to see him for treatment. My resources are for law-abiding citizens only. Criminals are to be killed and cut to bait, do you understand?"

Without another word, she grabbed Jones hard by his broken wrist and led him to a room in the back of the cottage.

Gurril sat on the front step of the cottage, wondering how to talk to his pupil. The door opened, and Pepper began the conversation for Gurril. "Gurril, was I supposed to kill that man?"

"You're training to be a town warrior. Your job is to do the town's bidding when it comes to people who would cause mayhem."

"This is my job, then? To kill people who get drunk and do something stupid? I feel terrible that I broke his wrist, to kill him..."

Gurril sighed. "You have to find a balance, Pepper. If you are too hard, they'll burn you on a stake in the middle of the night for being a tyrant. If you're too soft, they'll walk on you like a bear skin rug and piss on you like the trough in the back of the bar."

"Are you mad at me?"

"The nurse is probably mad at you. Some of the townsfolk who are sick of Jones getting drunk and causing trouble will be mad at you. I'm not."

"Why not, Gurril?"

"Because the hardest thing for a warrior to know is when to kill, when to be soft, and when to be something in the middle. I saw enough today to know that you'll probably teach me more about that than I could ever teach you about anything, Pepper."

The two had begun walking down the avenue as they spoke, and now they stopped and faced each other. Pepper put his hand on Gurril's shoulder as the warrior-teacher swallowed back tears. "Thank you, Gurril."

The man smiled at the ferret, and nodded his head in the direction of the carpenter's shop.

"Let's get your weapons, Pepper. Anyone ever tell you you're built like your mother was an oak tree and your father a slab of granite?"

"Oh, all the time." They laughed together, walking through their town.

126

The meeting of the elders that evening began as most did. Gurril stood at the front of the council room (this time with Pepper at his side instead of Coska), and elders shuffled into the room the way old people do. Gurril watched as they entered, and was amazed to see an extra elder. He was an extremely old man with bluish hair that stood on the very top of his head like an ice cream cone. The old man shook with a muscle wasting disease.

Trina, the usual spokesperson for the elders, stood up. "Gurril, Pepper… We have a new advisor to the elders for you to meet this evening." She motioned over to the old man with the blue ice cream head, and said, "Joseph, please introduce yourself."

This was a completely new situation to Gurril. There had never been an advisor to the elders that Gurril had known of, and no elder except for Trina had ever introduced himself or herself to Gurril. It was just assumed that the warrior should know or be able to figure out everything he needed to know about them. The man stood shakily, and Gurril could smell the reek of his breath from almost ten feet away. The smell was like rotting flesh and mildew mixing together.

Joseph smiled, and said wheezily, "Hello, Young Man. And hello Young Ferret. I'm Joseph. We'll talk more in time." With that, he sat back down and shook within his chair.

Trina took over speaking again. "It's been far too long since you've been patrolling, Gurril. Roy tells us that Pepper is ready to begin working with you as a warrior. How's his training coming?"

"He's got the basics, but there is still a long way to go before I'd put him in a real fight." At this, Pepper turned and looked at Gurril, offended.

"I can fight!" He interjected. "I handled the situation in the bar just fine."

Gurril turned and glared at him. "Quiet. I'll know when you're ready."

Trina smiled. "He's anxious. Good. You patrol—" She was cut off as Pepper made a painful sound and dropped to the floor. Before the eyes of the elders, the ferret shook and twitched and crunched and moaned as he shrunk back down to his smaller version. At the end of his transformation, he lay covered by his shorts. The cloth of the shorts rolled a bit, and the small ferret stepped out, and smiled his large toothy grin through the obvious pain he still felt.

Having to speak much louder to get the sound to go just as far, Pepper said, "Maybe I can stay back and train with my new weapons while Gurril has a nice patrol tonight."

Roy stood and looked at the ferret, concerned. He asked, "Are you sure you're all right, Son?"

Pepper nodded, still smiling. "The pain goes away pretty quickly, Sir."

Roy looked to Gurril. "Gurril, make sure Pepper is all right before you go on your patrol. Maybe a swing up and down the river banks; the air should be fresh tonight. Have a good evening, now."

Pepper climbed up Gurril's clothes until he was perched on the man's shoulder. The ferret couldn't help but notice a concerned look on Gurril's face as they left the meeting. Once they were out the chamber door and on the street home, Pepper asked, "What's wrong, Gurril? You look like you've got trouble on your mind."

Gurril shook his head a bit and said, "Roy's never been nice to me before."

Pepper's grin widened, and he said, "Maybe I've loosened him up a bit."

Gurril grunted a concerned sound, rubbed his chin, and said, "Maybe so."

Chapter 5: The Incredible Weapon

1

Gurril became nervous every time life fell into a routine. He had spent the last ten or so weeks patrolling for more rats, expanding the villa, and training Pepper, but nothing much of note had happened. Jones the fisherman made a common habit of dropping off a portion of his catch as a tribute to Pepper for not killing him in the bar, and Snick made her regular visits.

With a spot of help from Gary the carpenter, Gurril had begun renovating the warrior cottage. The extra space was needed now that the former second bedroom was a small courtyard for a tree, and a (sometimes) giant ferret needed a room with a bed and storage for weapons.

By now, Gurril had cut down the perimeter wall and roof over Coska's bedroom, so that it was like a small courtyard. A hole had been drilled in the floor and Coska's taproot held a tenuous grip in the hard dirt under his body. What was left of his human form still rested on the bed, but other roots had begun crawling from it, surrounding the bed. A stubby trunk rose about two feet from what had been Coska's sternum. Pepper was convinced that when Coska's transformation was complete, the trunk of his tree form would be huge, and that Gurril might have to think about moving more walls. As it was, Gurril had just completed adding two rooms to the cottage; the bedroom for Pepper, and a small stable for when enough money was saved to buy horses.

As he finished hanging the solid door to the stable, a door that had to be heavy enough and seal around the door frame tightly enough to block the smell of horses, Gurril grunted to himself in satisfaction. "Mmm. This is turning into quite the mansion."

From behind him, he heard the small voice of Pepper in his sixteen-inch-tall form. "Maybe the elders will pay you for some of this work. I mean, it really is their house."

"It is their house, yes. But part of the privilege of living here is making the cottage work for my needs with the salary they pay." He turned and faced his friend. "When are you going

129

to grow tall again? It's ridiculous to watch you train with those tiny weapons."

"Coska tells me that he's going to fix it so that soon I can choose to change my form at will."

Gurril grunted a reply that meant of *course he will*.

"Well," the ferret continued, "I'm off to finish training for the day."

"Are you sick of that stupid bow staff yet?"

"Almost. Next time I hit myself in the head with it, I'm going to throw it out. It's a shame I never got to train with the full-sized version."

"No it isn't. I'm planning on mounting it in a corner of the courtyard between two trees. We can use it to do pull-ups. I'll meet you out there in a few minutes. In the meantime, I bought you something for when you're large. It's under my bed."

The ferret bounded to Gurril's room and dove under the sheet that hung from the mattress to the floor. There he found a new sword, one that would replace the full-sized trainer he had been using. It was fully four feet long, five inches wide at the base, and three inches at the head, which narrowed into what was a broad, thick tip. The handle was polished copper with an ornamental red jewel on the nub. It was a beauty, and had Gurril fought with swords instead of hammers, he would have kept it for himself. Its sheath would strap around Pepper's back, and was made of leather. Pepper smiled, knowing that the leather meant he could unsheathe the weapon silently when needed.

An hour later, the two were training separately in the courtyard. Gurril was mutilating a tall log with his hammers, while a tiny Pepper swung his eight-inch-long wooden broadsword in parrying stroke, blocking a doll of a rat that was mounted to a spring-loaded metal rod on a rocker base. It had been left at their door with a signed note from Joseph, the elders' new advisor. They both were totally focused on their training tasks, and didn't hear Snick enter the courtyard.

The sight was not a new one for Snick, but it made her laugh anyway: In one corner, the town warrior, with a broad chest and bulging muscles. In the other corner, a sixteen-inch-tall ferret swinging around a tiny wooden sword. She covered her mouth, but it was too late. Both of "her boys" as she liked to call them, had heard her. They both halted their tasks and turned to her with smiles. Pepper was closest, and trotted over to her first, wiping his head with a wash cloth she had woven him to use as a towel.

He bowed deeply, and said, "My Lady! I assume you've come by for a meal of fish and a game of cards. Maybe later I'll show you my gigantic new sword." He winked slyly.

She smiled and bowed back at him. "I have indeed, my fuzzy little friend." She looked up at Gurril, who was standing in front of her, huffing big breaths and smiling. She added, "And my tall, handsome friend," winking at Gurril.

Gurril winked back, and walked into the house to bathe before dinner.

2

"Pepper," Snick said as she took a river salmon off of a cedar plank in the oven, "You should really make more people angry and then not kill them. All this free fish is great!"

Pepper, who sat expectantly at the table, pretended to think it over deeply. "Hmm. Maybe a farmer. We could use more vegetables with our fish meals." He smiled his (tiny) huge grin, and turned to Gurril. "What do you think, Python Arms?"

Gurril smiled and said, "A farmer, indeed. One who grows carrots!"

The three laughed at this— it was the sort of thing that a group of friends laughs at that people outside of the group would not understand. They had grown into a close fellowship. As they became closer, Gurril felt more and more physical desire for Snick's body. This desire, which over time was turning into lust, combined with friendship to become a sort of feeling he hadn't had in months. Snick was pleased to see that Gurril and Pepper had grown to be friends, and Pepper was glad that his only two friends in life seemed to be becoming a couple. In his tiny courtyard, Coska watched all of this and put his energies into becoming a tree in order to protect the fellowship that blossomed inside the cottage.

The group dug into their food, chatting a bit here and there. Pepper noted that he thought the mayfly hatch would happen soon, and it would be big this year. Gurril told his two friends about how boring his patrols had become, and Snick spent time talking about how she had taken David to a field to watch him hunt. Gurril winced inside when he remembered the dinner where he had yelled at Snick for talking about hunting with the hawk. He had been an ass that night, and he regretted it.

"I don't actually know how to hunt with a hawk, so I just release him and see what he does. Every now and then, he'll bring me something useful to eat, but today he kept on catching this type of weird creature."

"What kind of weird creature?" Gurril asked.

"It's a very funny animal. Like a mouse, but about five times as large. It looks kind of like a tiny little rat. The biggest one has been about a foot long. I suppose I could have eaten them, but they look so much like little rats, that it just seemed gross."

Gurril and Pepper thought this over for a bit, and dinner continued in silence until there was a knock at the door. Gurril left the table and opened it, finding Joseph standing outside. The old man smiled, and waved his shaky hand to the young warrior.

"Gurril," he said in his croaky voice that reeked of rot and mold, "I was wondering if I might come in for a bit of talking?" The old man sniffed the air, waving his head back and forth slowly while his nose twitched like an animal trying to determine where a scent is coming from. His eyes lit up, and he said "Ah! And more fish if you have it!"

3

The shaky old man sat at the table, smacking his lips. He shook even as he sat, and Gurril wondered how it was the man could even walk with such a shaking.

"Well," Joseph began, "I trust that you received my training aid, Pepper?"

"Yes, Sir."

"Good." Joseph turned to Snick. "Your name is Snick, right?"

She nodded. "Yes..."

132

He continued, "Very good fish you cooked tonight. Tender. With all of my teeth and both my jaw bones rotting from age... Well, tender things work a lot easier for me."

Gurril now understood the smell that emitted from the man's mouth. He had the disease that old people got when they didn't use a brush or chew on a stringy reed of carp grass after eating.

The old man sighed, and began again. "I came here tonight, because I thought that the three of you might be here together. You like to have dinner as a group on Tuesdays." He chuckled a bit, and Snick thought that the man must think himself to be quite the sly fox. "Well, first things first." He turned to Snick. "I've learned that you don't stay in any one place too long. That true, Young Lady?"

"I've moved around a bit." She shifted nervously in her seat. His next words turned her from nervous to ice.

"Yes... Must run before you get discovered as a witch, hu?" He eyed her sharply and she squirmed, ready to run out the door and make a hasty exit from the village. "No worries, Snick," he continued after a pause. "I've already talked with the other elders, and they agree that you are of no harm. In fact, with Gurril's history of working with a magic maker, you could be of some use."

She was stunned, and didn't quite believe the man. "I... I'm no witch, Joseph."

He chuckled again, and this time Snick was sure that the old man really *was* a sly fox. "Like I said, no worries." Pepper and Gurril exchanged a look. Joseph saw the look and addressed them. "Oh, no worries for you two, either. I thought that I'd come by tonight and do two things. First, I want Snick to know that her days of running can be over if she chooses them to be. Second, I wanted to tell you two boys about who I am..."

4

The last time I lived in Hearthstone was about three score ago. My father had been a helper to the town warrior, like you, Pepper. Of course, he was not an animal. No, my pa was just another guy with a set of throwing knives. Most of the time he farmed, but whenever there was trouble with rats or bandits, he'd take his knives out of the drawer and ride into town to fight alomgside the town warrior, a guy named Bradley.

Bradley retired when I was about twelve years old or so, and my dad tried taking up with the next winner of Beating Day. That guy— I don't remember his name— was no good, and my pa decided it was best to put his knives away for good before he got himself killed. Our farm ran into a spot of trouble that same summer. Well dried up, the sheep we raised all came down with anthrax, and my mom ran out of town with Bradley. They didn't have the retirement place back then for warriors; maybe the promise of a few maidens would have kept him away from my mother. Who knows. Anyhow, my dad couldn't take it all, and he hung himself in the barn. I found him swinging there one day when I got home from school.

My grandmother on my mom's side was a town elder. I moved in with her for about a year; then she got ill and died of a skin cancer. Having no more relatives in the village, I was sent to the boys' school in Belfenville. There I lived for most of my younger years. I graduated from school when I was nineteen and became a metallurgist's apprentice. That was when my trouble started. I met a young woman, a voluptuous woman who turned every head that walked by her. Not unlike you, Snick. Our romance was a whirlwind, and the next thing I knew, we were standing at an altar, and her belly was huge and round. It didn't take long before I realized that although a beauty, she was a horrible, horrible woman. Nothing can ruin a man's life like getting suckered into loving a bad woman. And what a sucker I was.

She used to wake me up in the middle of the night to spend an hour rubbing her feet. Then, I'd have to wake up and go to work at a hot forge the entire next day. I swear she was trying to kill me! Twice I got badly burned and almost lost my hands. Once, I even got a hot piece of tin in my left eye. I was blind for a week in that eye. But that woman... oh, she would have none of letting me rest.

"My feet hurt! My belly hurts! This kid kicks too much!" She never stopped.

Now, I have no idea what it really must be like to be pregnant, but this woman made it out to be a living hell. And she hated that kid. I used to pray every night that she'd die in childbirth so that I could raise the baby without her.

She smoked the sawweed when she was pregnant. We knew even back then that it was bad, but she did it anyway. And drink! She drank so much I thought our poor baby would come out smelling like a distillery, and stupid to match. I'd get home late from work— trying to stay there as long as possible not only to earn more money for the family, but to stay away from that nasty woman. But I'd come home late, tired and sore, and just wanting to relax and rest. She'd scream at me and whine because she was hungry. I'd run down to the market, pick up a dinner, cook it, eat while I listened to her ninny on about how hard her day was lying around being sore, and then I'd clean the kitchen to boot.

One night when I had been shaken awake to rub her feet, I stared down at her after the foot rub. She lay there asleep, and I couldn't see one beautiful thing about her. I had to fight every ounce of desire in my body, because that desire screamed at me to strangle her. I thought about the baby, and I couldn't do it. I watched her sleep, and left the house to go to the forge early to start work.

The forge was next door to the town alehouse. The alehouse in Belfenville was, at that time, a really no-good place. The worst kinds all hung out there. That night, as I worked alone in the forge on some iron wheel spokes, I wished over and over again for her to die. Eventually, my lack of sleep got the better of me, and I sat down to rest near the window, relishing the fresh air. Outside, I could hear two men talking. I recognized both voices; one was a boozer who made his living as a road repairman. The other was a night hunter. The night hunter was telling the boozer about a woman he'd been with a while back, and about how she had ended up pregnant. He said that the woman was a terrible person, but had a good body and lay well in bed. I'll save you the details, but the way he described her body and the way she worked him over during sex, I knew he was talking about the woman I had taken as my wife.

I learned that night that the child was just as likely his as it was three other men besides me or him. Turns out she was good in bed because she was practicing so much! It disgusted

135

me to wonder whether I was first or last in that line. I stood from the window and went to the town bath. I washed myself over and over, hoping to get her wretched stink off me. Every minute that I was away at work during our courtship and marriage, she was laying other men! I vomited, just to think of such a thing. I resolved to kill her before the sun rose. I didn't care if the kid was mine or not, I only wanted that bitch out of my life and out of the world itself.

I crept back to our house, and up the stairs to our room. I had brought one of my forging hammers home, and was going to dash her brains out with it. As I approached the bed, her eyes flew wide open, and she screamed. Her labor had started! I told her to stay calm and breathe. I no longer wanted the child, I no longer wanted the woman, and I no longer wanted my own life. She begged for help, but I denied her. She screamed for help, so I stuffed one of my shirts into her mouth and tied her hands to the bed. I watched as the baby began pushing out from her, disgusted that this woman had ever held my heart, or that I had ever put any part of my body inside of hers. She was nothing but a suffering whore to me during those hours.

The baby came out far enough that its head was fully free from her. She bled onto the sheets, and kept trying to scream through her gag. I raised my hammer... It took but only a few blows. Her dead body continued birthing the bastard child until the job was finished. I took the baby out the door, and was going to throw it into the river.

By the time I reached the riverbank, the sun was half risen, and people were beginning their days. I was witnessed, bloody, dead blank stare, holding a crying newborn by its feet. The town warrior quickly took me in, discovered my dead wife, and removed the child to the custody of an order of nuns in the town.

I don't know if you are aware, but Belfenville used to be one of the more forgiving villages. The town elders there sentenced me to fifty years in the tower. My only request was to be given books to read as I languished. I lasted there until my sentence was commuted, due to my good behavior, and the fact that it had been proven that the baby had lived his life and been killed as a bandit. His name... was

136

Tad Gallagher."

Gurril's eyes popped wide. "You... You are the father of Tad Gallagher and the grandfather of Seth?"

The old man nodded through his shakes. "Yes. When I heard what happened, and that it involved the warrior of my very home town, I resolved to return."

Gurril wasn't sure how to play this turn of events. His mind reeled as he tried to wrap his thoughts around what the old man had said. The old man, in turn, sat there shaking as he stared back kindly. It was Snick who broke the silence.

"Joseph, if you spent the better part of your life in the Belfenville tower for murder, how is it that you were able to come here and become an advisor to the elders? And how so fast? Forgive me, but of all the towns I've been in, I've never seen a group of elders so quickly give trust."

The old man smiled while he shook. "Young woman, you are a very smart whip. I spent decades reading books. Many of them about metals. One of the ways I am convinced that the two men Gurril has killed were of my descent was that they both took on engineering as a hobby. That's the sort of thing that runs in blood."

It was Pepper's turn to speak up. "So how did that endear you to the elders?"

The old man smiled again, and stood up shakily from his chair. "Originally, I came here only to thank whomever it was that killed those two descendents of the she-devil I married. Then, I found out a few things. One thing was that Seth had a rat spy who worked for him. He told this spy his whole life story... Seth knew about me. He and his father learned things as they travelled the area, raiding. The other thing I learned is that you have a much larger rat problem than you think you do."

Gurril sat up at attention. "How much larger?"

"They have an army, Gurril. The elders told me about how you took three of them on and killed them. Quite impressive. But they have an army of over eighty rats. And I have a way to kill them."

Gurril, Snick, and Pepper all stared, wide-eyed with excitement. "How?" Pepper asked.

"It's called a cannon. It's a large tube of metal that shoots out a chunk of iron at an enemy army. Now, Gurril, with proper planning you and your friend here— if he's in the right shape, that is— might be able to handle ten, or even fifteen, rats. This cannon, with these balls of iron that it shoots from it, can kill that many in one shot. If we build the cannon, and position it to fire into the advancing rat army, we can allow you two to properly defend the town if you gather a posse."

"This cannon," Gurril mused, "has to take a large load of iron. Where do you propose we get it from?"

"You've got a ton of it in storage at the elders' chambers. We'll use the iron that you lured Seth with and increase trade with other towns for the rest we need."

Snick sighed. "This is really a lot to take in, Joseph."

Joseph nodded his head in agreement. "Yes, yes. It surely is. Why don't the three of you think about this plan for a while. It's getting late for an old man anyway. Call by my house in a few days."

"Joseph," Snick said as the old man began shuffling shakily to the front door. "What is my part in all this?"

"I'm glad you asked." He smiled and scratched his chest, then sniffled back a bit of run from his nose. "I need you to mix up a powder or a gel that will explode in the chamber of the cannon with enough force to propel a fifteen pound chunk of iron out of the cannon and a quarter of a mile into the rats."

"Oh. I see." She immediately set her mind to the work, the wheels of thought turning furiously in her head, as if she couldn't help but devise a plan for this man.

He nodded again, and gave Snick a very serious look. "Remember: highly, highly explosive!"

In his small courtyard, Coska took in everything the old man had said. He had sensed when the man had arrived, and something seemed off to the tree. He thought about talking to Pepper or Snick about this feeling, then thought better of it. There may be a coming vision about the old man, and talking about him could cause an unwanted turn of events to occur. The wise tree stood under the stars, turning his feelings over and over in his mind. There was some connection between Coska and the old man, but Coska was unable to identify it. It could be trouble, or it could be almost nothing. Coska always felt that when unsure what to do, thinking about whatever thing was concerning him helped, so he decided to say nothing, and to think about the old man until he could sense what he should do.

6

After the old man had left, Gurril, Pepper, and Snick sat in silence for a bit. Pepper was the first to break the silence.

"An army of rats," he said, "And a huge metal tube that throws iron at them. Here I thought talk of mayflies was exciting."

Gurril grunted a slow, long, thoughtful sound. "We need to talk about this."

Snick stood and began turning a corkscrew into a bottle of wine. "I agree. It's a lot of information to think about."

The three sat quietly in the kitchen for a bit. Pepper began shuffling about in his chair in an uncomfortable way, and Gurril took notice.

"Hey," Gurril began loudly, drawing the ferret's attention with a start, "what's with the fidgets? You're making me nervous."

Pepper shrugged. "I guess I'd like to meditate with Coska before we talk about it. I'm still getting used to how things work between us and the elders, and he might have some good advice for me."

Snick concurred saying, "You know, Gurril, maybe sleeping on it isn't a bad idea. It would help us avoid group-think."

He turned in his chair, irritated that he wasn't going to get his way tonight. "Group-what?"

Snick felt herself blush a bit, and she repeated herself, this time a little more quietly. "Group-think. It means when people start to think the same way because... well, because that's just what people do in a group. We should all sleep on this, consider Joseph's idea for ourselves, then talk about it tomorrow. Whenever my father has a big decision that he has to make with his advisors, he has everyone sit alone for a bit to ponder it."

"Then what do we do tonight?" he asked.

139

Pepper slapped his palm on the table, and in a gleeful, excited tone, said "Fish poker!" loudly.

Gurril grunted, trying to make his acquiescence sound more begrudging than it really was. A game of fish poker actually sounded quite nice. Snick sat down, and began to shuffle out the three cards to each player. The thoughts of rats and cannons would have to wait; tonight was for friends and wine.

Soon, Gurril was swimming up the seven cards in the river as they were turned over one by one. He smiled as he watched Pepper overtake him and win the hand, while the wine began to make him feel more warm and relaxed. This was a good life; he finally began to see it during that card game, even though he still resisted the feelings of kinship with the others at the table out of a feeling of obligation to his old life.

The night grew late (not just for old men, but for young ones, too), and the cards were shuffled together and stored away into their box. Snick stood from the table. "Well, boys, thanks for a good night."

Gurril stood. "I'll walk you to the door. Let's meet tomorrow around lunch time to talk about this cannon business."

Pepper cleared his throat, and said "The mayflies might hatch tomorrow. If they do, we'll come and get you, and escort you back here to talk."

Snick laughed. "I think I can make my way through some mayflies, Pepper."

"Oh, not this year." Pepper said. "This year they'll be really bad. You won't be able to see your hand in front of your face, Pretty Lady."

"Hmph. We'll see." She stepped to the door, and Gurril followed her outside. She stopped in the moonlight and turned to him. In little more than a whisper, she asked, "Is your mourning over?"

He breathed in deeply before answering. "It never will be. But my life has to go on. I'd like it to start going on with you holding my hand."

He reached out and touched the curve of her waist, pulling her toward him. He watched her chin quiver with the anticipation of a kiss.

"I've never been with a man like you," Snick said, almost in a sigh. "When the time comes, Gurril..."

His words quivering with his excited, hot breath, Gurril replied, "I'll know what to do and how to do it. You may have brown skin and webbed feet, but you're still a woman."

"I don't know if I can love you."

He backed away from her lips, and said, "Then dream tonight, and if you love me in your dreams, let your body come and love me tomorrow night." She grabbed his arm lightly, and dug her nails into his muscle. She felt a heat inside unlike anything she'd felt before. She quickly let go of him, and backed away.

He watched as she began walking away, and she worked her legs in a manner that made her muscular, round cheeks wave goodbye. He knew that she was his in that moment, and he prayed that she wouldn't be taken away as Sheila had been.

As she walked, Snick could almost feel Gurril's eyes on her. She couldn't help but turn and look back at him once, standing there, staring. She waved delicately at him, and he returned the gesture. She felt warm, wet passion begin to come alive inside her. Part of her (a very specific part of her, in fact), begged her legs to run back to Gurril and her mouth to attack him with kisses. She forced herself to keep walking, turning away from the warrior who stared at her. The fact that he had been watching her made her heart pound so hard in her chest that she thought its thumping might wake up the neighbors.

Snick walked slowly after she knew she was out of sight of Gurril, promising herself that when she got back to bed, she would touch the warmest, most sensitive place of her body and dream of the arm she had held with her fingernails. She passed various empty streets as she strolled under the stars to her apartment. Just before entering, she noticed a mayfly buzz past her face. She smiled, and wondered how it was that Pepper could have known the hatch would happen soon.

Her smile turned to a yelp of surprise as a hand clamped down on her shoulder from behind. She turned to see a man who looked similar to Gurril, but shorter and thinner, with tall blonde hair. She stammered in surprise. The man smiled an ugly, drunken smile, and gripped her tighter.

"Coming back from my brother's house, are you?" He slurred the words, and his breath reeked of whiskey.

"Just out late," she said as she tried to turn back to her doorway. He spun her around to face him again, then used both of his arms to push her backwards into the wall. She yelped and hit her head, and was stunned for a second or two.

"That's more like it," the man said. As she shook the stars from her head, she felt his hips press into hers. She felt his hardness pressing against her, and fought the urge to vomit. "Come on, then!" He grabbed her arms with his hands, and although she struggled, the wine she had and the fatigue from staying up so late fought against her. She had little physical strength to fight the man who was now dragging her into the lawn beside the building that held her apartment. Snick struggled in vain against him as he threw her onto the grass.

He watched her fall, and then watched her body move as she tried to stand. This would be a prize for certain— no woman in the village had ever looked this good. And to walk around in such short dresses so often! As she got to her hands and knees to rise, he kicked her in the ribs, and she rolled into the grass again, coughing and shrieking in pain.

He knelt in front of her, forcing her knees apart. She reached up, trying to claw at him, and he punched her across the jaw. Her head snapped to the side, and she spat out blood. She tried mumbling something, and he punched her again, striking her just below the eye. When she turned her face back to him again, it was far less pretty. She bled from the mouth, and her cheek was swollen to the size of an apple. She mouthed words, but he couldn't see what she was trying to say.

She felt as the man reached into the top of her dress, a new yellow one that she had bought because Gurril mentioned how much he liked the color, and squeezed her breasts. He tore away the top of the dress to expose them, and a line of drool ran from his mouth. She tried saying "No," but nothing could come out of her blood-filled mouth.

She wanted to tell this man that she'd never had her chance to be with Gurril, that she wanted to be with Gurril, Gurril only, and this man never. She wanted to beg him to stop, to ask him why he did this. Just to scream the word "why" over

142

and over again if she could have spoken, as if this simple
question could have given her any relief from the fear and horror
she felt. She wanted to be warm and safe in Gurril's arms, or in
her own bed, or anyplace but on this grass, with this monster.
She could smell his rotten, drunken breath, and hear the animal
sounds he made while he pawed at her. She felt fear, she felt
pain, and she felt hate.

But the man cared for none of her feelings. The thing he
wanted was beneath the skirt of her dress, and he clumsily
yanked her underwear, light colored panties bought with the
dress, down to her ankles. Snick could hear a tearing sound as
his hands yanked at her panties. She tried to move away, but
was punch drunk from his beating to her face, and she could only
watch as he pulled down his pants to reveal a tiny pink penis
surrounded by tangly tufts of blond hair. He smiled as he looked
down at her. "You'll be a good fuck."

Angus was trying to get his pants the rest of the way
down when he heard a piercing shriek. He saw nothing, but felt
a horrible tearing at his head. The shriek came again, and he felt
his scalp being shredded and hot blood run down his face. He
reached up to swat at whatever form of hell had attacked him,
and there was nothing there. He stood with his pants around his
knees, looking up at the sky. Nothing. Blood poured down from
the shreds of his scalp.

Snick tried to use the time that David the hawk had
bought her to gather herself. She started sliding her panties up,
when Angus turned back to her. David had swept down and
used his talons and beak to tear flaps of the man's blond scalp
open, and it flopped around as he turned to face her.

"You're not going any—"

She saw the hawk swoop from seemingly nowhere down
to the man's crotch. Angus screamed a high-pitched womanly
shriek, and there was a sound like tearing fabric. The hawk was
gone just as fast as he had come, and the man's penis now hung
by only one last tendon, dangling between his thighs. Blood
spurted out from the wound where the man's tiny pink thing had
been, and he screamed in horror, rage, and pain.

Angus staggered backward, screaming, as the hawk
made one final descent. Snick had gained enough of herself to

stand as she watched the hawk attack the man's face. His screaming turned to gurgles as she ran to lock herself in her apartment. When she was safely locked away, she opened her window, and David appeared without being beckoned. She locked them both in for the night, not knowing where the man who tried to rape her had gone. Mayflies tapped here and there on the outside of her window, gathering in the atmosphere around town.

7

On days when the sun was blocked by rain or thick clouds, Gurril usually ended up sleeping in. When he awoke the morning after Joseph's visit, he sensed that it was later in the morning than his usual wakeup time. He sat up in bed, rubbed his eyes, and stretched. He turned to look out his window, expecting to see a misty rain or an overhead carpet of clouds.

Instead, what he saw was a thick blanket of mayflies swarming outside his window. The swarm moved and flowed almost as if it was a liquid being shaken inside a jar, swirling and waving. A living atmosphere, more bug than air, danced a seemingly endless and random dance. The grayish color of the insects at first seemed to be fog, as if the mayflies were actually ghosts of the previous year's hatch. Gurril supposed that in a way they were, since these were the offspring of last year's spectacle, come to life to follow their parents' unspoken instructions. One day and night of excitement, sex, birth, and death, all under the two moons, and all in such a short span; the sheer volume of space the creatures used up pushed all other life into taking the day off to stay huddled in shelter. The sky was clear, the wind was still, and yet the whole world, as far as Gurril knew, was tucked away watching from a safe place, as if a storm raged around it. It was a wonder, he thought, such bugs could exist with so much power, yet be so delicate and short-lived. Life's mystery danced in front of his window, and the warrior watched the scene, forgetting any dreams he had, any waking thoughts, and feeling the wonder of a little boy. He grunted an expression of amazement and left his bedroom for breakfast.

As usual, Pepper had awakened first. He sat at the kitchen table playing solitaire, a half-eaten jelly sandwich in front of him. It took a second or two for Gurril to realize that Pepper had transformed into his taller self. Gurril grunted at Pepper, and the huge ferret looked up from his card game. He smiled his large, toothy grin, and called out a hello to Gurril.

"Looks like you were right about that mayfly hatch, Pepper. How'd you know?"

"I lived in the woods for a long time before coming here. I'm in touch with wild things."

"How's the jelly this morning?" Gurril asked as he made his way to the kitchen table.

"Extra sweet." Pepper shuffled the cards and began dealing a game of rabbit. "Looks like we'll have a nice day to stay inside and talk cannons with Snick."

"When did you transform?"

"In my sleep. I had a really odd nightmare… I must have had it because of transforming."

"You should ask Coska about it. Sometimes dreams mean things. What was it about?" Gurril slopped jelly on his bread and poured some berry juice from a pitcher. He was mostly making conversation when asking about the dream, not really expecting much in return.

"I dreamed that a rat was trying to chew Coska's bark so that he was girdled, the way farmers kill trees to clear a new field."

Gurril could see from Pepper's face that the dream had disturbed him.

"Well," he reassured his friend, "it probably is nothing."

Gurril quietly bit into his sandwich, remembering his recurring nightmare of Sheila, and shuttering the slightest bit. He swallowed, and sipped more juice. Pepper motioned for him to pick up the cards he had just dealt.

Gurril did, grunted, and said, "You're the rabbit." He laid down the king of spades to indicate that he was the hawk of the game.

"When should we pick up Snick?" Pepper snapped down the queen of hearts, and Gurril grunted in fake pain, feigning a look like he had just been punched in the ribs.

145

"Nice card. Let's pick her up after the game; we can treat her to breakfast. I draw." Gurril took a card from the stack in the center of the table.

Pepper scratched his nose, and replied, "I hope she enjoyed the fresh air on her walk last night. Once all these mayflies die off, it's going to stink for a few days."

In her apartment, Snick sat on her bed, rocking back and forth. Her broken cheek bone was still the size of an apple, and she couldn't see out of her left eye. Three of her teeth were loosened by the first punch she endured, but thankfully none had fallen out. David the hawk sat perched on the foot of her bed, staring at her and chirping lightly from time to time. She was convinced that the bird was trying to tell her that everything was all right, that he would protect her when Gurril couldn't.

Her bed was still made, having not been slept in. She wore her red dress, the one she thought made her look the least attractive. She wanted to buy a pair of pants, and a belt; anything that would keep unwanted hands from clawing at her bare legs again. She looked to the garments she had brought from her island home, piled up in the corner waiting for a wash, and told herself she would never, ever wear the old clothes of her former life on Flamingo. There was a knock at the door, and with every rap, she jumped in fear. Before coming to Hearthstone, the most fear she had ever felt came while she was first outrunning her countrymen. After that time, she left any town long before being discovered as a magic maker.

Since coming to Hearthstone a few months ago, she had nearly been eaten by rats, discovered as a witch, and had been assaulted for sex. If she hadn't fallen in love with Gurril long ago, she would have left this town behind. The knocking came again.

Hesitantly, and trying not to burst into tears when she spoke, she asked, "Who is it, please?"

Her right hand, shaking with fear and lack of sleep, crept to a small dish of a powder she mixed up in the night that she could fling at an attacker's eyes. The response from the other side of the door was the most welcome sound she had ever heard in her life: Pepper, his voice deep enough that she knew he was his larger self, said "It's your boys! I told you we'd pick you up if the mayflies came."

"My boys!"

She leapt to the door and flung it open with excitement and relief, tears bursting forth from her eyes. Both Pepper and Gurril instantly could see that her face had been broken and that she had not slept a wink. Gurril held her tightly as she wrapped her arms around him and bawled into his shoulder, soaking his cotton shirt in salty tears. He put a bit of space between his body and hers, held her shoulders tightly, and looked closely at her wounded face.

He winced when he took in how badly she had really been hurt and asked, "Snick, what happened to you?"

Pepper had already drawn his sword and taken a defensive position in the hallway, the way Gurril had trained him to do if defending a room within a building. Over his shoulder, he asked, "Were you attacked? Did they leave the building, or can we kill them?"

Snick buried her face into Gurril's chest and wept. "He's outside. It was last night, in the park beside the building. David saved me, or it would have been horrible."

Pepper ran down the stairs and to the front door of the building to look outside. Gurril stepped away from Snick and stood in the door to her apartment, taking up the defensive position that Pepper had recently occupied.

Gurril had no worries for Pepper's safety. His training, even in his sixteen-inch-tall form, had been excellent, and Gurril knew that Pepper would not be beaten by anyone other than an incredibly exceptional fighter. The ferret was back after what Gurril estimated to be two minutes.

"Gurril, I found blood on the grass but no sign of anyone still around out there."

"With all these mayflies, you wouldn't see him if he was three feet away from you." Gurril turned to Snick. "Let's get you back to our house."

As they made their way to the door, David flew up and landed on Snick's shoulder. She turned to him and said, "You're such a good bird."

They walked in line, Gurril first, then Snick, gripping a
hunk of fabric on the shoulder of his shirt, and finally Pepper, his
hand on Snick's shoulder. The thick blanket of mayflies in the
air made vision impossible, and the small bugs bounced off
everyone's faces. The normally eight minute walk was increased
to over fifteen minutes, with stops from time to time for Pepper
and Gurril to compare notes about where they thought they were.

When they finally made it home, Gurril swung open the
door and hurried Snick and Pepper in. A batch of mayflies
entered the house, as well. David took off from Snick's
shoulder, flying through the space of the house and snapping
them up one by one as Pepper and Gurril ushered Snick to a seat
in the living room. Gurril crouched in front of her and looked
closely at her cheek. He touched it lightly, and she winced.

"Snick, this is broken. I should get Cami."

"No, no. Gurril, it'll be fine. I've been putting a cream
on it…"

Pepper frowned at her. "Snick," he said, "are you sure
that it will work?"

She smiled at him lightly, "You should have seen it last
night."

Gurril nodded. "Okay. You've got the cream with
you?"

"No, but I think you'll have everything I need to mix it
up. Can I go to the kitchen? While the cream rises, I'll make
you boys some lunch."

"No cooking. Rest," Pepper insisted.

"Pepper, please. Let me. It'll help me feel better."
Pepper looked to Gurril. Without saying a word, the two
discussed it with eyes and shrugs, then Gurril turned back to
Snick.

"As long as you promise that after lunch, you'll use our
bath and then spend the day resting and healing."

She nodded. "I need rest in a safe place. I was too
afraid to sleep last night."

A few minutes later, Snick had gathered some herbs, the
water from the eye of the previous night's fish, a bit of spider
web from a corner, and thick whipping cream. She mixed them
in a bowl, sprinkling in a few of her own eyebrow hairs. She

hummed out the words, "Stitch and paste," over and over again as she mixed the ingredients.

Gurril listened as he looked over his bookshelf, knowing that the woman liked to be alone when she incanted. He thought it odd that so many of the magic words Coska had used made no sense to him, and so many of hers seemed like random singing. When the cream was finished, she smeared some on her wounded face, then washed her hands and made a few sandwiches.

Lunch was silent, and shortly after the meal was finished, Snick walked quietly to the bath and closed the door behind her. Pepper stared out the window at the swarm of mayflies as the hawk sat perched on the back of a kitchen chair.

"Gurril, what should we do when we find out who did this to her?"

Gurril sat in the living room on a stuffed chair with a book in his lap. "One of the town warrior's duties is to keep peace and order. I'll go to the elders first, and present my case. If possible, I'll do this today. That's assuming we can identify the man. My guess is that even if Snick can't give us a good description, we'll still be able to find him by his wounds. The talons on that hawk can do some serious work."

Pepper turned to David and cooed, "Good boy, Hawk."

"After getting the order from the elders," Gurril continued, "we'll find the man. If Snick is too afraid to be alone, we'll search for him in turns. Whichever of us finds him will make quick work of it. He's to be killed, and given to the fishers for bait cutting."

"Do you think she's been honest that David got to the man before he had his way?"

"I know her well enough to know she doesn't lie. You know her well enough to know that, too. We'll take it on her word."

Pepper went back to staring out the window, and Gurril picked his book back up. His hands shook with fury as he tried to focus on the words printed on each page; had the book been made of metal, he might have crushed it with his grip. As Pepper stared at the innumerable insects swarming outside, he sighed and thought about what it would be like to kill a man.

A few minutes later, Snick emerged from the bath, dressed in Gurril's soft woven sleeping pants and shirt. She looked better, and Gurril was happy when she asked if she could lie in his bed for a nap.

As he kissed her unwounded cheek while she lay under his blanket, he told her, "When you wake, we can talk about whatever you like."

She smiled and nodded, then rolled onto her side and fell into sleep within a moment.

8

The world was glass. A thick snowfall, with flakes great and bulbous, blinded Snick. She wandered through an empty village, screaming for help. Above her, an angel with a bronze face swept down close, put its finger to its pursed lips, and went *shhhhh!* A hand shot out of the white and grabbed hers, squeezing it tight. She didn't know if the hand meant to guide her to safety or pull her to hell. The body that belonged to the hand was lost it the snow and haze.

A voice from nowhere said "We're all dead, Snick. You could have saved us."

Snick shivered as the falling snow made scratching sounds on the glass world. She looked down to her body, and saw that she was dressed again in her old garb of a tiny swimming top and tight, small bottom. It was cold here, and nobody was alive, except for the hand that held hers somewhere unseen in the snowfall. She felt blood run down the insides of her thighs, staining the snow beneath her.

9

Pepper came in to check on Snick as she slept, and noticed that the blanket had fallen to the side of the bed. She shivered lightly in her sleep, and the ferret gently laid the blanket back over her again. She inhaled deeply in her sleep, the shiver leaving her. Pepper noticed that her cheek had almost returned to normal, the cream she had spread on it now a dry crust.

Pepper made a mental note, thinking, *If I'm ever hurt badly, I'll skip the nurse and go directly to this lady.*

150

Pepper and Gurril ate lightly and played a few games of cards. They watched the swarm through the window, opening the front door once to let David out for a few minutes. He returned and tapped his beak on the door to let them know he was back. They opened it, and he resumed his earlier activity of chasing down mayflies that had made their way inside and gobbling them up with snaps of his beak.

It was nearly time for dinner when Snick emerged from the bedroom, her white hair tussled and her green eyes squinty with sleep. She still wore Gurril's sleeping clothes, and stretched as she entered the living room.

She smiled lightly at Gurril and Pepper, and asked, "How about some dinner? I'm hungry."

Pepper looked to Gurril, and could see by the look on the warrior's face that he too had noticed something amazing: Snick's cheek had completely healed.

Gurril stood to greet her, and pointed to her face. "How?" He grunted the word more than saying it, but she understood.

"The cream. I think the spiders you have here produce especially good webs. The only person who saw that I had such a bad injury besides you two was the guy who attacked me. I thought if I used a cream and healed quickly, maybe nobody else needs to know."

Pepper cleared his throat, bundled with nerves. "Snick, do you think you can tell us who did it? Hit you, I mean?"

She briefly looked to the floor, then answered the question, having resigned herself to the fact that she would have to eventually tell them about the experience in detail. "I've seen him from a distance around town, but never while I've been with you two. He was a blonde man. He looked a bit like you, Gurril, but was short and skinny."

Gurril's eyes widened. "How long was his hair?" Pepper and Snick couldn't help but notice that Gurril spoke this sentence through clenched teeth; it was a bit frightening for them both to see him quiver with rage. Pepper became suddenly thankful that if he ever fought a battle, this man would be by his side rather than facing him.

She considered for a moment, and then answered, "A bit shorter than the typical man's hair, but he wore it straight up. He actually looked a bit like a wheat stalk." She stopped, seeing that Gurril was seething, and even growling a bit under his breath.

"Pepper," he growled through his clenched teeth, "Stay here." The muscles of his jaw bulged as they flexed, and Pepper thought that the man must have incredibly strong teeth to stand up to such pressure.

Pepper nodded, and Snick began to question Gurril, but Pepper stopped her with a quick shaking of his head. The ferret held her hand while Gurril walked to the door, picking up his largest battle hammer as he passed it. They watched as the door swung open, and Gurril was swallowed up by the swarm of mayflies outside, as if he was walking into a fog bank.

By the time Gurril returned, Pepper had explained to Snick that the man was Gurril's brother. They had eaten a light dinner, saving bread and warm vegetables for the warrior. He silently walked into the house, set down his hammer, and sat at the table. Pepper and Snick both faced him nervously, each afraid to be the first to speak.

Gurril looked at them and said simply, "He never made it home last night. Probably got lost in the clouds of mayflies out there. Maybe by now he's bled to death."

He picked up a chunk of bread, dipped it in the wooden bowl of butter that sat on the table, and began chewing into it. Pepper saw that Gurril didn't ferociously chew the bread as if he was gnawing Angus to death, and thought that the walking must have calmed him down a bit.

"Do you really think he... your brother Angus, might be dead?" Snick asked softly. She reached out a hand and rested it on Gurril's forearm. He nodded and grunted an affirmative answer.

Between mouthfuls of bread, he said, "You said that the hawk tore his scalp up badly."

"Yes. And other portions of his body." While Gurril was gone, she had shared the rest of the details of the event with Pepper. The ferret looked down to the floor and shuddered as he thought again of the injuries that she had described.

"So he was bleeding a lot?"

"Very much, yes."

"He probably had trouble getting back to his house because of the wounds. When the swarm hatched, they made it impossible for him to make it home torn up and drunk. They feed on new kill, and by now they probably have eaten most of his body. We'll find bones, I suspect, tomorrow when the swarm dies."

The group was silent for a moment, and all of them heard a strange scratching sound come from the walls.

10

Billy looked to the bubbling cauldron over the fire in the tiny cottage he had taken over outside of town. He inhaled deeply, relishing the smell of the flesh boiling in the pot. Most rats loved human flesh raw, but ever since the incident in Stonecorn Field, Billy craved cooked meat. Seth's was the last human body he wanted to ever eat raw.

He leaned over the cauldron, stirring it and taking another deep whiff of the smell of cooking human flesh. Outside, the mayflies swarmed. Inside, Billy cooked a blonde man who had wandered to the cottage, injured and whining for help, unaware of the fact that he whined and begged to a rat. Billy had been wearing his clever disguise, and looked as harmless as a fly to this man. Billy smiled, took him in, and told the injured man he could soothe him for the evening. In the morning, Billy promised, he would take him to the nurse. The blonde man with the torn-apart scalp and blood-soaked pants had thanked Billy, and stumbled inside the cottage.

Billy descended upon the man as he lay weeping on the stone floor. Remembering the look on the man's face made Billy chuckle. Such surprise! Billy had whacked the man in the already-injured head with a log for the fireplace until his skull collapsed. Undressing him for deboning, he noticed why the man's pants were so blood-soaked. Billy made a note of the information, and went about his business of preparing the man for a large dinner.

The man had been surprised, and Billy chuckled again at the look on his face. What must he have thought, Billy wondered as he peered into a mirror at himself. An old man, an advisor to the town elders, shaking with weakness no less, picking up a log and smashing it down into his face. Billy smiled with the face of an old man the people in the village knew as Joseph, his breath fogging up the mirror he looked into. Dinner would be ready soon.

11

Billy's transformation happened at the same time as Pepper's. He had been in the field, and a residual bit of magic splattered onto him. This caused the connection with Coska. Neither Coska nor Billy knew they had any sort of connection, even though they both felt it a bit. To Coska, Joseph was a mysterious old man who smelled like trouble. To Billy, the tree was a nuisance that would someday be chewed to the ground.

Billy's change into the human form of Joseph took longer than Pepper's change, but was somehow more at his own control than Pepper's. Joseph hadn't once wanted to change back into his rat form, and had been successful at staying in a human shape so far. Although, he noticed that the longer he stayed shaped as a human, the worse he shook. With no understanding of magic, Billy/Joseph did not realize that the spell to look human took energy, and that he would have to spend time in his rat form now and then to recharge and rest.

After being splashed with the bit of magic, Billy came into town and ate the corpse of Seth. Billy was convinced that this was where his sudden knowledge of engineering and physics had come from. He learned nothing after eating Angus, and suspected that in the hours after his transformation, he was somehow able to absorb knowledge like nutrients out of a freshly dead brain. It was after eating Seth that Billy hatched his plan to destroy the village. He and his new mischief of small rats, broken individual pieces of the larger mischief he had transformed with his new powers of magic, could then eat the flesh of the dead humans, and enslave the beaten-but-still-living ones. They could begin a breeding program, and as Billy reassembled the tiny rats into the old mischief again, he would not only have a source of his favorite food for the rest of his life (which he was convinced would be long, indeed), but he would be revered as a hero to the mischief for generations to come.

12

Talk had trailed off at the kitchen table until Snick proposed making a pie from some apples Gurril and Pepper had on the counter. They both smiled at her and offered to help.

She declined, saying "I'm almost all the way better, boys. A little more time to think about other things, and the old Snick will be back again. I promise."

She began mixing ingredients for dough, and asked Gurril over her shoulder, "Were you ever close? You and Angus?"

Gurril grunted. "No. He was an ass. The last time we talked, Coska was still…" He almost said alive, then realized that Coska hadn't died, just started turning into a tree. "An animal, not a plant. Anyway, Coska nearly cut his head off with a sword we took from a dead bandit."

"That's why his hair was a bit short?"

"Yes."

Pepper joined the conversation. "Do you have any other family, Gurril?"

Gurril shrugged. "My mom, I guess. Although she's no better than Angus was. She's addicted to the sawweed, did it even when she was pregnant, I'm sure. She does only what will bring her more coins to buy leaf with. My father died, but he wouldn't like me."

Pepper said, "Didn't you tell me that your mother wanted you to put her in a will?"

Gurril nodded. "It was the night that Coska gave Angus a haircut. I threw them both out of my life."

"How did your father die?" Snick asked.

"I was about nine. He was a fisher. Fell off the boat in a storm."

"Really?" Pepper asked. "Which lake? Or was it the river?"

"Chicken Coop Pond."

The ferret smiled. "Well, what do you know! We've got a thing in common!"

155

"What's that?"

"I had a whole mess of family, and no less than two of them have drowned in Chicken Coop Pond."

Gurril and Pepper stared at each other for a moment, then began laughing.

Snick turned to them from her task with a frown, "You boys! You're terrible! Laughing at a thing like that." She huffed at them, and then asked Pepper, "What about the rest of your family?"

The ferret immediately stopped laughing and swallowed hard. Very quietly, he said, "I don't think I'll ever see them again. After what's happened, I'd be forced out. They wouldn't trust me after being so close to humans."

Snick wiped her hands clean and walked to the ferret, hugging him from behind as he sat in his chair. A few tears slipped from his eyes, and she rubbed behind his left ear. "You'll always have us, Pepper. We three are a family now, I think."

Gurril reached out and patted the ferret's fuzzy, part-human, part-animal hand, and grunted. Amazingly to Pepper, the grunt sounded sympathetic.

Pepper sniffed and wiped at his eyes. "Thank you both. I know that there are no other creatures like me in the world. I'll never mate, and I'll never be loved in any way other than this. When I die, I'll have been the only one of my kind." He sniffed again, more tears rolling down his long nose. "Part of me really wanted to have pups some day. There was this female, her name was Ginger."

His bottom lip quivered, and he buried his head into his arms, sobbing. The thought of never having the chance to love hit Gurril very hard, and he realized that he had been incredibly lucky to have loved once in his life. Now, he was faced with that same chance for luck again. He looked to Snick, his eyes full of tears ready to spill. She smiled at him, and he knew that he could love her if he let himself.

Pepper cried until he had to excuse himself to the restroom. When he had left the room, Gurril stood and faced Snick as she returned to her task of making pie dough.

"Sweet Lady," he said, "when the time comes that you are tired of running from town to town, and ready to be more than a friend—"

She turned to face him and pressed her finger to his lips.

"Shh. We can talk about that later. Don't worry, I'll still be here for you for a long time. We have Joseph to protect me from a burning stake, remember?"

Gurril smiled and nodded. In the silence, they both heard another scratching sound within a wall. Gurril furled his brow. "What in the world," he mused.

Snick turned back to her pie dough, and said, "Probably just some mayflies that got into the wall."

Pepper returned from drying the tears on his fur, and sat down. "Well, Snick. Your turn. Tell us about your family."

Snick shrugged. "You've both heard all of it already over so many card games. I was a princess. I was a witch. I ran away."

When she was finished mixing ingredients, they sat quietly at the table until the pie was baked. There was nothing left for them to learn about each other, and soon they would have to discuss the cannon. It wasn't until the pie was out of the oven that Pepper broached the subject. He began by taking in a big sniff of the air.

"Great smelling pie, Snick. Now how about that cannon?" He smiled widely at his friends.

"I've never heard of anything like it." Gurril said.

"I'm still trying to figure out the whole concept." Snick added.

"Well," Pepper said, "for what it's worth, I think that it is a dangerous weapon. Very powerful. Very good at defending the village, but very dangerous. What happens when the next village hears about it? Rat army or none, they'll be worried that *Hearthstone* is raising an army. Maybe even trying to put a king in power."

Gurril looked to Pepper. "Is there any way you can consult with Coska on this? He's a very wise... well, tree."

Pepper nodded. "Yes, but not tonight. I should wait until the mayfly infestation dies off tomorrow. I don't think I'd be able to meditate very well in that swarm." He turned to

Snick. "Snick, can you really mix up the gel that Joseph talked about?"

"I think can come up with something, yes. What do you two think of Joseph? His story? I don't entirely trust him, and still don't understand why the elders have taken him in so fast, rat army or none."

Gurril grunted. "I've been turning that one over in my head. There would have been a record of his history... long ago. It may not still be around. One of us could travel to Belfenville if there's no record here. That would be the next logical place to look for a record."

"But to access the records," Pepper said, "you'll have to get permission from an elder. Whomever you speak to will surely tell Joseph."

"You're right," Gurril mused. "Maybe the best way to do it is to talk directly to Joseph, show him our cards as it were. If he is true to his word, he'll have no reason to try and hide anything. If he's some sort of... What *would* he be if not true? I mean, why would he be here, and why would he try to build this cannon of his?"

"Maybe he wants to be a king." Snick said.

Gurril shook his head. "Too old."

"Unless he's a magic maker, disguising himself to be an old man." Pepper interjected.

"That's truly possible," Snick said. "Gurril, do you think you could access the record room under a false pretense?"

"What pretense?" He sat up straight, trying to think of a good lie.

"What else would they have records for?"

"Births, deaths, who held what jobs."

Pepper threw up his hands. "Boring stuff! Do we even believe that the rats have an army they are putting together to attack us?"

Gurril scratched his chin. "I've been patrolling a lot less since you came around, Pepper. Maybe they think I'm weak or sick. Surely they've watched me patrol and figured out when and where I walk nights."

Snick asked, "Are they that smart?"

"I could see their intelligence the night I fought them off you. They're smarter than we've been giving them credit for. And those three were organized. I think it's entirely possible that we may be facing the real threat of a rat army coming to Hearthstone."

"What about the cannon? I mean, could it be used against another town?" Snick asked.

Pepper nodded his head. "Why not? If it is as powerful as Joseph says, then it could knock down walls."

Gurril scratched his chin. "How do we confirm that it isn't going to be used for tyranny, then?"

The three sat in silence for a bit, considering this. Snick snapped her finger, and almost shouted, "I've got it! We have to keep the cannon here in Hearthstone. If it can't be moved, it can't be used to attack another town."

Gurril smiled at her, and said, "You're as brilliant as you are beautiful!"

"It sounds," Pepper said, "like we've got to confirm Joseph's story, while we somehow make sure the cannon that's built is not a mobile weapon."

"How do we do that?" Snick wondered aloud.

"It's got to be heavy," Gurril said, "so maybe it just *can't* be mobile. It's a lot of iron from the way Joseph spoke about it."

"If that's true, then we're in luck on that front." Pepper stood after saying this, and asked Snick, "Now how about that pie? Snick, this is just too much thinking without baked fruit!"

"Before I cut it," she teased, "let me make sure I know the plan. Gurril, you'll think of a way to get Joseph's record. And when we talk to him next, we'll make sure the cannon can't be moved after it's built."

"Agreed," Gurril said.

Pepper smiled. "Agreed, now cut the pie!"

13

The next morning, Gurril woke from an uncomfortable night's sleep in one of the large chairs in the living area of the villa. He rumbled around the house for a while, preparing some tea and peeking out the windows at the piles of dead mayflies

159

that lay in mounds around the village. He was astounded by them again, this time at the thought of the millions of tiny souls that had escaped to another world. He wondered what must become of the mayflies after death. Their carcasses filled the streets, covered roofs, and tricked the eye into thinking that a layer of dirty snow lay over the grass. The dead bodies were eaten by wild animals, mostly birds, as they lay. A few groups of fishers collected as many of the dead bugs as they could fit into baskets, the flesh not wasted when it could be used as good bait.

Twice Gurril heard the strange scratching sounds in the walls again, but by the time Pepper strolled out of his bedroom and Snick walked lightly out of Gurril's bedroom, the scratching sound was gone.

Snick sniffed long and loud as she enjoyed the flavor of the tea-scented air. "Mmm, Gurril. Green tea!" She made her way to the kitchen and began cutting bread into hunks that the three of them could eat with jam.

Pepper stepped into the courtyard to check on Coska. The tree that he had grown into stood a full seven feet now, with a thick set of roots extending from the bed and into the floor. Pepper sat in the chair next to the tree and noticed that the green color of the bark was now fading into a gnarly brown, and the long trunk was sprouting a few new branches here and there. The weather had been good for growth. The ferret looked up at the tree, noting that the wide trunk would soon encircle the bed that Coska had lain in before his transformation.

"Well, aren't you quite the tree today? No damage from the mayflies, then." Pepper hadn't noticed, but the tiny courtyard that had once been a bedroom was completely free of any dead insects.

From inside his head, Pepper could hear Coska's reply. As usual, it didn't come in words, but more as a set of known things that Pepper previously could never have even guessed at. This morning, it was nothing of much importance, and Coska filled Pepper's head with sights and sounds of things the ferret's family had been doing. He saw one of his sisters snapping up the few remaining live mayflies that buzzed around her den, and one of his brothers was rolling in dirt and spraying musk. These

160

visions relaxed and pleased Pepper after his fears of the previous night. His family was, on this morning, all healthy and happy in the wild.

The ferret knew that even if he could never see his family again, as long as he had Coska he could look in on how they were doing from time to time. A very sad thing occurred to Pepper, though. He knew that in all likelihood he had inherited a longer life span from Coska. In addition to having hands that were more human than ferret, knowing how to speak, and walking on his hind legs, he would far outlive every member of his family and their next few generations.

Pepper had only known a few ferrets that had lived to six or seven years. One uncle of his mother had even made it to nine years. By the time Pepper died (unless he broke a rule of knowing, and told anyone about his vision at the wrong time), any wild ferrets he was related to would be at least great-great-great ancestors of his brothers, sisters, and cousins.

Pepper sniffed away a tear, and patted the tree. "Thank you, Coska, for showing me that they're all right."

Inside, Gurril and Snick shared tea. They sat at the table making small talk about the mayflies, until Snick broached the subject of her attack.

"Gurril," she said directly, "Pepper told me a little bit last night about your brother Angus. You're sure he's the one who tried to hurt me?"

Gurril grunted a positive response, and sipped his tea.

Snick continued, "Then it is part of your job as the protector of this village to find him."

Again, Gurril grunted what sounded like a positive response.

Snick sighed. "Then I should look for a record of Joseph while you do that. You, Pepper, and I can go to the elders today. Pepper can talk to Joseph about the cannon remaining immobile and our concerns that other villages might believe we are becoming aggressive. I can look up Joseph's record, and you can search out Angus."

"How will you get into the records room?"

"I'll tell the elders that you want me to look over the records for any history of similar attacks. I'll tell them the attack was related to the town's defense, though. Maybe a man, working for the rats, was attempting to steal a potion that could be dangerous."

Gurril mulled this over for a bit as he sipped his tea and ate his bread and jam. He nodded. "Sounds like as good of a plan as we'll have." Pepper walked in from his visit with Coska, and Gurril waved him over. "Snick has a plan for the day. Eat while she tells you."

Snick began sharing her plan with Pepper, when about halfway through her explanation, the ferret grimaced in pain and doubled over. "Pepper, what is it?"

Pepper snarled and tried to talk but couldn't.

Gurril grabbed him by the shoulders. "Are you becoming small again?"

The ferret nodded, and Gurril helped him onto the floor. Snick and Gurril watched as he thrashed about in pain for a few minutes, shrinking slowly before their eyes. It was a full half hour before the shrinking stopped and Pepper quit moaning in incredible pain. When the process was finished, he lay on the floor, panting. Snick sat down beside him and gently petted his fur.

He looked up at her and said nothing, but with eyes that showed incredible gratitude at her compassion.

"It's all right, Pepper. We're both here," she cooed.

Gurril sighed, and began putting away the breakfast dishes.

An hour later, they were bathed and ready for the day. Pepper had assured Snick and Gurril that he was now fine and could have a conversation with Joseph without a problem. By the time they walked to the council chamber of the elders, Pepper had regained his usual smiling persona, riding along on Gurril's shoulder and watching the world go by.

He jokingly said to his friends, "I talked to Coska today. Maybe I should have asked him to get moving on his plan for me to control my size better."

Gurril said, "How often do you two talk?"

"Oh, almost daily."

Snick nodded, and said "Me, too. Coska and I talk often. He's close to being ready to let you control your size, Pepper."

Gurril growled, and said in a low voice, "Why won't he talk to me?"

The warrior wasn't asking either of his companions, but only wondering aloud. Snick and Pepper shared an uncomfortable silence. Coska hadn't told either of them why he wouldn't talk to Gurril, but they both had a strong suspicion that it had something to do with a vision. Pepper suspected that the vision must involve Coska's possible death. The thought of this chilled him. Snick believed that it must be about Coska's vision of her future, and this intrigued her. Neither of them knew (or could know) that Coska was preventing Gurril's death by not communicating with him.

The rest of their walk to the chamber was silent. They entered the main door and Gurril called out a greeting. As they waited, they heard what sounded like a scurrying sound within the walls of the chamber, and exchanged a look that told each of them that this scratching sound was a matter to be discussed when they were together again in private. A few moments later, one of the elders who Gurril did not know very well emerged from the door the elders used to enter and exit the chamber. Her name was Glance, and she was a plump, jolly-looking old woman with a tall blue beehive of hair.

"Yes, Gurril?"

"Madam Glance. I believe that Joseph has had a discussion with you about Snick playing a role in the defense of our town."

Glance smiled toward the group and approached them. As she walked near, all three of them could notice that she smelled heavily of a combination of vanilla and mint. Behind the pleasing odor was something else, but none of them could quite put a finger on what it was. Glance now stood directly in front of them, rather than behind the council meeting desk, where Gurril usually saw her.

"How did you know someone would be here today, Gurril?" she asked kindly.

"There's almost always an elder somewhere in the chamber. I thought that after the mayflies last night, there might be a lot of townfolk with issues to discuss, so the odds of an elder being here would be even more so than on a usual day."

Glance's smile widened. "Smart boy. Your muscles tell lies about the workings of your brain. Yes, there have been a few people in today about cleaning up the village. And yes, Joseph has told the entire council that Snick is, indeed, a witch."

Snick shrunk quickly back from this statement, almost as if she had been slapped. Glance gently, grandmotherly in fact, touched her cheek.

"Dear," Glance reassured, "you've done nothing but show kindness and help to everyone in this town. There's no evil magic in you. Gurril has worked well with a magic maker in the past. He'd do well to make you part of his plans for our town's defense."

Snick swallowed, and said "Thank you, Ma'am."

Gurril addressed the old woman again. "Glance, has Joseph also told the council about his plans for a defensive weapon?"

"Yes. It's called a 'cannon,' I think. Sounds loud and heavy though, if you ask me." She giggled a bit. "He asked you three about it a few nights ago, did he not?"

Gurril nodded. "Yes. We'd like to discuss it with him more, if you know where we can find him. I'd like to assign this task to my companion warrior, Pepper." The ferret stood up on his hind legs (which he found was quite easy, even though at this size, his features were more ferret-like than anamorphic), and waved at Glance, giving her his biggest smile. The ferret loved mint and vanilla, and his nose, although usually quite keen, was blinded to the identity of what other scent it was he could detect.

"Glance," Pepper said, "I have a few questions about the cannon for Joseph before we can agree that it is a good idea."

"Understandable." Glance smiled at the ferret. "Tell me, Pepper, why will the three of you not talk to him together?"

Pepper's smile stayed just as wide and sincere as he spoke to the old lady. "Well, there was an attack two nights ago, after Joseph told us about the cannon."

"Oh, my! What sort of attack?"

Gurril began to speak, working to keep himself calm. "Snick was mugged, Glance." As Gurril said this, Pepper's demeanor changed. His smile faded, and his eyes became very serious. One of the most important lessons he had learned from Gurril was to be an actor when the situation called for it, if it could help the mission.

Pepper continued the story, bending the truth as he went. "A man came at her, and stole one of her potions. We don't think the man knew it was magic, but the potion was very powerful. It turns wood much harder, almost like iron. If this fell into the hands of an enemy…"

"A wooden plank that could be as damaging as an iron mace," Glance continued. "Sounds dangerous. Snick, were you injured?"

Snick attempted a smile and to have an air about her that said she was shrugging off the attack, which had been very different than what Pepper and Gurril had described. "Fine. A bruise or two, but I've got mixtures to heal those."

Glance patted Snick on the shoulder. "Good, Dear. Go on, Pepper."

Pepper continued, "Well, Gurril should begin a search for this man immediately. But due to the darkness, Snick couldn't see the man very well. So while I'm talking with Joseph, Gurril will search for men who match the description of Snick's attacker, and Snick would like to search through the town record archive to see if there is any history of this type of attack occurring here in the past."

Gurril bit his cheek to keep from smiling. That wily ferret! He had become an excellent actor, executing the ruse without once putting on that they were suspicious of Joseph! It was a wonderful performance, and Gurril silently promised himself that he would thank the ferret later for how well he'd done in carrying out the plan.

Glance nodded, eating every word that Pepper fed her. "Yes, that sounds like a good idea. You three will be busy today. Best get going. Pepper, do you know the old cottage that the Emmers family used to own, down by the bend in the river where there's a stand of pines?"

Pepper shook his head. "No, Ma'am. I'm still learning some of the geography of this town."

Gurril cleared his throat. "I know it. Is that where Joseph is staying?"

"Yes. Why don't you take Pepper there as you begin rounding up suspects."

Gurril nodded. "I'll do that."

Glance put an arm around Snick. "Come with me, Dear. I'll show you where the records room is."

14

Joseph sketched on a piece of sheepskin, drawing out the cannon. As he filled in numbers for thickness of the iron barrel, there was a knock at his door. He opened it to find Gurril standing outside the cottage with Pepper on his shoulder. The ferret had a tiny wooden broadsword strapped to his sixteen-inch-tall frame and smiled when the old man's door swung open.

Joseph looked a bit startled, then smiled at the pair. "Gurril! Pepper! Come in, come in! Here to talk about the cannon, I expect."

Gurril stood outside while Pepper leapt down from his shoulder and strolled inside.

The ferret looked up at the man, and said, "Gurril's on a manhunt. I'm here to ask you a few more questions about the cannon."

The old man looked startled. "A manhunt? Has something serious happened?"

"Snick was mugged the night you visited us," Gurril replied. "I've got an idea of two or three men who it could have been."

Joseph thought back quickly to the man who had stumbled into the cottage with the torn up scalp and the pants soaked with blood. He said to Gurril, "Anything in particular I should keep an eye out for?"

"I think that David, Snick's hawk, may have attacked the man to the point where he is walking injured." Gurril saw the old man's eyes widen, and wondered what he was thinking. The old man/rat in disguise, was in turn realizing how it was that his meal from the other night had become injured. The fact that now

166

the town warrior was searching for that same individual might be tricky for Joseph. Most of the bones had already been ground down and tilled into his small garden out back, and the clothes burned in the fireplace. But Gurril was a smart lad. Joseph would have to come up with a plan to find out who it was he had eaten, and come up with a few false leads to offer to Gurril to explain away the man's disappearance.

"Well," Joseph said, "good luck with your search, Gurril. Pepper, would you like a shot glass full of tea? I was just working on the plans for the cannon, and I'd like you to see them as you ask me your questions." The old man ushered the ferret into the house, and Gurril left to visit Angus's farm and finish his business. He had decided that the way to deal with only Angus and not have to round up others would be to kill Angus when he was away from any witnesses, then claim to the elders that his brother had admitted to attacking Snick.

15

In the records room, Snick sat alone. Glance had left to do whatever it was the elders did deep in the bowels of the chambers. Snick often wondered about what their activities must be, and thought that if nothing else, they must sit and drink coffee while sharing stories of the old days the way elderly people do and have done for as long as time. She wondered what it must be like to grow old by sixty or seventy, the age at which most Flamingoans were just beginning the prime of their lives.

As she thumbed through the tomes, trying to find Joseph's record, she heard scratching within the walls again. She stopped for a moment to listen to the sound, and went back to her work when the scratching stopped. She looked through records from about the time that Joseph would have been a boy, trying to find anything about him, his mother, his father, or the town warrior who his mother had run off with. Finally, she came to an old piece of paper that described a boy named Joseph who was the grandson of one of the elders. She pulled the paper out, and began reading.

167

Gurril strolled up the lane leading to Angus's farm. Angus had no children yet, and his wife Kelly stood alone outside the door of the huge, two-story mansion. She looked off to the horizon, waiting for a husband who was never coming home again. The house had been built with the intention of being filled with a family. It was painted a dull yellow, and stood in front of a barn of the same color that was slightly smaller than the house. As Gurril approached, she ran to him.

"Gurril," she shouted as she ran, "Where is Angus?" Gurril could see that she had been up all night by the bags under her eyes as they glistened with tears of worry.

Gurril always felt bad for Kelly. Angus had bought her from her parents after they defaulted on a loan for a fishing boat. He used to boast to Gurril that she was the best investment into a whore he'd ever made, and before they were married for even a full year, it was obvious to everyone that Angus was going to continue playing with other women. Gurril always knew that his brother would leave her widowed by bringing himself to an early and violent death, but he thought it would be by the knife of a jealous husband, not an attack by a hawk defending its owner.

He shook his head. "I think he might be in trouble, Kelly. We should go inside."

She began weeping, and turned to enter the farmhouse. Gurril followed, watching as her short, plump but not unpleasantly-shaped body and curly, tangled mess of light brown hair passed from the sunshine of the outdoors into the dim light of the house.

She entered the house through the kitchen door into a space that was large and square. The farmhouse was far more luxurious than most. The kitchen had been designed to accommodate a large family, and to be run by a slave. Gurril always thought it revealed much about Angus that the man saved money to buy a slave after buying a wife, even though both practices were frowned upon in the area. The result of the kitchen's design was a room that looked like it belonged in the back of a restaurant instead of the front of a home. It felt cold, with a stone floor and heavy wood trim. The walls of the kitchen were panels of pine, and Angus would, from time to time, carve a wheat stalk into them while drunk. Rather than looking like the wonderful art Angus took the reliefs to be, they looked like something a naughty child had done after getting hold of his daddy's whittling knife.

Kelly calmly sat at the large table that stood next to the kitchen in an equally industrial-looking dining room. Gurril followed suit, telling himself that if Angus ever had children, he would have made them line up like soldiers for inspection in this room before receiving their dinner. He pictured Angus yelling at one of them, because they hadn't lined up tallest to shortest. The loss of his brother seemed to Gurril to be the best thing that could have happened to those kids, who now had a chance at being born to a decent father instead of a tyrant.

Kelly looked Gurril in the eye, and spoke through her tears. Gurril knew she didn't cry out of love for Angus, but out of worry for what would happen to her, the widow out alone in the empty house. She had never been alone.

"Do you know where he is, Gurril?"

Gurril shook his head and grunted a negative.

She took a deep breath and let it out purposefully. Gurril was impressed by her demeanor under the pressure she must have been feeling. She swallowed and spoke again. "Do you think he might be hurt?"

"Kelly, I'm going to give this to you as straight as I can. I suspect Angus of attacking a woman during the mayfly hatch, shortly before I came here looking for him, and being injured by a passerby." Gurril didn't mention David the hawk; he was afraid that if people found out that the hawk had viciously attacked a human, even a criminal, they would demand that the bird be put down. "If he never arrived here... I think he's out there, hurt somewhere."

"Or dead." She said these words softly, calmly, and with sheer terror in her voice. "Why did he attack the woman? I know you wouldn't tell me such a thing unless you knew it to be true without a doubt. When you came here looking for him, you only told me you wanted to talk to him. I assumed that he had gotten stranded at a neighbor's farm. Why didn't you say anything to me then about the attack?"

"I wasn't sure yet how to handle this."

"Why did he attack her?"

Gurril groaned audibly. He knew that Kelly would find out eventually; he just didn't want to pile on more bad news. He scratched at his chin.

"Rape?"

Gurril looked away from her, and answered, "Please keep that part a secret. For the sake of the woman. He wasn't successful. The passerby—"

"So you'll kill him, then? Kill him and have the fishers cut him into bait?"

"His injuries were more than just minor cuts. If he didn't find help, I think I may not have to pursue justice."

Kelly laid her head on the table and wept, afraid of being alone. Gurril sat across from her, looking out the window. He felt sorry for her, and hoped that in time another man (one better than Angus) would take the pretty lady for a wife.

17

Joseph poured Pepper a shot glass full of fruity tea and asked him to sit by the plans he was drawing. The ferret (amazed that the man's shaking hands hadn't spilled any tea) obliged, and Joseph put a distracted look on his face.

"Pepper," he said, "Why are you wearing that wooden sword?"

Pepper smiled his large, toothy grin. It was a bit more difficult at his ferret size than it was at his human size, but he had grown fond of the feeling of grinning. "I've chosen the sword as my weapon, and until my metal is forged, I'm wearing this one to get used to the feeling."

"So, you like the idea of being a town warrior, huh?"

"Well, I have to assume that this lot in life has been cast for a reason. I only hope to fill my role in a wise and just manner."

"Gurril has been teaching you well. Have you ever killed?"

"I hunted quite a bit before I transformed. But that was different, somehow."

The old man nodded. "I've killed and I've hunted, and they are two very different things. Knowing my history, Pepper,

170

aren't you the least bit afraid that I may try to harm you? I *did* spend a lot of time in a tower for murder."

The ferret shook his head and answered, "No. You killed after being pushed into it by a horrible woman. She cheated on you and made you ashamed. Besides, I see how aged you are, and if you did decide to try to hurt me, I could run away easily enough."

"And then come back and kill me when you grow seven or eight feet tall again," the old man finished.

Pepper nodded solemnly.

"Hmm. So, why don't I show you my drawings for the cannon. Maybe that will answer some of your questions."

"Please do."

Pepper and the old man leaned over the sheep skin parchment, and Joseph pointed to the long barrel of the weapon.

"This part," he lectured, "is the barrel. It is made of thick iron, and a projectile, also of iron, shoots forth from it at the enemy. This part down here," Joseph pointed to the base, "has to attach to the ground in a way that will let it swivel around."

"So the cannon can't move? I mean, other than to swivel around?"

"No, no. I thought about some kind of wheels, but we'll be using every bit of iron we can muster for the cannon and its projectiles. Wood couldn't handle the weight."

"How does it shoot the projectile?"

"That's what I need Snick for. We put some explosive material back here," he pointed to the chamber of the cannon, "and detonate it. The pressure from the explosion is what pushes the iron slug out at the enemy."

"I see. And what if another town thinks that we're building this in preparation for a war against *them* instead of rats?"

Joseph sat back and blinked his eyes at Pepper. "War? With another town? Who ever heard of such a thing?"

Pepper realized that he may have been too direct with Joseph. The ferret watched as the shaking old man looked at him, aghast. He tried to shrug it off.

"I guess it must be my wild side coming out. You're right, no civilized humans would ever go to war against other people." He smiled, trying to make himself look embarrassed.

Disguised as Joseph, Billy had done a good job acting human. This was an odd turn, though. He realized that the town defenders he had enlisted to help with the cannon were afraid that he had ulterior motives. He would have to play this smartly in order to carry out his plan. Coming from the wild himself, Billy knew that there might be skirmishes amongst clans of animals, but true wars were unheard of.

He tried to look a bit disgusted at the ferret, and said politely, "We humans are a higher order of beast, Pepper." He patted the ferret's head gently, in a grandfatherly way. "Tell me, Pepper, how do you like the tool I made you to help train?"

"Oh, the rat doll on the rod and spring? I love it. Gurril says it's good to have a moving target that I can walk through maneuvers with at this size. Thank you, Joseph."

Pepper was now convinced that the old man had bought his excuse for asking about war. He thought he probably had all the information he needed; the cannon was not mobile and apparently other towns would not think of it as a threat. The shaking old man, Pepper concluded, was probably himself not a threat.

18

Snick paged through Joseph's official history, checking out his story point by point. The written record matched what he had said, with no exceptions. She was reading the final entry in the record of his childhood when the door to the records room creaked open. Glance poked her head inside and smiled at Snick.

Snick froze for a moment, then lightly lowered the record, hoping Glance had poor eyesight and would not see it. Snick smiled at her, and said "I think I know who the suspect is."

Glance's smile widened. "Really? Who?"

"A man named Angus. He's Gurril's brother." Snick hoped upon hope that the old lady would not ask about the record.

Glance looked shocked. "Oh, isn't that a spot of trouble? Do you think I should talk to the elders about Gurril's interests being in conflict with the town's well-being?"

Snick shook her head, now moving her arms so they lay on top of the record she had been reading. "No. Gurril already thought that Angus might be who it was, based on my description. Gurril was very unbiased about it. Angus was on his list of people to question today." She smiled nervously, hoping that Glance would take her bundled nerves for a feeling of awkwardness about the situation with Angus and Gurril.

Glance nodded at her. "Well, why don't you finish up in here. I'm sure you're ready to go home by now."

"Yes, Ma'am."

19

They all arrived home at about the same time. Gurril picked up a chicken from a farmer on the way home. It hung limp from his hand, the wrung neck making its head bounce back and forth as he walked. When Gurril entered the villa, he heard Pepper in the courtyard making battle sounds of "Ya!" and "Hoorah!" Gurril stepped into the courtyard lightly, holding the chicken upside-down by the feet. He watched the ferret swing his wooden sword around at the spring-loaded rat doll trainer that Joseph had made. It was entertaining to see a sixteen-inch-tall fuzzball engaged in swordplay. Without a word, he turned again, and entered the kitchen to pluck the chicken's feathers.

Snick arrived a few minutes later, and by the end of an hour, the three were sitting in the living room, sharing the stories of their day. They stopped to eat the chicken, and after dinner, Gurril asked Snick if she would mind excusing Pepper and him for a few hours so they could train together.

She smiled, touched his arm and said "Gladly. I've got to pick up some fabric."

"Fabric?"

"I'm going to make myself a few more dresses. I can't go walking around in the same three of four things every day. Maybe some pants, too." Gurril understood, and nodded in agreement.

Pepper stretched his neck by craning his head back and forth a few times. "We should compare notes on Joseph first."

Snick nodded. "Right. The records confirm his story. Oh, and I told Glance that we're relatively sure Angus was the one who, um," her eyes darted away for the last words, "mugged me."

Gurril grunted approval. "Good work. Can't find Angus. His wife Kelly thinks the worst has happened. I agree with her. We'll probably find his bones somewhere, and you do not have to worry about him in the night, My Dear."

Snick shuddered. "Poor woman, I'll bet she's a mess right now."

Nodding, Gurril said, "I think she's more afraid to be alone than anything. Angus didn't treat her well." He turned to Pepper. "How did it go with Joseph?"

Pepper shrugged. "He seems all right to me. The cannon is too heavy for wheels, and he's building it on a fixed base that will allow it to swivel. There will be a building around it to protect it from the elements, and the building will have long window openings for the cannon to fire out of."

With that, the group had decided that Joseph was probably not a threat, that the cannon was probably not going to lead to an arms race with other villages, and that they would have to begin spreading the word to the town that Angus was missing.

Snick believed Gurril when he said that Angus was probably dead, and that she shouldn't worry about him. She debated to herself where to sleep. She knew that eventually she had to be brave enough to walk the street in the dark and sleep in her own room again, but the thought of it made her feel the way she felt the day she threw her belongings in a boat and escaped Flamingo. She excused herself from the table and left the villa. She told herself again that Angus was most likely dead, and as she walked to the town's general store to find fabric for dresses, she couldn't help but hope to herself that the evil man had suffered.

20

In the days that followed, Joseph recruited three men who were familiar with iron works, and the elders began buying iron from the surrounding areas. Coaches weighed down with the metal began rolling into town, and near the center of the village, under the cover of a temporary building, the work of heating the iron and pounding it around a large, smooth log began. Joseph explained to Gurril that the log would act as a cast, and when the iron was done being formed around it, the log would be burned out of the center. This iron barrel would then attach to the chamber where the explosion would happen, throwing out the iron slug toward the rat army. Beneath the area where the chamber would sit was a large rotating cuff. Joseph explained that this cuff would allow the barrel to rotate in order to point toward the rat army, no matter what direction it approached from. A hinge on the cuff would allow for the cannon to point higher or lower, throwing the slug farther or nearer. None of it made much sense to Gurril, but the more the shaky old man explained it, the more it seemed like it would work.

Gurril was making regular patrols, but found no sign of any rats. He would go out almost nightly, looking for anything that would indicate that there were a large number of the beasts in the area, but nothing was ever found. He doubted Joseph's story a bit, but nonetheless was constantly pushed by the elders to continue patrolling. They would give Gurril certain sectors to patrol, saying that there had been reports of rats in that area. He would follow their instructions, but night after night, no evidence was found.

Pepper remained in his small form, and the ferret regularly sat under the branches of Coska, meditating and communicating with the tree that had once been a man. Now and again, Snick or Gurril would join him. Snick always reported getting a few messages from the tree. These messages were mostly innocuous things, like "You should make a red dress, you have too many blue ones." Every now and again, however, she would get a flash of a vision or a reminder about the rule of knowing regarding the first vision that Coska had shared with her.

The season went on this way until one day, while Gurril and Pepper were training, Pepper simply dropped his tiny wooden sword and said, "He's found the answer."

Gurril turned, breathing heavily from practicing heavy hammer swings, and asked, "What did you say?"

The ferret turned toward Gurril. "Coska. He's got the answer."

Gurril was confused. "The answer to what?"

"To me. To my size. He's sprouting leaves! They'll be poison to anyone but me. If I eat them, I'll grow large. I wonder if I could make them into a tea?" Pepper rubbed his tiny chin and thought about it for a minute. He turned back to Gurril. "I've got to talk with Coska. I hope that with this leaf-eating system of his, it will hurt less when I grow large. He promised me before that when he had an answer, it would hurt less."

The ferret turned to walk over to the tree, and Gurril went back to training. Pepper climbed up the bark of the trunk, past a branch that looked faintly like a leg and foot, and into a Y-shaped branch end toward the top of the tree. The entire set of limbs was sprouting small, bright green leaves. Pepper sat in his meditation pose, with his back straight and his front paws resting on his knees. He closed his eyes, and let his mind wander.

The first thing he heard was, "It will still hurt. Just not as much."

This conversation, as every conversation between the tree and the animal, was telepathic and silent to the outside world.

Disappointed that he would still go through pain, he asked Coska, "How long will I stay large?"

"Each leaf will give you a certain period of growth, but I don't know exactly how long each leaf will keep you large. If you eat a few leaves, you will stay large longer. Eating three or four full-grown leaves should keep you big for two weeks or so."

"Can I make the leaves into a tea?" After asking this, the ferret heard Coska laugh.

"Yes, Pepper. You can make them into a tea. It may not taste very good, though. And the effects won't last as long."

Pepper now asked a question he had wondered for a very long time. "Why did you do this to me? I was happy before just being myself."

Pepper felt the tree sadden. He was amazed at how different this tree was than any other tree in nature. No tree he had ever encountered had emotions, or could communicate.

Coska replied, "Pepper... I'm sorry. I never meant for this to happen. In this new form, I've been able to communicate with a million others like me that are forever unfound. Wizards who everyone thought had died, but they didn't. They're out there; many are trees, but some are vines or bushes. One of them is even a sort of island, lost, lonely, angry, and floating around a vast sea. They all seem to turn to me, to find me. Maybe it's that most of us root into the same dirt. The point is that I've learned many things from them, and they've learned many things from me. What happened to you happened because I had more power inside of me than my body could handle. When my body came so close to death, it couldn't hold that power any longer. It had to leave my physical form."

"Why me, though?"

"Because you were simply standing where the beam of power landed, My Little Friend. If the weapon that had injured me had moved just a bit faster, and if it had just a bit more power, it would have killed me instantly. But the power inside of me would have kept my body alive, and I would have become something very dark, very evil."

"What?" Pepper couldn't understand how anything evil could have come from the Coska tree.

"Pepper, you will have other adventures, other challenges. Remember this as you have them: a wizard whose body has died, and is being kept alive only through his magical power is a dangerous thing. Most wizards in such a state don't know they've died, even as their body rots around them. They'll kill entire areas of life, creating a dark force."

"Should I be worried that I may have to face one of these creatures?"

"Not soon, but someday in the future you will. For now, just remember the vision I gave to you, and remember the rule of knowing. If you want to survive, don't tell a soul about the vision until after you've gone through the pain."

21

Snick had created a series of dresses that were every color and pattern of fabric she could find. Her previous method of dress had either fitted her form more like an advertisement than a fashion statement or had been baggy. These dresses, however, were designed by the woman herself, and they hinted perfectly at her wonderful shape. She also made a few pair of pants, but realized as she sewed the fabric that she really did prefer a dress.

After a full day of training, most of which Pepper had spent up in the branches of the Coska tree, Gurril looked forward to seeing the woman when she arrived for dinner, and what new dress she had chosen to wear. He bathed, and sat reading in the living room when she arrived. He looked up at her, saw her beautiful shape under the dress, and decided that he couldn't take any more.

She looked at him with suspicion. "Gurril, what is that look you're giving me?"

He growled lightly. "I know this isn't romance. Pepper is asleep in the tree. I need to take you. Now."

He looked over her body, noting that he could see how hard her nipples were under the light cotton fabric of the dress, and knowing that her breasts, legs, and every curve of her body would feel so good under his fingers, his hand, and his tongue.

Despite her brown skin, she blushed. "Gurril..." He stood from his chair and walked to her. He ran his fingers through her hair with one hand, and slipped the other hand inside the opening of her dress between her breasts. She took a surprised breath. She tilted her head back to look at him, and they kissed. Before she knew what was happening, he had picked her up and carried her into his room. He lay her down on his bed, and began kissing her body from top to bottom, sliding the dress off her curvy form as he went.

The dress was the first fabric to hit the floor. While she lay before him, naked except for a pair of green cotton panties, he slipped his tunic over his head. She clawed at his chest, leaving light red trails behind. He shivered in excitement, and dropped his pants and undershorts.

He stood in front of her as she lay on the bed. She watched the way his erection throbbed, and her mouth watered. Gurril looked at her body, and every curve of it made him want her more. Snick reached out to Gurril, grabbing his ass and pulling him toward her. As she lay on her back in the bed, she took him into her mouth.

He slipped his fingers under the seam of her panties, and she moaned with him still in her mouth. The green cotton underwear was the last fabric to hit the floor, and he pulled back from the satin heat of her tongue. She lay naked on the bed, wetness flowing from her almost as if she were a spring.

She watched as he knelt and kissed her toes, then her calves. He ran his tongue up her thigh. As Gurril approached her with his tongue, he could see that there was already a wet spot under her. Snick excitedly shuddered as her view of Gurril's mouth was blocked by her hairless body. He licked and tasted, teasing her with soft, round motions. She came almost immediately, and wasn't sure if she should force him off or continue to enjoy the feeling until she thought it would cause her to scream. She took it for as long as she could allow, and then pushed him away. To him, using his mouth on her was like sampling a special candy, a naughty treat. The taste, the sensations, the feel of her clit against his tongue... it was all the stuff of fantasy.

She looked up to him, and he saw again how beautiful her body was, hot and quivering. As he penetrated into her, she bit her lower lip and grunted in pain for a second, then kissed him with her mouth open, her tongue anxious to be massaged by his. He felt himself slam deep into her, her tight warmth surrounding and gripping him.

They kissed each other in an almost animal manner. She clawed and bit at him as he pounded into her harder and harder, the sound of their slapping skin creating a natural rhythm that combined with moans and grunts, then screams. Their fucking became raw power and passion, teeth and claws mixed with sweat and desire. She climaxed, her fingers clawing him relentlessly and her back arching while she yelled out unknown words to unknown deities.

They rolled over, and she straddled him. He squeezed her ass and watched her perfect breasts bounce as she rode. She screamed again as she came hard, and as she screamed and threw her head back, Gurril felt his own orgasm nearing. As Snick came, Gurril could feel her spasm and push out more wetness. This drove him over the edge, and he began screaming with her as they both came together. When they finished, Snick flopped down onto Gurril, both of them sweating and wheezing a bit from exhaustion.

Afterward they lay together, the bed soaked with the sweat, blood, cum, and saliva they had expended. The muscles of her thighs still quivered as her cum dried on them. She looked at Gurril lying beside her, his heart thudding in his chest harder than it ever had before in his life. His left shoulder bled from where she had bit him hard, and his back and chest bled from the deep grooves her nails had torn into his flesh.

With sleepy eyes, Gurril smiled at her. It was the joyous, victorious look of a strong man who had just given all of his essence to a woman in a blast of pure passion. Snick knew that although Gurril cared for her, it was not his heart that had driven him to take her in such a manner.

He spoke through a battered, hoarse voice. "Why don't you have any body hair? Have you removed it?"

"My kind doesn't have any hair except on our heads, Gurril. It helps us swim quicker. We've been living out on the ocean for so long, that we're a little different from you. It's the same reason I have webbed feet." Her vocal cords were equally as battered as his.

"Did it hurt?" Gurril couldn't help it, but he thought back to breaking Sheila's hymen, and how she had cried in pain. Snick, on the other hand, almost seemed to enjoy the sensation.

She smiled and held back a chuckle. "Gurril... you know I wasn't a virgin, right?"

He turned red and stammered "Um" a few times, and Snick became suddenly and deeply embarrassed for Gurril. Afraid he might reject her or accuse her of misleading him, she attempted an explanation.

"I'm sorry, Gurril. I think I might be different from mainland women in that respect. On Flamingo, it is common for boys and girls to take lovers early in life. I was thirteen when I had my first."

"What else is different about you?" He accepted her words plainly, understanding that he was not in any position to judge whatever past she might have. Her culture was different from his, and it was only polite at this juncture to accept that fact. He had been no picture of purity in his life, and he knew that.

"Well, let's see." She thought for a few seconds, relaxing as she saw that he would not reject her. "I have a lifetime that is far longer than yours. I'll most likely live to be well into my hundred and thirties. I can hold my breath for a very long time, and handle extreme pressure changes. Those things allow me to swim to great depths and back again. Oh— I can drink salt water, too."

"Salt water? I've read that drives people mad."

"People like you. It would kill you." She sighed, and combed her fingers through his short hair lovingly. "I don't want anything to ever happen to you, Gurril. I've wanted to be with you like this for so long. My heart—"

"Shh." He kissed her, and they fell asleep covered in sweat, blood, and cum.

Chapter 6: Return to the Kingdom of Flamingo

1

Like many couples when they first find each other,
Gurril and Snick made love together as often as they could. At
times, they would lie in a bed or on a blanket three times a day.
Snick created a cream that she would spread onto Gurril before
he entered her, to prevent herself from becoming pregnant.
During the times when Gurril was training or patrolling, she
worked on the gel for the cannon.

She was in her apartment, mixing different ingredients
into a cauldron, daydreaming about her next chance to see
Gurril. It was difficult for her to create the gel that Joseph had
requested, but she felt as if she was getting close to a working
recipe. She stopped mixing, and watched as the thin liquid
congealed into a gel. She scooped the mixture out, and took a
handful of it to the park beside the apartment building.

Snick stood in the park, a missing person poster with a
drawing of Angus on it nailed to the tree behind her, and plopped
the handful of gel onto the ground. She used a set of striking
stones to light a small branch on fire. With a small sigh of hope,
she watched the branch end burn as she held it over the pile of
gel. Snick dropped the branch into the gel to see if it would
ignite.

In the courtyard where he trained, the sixteen-inch-tall
Pepper stood taking a drink of water out of a small jar that had
originally held a few olives. He looked over at the Coska tree,
noting that the leaves were now big enough to eat. Pepper
steeled himself, and walked toward the trunk of the tree. He
scrambled up the trunk, and began plucking leaves from
branches. He decided that it was best to grow large for a longer
period of time, so he plucked four leaves. The leaves of the tree
were broad and flat, with slightly scalloped edges. They were a
bright green color, and smelled almost like mint.

He took the collected leaves into his room and sat on the
bed, staring at them. He knew the pain would still come, just not
as intense as before. Before, he had grown large at seemingly
random times. Now, he had to choose the pain. He closed his
eyes, and began chewing a leaf.

As he chewed on the leaf, he wondered if this was really worth it. Maybe it would be better to just run away. Why should he go through such pain just to protect a village? The humans of the village hadn't ever really accepted him. Gurril was the closest friend he'd ever had, and maybe that friendship made the pain worthwhile. Even when the warrior had just met him and didn't like him, the man had been kind to him. It was annoying to listen to Gurril and Snick having sex over and over again in the next room, but he loved them both.

It was the thought of Snick that made him decide to stay. He adored her and knew that if the village ever needed to be protected, he would fight against any threat for her. He loved her in a way that was not romantic, but was instead a sort of idolization. Pepper took a deep breath to calm his nerves, and continued eating the first leaf.

Gurril had been on patrol. He strolled back into town, enjoying the feel of the sun on his back. He walked proudly, having enjoyed his time on patrol. Although making love to Snick was pleasure beyond his wildest dreams, he knew he needed time to let the scratches and bites she left on his body heal. He was also sore between his thighs. It seemed that no matter how often they were together, she could still pull him in and squeeze him with her internal muscles. He loved the sensation, but it was giving him a bit of a battering down there. He never mentioned it to Snick, partly out of male pride, and partly out of a certain bit of naughty pleasure the soreness gave him.

He smiled at this thought: His troubles today were limited to the sun being so bright and warm that it was hard to see when he walked into a shadow and his body being sore from having sex with a woman who loved like a crazed beast. As he approached the front door of his home, he heard a loud *thump!* inside, and then the horrible, wild screaming of an animal in pain. He quickly threw open the door and ran inside.

"Pepper!"

The scream came again, and Gurril ran to the ferret's room.

In the room, he saw Pepper growing into his large form. The ferret's body popped and made tearing sounds from inside as he writhed on his bed in pain, squealing. Pepper opened one eye and looked at Gurril with a pleading expression.

Gurril kneeled beside his friend and said in a soothing voice, "It's All right, Pepper. It won't hurt for very long."

He watched while a loud crunching sound added a few inches of length to one of Pepper legs. Gurril realized where the loud thud had come from when he saw there was a hole in the plaster of the bedroom wall. One of the animal's arms or legs— or maybe his head— had done that.

As he watched Pepper's agony, a loud bang came from somewhere in the village, and the ground shook with the force of a small earthquake. Gurril instinctively ducked for a second, then looked over his shoulder. Of course, all he could see was another wall. It was silent outside again for a few moments, then a hurried pounding sounded from the front door.

Gurril could hear the urgency in the pounding, and he left Pepper's side, saying "I'll be back for you, Friend."

A woman with pure panic on her face stood at the front door, pounding. She continued rapping the side of her fist at the air as Gurril opened the door.

She pointed toward the other side of town, and said in a frightened voice, "That woman you go with… the one with brown skin… she just exploded!"

Gurril ran from the doorway as Pepper screamed in pain behind him, the ferret's voice now sounding more deep and full instead of like a shrill animal cry. The warrior sprinted to the apartment where Snick lived and saw that the park beside the building had a large, smoking crater in the center of it. The trees that had been around the crater were smoldering, and a few had even fallen down.

A crowd had gathered around the crater, and Gurril shouted to them, "Where is she?"

Nearly every window in this part of town, Gurril noted, was shattered. The people in the crowd just looked at him and shook their heads, none of them knowing where Snick had gone.

One random man said, "She must be in a million pieces somewhere."

Gurril stepped into the crater, which was about three feet deep. He fell to his knees, and buried his head in his hands. All

185

over again, the feelings he had when he lost Sheila came back to him. Another woman he loved… gone. He wept and fell from his knees onto the burnt ground of the crater.

From behind, he heard Joseph's voice. "Gurril, it may not be safe inside there."

He ignored the old man. Joseph stood in the crowd, staring down into the crater, amazed at the size of it. He hoped that there the woman had made more than just this batch of gel before blasting herself into kingdom come. The crowd stared at the bawling warrior, and soon Joseph was joined by Pepper.

The tall ferret tapped the old man on the shoulder. "What happened?" he asked.

Joseph took Pepper's hands in his own. "It's Snick, Pepper. I'm afraid that she made a gel that worked better than she expected. She's gone."

Pepper's breath disappeared, and the ferret felt like he would throw up. He turned and looked toward the crater, noting that there were shredded pieces of a green dress littering the area. One of Snick's sandals was on top of the roof of her apartment building, while the other was stuck in a tree branch about thirty feet high and in the opposite direction. Pepper began to shake, and he bit his tongue to keep from crying. The river ran behind the park; from it Pepper began to hear an odd splashing. Soon, the weeds and trees that lined the river began to rustle, and from them emerged the greatest sight the ferret had ever seen.

Snick stood from the water and walked through the trees and weeds of the river bank. She was naked and soaking wet, her dress and shoes having been blown off by the blast. She had a look on her face that told Pepper she was just as surprised to be alive as anyone else was to see her alive. She walked shakily to the crater, her modesty nonexistent in her happiness not to be dead. The crowd parted as she walked, as if afraid that she might somehow explode again. Snick entered the crater, and knelt next to Gurril.

She touched his shoulder gently, and whispered "I'm alive," gently into his ear.

He opened his eyes and looked up to her in disbelief. He smiled brightly, grabbed her, and pulled her into a hug. He loudly wept, squeezing her so hard that she thought she would

186

suffocate. Gurril let go and began running his fingertips over her cheeks. He shook badly, and tried to talk to her, to tell her how happy he was that she was alive. All that came out were whining squeaks as his voice betrayed him. He covered her face in kisses while she held him close to her, feeling his body shake and sob. They hugged there, rocking back and forth, Gurril unable to do anything but hold his lover and cry.

Beside the crater, Joseph leaned over to Pepper and said, "Looks like we've got a good gel for that cannon of ours."

Pepper stared into the crater, his jaw unhinged with surprise. In the air around him, smoldering shreds of dress and a missing person poster slowly floated to earth.

2

There were four of them at the dinner table, staring silently at each other. Snick, who was embarrassed by her mistake earlier that day; Gurril, whose body still shook a bit from the earlier emotional rush, and who couldn't stop smothering the woman across the table from him with kisses in the hours after the blast; Pepper, still working out the last cramps and aches of his transformation; and Joseph, shaking so badly the soup sloshed out of his spoon before he could get any of it into his mouth. He slurped up the last bit in the spoon's bottom and made a rattling *mmm* sound.

"Pepper," the old man said, "I didn't know you could make such a delightful dish."

The giant ferret smiled his familiar toothy grin at the man. "Neither did I until I actually mixed it all together today. Maybe my happiness that Snick isn't dead helped me pick good spices to add."

He winked at Snick, who shied away. He reached out and squeezed her hand. "You know, Snick..." the ferret sighed, then continued, "They say that every genius blows themselves up at least once."

She looked incredulously at Pepper, and tried to resist the smile that started to form on her face. He made a goofy look at her, and Snick couldn't resist laughing.

She patted Pepper's hand, and said, "Even when I just want to sit here and be upset, I can't when you're in the room. Thank you, Pepper."

Joseph chuckled and cleared his throat. "I'm quite surprised that you could have survived such a thing, myself. You see, when a material explodes, it creates this large wave of pressure and heat. That's what tore away and burned your dress. Luckily for you, your clothes stuck around long enough to take the brunt of the heat. The pressure, though. I'm quite surprised... Oh, but wait! I seem to recall something about people from Flamingo being less sensitive to pressure changes..."

She smiled. "That's right."

The old man chuckled again, this time at his own knowledge. "Hmm. Your face does look a bit burned, though."

"I already started a cream for it. It'll be better by tomorrow this time."

Now Gurril chimed in with a worried tone, "You aren't sore, though? You don't hurt?" He looked ready to leap up from his chair and begin administering first aid at any moment.

The woman shook her head. "No, dear. It doesn't hurt. I'm a bit stiff, but really none the worse for wear."

Gurril grunted approval at this, then said, "Unfortunately, the entire town will see now that you're a witch."

Joseph slurped another bit of soup from his spoon, and said, "Not to worry, Gurril! She's under the protection of the council. We've had her permit to conduct magic on file for weeks now."

They ate in silence again for a few minutes, then Pepper perked up his head and turned it slightly to the right.

Joseph turned to him. "What is it, Pepper?"

"Scratching. In the walls again. It's the oddest sound."

The old man's spoon steadied as he set it back into the bowl of soup before him. He waved his hand in the air. "Nothing. What else have the bunch of you been doing of late? It's been an age since we've spoken."

Gurril took a sip of soup and said, "We've been trying to search out my brother, Angus. He assaulted Snick—"

"It was only a mugging," she interrupted.

"Yeah, a mugging. Anyway, it was the night of the mayfly hatch. He hasn't been seen since. Any ideas about how to find him?"

The old man looked straight down into his soup. Joseph thought very hard for a few moments. His entire plan relied on everyone being convinced that he was really an old man, not a rat in disguise.

From his small courtyard, Coska tried to peek inside Joseph's mind. Something was off with the old man; Coska could sense that Joseph was struggling to keep some sort of magic active. The tree was becoming more and more sure that the man was a danger, and he wanted to try to see inside his head for what might be motivating him. This had to be done carefully, so that the man did not sense any intrusion by the tree. Coska tried multiple ways, but was unable to peer inside the old man. Had he seen the plan the old man was putting in place, the tree would have summoned all his powers and killed Joseph immediately.

Joseph could feel his grip on a human form waver slightly as he looked straight down into his soup bowl. He wondered if he'd have to change back to a rat for a bit, and if so, how soon. He looked up to the group, the three of them expectant of his reply.

"Well," he said cautiously, "when was he last seen?"

Snick answered, "When I saw him. David, my hawk," (Joseph tried not to sneer at the mention of the hawk,) "attacked him and tore up his scalp and... other areas." She knew that it was to be a secret that David had attacked the man, but she trusted Joseph completely, and knew he would never take the hawk away from her.

Joseph bit down hard on his tongue in an attempt not to smile. The woman had been lying! Joseph himself had seen those "other areas" that had been ripped apart by the hawk. Angus' penis was almost entirely removed. He hadn't mugged her, he had raped— or tried to rape— the woman. Joseph shook his head, knowing that he would laugh in that giddy *I know something you don't think I know* way if he opened his mouth or looked away from his soup.

Gurril added, "With his injuries, I think that maybe he fell dead somewhere."

Joseph's head popped up, and a bit of a laugh escaped him. He pretended that the laugh was a cough from swallowing his soup wrong, and he covered his face with his hands and let himself laugh it out. Pepper gently patted him on the back, saying "Maybe I used a bit too much spice. Are you all right?"

This only made the old man laugh harder, and now he felt tears squirt out of his eyes. These fools! These damned, stupid fools! It was a wonder the rats never overtook the village before! Joseph huffed out the last few laughs, trying as hard as possible to cover them with fake coughs.

He sat up straight, looked at the group, and said, "Perhaps the mayflies ate him to nothing." This almost caused him to laugh again, but he held it back.

"I've considered that," Gurril said, "but there at least ought to be bones somewhere. Or maybe clothing."

Joseph shook his head. "Mayflies will eat most cloth. I've seen it myself. And between the various wild animals out there, his bones have probably been scattered to the winds."

As Joseph sipped more broth from his spoon, Pepper added, "It could even be that a rat got him."

Joseph couldn't handle this, and soup flew from his mouth in a spray over the table. He doubled over once more, and this time his laughter really was mixed with coughs as he inhaled some of the soup.

3

At a port city many days' ride away from Hearthstone, a young warrior with white hair, striking green eyes, and brown skin walked up a dock to the office of the harbormaster.

"Excuse me," he said. "My name is Atticus. I'm looking for a woman with dark skin, white hair, and green eyes."

The harbormaster peered out his window at the man. "You mean she's Flamingoan? Like you?"

The young warrior named Atticus nodded, and the harbormaster shrugged, saying, "Never seen one of your women before."

4

Joseph retired to his cottage, locking the door swiftly behind him as he entered. He collapsed to a stuffed chair, and began letting himself transform into a rat. His change was far less painful than Pepper's transformations, and Billy/Joseph knew that this was because the size differential between his rat self and his human self was far less substantial that Pepper's was. Even though he planned on killing the ferret, Billy couldn't help but feel a bit of empathy for the animal. This feeling, empathy, was almost unheard of in rats. They were aware of what empathy was, but seldom if ever let themselves succumb to what they saw as such an ugly and weak emotion. Billy supposed that he must feel it a bit stronger due to the same process that allowed him to absorb some of Seth's engineering knowledge. What he couldn't have guessed was the *real* reason for his readiness to feel empathy: his connection to Coska, unknown to both rat and tree.

It took about fifteen minutes, and in the end, Billy the rat lay curled up in front of a fire, living the life of a king rat. It was beyond any of his wildest dreams. As he began to doze off, he thought of the many females in the mischief, and the various acts he would force them into once they were restored to their normal selves. With rats, sex was always crude and often violent. Billy dreamed of twisting back a female's head while penetrating her, until he could feel the tendons in her neck begin to snap. He drifted off further and soon was asleep, the pink, pointed shaft of his penis exposed from its fur foreskin.

Conscious wishes and the shadows that rumble in the unconscious are seldom a good match. Rats, like people, often wish that those sketchily-remembered dreams projected on the screen of their wishful mind when beginning the journey to the land of Queen Mab would continue to push them along into a sleeping paradise. When Billy's initial thoughts of sex faded, he had no dreams at all for the first few hours of sleep. Then, all at once, his brain alit with the dreams of his undermind.

Around him was chaos. Pounding footsteps, odd shapes of things flying through the air. The sky not quite the right color, but at first Billy couldn't quite decipher what color the sky actually *was*. Billy ran along with a crowd, his human self melting away until everyone around him, the crowd a mixture of rats and humans, could see what and who he was. Now the pain of stinging bites, moving methodically from his feet up to his face. He couldn't see the thousand mouths that bit him, but he could feel them. Their small, pin-like teeth sunk deep into his flesh, puncturing it so that blood oozed from him as if he was a sieve. The sky above now took on a definite color: pink.

Billy slept through the dream, and into the next afternoon. When he awoke, he decided to take one more day of rest in his rat form, and then change back into a human until his plan was finished.

5

In a tall field of soft grass, they held hands in the night, walking side by side under a blanket of stars and two moons. The reflection off the moons made the prairie they walked through bright, and the gentle breeze of evening rustled the grass around them. Gurril enjoyed the fresh smell of the night air, and Snick enjoyed the feel of Gurril's large and strong hand holding hers. She had been slightly afraid of the dark ever since her close call with the rats in Stonecorn Field, but this fear was allayed completely when she was with the warrior she adored. No fright entered her heart when her love was at her side. His security, his strength, his protection, was greater than any spell she could have cast to keep herself from harm.

Under the moons, she stopped, and placed Gurril's hand on her behind. Tonight, they would make love again, the air around them full of the peace that only resides in a place of beauty and nature.

6

Under Joseph's direction, Gurril and Pepper had of late begun making extra patrols for rats. Joseph would visit them every day or two, and give them instructions for locations to patrol, based on areas where he thought rats might be readying for their attack. The increased patrols, it was reasoned, would also keep any rats from discovering the cannon by keeping them from encroaching into the territory of the village on scouting runs. The duo never seemed to find any evidence of invaders and reported thus. Joseph would smile, politely thank them, and then go back to the council chambers.

Pepper was due to patrol this mid-morning, and the ferret decided that after breakfast, he would begin his patrol by walking over to where the laborers Joseph had hired were toiling away on the cannon. As Pepper strode through the door into the small building that had been erected around the still-under-construction cannon, the workers stopped and waved hello to him. He was extremely popular with the men (mostly due to his willingness to help them lift some of the more heavy loads), and they all greeted him with smiles.

Trina, the elder, was supervising some of the work. Pepper approached her with a morning greeting.

"Hello to you, Pepper," the old woman said. She smiled at him and took a deep breath, coughing it out when she exhaled.

"Are you all right?" he asked.

"Oh, never better, never better. I love the smell of an iron furnace, but damn if the soot in here doesn't make me cough till my lungs ache. Let's go outside." They walked outside of the building, and Trina turned to Pepper and smiled again, squinting her eyes against the bright morning sun. "Both moons were out last night. Did you see them?"

Pepper nodded. "They gave off so much light, I decided to do some night training. I'm still learning to fight in the dark, but Gurril says that in a few weeks, I should be ready to take on some night time patrols."

She patted the giant ferret's thick shoulder. "Good! Good! Let's hope that we get this cannon done in time for the rat attack. Times are frightening, you know."

"Yes, they are." As a normal ferret, Pepper had never experienced anything like an impending battle, hordes that attacked, or even much of a fight beyond a minor scuffle or two over territory. He was amazed and frightened at the scurrying rush toward death obsessed upon by both humans and rats. "Trina, is Joseph here? I wanted to tell him hello, but I haven't seen him for a couple of days."

She shook her head. "I haven't seen him either."

The woman coughed lightly, and Pepper was taken aback by the foul reek of her breath. He furled his brow.

"Perhaps I should check in on him. My patrol isn't too far out of the way."

The old woman smiled and patted Pepper on the arm. "No, boy. He's fine, I'm sure. Probably just busy. Wait another day and see if he turns up."

"But I would feel so bad if he was hurt or sick, and it really isn't—"

"*Don't break from your patrol!*" The old woman barked. The workers in the cannon's hut stopped for a second to look over at her, then at each other in shock. Pepper was taken aback and stared at her with wide, wondering eyes. She saw this, lowered her eyes, then looked back up at him. A bit sheepishly, she told the ferret, "It's just that we've planned patrol routes that will give you the best chance of seeing if there have been any movements by the rats. I'd be upset if you missed something."

Pepper nodded his head slowly. "Of course. I should go."

Trina nodded and waved him good-bye. He turned and walked toward his patrol route, one that would take him four miles out of town, and then loop back again to within a half-mile of Joseph's house. Pepper decided to himself that there was a problem, but he would need to investigate to determine what it was. Part of that investigation would mean checking in on Joseph. Surely, Joseph would tell Trina that Pepper dropped in, unless the old man was dead (a possibility the ferret gave heavy weight to).

As he walked from town, adjusting the strap of the sword sheath that lay against his back, Pepper began trying to think of excuses to stop by the small cottage where Joseph lived.

7

Atticus had visited town after town. No one in any of them seemed to recall seeing a woman from Flamingo. He walked on, passing by a forest and wondering how he would approach Snick once he found her. He instinctively ran his fingers along the knife that hung at his waist. The weapon was almost as long as a short sword and made out of shark's teeth mounted to a shaft of whale bone. The yellowish bone and white teeth made the knife look smaller than it really was as it hung next to the dark-skinned man's leg. The handle was round, with a carved-in knob on the end and divots for Atticus's fingers to wrap around to keep it from slipping out of his hands when fighting in water. The shank of the long blade was a continuation of the same bone as the shaft, and holes had been drilled into it using small, hard stones with tiny, sharp crystals all around them. Atticus remembered drilling those holes and how the task had made his fingers bleed for hours. The shark teeth were glued into these holes using a paste made of ground up fish scales, along with the blood and blubber of the very whale the bone had belonged to. The teeth stuck out from the bone about half an inch, creating a serration-upon-serration effect. The tip of the knife was shimmed into a point, and had penetrated three men's chests in its lifetime.

Atticus had made the knife himself and would not have traded it for the world. Nothing could survive a strike from it; the teeth and pointed bone tore viciously into man or beast, and Atticus had the muscle power to pull the knife back out, tearing apart flesh and bone as it ripped into and back out of a body. On two occasions he had pulled out entire internal organs. The first time, when fighting a rival to the throne of Flamingo who had threatened the king's life, he had pulled the knife out of the man's chest to find his still beating heart skewered by it. Atticus had looked at the heart with wide eyes, thrown his head back, and screamed his father's name, *Kalima*. The second time, when a stray saltwater crocodile had swum to the island, he jumped on the beast, plunged in the knife, and pulled out what he believed to be a kidney. The man whose heart he pulled out had died immediately, but the croc flopped around, chomping at Atticus with its wide, angry mouth for a good ten minutes before finally dying of blood loss. Every other man and beast he had fought with the knife bled to death seconds after being stabbed or died instantly upon attack.

A carriage came toward Atticus from behind, and he turned to wave a greeting at it. The coachman returned the greeting as he passed by. Atticus stared at the horses and carriage after it passed, amazed at the land animals and the power they must have to carry such a vehicle. For his part, the carriage driver was amazed to see a muscle-bound young man with brown skin walking down a dirt road wearing what looked like light brown cotton swimming trunks.

He walked until nightfall, and set up a crude camp just inside the cover of a field of sunflowers alongside the road. Atticus had hoped to find shelter at a town, but was confident that he would be safe on the roadside. He lay in the grass and stared up at the stars as he heard two more horses trot by on the road. Their hooves were soft in the dirt, and Atticus could hear the conversation the two riders shared.

"How many are on it?" the first rider asked.

"Three, plus the driver," the second replied.

Atticus slowly sat up to spy on the riders from between the tall stalks that hid his bed in the sunflowers. If he was lucky, they would mistake his white hair for weed tassels, and his dark skin would blend in with the night. He had a bad feeling about these two men and wanted to stay hidden if he could.

The first rider spoke again, saying, "I thought I saw a woman. I could use a good piece of ass tonight."

"You had the first try at one last time. Let me go first tonight." The second rider smiled as he said this, and Atticus watched the two men's horses trot by.

He stood behind them, and jogged along in the grass about twenty yards behind, his quiet footfalls masked by the clopping of the horses' hooves. They went on like this for miles, and Atticus pieced together that these two men raided carriages. Tonight they were out for a woman slave as much as for gold and goods. Atticus ran his finger along the blade of his knife again while he jogged behind the two men.

Finally, they approached the carriage. It was pulled to the side of the road, one of its wheels off the iron axle that held it. Without slowing, the two men approached, and Atticus crept from his position behind them into the high grass and sparse sprinkling of trees that now shrouded the road. The first rider held up a hand in greeting to the coachmen, and Atticus could see a young woman and two older men standing near the carriage. The two men were trying to impress the woman by lighting a campfire; they couldn't actually light the small pile of sticks in front of them on the road, but they argued with each other over which of them was the cause of a failure for their kindling to catch and burn. Atticus surveyed the road, and saw that the raiders had set up a crude trap to break the coach's wheel. They had buried a large boulder so it stood up from the dirt of the road with a jagged face. It was high enough to trip a horse or break a wheel, but not so high that a coachman would be likely to see it in the limited light of the stars and moons.

The coachman and first rider talked for a bit about the best way to fix the wheel. The coachman asked for a ride to the next town, and behind this conversation, the second rider uncoiled a long whip. Atticus crept closer to the edge of the grass, and was within ten feet of the road. He would wait until the two raiders attacked, then catch them off guard as they surprised the group of people on the road.

The second rider, quick as a flash, struck his whip out to one of the older men, snapping it around the man's neck and yanking him to the ground. The coachman saw this, and immediately reached for a spear that was sheathed on the side of the coach. Before he could grab it, the first rider kicked him in the face from his mount, knocking the man to the ground. Atticus ran from the grass, screaming a battle cry as he leapt high and forward, his knife in hand. The Flamingoan warrior rammed the knife home into the second rider's thigh, tearing it out as he landed on his feet. The jagged teeth of the knife ripped out a huge gouge of flesh from the rider, and he screamed in pain, dropping his whip. The rider fell from his mount and had barely hit the ground before Atticus swung the knife downward in a smooth arch, beheading the man.

The first rider turned his horse around as this happened and charged toward Atticus. Blood pulsed out of the beheaded raider's neck in gushes, creating a slurry of dark mud in the middle of the dirt road. Atticus leapt straight into the air as the unarmed rider came to him. With a fast, devastating swing, Atticus plunged the knife into the horse's forehead and ripped it out again, splitting open the animal's skull. The horse dropped to the ground, throwing its rider forward onto the roadway. The man who had been on the horse tried to crawl away, gasping for breath. Atticus knew that sound well from other battles. It was a rattling, wet gasp, telling Atticus the man had broken ribs that had torn through his lungs. The warrior from Flamingo walked to the struggling man and knelt over him. He reached down and flipped the man over, looking into his eyes. Atticus's own eyes burned as he looked into and then through the man.

"Tonight you die slow and painful at my hand. You'll get to hell and tell them 'Atticus sent me here.' And when I get there someday, I'll kill you again and send you to the next place."

The passengers and driver of the coach stood huddled in horror. The man who had rescued them was a broken savior. He relished watching the raider die slowly and painfully. He held his knife before the dying man, as if to taunt him with a mercifully quick death that was so close but would not be delivered.

The raider took an hour to die, and just before death, as the rattles inside of him told Atticus that the end was near, the warrior whispered, "When I get to hell, I'll make your death tonight look like paradise. Fear me again in the next life."

8

Pepper's patrol was coming to an end. He walked over a hill, and looked in the direction of Joseph's house. He could see a grove of trees near the house, and smoke from the chimney. Pepper decided to go to the cottage; his excuse would be that he thought he saw a rat in the trees nearby and wanted to check out the situation.

He worked his way down the hill, the sun having set an hour ago at his back; Gurril would be upset that the ferret had stayed out so late. The shadows stretched long as both moons rose, and Pepper had a nervous feeling. Something seemed wrong, and he wanted to know what it was. The dirt road that ran in front of the cottage was kicking up a bit of dust as the night wind began to blow. Pepper's fur ruffled on his arms, and he stopped for a moment to sniff the air. Any smells coming from the cottage were going to escape him as he approached due to the wind at his back, but with his nerves on edge the way they were, Pepper wanted to take in every piece of input his body could process. As he looked, listened, and smelled, he put each sense's reading into a centralized area of his brain to analyze.

Everything kept showing up as normal. There was nothing yet to indicate a problem. He walked again, continuing to descend the hill.

Inside the house, Billy was waking up from his last nap as a rat. He stirred lightly, then stretched out and opened his eyes in a lazy way, looking at the fire the way a lover looks across a pillow. Soon, this life of paradise would be his forever, and the other rats would bow to him. The humans would be served up on platters every night, and the fire in the cottage would never stop giving him joy.

It wasn't necessarily the heat from the fire that Billy loved. It was something more primal, deeper in his genetics than he could understand. It was something common to most rats, but not all, this feeling of pleasure to watch a fire. In a wildfire, rats would stay close to danger as long as possible, watching the forest or prairie crackle and burn around them. Many a rat stayed too long and watched a fire advance until they were consumed by it. Those that didn't suffocate from the heat and smoke often times would orgasm as they watched their own fur begin to combust. Billy watched the fire and imagined holding a female rat's head over the flames while he corrupted her. That was the first moment he felt the retransformation into Joseph begin.

It started in his left foot. A sort of cramping pain that radiated up his leg. Before long, he was writhing on the floor the way he did the night he ate Seth. He kicked out a leg, knocking over a table that sat beside his favorite chair. An arm flung out and hit the chair hard enough to force it out of its regular resting spot. The voice that cried out in pain was neither Billy nor Joseph, but some molding of the two. The screams gurgled with saliva that made Joseph (for he was now more human than rat), choke and cough.

Pepper was only a few hundred feet away from the cottage. The wind died down for a brief instant, and he thought he heard a gurgling scream come from the cottage. It was quite low, however, and Pepper wasn't sure if he had heard anything or not. He froze in his tracks, every sense now on edge. There was silence. Now that the wind had died down a bit, Pepper sniffed the air again. He smelled nothing out of the ordinary.

He could see the cottage quite well now, but the windows were all made of cheap, warped glass, and he could not see inside from this far away. He continued to approach with caution.

As Pepper slowly walked forward, there was a definite *thump* from inside the cottage. The ferret decided that the best thing to do was approach quickly now, in case there was trouble with the old man. A terrible voice inside Pepper's head said to him, *The old man is dying right now! You've moved so slowly that he'll be dead before you get to him, and you'll be the one everyone thinks pushed him over the edge of life into the abyss!*

This caused Pepper to trot rather than walk to the cottage, and when he approached the door, he could hear heavy breathing and groaning inside. Pepper tried turning the handle to the door and found it locked. He stepped back, then thrust his body forward while kicking straight out, striking the door right next to its handle, the way Gurril had taught him to when breaking into (or out of) a locked place.

Joseph didn't hear Pepper coming. All he knew was that one minute he was urinating on himself from the pain of transforming, and the next minute, his front door was smashed open. In his confusion and haze from being in shock from the pain, Joseph thought that one of the rats from the mischief was coming to assassinate him. He looked up in a confused way, his naked body shaking, and realized that it wasn't a rat, but Pepper.

Afraid that he had just been discovered as a rat in disguise, Joseph stammered out, "Pepper... Don't tell anyone..."

Pepper looked down. What he saw was a hurt and frightened old man, covered in urine and shaking in pain.

Pepper knelt beside him and said kindly, "It's okay, Joseph. I won't. Everyone falls down sometimes. Let me help you up, and we can see if you're hurt."

This didn't make any sense to Joseph, but he nodded anyway, and held up his hands so Pepper could aid him in his attempt to stand. Once on his feet, his mind began to clear, and Joseph looked down at his body. He feigned embarrassment at his nudity and loss of bladder control.

"Ah, Pepper... Do you think I could have a few moments to wash off?"

200

Pepper shook his head. "We should get you checked out, Joseph. You were pretty shook up."

The rickety old man smiled politely at the ferret. "I'm fine, Pepper. Just had a bit too much wine last night, and woke up confused and afraid. It's a thing old men do from time to time. I'll wash off and get dressed; then you and I can sit down, and you can tell me about your day. I could use a bit of company."

Pepper bit his lip and thought for a few moments. "Better yet," he told Joseph, "why don't we go back to my and Gurril's house for dinner. You can play fish poker with us both."

Joseph smiled politely and nodded, then walked shakily off to his washroom.

9

The sun rose over the waking coach passengers as Atticus stood guard over them. They feared him as much as they feared any raider. When the sun was high in the morning sky, another coach came by. It slowed to a stop as the driver of the broken down coach stood and waved his arms over his head, then ran over to the now stopping carriage. Atticus watched from a distance, hearing bits and pieces of the conversation between the drivers. When it was over, the two men nodded to each other, and the driver of the broken down coach strolled over to the passengers and Atticus.

"The other driver," he drawled slowly from his lack of sleep, "said he can take all of you who rode with me. Atticus, if you'd like to help me fix this wheel, I can give you a ride to the next town."

Atticus nodded and asked, "What is the next town called?"

"Hearthstone. They've got a nice hotel there over the ale house."

The passengers transferred their luggage (with the help of Atticus and the drivers) to the second coach and rode off. The dust trail of their departing horses had begun settling when the coach driver held out his hand for Atticus to shake.

"I caught your name earlier, but don't think I gave you mine. I'm Blake."

Atticus firmly shook Blake's hand and responded, "They were afraid of me."

"Yes. Yes, they were. Atticus, I don't know how you do things over in your part of the world, but to see you be cruel to that dying man last night... It was a scary thing. Grab that chisel over there, and let's pry off this wheel, so we can change out a wheel quarter."

They began working on taking the wheel off and replacing the broken section. Atticus could see that the wheel was designed so that a quarter of it could be replaced by another quarter section that was held in a large baggage compartment on the back of the vehicle.

It was well into the afternoon before the two men finished. The sun was high, and baked their skin, while their empty stomachs rumbled like two angry dogs.

"Looks about good," Blake said with a smile. "Thanks."

"Can I ride on the driver's bench with you?" Atticus asked. He wanted to enjoy the scenery around them as they rode.

"Well, sure. Hop on up." They mounted the bench together, and just before snapping his bridal at the horses, Blake said lightly, "You know, I think there might be a girl in Hearthstone from that island you said you were from."

The driver couldn't see it, but Atticus's eyes narrowed, and his right hand tightened around the hilt of his shark tooth knife.

10

There were some days when Gurril looked forward to supper because it would be a break from training or patrolling. Today he looked forward to the meal with an absolute lust for food. He had been running a lot of extra patrols lately and spent a lot of time training in preparation for the attack that Joseph insisted was coming from the rats. The extra work was making his body scream for calories.

The whole scenario of rats forming an army seemed outlandish to Gurril, but he had come to trust the shaking old man, had even grown fond of him. So this night, when the time for supper came, and Gurril's body was begging for protein and calories, he silently looked forward to when the old man would stop by for a meal. His bulging left bicep twitched, as if crying out for food as he sat down to the smell of a pot of squirrels that David the hawk had hunted down with Snick earlier in the day.

Snick stirred the pot of squirrels, and smelled the steam that rolled off the stew. She smiled at Gurril, and he smiled back. Tonight few words had passed between them; they seemed to be sharing a common mental bond. Gurril could hear Pepper training in the courtyard with his broad sword. The progress the ferret had made was incredible so far, and Gurril knew that if they had to fight together, he would completely trust the furry giant to fight well.

A light knock at the door meant that Joseph had arrived again for dinner. The group enjoyed the old man's company. The only drawback was his horrible breath that seemed to ooze out of him like the musty odors that come from a moldy carpet. Pepper trotted in from the courtyard and opened the door. Joseph stood there smiling and strolled in. He had a large wine bottle with him. So it was that many evenings had come to begin lately, and the warrior's cottage was a happy place. As the four sat down together, there was much they didn't know. Gurril didn't know the visions that Coska had shared with Pepper and Snick. Pepper didn't know that soon the village that loved him would turn on him and demand his death; Joseph didn't know that while he plotted against the village, a plot against him boiled in the minds of his mischief cohorts; and Snick didn't know that soon she would begin her return to Flamingo.

The squirrel stew and wine were almost finished. The group laughed and talked. Joseph told everyone that the cannon would be ready shortly.

Snick turned to him and said, "I've got enough of the explosive stuff made for about five shots. How much more do you think you'll need?"

Joseph looked up at the ceiling and scratched his chin. To Pepper, the chin scratching sound was similar to the mystery scratches he kept hearing come from the walls.

"Well," Joseph said, "I suspect that it won't take too many more than five, but it is better to have plenty of shots. Make a few more in the next days. I think that the rats will march on us very soon. I'm glad we have what we need for defenses. Pepper, how is your training coming along? Have you—"

He was interrupted by a knock at the door. Gurril stopped Pepper from standing by placing his hand on the ferret's shoulder. "I'll get it. Tell Joseph about your training."

The warrior stood and walked to the front door. He swung it open to see a Flamingo warrior on the other side. Gurril quickly stopped the door from swinging all the way open. He calculated the situation instantly. Snick was a witch, who was running from a burning stake. This was a warrior from her kingdom. It took no genius to see why he was here. Gurril managed not to look as on guard as he was.

"Can I help thee?"

Pepper stopped talking at once and stood from the table. He and Gurril had worked out a simple code; the use of any words like thee or thou meant trouble. Pepper put his finger to his lips in a shushing gesture to Joseph and Snick. As quietly as he could move, the ferret crept over to his broad sword, sitting in a corner hidden from the view of the doorway and began buckling it to his back.

Atticus smiled at Gurril. He knew there was a game about between the two of them. "You are Gurril. My new friend, Blake the coachman, has told me that you are town warrior here. I'm Atticus."

The use of the term "new friend" to describe Blake was meant to relax the warrior who stood on the other side of the door threshold from Atticus. They were roughly the same size. Atticus was a bit taller, but Gurril had more muscle bulk. Atticus detected no weapons on Gurril, and Gurril had already scoped out the knife Atticus wore on his waist.

Gurril noted that Atticus was dressed in what looked like a bathing suit, the same way Snick had been many times on warm days. He tried sizing up the Flamingoan's weak spots in case of a fight and noted that with his long-handled, medium weight hammer, he could stay out of reach of the knife and still deliver relatively quick and powerful blows. He would aim first for the man's knife hand.

As these thoughts raced through Gurril's mind, Atticus reasoned that any attack would probably be folly. Blake had told him about Pepper, and although Atticus hadn't seen the ferret, he knew that the animal would probably be close. If it came to a fight, he determined, he would try to strike quickly at Gurril's legs to gain a mobility advantage. That way, he could stay out of reach of the skilled warrior while he fought with the ferret, who was new to the fighting game and probably not well trained yet.

In these ways, the warriors thought, planned, and schemed as they stood staring at each other through the doorway. Pepper could peek a bit through the crack between the door frame and door. He saw that the person outside looked like Snick and thought that this might be an attempt to kidnap or execute her. He finished buckling on his sword and silently motioned to the woman to hide in the cabinet near the sink. Pepper motioned to Joseph to stay where he was, silently drew his sword, and crept around the corner so he was behind Gurril but out of sight of whoever was in the doorway.

Joseph watched this quiet drama play out in the few seconds it took to develop. His mind spun, trying to figure out what was going on, and in the end, he decided to just go with the situation, and hope that it turned out to benefit his plan somehow.

"Hello Atticus," Gurril responded. "Is there something you need me for? Someone in town perhaps has tried to commit a crime against you?"

Atticus shook his head. "Not quite that. I think you know why I've come calling on you tonight."

Gurril positioned his foot so that it was reinforcing the door. If Atticus tried to push in, the door would not open any wider than it was already, blocked by the foot and lower leg of Gurril.

"I think not. Perhaps you could help me understand."

"May I come in?"

"Not while armed. You'll have to leave that knife outside the door." Gurril hoped that Pepper had the foresight to hide Snick.

"I'm a careful traveler. I go nowhere without my knife."

Gurril nodded. "And I am a careful town defender. I don't let armed strangers into my home. Perhaps we can meet at the alehouse in a few minutes?"

Atticus knew that Snick would be in the house. The reaction by Gurril had told him that much. He at least needed to see her, to get some sense of how to handle this. The last thing he had expected is that she would be under the protection of a powerful warrior. Atticus clenched his jaw, and pulled his knife from its sheath at his waist. Gurril was ready to step back and slam the door into the man if Atticus came at him with the knife, but instead, the Flamingoan warrior set it on the ground outside the house.

"I'll unarm if we can speak here." He smiled again at Gurril.

Gurril didn't trust the smile, and stayed on guard as he opened the door a bit more to let the man in. Atticus entered, seeing first Pepper standing behind Gurril, his sword at the ready. He smiled at the ferret.

"Careful indeed. You must take very good care of your city."

He walked casually to a seat in the living area of the cottage and sat down. Gurril grunted to Pepper, and the ferret put his sword back into its sheath. Gurril sat across the living room from Atticus, and Atticus noted a shaky old man sipping stew in the kitchen.

Atticus motioned to the man. "Your father?"

Gurril grunted a negative. "No. Friend and advisor to the town elders."

"It may be better if we speak without him present. Both of our best interests are in play for this conversation, Gurril."

"He'll stay, as will Pepper."

"Both of us are unarmed, Gurril. But your animal friend... that sword is almost as big as me."

"Like I said, we're careful. We're in our home, he'll stay armed. Now tell me what you are here for."

Atticus decided that it was best to cut to the chase. He never enjoyed playing mind games, becoming bored quickly with them; if a fight was coming, he just wanted to get to it and get it over with.

"I'm here for a woman from my kingdom. Where is she?"

Gurril knew that he could only lie so much to this man. The townsfolk had no doubt told Atticus that Gurril and Snick were a couple. She had been seen around town as little as a few hours ago and was probably last seen entering the cottage. He began with a small lie, meant to test the man across from him.

"She heard that someone was coming from Flamingo. She told me goodbye and left through the field behind the house."

Atticus weighed this story in his mind. It could be true. The coach passengers arrived in this town hours before he did and would have shared their story about the man with brown skin, green eyes, and white hair who had saved them. He would need a way to test the validity of the story. If Snick was hiding nearby rather than running, she would probably be in the house, within earshot. He spoke his answer somewhat loudly, hoping that if she was nearby, she would hear.

"Her father has died. She's the queen of our village, although as a witch she can never take her throne. The people despise her for what she is but need her skills of magic. For a long time, it has been the royally-ordered duty of any Flamingoan to kill her on sight. Only recently did this change."

"Did you come to kill her?"

Atticus shook his head. "No. I came to take her home. Our kingdom is under siege from the Mer. They killed fully a third of our entire population before I snuck through their lines to come to the mainland to get her. We need her magic, or we will all be killed."

Snick could hear every word of this. She knew Atticus well and knew that he would lie to get what he wanted, but that he also would take any advantage he could get in a battle against a foe like the Mer. He had served as her father's primary guardian and would not leave his side. Yet he was here alone. Perhaps he really was telling the truth. The Mer had long been to the Flamingoans much like rats were to the people of Hearthstone.

Joseph stood from his chair in the kitchen. What Atticus had said, and what he was here for, would help Joseph's plan perfectly. Explosives for five shots were all that Joseph would need, and with Snick gone, there was one less dangerous person around to stand in Joseph's way.

He hobbled from the kitchen to the living room, and waved a shaking hand in the air. "Hello young man. My name is Joseph."

Pepper stepped aside to let Joseph through.

Atticus bowed his head to the elder. "Good evening, Joseph. As a friend and advisor to the town elders, I know that you must be unhappy to learn that a magic maker has been in your midst."

Joseph chuckled, always loving the feeling of knowing more than the person to whom he spoke. "Indeed. But as an advisor to the town elders, I also understand the need to defend your kingdom. Snick is –"

Pepper cut him off, before the old man could reveal that Snick was hiding in the kitchen. "We have to test your truth, and I know how to do it," the ferret said as he stepped from the living area to the small courtyard where the Coska tree grew.

Gurril was nervous. If this man was lying, it meant there would be one hell of a fight. If he told the truth, Gurril's heart would be broken when Snick left to go fight the Mer (whatever *they* were).

Pepper found a small switch from a lower branch of Coska and tore it off. He used his sword tip to sharpen the base of it to a point and approached Atticus. Pepper had no idea how he knew this method of lie detection would work. The knowledge had just popped into his head. Coska had put it there while he listened to the conversation outside his courtyard.

Pepper looked to the Flamingoan warrior, and stood directly in front of him. "Hold out your arm," he commanded.

Atticus shook his head as if to say no, but Pepper plunged the switch forward anyway, and before Atticus knew what was happening he had a small tree branch sticking out of his body. He reached over with his other hand and tried to rip it free, but the branch had somehow grabbed onto him and was rooted there.

"What sort of evil is this?" He yelled out the question, on the verge of panic.

Pepper knelt in front of Atticus so he could look him in the eye while he sat. "It's a special tree. If you tell me the truth, the switch will fall out of your arm and you will heal. If you lie to me, it will poison you most horribly. Why do you want to find Snick?"

Atticus swallowed with an audible click. There was a voice in the back of his mind (he would have identified it as Coska, had he ever known the man), that said to him "Tell the truth or become compost, Atticus."

Atticus took a deep breath in, and began speaking.

11

About three months ago, the attack of the Mer started. They swam up during a high tide, when the island was covered with water, and ripped up all the sea corn we had planted. Before the tide rolled back out, they left and hid in the deep water.

We came back from fishing, and the three men who had been farming the corn were found dead, their throats slit and the meaty parts of their bodies eaten. It looked like a Mer attack, but we were unsure until we found the sea corn gone. Tearing up crops is meant to starve their victims into an attempt to flee across the sea; it is a common tactic for the Mer. Our hope then was that it had been a small roaming band. The next day, we decided that it was best for most of the village to stay on the island during high tide rather than leaving to fish. I remember watching the few fishing boats we sent as a test go out, and as soon as they hit high water, they disappeared under the waves, one by one.

All the warriors met with the king to plan a strategy. Two of our best swimmers went out a bit and tried to scan the waters, but the Mer were too deep to find. By observing them as they came in from time to time for raids, we've determined that there are no less than five hundred.

We have only three warriors in our village, much like you have only two here. We could never take on such a force. We picked off a few of them, using spears. Snick's father even devised a way to fish for them using meat from our dead and dying villagers. We killed twelve of them, while we were losing now between fifteen and twenty Flamingoans per day.

The Mer come mostly at high tide, during the middle of the day. They blend so well with the sea bed that we cannot detect them from above the water. But sending anyone into the water is madness. Even we cannot fight underwater as viciously as they do. They will leap from the water into a hut and use their claws to clamp onto a victim. They wrestle him into the water, and eat the person.

They moved in close enough so that at night you can see where they are in the water by their glowing eyes. Have you ever seen one? They look like a nightmare. They are long, between seven and ten feet when grown to adulthood. They have arms like yours or mine, only their hands are more round than long, and the webbing between each finger runs from tip to base. They have large claws that drip with a clear poison that make the victim cramp up, and unable to swim away from them. Their legs are connected down to the knee, and their feet are round and webbed like their hands, but without the claws. They swim like dolphins, arching their backs. The skin on most of their bodies is green, with black nipples and lips. The females only grow breasts when they have young to feed, and that is the only time you can tell the males and females apart.

It is their heads that are the most frightening, attached to their bodies with no necks, and with eyes like an alligator's, high up on their head. When they stand out of the water, they must lean forward a bit to see in front of themselves properly. In the water, the position of their eyes allows them to see in front as they swim and hunt. Their mouths are like beaks that lie close to their bodies, with jagged edges. This beak can pull apart any flesh. They have a skin covering over the beak, so that they have lips. When they draw back those lips to bite, the beak is exposed. The beak is a horror, orange, and jagged. When a victim is bit, it goes so deep into them and they bleed to death very quickly.

We need Snick in order to survive. She can make potions to help us, maybe one to put in the water to kill the Mer. Or perhaps a potion that we can use to make our skin like iron that cannot be bitten through. Without Snick, her kingdom, like her father, will be pulled under the water and eaten to nothing by the beaks of the Mer.

I've come here today after searching her out for many days. She left Flamingo years ago and we thought she was probably dead. Our only hope was that she hadn't been caught on the mainland and burned at the stake. If Snick chooses not to come with me, I cannot force her to come. I will not take her without her consent. I would prefer not to fight you, but if she is a slave to you and wishes to come with me, I will do everything I can to take her from you.

My greatest fear is that when I return, whether Snick is with me or not, there will be no one left alive. If that is so, I think it would be the best death for me to simply swim as far out into the deep water as I can and let them have me.

12

The small branch sticking out of Atticus's arm fell to the floor. The wound that Pepper created by jamming the branch into the man's flesh sealed itself up. Only a few drops of blood remained. Atticus looked from Joseph to Gurril to Pepper. Each one of them gave him sympathetic eyes, but Gurril also silently counted his concerns. If this man took Snick, would she be killed by the Mer? Or, would they get to Flamingo and find that everyone was dead, then go to work creating more of their race? Either way, he only saw a life ahead of him void of the woman he loved. Yet, he knew he could not stop her if she chose to go.

The cabinet near the sink creaked open, and Snick removed herself from the cramped space. She walked to the living area, and Atticus held back a gasp when he saw her.

He stood, bowed, and said, "My Queen. Did you hear my reasons for coming to you?"

She answered, "Yes. And I will return with you. Not because I feel any loyalty to the island kingdom that threatened me with a horrible death, but because I do not wish to see so many innocent lives lost to something as evil as the Mer. I have no more loyalty or obligation to that place, Atticus. Hearthstone and Gurril are my home, now. I've done what I can do to help this place with their problem.

"I can make a powder that will poison the Mer. We can put it into capsules that taste like fish. They have evolved far enough away from their human forms that they'll go for such bait." She turned to Gurril, and said, "My love. I promise you I will return, no matter what."

He rose from his chair, then held her in his arms.

They kissed briefly, and she said in a matter-of-fact tone, "I've got to get to work. I'll be in my apartment." She turned to face Atticus again. "We leave tonight. We can rent a coach and go directly to the coast. I've saved money the entire time I've been on the mainland and can surely afford the trip. I am going to mix up everything we need. You and I will put it into capsules on the ride to the coast."

Atticus stood, and asked, "What should I do while you're busy?"

"Find a coachman who will take us, and then get yourself something eat. We don't have time to waste, so you need to be ready when I return here."

"Yes, My Queen."

Behind Snick, Joseph smiled. The witch would be gone when he pulled his plan, and there would be one less dangerous person to fight. He had drooled at the thought of eating the woman's flesh, but the plan was the primary goal. He watched with glee as the rest of the night moved quickly. Gurril went to Snick's apartment to stay by her side for as long as he could. Joseph knew the young warrior had too great a sense of honor to try to talk the woman out of her plan. Instead, he would hold her hand, cry, and (if he got really lucky) make love to her one last time.

Pepper went to the kitchen and made a plate of the squirrel stew for Atticus. He put a whole loaf of bread to the side of it and poured the last of the wine for the man. Joseph sensed that Pepper disliked the man for taking Snick away, but also knew that the ferret, like Gurril, had too great a sense of honor to treat Atticus with contempt.

Honor! What a sham! The only honor that Joseph believed in was the honor of conquering an enemy. That enemy could be another rat, a human, or some ocean freak like this man from Flamingo. Any way you looked at it, the honor of telling the truth and standing for justice and peace was usually rewarded with tears.

By the time the moons were fully up, Atticus had sought out and found Blake. He hired the man's coach for the trip to the coast, and when Snick and Gurril arrived back at the warriors' cottage, the coach was outside waiting. Blake briefly introduced himself to Snick and accepted her fifteen gold pieces for the trip. Pepper, Gurril, and Joseph were lined up outside the cottage, helping her load three large boxes of mixed powder into the passenger compartment of the coach. Overhead, David the hawk circled through the moonlight, watching down over his mistress.

Snick stepped to Joseph and took his hand. "Don't worry, My Dear Friend. My gel will work for your cannon. Thank you for saving the place I love while I go to save one that doesn't deserve my love." She stepped to Pepper next, saying, "All the friendship in my heart belongs to you, Pepper." She whispered the vision that Coska had given her into Pepper's ear, then asked him quietly, "Should I tell Gurril?"

Pepper smiled at her sadly, then shook his head to say no. He leaned forward and whispered into her ear, "Maybe later."

A tear slipped from her eye as she held her body close to Gurril's. "My Love, My Love, My Endless Love," she cooed.

He held her close, squeezing her almost to the point of painfulness. Earlier in the evening, while she took a break from mixing her powder to poison the Mer, they had made love. Now she remembered how warm he had felt inside her body, and she relished it. They kissed, and pressed their faces together. Their tears mixed, and as the salty drops fell in the moonlight, they glinted like tiny diamonds. Atticus boarded the coach silently, nodding to Pepper and Gurril, knowing he was the cause of their heartbreaks this night. Snick boarded after him, and they were off.

13

Their first stop was to be the town of Belfenville. There, Blake would rest the horses and himself. They would push on after a minimal rest period, forcing the horses to run nearly eighteen hours a day. Blake was sure that at least one of the horses would die at this pace, but Snick assured him that she would replace any of the animals that dropped from exhaustion. She only briefly considered making a potion to allow them to run further, but decided to focus solely on the poison.

On the way, Snick changed from her dress to her old getup of swimming gear. She and Atticus filled up small cellulose capsules with the poison. The capsules were about the size of Snick's pinky, and the smell of the poison easily wafted out of them. They had filled up a few dozen pills using a small spoon and funnel, when the coach pulled to a stop in Belfenville. The sun had risen just a few minutes earlier, and Blake dismounted his driver's bench.

The man leaned into the open window of the coach. "I'll find a livery for the horses. We'll take eight hours here, then be on the road again. I'll be back soon. We can leave the coach here after the horses are in for the day. I think it's best to keep running them at night so they stay cool."

Snick nodded, and said, "I'll pay for the livery if you send a boy here to collect."

Blake nodded, then stepped away.

She turned to Atticus. "We should be there in three or four more days. We're doing well on the capsules."

Atticus rubbed his eyes, then his stomach. "Snick, I'm hungry. Do you think we could find some breakfast?"

She nodded, and opened the door of the coach. They stepped out, and Snick remembered that Belfenville had been the town where Joseph had been imprisoned in a tower. She scanned the small town, and saw a tower about thirty feet high. At the top, there were three small windows with the rising sun shining through. She decided that after a bit, she would visit the tower, to see what the old man had endured for so long.

The day came and went, and the eight hours were nearly through when Snick finally pulled herself away from the capsules to visit the tower. This was supposed to be a break period, and she decided that she needed to just walk away from the poison for a bit. Relaxing for a few minutes would allow her to focus more keenly on the task of filling capsules when they got on the road again. At first Atticus began to follow her, but she turned and shook a finger at the man.

"Keep on with the capsules. We've only got a few dozen, and we'll need hundreds. I've got an errand to run. You already had your break with that big breakfast."

There was a guard at the base of the tower. He was armed with a spear, and said, "Halt, madam," as she approached.

"Good Sir," she began, "I know a man who was imprisoned in this tower for many years. I was wondering if I could see the cell he was in."

"No tours, madam. Sorry." The guard had a look on his face that told Snick that there was no questioning this order. No tours. She frowned.

"Maybe you could tell me a bit about him," she said. "Surely he was here when you were."

The guard looked confused. "Only one man in the tower at a time, Madam. This one's been here since before I was born."

"Is there another tower in the town? Or another prison, perhaps?"

The guard shook his head. "No, Madam. Maybe you have the wrong town."

"I could have sworn he said Belfenville. His name is Joseph. He's a very old man."

Now the guard looked even more confused. "Madam, did you say Joseph?"

"Yes."

The guard motioned over his shoulder with his chin. "That's the name of the old man in the tower right now. He killed his wife years ago, for whoring with half the men in town. He's there for life."

Snick stepped back in fear, confusion, and anger. She had been lied to. Gurril and Pepper could be in danger. "Sir, I am the queen of Flamingo. I need to see the man in this tower. There is another man, in Hearthstone, who claims to be this very prisoner!"

"I'll need to get a town elder, Madam." The guard could see that the woman before him was telling the truth. He turned and rang a bell, worried that somehow the man in the tower was a doppelganger, and the real Joseph had escaped. Within seconds, two town elders appeared, along with the town warrior for Belfenville, a thin, tall man named Henry.

Snick explained her story to them as Atticus and Blake approached from behind her.

"Snick," Atticus said, "We have to keep going."

She turned to him. "Give me half an hour. This is important." She turned back to the group that had gathered, and shared Joseph's story with them. They agreed that there was a sham somewhere, that they needed to find out if they had the right prisoner, and if so, why someone would want to impersonate him. They entered and climbed the tower. As she walked the steps, Snick noticed that the dank and dirty prison smelled of human waste. She turned to Henry and asked, "Why does this place smell like a sewer?"

"It leads to our sewer. The waste is taken from the town to a swamp a few miles away. We left it open here as a punishment to the prisoner at the top to remind him that he's also human waste."

The group came to the top of the tower, and the guard slid open a small door at eye level on the main door. It had a few bars in it, and allowed a visitor to view the prisoner inside. Snick peered in to see a frail old man, rocking himself back and forth. He looked nothing like the old man named Joseph she knew.

"Old man, Joseph!" she demanded.

The man opened his eyes and looked at her. He smiled a toothless grin.

Through his gums, he said to her, "Another friend? Are you another friend? I miss Billy."

"Who is Billy?" she asked.

The old man smiled again. "I told Billy all about my life. About my ideas. I miss Billy. He's a good rat. Are you another friend?"

Henry ordered the guard to slide the viewing door shut. He turned to Snick. "That's our old man, for sure."

"Who's Billy?"

"I don't know."

"Why would he say that Billy was a rat?"

"I don't know. I only know that we've never had a rat in this town. *Ever*. The old man is clearly delusional."

"Why would an old man come to Hearthstone and claim to be this one?"

"What has he done in Hearthstone?"

"He's an advisor to the elders there."

Henry smiled at this and patted Snick on the back the way he would have patted a small child on the head, and said to her, "The town is getting a bit of a con, I think. It's a good life to be an advisor to town elders. If the old man isn't hurting anything, then there's no harm."

At this point, none of the elders or Henry would listen to Snick's complaints as they shooed her away. She was torn, and told Atticus that she was having second thoughts. He furled his brow at her.

"You are coming with me, Snick. There is no time to turn this carriage around, and I need your help with these capsules. We're going to Flamingo. Both of us. When the battle is done there, I'll come back with you and help with your fight in Hearthstone." Then, yelling so the driver would hear him, he said "Blake! Get us moving!"

With that, Blake started the horses on their way, and Snick and Atticus were rolling again toward the coast.

14

They worked, it seemed, for hours and then days without stopping, although Snick knew that they had stopped to rest, to eat, to walk, and to breathe. By now, the sun had set and risen three times, and they had camped on a roadside or slept in an inn each morning, travelling mostly at night. One horse had dropped dead of exhaustion, and it was replaced as they passed the last village before the coast. Snick played the scene in Belfenville over and over in her head, wondering why an old man would impersonate Joseph. The most plausible idea was the suggestion that he was now able to reap the rewards of being an important person to the town elders. Perhaps this was the type of con that an old raider would enjoy during retirement. Somehow, she doubted it.

Snick and Atticus sat side by side on one bench of the coach, filling capsules with the poison she had mixed. On the other bench was a large wooden crate, bought prior to leaving Hearthstone. It was stocked almost to the top with filled capsules. Snick guessed that there must be thousands of them in the crate. She took a break to stretch her fingers, and the knuckles on each one cracked loudly as she flexed them and then bent them straight again.

Atticus sighed heavily. "Queen Snick," he began, "At the coast, I think it best if we find the boat I left and take it toward Flamingo. I don't know what to do to get through the Mer lines, however."

She thought for a few seconds. "They have the island ringed, and are staging intermittent attacks, mostly during the day, correct?"

"Yes."

Snick closed her eyes and rested her forehead on her palms, trying to devise a plan. She wished that she had Gurril with her. He had a mind for battle and would have come up with some way to either get through the line or... Snick's eyes widened, and she began speaking out a plan to Atticus. Together, they refined the plan. By the time they reached the coast, it was finalized.

Blake stopped the coach near the docks, and the wheels had barely stopped rolling when Atticus jumped out, the crate of capsules in his hands. Snick followed, handing a satchel of coins up to Blake. She smiled at the man.

"There is enough to cover all of your expenses back to Hearthstone. I've given you a bonus to pay for any more horses you lose in the next few days. Take a rest for them, and for yourself. Between what I've given you here, and the fares of passengers you take back with you, you've made more than I guess you normally would in an entire year."

Blake smiled back at the lady, sneaking a long look from her legs all the way up to her wonderfully light eyes. "Aye. I hope to see you again, Queen Snick."

She smiled and nodded, then turned and walked to the boat where Atticus was loading the crate. Blake watched her walk the whole way to the boat, thinking that her body was the most incredible thing he'd ever seen. The coachman wondered how it was that such a lady could walk outside of a dream, and thought it no surprise that men in every town they passed had gawked at the brown skinned woman with the long white hair and brilliant green eyes.

By sunset, the boat lay low in the water, filled not just with the crate of poison capsules, but with as many provisions as could be loaded into it. Snick had bought food and medicine for the Flamingoans. Atticus had bought a long spear. He thought it might be handy to have a longer weapon to try to spike the Mer if they got too close to the boat. The horizon was orange and pink as they pushed the twelve-foot-long wooden craft from the dock. Atticus began rowing out as Snick raised the stubby sail of the boat to try to catch the wind.

The moons above were both at a quarter of their full selves, providing only slivers of weak light onto the water. It was a dark night with few stars, and in the first hours of their voyage to Flamingo, Snick thought of her father. She had asked no details of his death, and did not want them. Death by an attack of Mer was a terrible way to go. Their hard, sharp beaks tore off flesh in bloody, quivering hunks. Often, the victim bled to death as they drowned, screaming for mercy. By the time the Mer were finished feeding, there was little left of the body but a few scraps. The bloody scraps never attracted sharks; the beasts could detect the mixed smell of Mer with the chum and would stay out of the area.

The swell in the open sea was low, and the few stars that shone this time of year in this latitude offered no comfort. Snick listened to the sound of Atticus's regular breathing and the push of water as he rowed. The light breeze gave them only a hint of a push, and Atticus began slowing his rhythm, wanting to save his energy for any Mer they might encounter.

"My father…" Snick said, "Was he able to do anything to help the island before his death?"

Atticus smiled. "Your father was a great king. I guarded him for forty years."

"Really? That had to be most of his reign."

Atticus nodded. His speech came in cadence with his rowing. "I was twenty-two. Just a little boy. Your grandfather was eaten by a shark while out trying to rescue some fishermen who had a damaged boat. Everyone on the island thought it foolish that a king would do such a thing."

Snick smiled. "I don't hear many stories about him—my grandfather, I mean."

"A good king. When he died, his protectors decided to retire. I began training at twenty, so I was ready for my job when your father took his place as king. Did you know I was there when your parents met?"

Snick gasped and sat upright. "Mother! Is she—"

"She's fine, Snick. She's lonely, and the new king, your brother..." Atticus trailed off, sighing.

"What, what about him? I've never met him and don't know who he is, so nothing you tell me can offend."

"He's fifteen. A baby. But a tyrant." Atticus shook his head and looked to the horizon. "I only hope he can learn to be more like your father and grandfather. He keeps your mother sequestered, and will go to her for advice now and again, but she sits alone in a hut, locked away like a prisoner."

"Does she miss me, do you think."

Atticus stopped rowing and trailed his hands in the water, then blew on them a bit. "Those oars, they really make the hands sore."

"Does she miss me, Atticus? Just tell me."

He swallowed hard and looked away from her face. "She denies that you are her daughter. She says that there must have been an evil wizard who stole her real daughter as a baby and replaced her with you."

Snick felt like crying. Her own mother! She began to regret deeply coming on this voyage. Damn the island! Damn every one of them! The only one worth saving was the man in the boat with her. He had never judged her, had never denied her right to exist.

"Atticus, when we are finished on the island, I want you to come back to Hearthstone with me for good, not just for the battle against the rats."

He shook his head. "I can't do that, Snick. I've made a commitment to spend my life protecting the royal family."

"And how many times now have you called me 'Queen Snick,' Atticus? I am the royal family member who is rightfully the heir to the throne."

"That is what I believe, too."

"So stay in Hearthstone. It's a good place. You can find friends there and good work. They'd give almost anything for a fisher as good as you, I bet."

He smiled at her, picked up the oars, and began rowing. "I'll consider it."

Snick smelled the salt in the air, and looked out at the horizon. In the water, a few reflections of stars shone, and as they moved through the sea, Snick instinctively knew they were drawing close to Flamingo. The swells made the boat lightly rise and fall, and Snick stared at the reflected stars in the water, wondering if those stars had orbiting worlds of their own, as the one she lived near did.

As she watched, she suddenly came to a horrible realization that made her come close to losing control over her body's waste functions. The lights in the water were moving slowly toward them. They were never reflections of the stars above, but the eyes of a group of Mer, following them now for at least the last half hour!

15

As hawks go, David was among the smartest. He had known this, even though his interactions with other hawks had been limited to those he randomly came across while hunting and to the few hawks he had been trained with. There had been three of them, all learning to hunt together. That was back when Sheila had been his master. Sheila, with the blond hair and strong muscles. Landing on her arm was like landing on a thick branch. He remembered her dying, replaying the images over and over in his head. He felt that he could have protected her if he hadn't been so focused on the damned stag he was tracking.

Not long after, he had acquired a new master for himself. She wasn't as strong as Sheila had been, and sometimes her arm would waver at his weight when he landed on it, but she took very good care of him. He protected her against a man who had meant to hurt her deeply; had intuitively known that the man would die after the attack. David felt joy in this. To him, it was noble to kill those who meant to harm one's master.

So it was with deep regret that he stayed behind in Belfenville. When his new master, Snick, had left for a battle David followed high above. He had watched the events in Belfenville, and had thought them quite odd. He survived mostly by his intuition, so when it told him to stay and investigate the old man in the tower, he knew it was what he must do for the good of Snick.

Now he stood in the window of the old man's cell, watching him sleep. The two thin moon slivers behind him reflected just enough light into the cell to allow David to see the space clearly. The hawk's intuition told him that Snick was far more able to care for herself than she knew and that there was danger in David's home that the hawk needed to attend to.

He stared down at the old man, then scratched at the stone frame of the window with a talon. The light scraping noise made the old man stir a bit, and David scratched again. He had a hunter's patience, and wanted to wake the man quietly, so the guard below would not know that a visitor had arrived. Scratch, scratch, scratch. Shift and snore. This went on for a bit of time, until the man finally fluttered his eyes open. He looked to the window, and his eyes widened as he saw the hawk there. The man smiled, showing a mouth full of gums.

"You... you... a friend?"

David faced the man, staring at him.

"A friend, like Billy?"

David scratched the stone wall again. The man chuckled to himself. "Well, Bird. You may be a lot smaller and less talkative than Billy, but I think you'll make a good friend. Sit, while I tell you my lot."

16

"Psst! Atticus!" Just over a whisper.

Atticus looked up from his rowing, letting the oars stop their work. Snick pointed to the eyes in the water. Three sets.

Atticus nodded, and said quietly to her, "We're very close to where the Mer have set their siege line. These must be guards of the outer ring."

Snick nodded back, and grabbed three capsules from the crate. She threw them one by one, so they landed a few feet in front of each set of eyes.

Mer ancestry had been human once, long, long ago. They evolved for their ocean life, and as their bodies became less human, so did their minds. The saltwater variety of Mer are extremely talented at swimming, hunting, and laying siege to both flotillas of boats and small islands, but in the end, like most other sea life, their stomachs were typically the organ that guided their lives. The sieges they laid against boats and islands were mostly a tactic to eat, once a tribe had cleared out all of a fertile fishing ground. So it was with these Mer— the three that Snick had seen, and the fourth under the boat. The fishy-smelling capsules had been irresistible, and one by one, each of the three capsules was snapped up by the deadly, horrible beak of a Mer.

The first Mer to eat a capsule was a female. She still had large, bulbous breasts from her last clutch, and they bounced in the water as she broke the surface briefly to snap up the capsule. Her thought was that a fishing vessel had wandered off course, and that they had thrown out some chum in hopes of attracting larger game fish. She was just finishing this thought when the poison took effect, causing her stomach to burst, and the blood inside her body to turn into a thick goo that could not pump through her heart and veins. It took her three seconds to die after chomping down the capsule. The second and third Mer had almost the same thoughts as the first, only they decided that they would immediately attack the boat after their snack. They took one swimming stroke toward the boat, then died side by side.

The fourth Mer looked up from the water at the boat above him. Snick and Atticus were unaware of the fourth Mer, and the fourth Mer was unaware that his companions had just gone belly-up around him. He could hear the people in the boat shuffling around, could hear their voices, muffled in the water. The fact that the other Mer had not attacked the boat made this one cautious.

Atticus watched as the Mer around them bobbed in the swell, their eyes now dark instead of glowing an eerie greenish-yellow color.

He turned to Snick. "Will they bleed?"

She shook her head. "I made it so that they won't bleed, only die. Mer will cannibalize their dead. It should also kill those who stumble across these and eat them."

"What if a shark or other animal eats the corpse?"

Snick looked to Atticus and shrugged in response, as if to say if there was collateral damage that was just too bad. Atticus nodded gravely, and began rowing again. He had only made a few strokes, when the male Mer who had been beneath the boat suddenly thrust up from the water with a loud splash and scrambled into the boat, snapping his beak and grunting.

Snick screamed and rolled off her bench seat to the back section of the boat, while Atticus instinctively grabbed for his knife. The Mer flurried about, scratching the boat and reaching out for Atticus with one clawed hand. Atticus held out the knife before him, hoping to either strike the Mer when it got close enough, or to cause the Mer to hesitate long enough for Atticus to grab hold of his spear. As it was, the Mer didn't allow for either of these things, staying out of knife range, but close enough to prevent Atticus from grabbing the spear.

Snick watched as the Mer rose to his hind legs and stood wobbly in the center of the boat. She thought about simply rocking the boat back and forth to make the beast fall into the water, but was afraid that the Mer's fall might capsize the boat, and they would lose all their capsules. It was an impossible standoff, with Atticus holding the Mer at bay, and the Mer unable to move forward against Atticus.

17

David had heard enough of the man's story to know that it matched what the imposter in Hearthstone had told them. As he beat his wings toward his master, he clutched a message in his talons that he hoped she would understand.

The tiny slits of reflected moon rippled gently on the swell below, and the hawk gulped down his fear. He had never been out of sight of land before, and was flying on bare instinct. He had understood enough of Snick's plight to know that she was heading first for the coast, then straight west to Flamingo.

David scanned over the open water, watching a small flock of flamingoes swoop beneath him, wondering how the large pink birds must taste. He decided that if he had the chance to try to attack and eat one when he was hungry later, he'd do so. It would be a challenge to take such a large bird, but the thought of a new and possibly delicious food was interesting to the hawk. He watched a school of bait fish and wondered about their taste, as well. Right now, all he craved was a squirrel. They were a favorite treat that he liked to sneak while hunting, and he imagined a nice, fat black squirrel in his talons instead of the stinking cargo he carried now.

David could see a small boat ahead, and he began to smell the odor of slimy fish. The hawk swooped close for a look, clutching his message for Snick tightly as he flew.

18

The standoff had to come to a resolution soon. Atticus knew it, Snick knew it, and the Mer knew it. None of them could move. Snick thought about offering the Mer a capsule, telling him it was fish, and hoping he'd go for it. She somehow thought this wouldn't work, and so stayed cowering near the crates of poison, food, and medicine.

The Mer grunted a few times, and snapped his beak threateningly toward Atticus. Atticus shook his head, staring into the glowing eyes of the beast.

"No, My Friend. I snap my beak at you!"

Atticus twisted the knife in the air at the Mer. What happened next seemed to Snick like recalling a dream that had been forgotten but never far from memory.

Through one sliver of moonlight, the shape of wings silently and with incredible speed shot out of the almost starless night. There was a *thump* as the shape struck the Mer in the side of the head, knocking it just a bit off balance. The Mer didn't fall, but did turn his head to see what had hit him. As he turned to look, Atticus kicked up the head of the spear and grabbed it. The Mer turned again to face him, and the warrior, holding the sharp end of the weapon, jabbed the blunt end into the Mer's chest.

The Mer stumbled back just a bit, and Snick kicked as hard as she could at his back, right beside his spiny dorsal fin. The Mer now careened forward again, and Atticus swung the

225

spear's blunt end in a high arc at the top of the Mer's head. The blow brought the wretched beast to its knees, and Atticus now delivered a second wide, arcing blow to the side of the thing's head. The Mer rolled out of the boat, and the small craft tipped precariously close to turning over. Snick dove for the opposite side, grabbing the crate of capsules with her free hand as she clung to the high side of the boat and hoped that it would not capsize. She looked over and saw that Atticus, too, was putting all his weight toward the high side of the boat. It teetered there for what seemed like an eternity; then, just as quickly as it had tipped up, the boat dropped bottom side down safely into the water.

The first thing Atticus saw as the high side of the vessel splashed back down was a glowing set of eyes in the water just in front of his. There was a loud splash, and Atticus had just enough time to register that a claw was coming at him. He tried to back away but was too late. Snick watched as the Mer's claws caught each side of Atticus's face, near his ear, and tore wide paths of destruction across the man's skin. Atticus threw himself back away from the claws, howling in pain, and holding his hands up to his face as it sprayed blood into the water.

Snick grabbed a capsule and threw it into the water near the Mer, who was now trying again to enter the boat. She grabbed the spear that Atticus had dropped, and shoved it into the eye of the Mer, who croaked a painful sound and splashed back into the water. Snick watched as the one remaining eye of the Mer circled the boat. She saw that above, the thing that had thumped the Mer's head circled directly above the sea beast.

The eye completed three full circles of the boat as Snick watched and Atticus bled, screaming in pain. On the final circle, it stopped just below where the capsule floated in the water. Snick watched as the eye came to the surface, and saw the Mer's beak snatch up the capsule. A few seconds later, the monster's body floated silently to the surface.

There was another sound of claws on the wood of the vessel behind Snick and she turned, frightened. There behind her sat David the hawk, looking up at her in a loving way (to those who know birds, at least).

Snick knelt down near Atticus, and tried to shush the howling man.

"Atticus, Atticus, it can't be that bad. You got away quickly."

The warrior's only reply through hands that covered his face was a kind of raw "Gaa" sound.

Snick pulled the box of medical supplies she had bought close to her, and gently pulled at Atticus's hands. In the dim moon- and star light, Snick saw the remains of Atticus's face, and vomited into the water as blood sprayed from the man's wounds.

His nose was completely gone, leaving a hollow black hole that sprayed blood. Flamingoans have a small artery that runs through the base of their nose to feed muscles inside the nose, allowing them to seal their nasal passages shut on deep dives. Snick knew that the Mer had torn the artery behind Atticus's nose. The man's cheeks had been torn wide open, so that his teeth showed all the way back to the hinge of his jaw, and his tongue had been cut off near its base. Snick could see the man's cheek bone through a deep cut on the left side of his face. The worst wound of all, she knew, was the most horrible to look at. Both of Atticus's eyes had been sliced open and ran down his shredded face in oozing trails of clear jelly.

She gave him a pain-killing medicine and pressed a towel to the artery behind the space where his nose had been. He lay back and shook in pain and fear, until shock overcame him, and then passed out into a deep sleep.

19

Snick opened her packets of ingredients she had brought for making potions, and found nothing that would save the warrior. Blood had soaked through the towel, and his normally brown skin began to take on a more grayish color as he drained of blood. Snick tried to hold back the tears that rolled from her eyes and thought to herself that if only she had thrown out a few extra capsules of poison, the Mer that had done this would have been dead with an exploded stomach and thick jelly for—

Thick jelly for blood! Too thick to pump through the vessels! Too thick to bleed! Snick turned, and grabbed a capsule. Carefully, she opened it, and held it so the powder would not fall from it. Then, she removed the towel over Atticus's face, and blood began to spurt out again. She turned the capsule and sprinkled the powder onto the wound; quickly and with the greatest of care she worked, and as she sprinkled the poison onto Atticus, the blood quickly congealed and clotted. Before five minutes were through, she had sealed the artery, and Atticus lay unconscious at her feet, no longer bleeding. Snick looked up to the night, noticing that now there was a shimmer of orange on the far horizon. Soon, the sun would rise. She turned to David, her ever-faithful hawk, and clucked her tongue at him to come to her.

David hopped over to his master, dropping his message for her at her feet. She pet the hawk's head with her fingertips, taking his message for a lunch that he had caught for himself. This irritated the hawk, and he nipped at her fingers, then hopped down to the pile of fur below. He pecked at it, then looked up at her.

"David, what are you…" Snick trailed off as she looked down and saw the oddest thing: There was a rat, but much smaller than any normal rat she had ever seen. The beast was no more than a foot long.

The sun rose over Snick as she drifted, wondering what to do. Her plan with Atticus had been to circle the outermost ring of Mer, dropping capsules in the water to slowly thin their ranks from the outside in. Atticus and Snick both knew that the Mer used the outer ring of a siege as a resting point, so the beasts there should have been easier to battle had they attacked the boat. Now, with Atticus so gravely injured, she wondered what to do. Snick turned to the hawk standing on the bench seat beside her.

"David, you've been so loyal to me. I know that you are trying to tell me something with that tiny rat, but I don't know what. And I don't know how to attack the Mer. I'm just one person, alone in a boat." Snick lay back and looked up at the sky, letting tears pool in her eyes and flow down her cheeks in tiny, salty rivers.

She heard David rustling about, then heard the whooshing sound of his wings pushing him into the air. She watched as the bird took off, ascending through her vision. Snick noticed that his talons seemed to be gripping something, and she wondered what it could be that the hawk had taken with him this time. Sitting up, she watched as the hawk flew high into the air, arcing around the boat in the direction of Flamingo. Snick determined by the position of the moons shortly before dawn that Flamingo was just out of her sight. She thought that the hawk must surely be able to see it from his position in the sky. David flew far enough away that Snick could barely see him, and she watched as he seemed to dive toward the water, breaking off his dive about thirty feet above the surface. Then, he pumped his wings hard and returned to the boat. He chirped at her briefly as he approached the boat, using his fully stretched wings as an air brake to descend straight down toward her. David peered down and landed—just for a second— in the crate of poison capsules. He filled both talons full of the poison capsules, and beat his wings again, pulling himself high above Snick.

He repeated his arc once more, and returned to the boat again. When he landed this time, he set down on the bench seat where Snick had sat, watching him. She could see before he landed that his talons were empty again, and she realized what the bird was doing: he was making bombing runs, dropping the capsules into the heart of the Mer lines.

David was hungry. It had been a long flight, and his bombing runs had fatigued him more easily than he would have liked. He rubbed the top of his head on Snick's leg, and flew off in the opposite direction of where he had been dropping capsules to the Mer. He flew until he found a small school of bait fish, and dove into them the way he would have dove into the river for a pike. Before long, he was back to the boat, enjoying his meal. This new fish tasted a bit different from his usual freshwater fare back home, but he enjoyed the experience, promising himself to try to find a different type of fish each time he took a break to eat.

The sun seemed hotter to David than it had on land, and the salt in the air bothered his nostrils a bit. He was happy that he wasn't a sea bird and watched curiously as another flock of flamingoes passed over the boat. After his meal was finished, he hopped into the crate of poison and took off for another bombing run. He flew high into the sky and took stock of the positions of the Mer. He had watched very carefully as the Mer swam around the boat the previous night, and could easily spot them from the air. They had three main siege lines surrounding the island of Flamingo. Every now and again, one line would send a group of charging raiders in close to the island to try to pick off a Flamingoan. The tide was rising, and David knew that the attacks would increase in frequency as the water covered the island, and the people living there took shelter in their raised huts.

The hawk flew to a point where a group of Mer congregated, and he swooped in low to drop the capsules into their midst. He thought it odd that these things had evolved from humans and that, as their bodies became more and more adept for the sea, their minds became more and more stupid. He watched as the capsules splashed down, and the Mer closed in on them quickly. The beasts would make a ruckus in the water as they snapped up the capsules; then a few seconds later, the lot of them would turn belly up.

David the hawk repeated this process until nightfall, then found more bait fish to eat. When the sun was set and he was full, he nested himself into the bow of the boat, near Atticus's head, and fell soundly asleep.

It was dark. Pitch dark. Snick knew this was the last night with such little starlight, and that tomorrow would be the new sky phase. The black blanket that covered her this night would be replaced with so many dazzling lights that the reflection off the water would make the night almost as bright as an overcast day. She waited, thankful for every minute she looked over the edge of the boat and didn't see any sets of glowing eyes coming toward her. She stayed awake for the entire night, knowing that Mer were far more likely to attack during the day, but still afraid after what she had gone through with Atticus.

In the morning, David began his bombing runs again. Snick woke Atticus in the early morning, worried that he had spent too much time asleep. She gently gripped and shook his shoulders, and he woke with a moan.

"Atticus, it's me, Snick. You need to drink water and eat, Atticus."

The man, who had once been so strong and mighty, now lay helpless, unable to see or speak, and barely alive. He moaned at her a bit louder when she mentioned water and food. Snick took this to mean that he was hungry and thirsty, so she gently poured water from a canteen into his massively wounded mouth.

It hurt to drink. It hurt to breath. It hurt to moan. It hurt to not be dead. But the water was soothing when it got to his stomach, and Atticus drank. Snick cut food into tiny bits, and while Atticus listened to Snick telling him about David's bombing runs, she dropped the tiny bits of food into his mouth so he could swallow them. He would reflexively try to chew now and then, but the action hurt the stump of his tongue too much, and food fell out of his torn open cheeks. Every beat of his heart brought on a pounding pain throughout the whole (or now would it be best to say "the hole"?) of his face.

Three days went on like this. Snick prayed for life. Atticus prayed for death. David prayed for another one of those small yellow fish that tasted to him a bit like a bluegill.

20

Gregor, the new king, sat alone in his hut, watching the ocean before him. Since the old king had died, taken by the Mer, torn to shreds by their beaks and eaten, the Flamingoans were down from a population of about six thousand to only a few hundred. Times were bad.

Atticus, the primary bodyguard of the king, had left on some cockamamie scheme to go retrieve Snick (not just competition for the crown, but a witch, no less!) from the mainland. The islanders were outnumbered, and some of the warriors in the group had begun to talk about burning the island, trying to use fire as a diversion so they could escape. Gregor sighed, and thought to himself for the fifteenth time that day, that times were bad.

It had taken a little girl to see the island's savior. A little girl who looked to the horizon one morning, pointed to what looked like some sort of crazy, dive-bombing sea gull, and said, "He's pooping on the bad guys!"

The island's one and only telescope had revealed the true story. The bird, some sort of predatory beast with eyes like fire and talons that were more fierce-looking than the claws of a Mer, kept swooping down and dropping things into the water. The telescope further confirmed that the Mer would attack these things, then turn up dead. Times were getting better.

By the end of three days, the Mer numbers had thinned to the point where the warriors were now making attack runs with some of the more stable boats. It was on one of these runs that Snick and Atticus were found.

21

Night time. Four days at sea. Not much food left. Snick hadn't seen any Mer since she and Atticus had been attacked, and David's bombing runs were taking him further and further away. She could only take this to mean that the Mer were being wiped out. Good thing, too. Around sunset, David had taken off with the last of the capsules. Snick hadn't slept in days and days and hour and hours. She was almost as delirious as Atticus was. The thing that kept her going was her will to stay alive and go home to Gurril and Pepper. She fell asleep just an hour before a boat full of Flamingo warriors came upon them.

Snick awoke to the sensation of her vessel being pulled through the water. She sat up and screamed, thinking that the Mer were taking her away for a snack. She looked around the boat wildly, and saw a warrior she recognized sitting on the bench in front of her. Atticus was gone. She looked around frantically once more.

The warrior placed his palms on her shoulders, and said "He's on the other boat. Looks like you saved him after a big fight, no?"

She nodded. The warrior smiled at her, and petted the bird with his fingertips.

"This one," he said, pointing at David, "is our savior. King Gregor has been calling him the bird-god!" The young man laughed, and Snick knew that her battle against the Mer was over.

22

Her homecoming was not glorious. She was shunned immediately, and heard whispers as people blamed her for Atticus's injuries. She was only home a few hours when Gregor approached her.

"Please," he said to her, "Come with me to the leadership hut."

She quietly obeyed, taking one last look at Atticus as he lay injured in the hospital hut, three nurses attending to his grotesquely injured face.

Gregor sat on the floor of the hut and looked up to Snick. "Sit, Snick. Please." She complied. "Our father—"

"I know. Atticus told me. So am I to be shunned rather than take the throne as queen? Or am I to be burned?"

Gregor shook his head. "No, you will not be burned at the stake. You saved Atticus, that is clear to me. You saved us from the Mer with your magic. And you brought us the bird-god. But you will always be an outcast. You may stay here and rest for two more days. You can visit Mother if you like, but I doubt if she wants to see you.

"Our few remaining artisans are completing a statue of the bird-god, and most of the island wants to keep him here. But I can see that you belong to him, and he will not let you go anywhere without him."

"You're letting him come with me? I'm surprised. All I've gotten from you people is hate and denial about who and what I am. I came back here to save lives but not because I care about any one of you. I want you to know that and to know that even though I care nothing for any individual here, it was a care for life itself that brought me back."

"It isn't kindness that keeps you together with the bird. I'm afraid that if I don't send the bird with you, he'll become angry. I saw what he did to the Mer. You and he have powerful magic together. He loves you as only a master can love his pet."

"So when the statue is done…"

"You must leave here and never return."

"I want to take Atticus with me."

Gregor's reaction to this was swift and angry. "Never! Try to take him and you will be killed. He is a Flamingo warrior, and we will not let him go into the clutches of a witch. It's better he die here with his people than be turned into a toad or his organs used as ingredients for some magic potion. Be happy we're letting you leave here with the bird and your life."

Snick reached into the small bag she carried with her to hold her dearest items. Inside was the copper coin she had flipped to decide whether to stay in Hearthstone or not. She knew she would never have to flip it again. Flamingo was no longer her home, and the decision about whether or not to tell Gurril about the vision that Coska had shared with her was made.

Chapter 7: Attack of the Rats

1

Between the walls, eyes glowed; under the floorboards, eyes glowed; creeping sly through the gutters in the night, eyes glowed. They snuck into granaries and stole bits of food. They padded lightly over sleeping humans. Sharp teeth glistened, and claws were sharpened on wood. The rats were small now, small ever since Billy had cursed them. They were small now, yes, but there were a thousand of them, and they were ready to feast on the flesh of men.

Pepper, in his large form and filling up the bed he lay in, awoke to the scratching sound in the walls. It nearly drove him mad sometimes. He listened to the scratching for a few seconds, then left his bed, stretching with a yawn. He walked by Gurril's room lightly, not wanting to wake the warrior who was still trying to get used to sleeping alone again.

Coska's courtyard lay free to the morning sun, and Pepper entered it with a smile, relieved to be away from the infernal scratching that had kept him up all night. His hearing was much better than human hearing, and he seemed to notice the noise more than Gurril. Joseph, it seemed, could barely hear the scratching at all. Pepper took this to mean that the old man was close to deaf. In reality, Joseph had stolen Pepper's trust just like he had stolen the trust of so many others. A dangerous sort of traitor, he had come to them out of the blue and promised hope in the face of danger. Forgotten to people was the fact that the danger had never existed before Joseph arrived.

Pepper sat down in front of Coska and took a deep breath. He closed his eyes and meditated. The Coska tree stood squat in the courtyard, his thin bark a color somewhere between brown and green. His trunk was very large, but he reached only just past the roof of the house with his branches. His leaves were broad, thick, and waxy. To Pepper, they tasted bitter but not unpleasant. Birds would land in the Coska tree from time to time, but they never nested. Pepper thought this was probably because Gurril's two cats had taken up residence in the tree's branches. They lay in the tree this morning, purring, basking, and lazing in the bright, fresh sunlight.

235

Pepper meditated, and communicated with Coska telepathically. Pepper would thank Coska for the gifts he had given him, and thoughts, visions, or ideas would spring into Pepper's head. This morning, the first and only thought that came to him was this: Your vision of challenge and possible death will come true soon. Pepper's heart jumped in his chest, and his eyes sprung open. He looked to Coska, afraid of the vision. It would be painful. It would be frightening. Pepper wasn't like Gurril, who would walk up to a fight and growl. Pepper didn't want to get hurt; he didn't want to fight.

He was thankful to Coska for giving him the gifts of magic, intelligence, and friendship, but was also sorrowful, because he was damned in certain ways. Pepper would never find a love. He was no longer an animal, but he wasn't human, either. When he had first met Snick, he had wanted her the same way Gurril had, but he knew he couldn't pursue her. He still dreamed of what it must be like to touch her long, slender legs with anxious fingertips. He still thought of her at night while he gave himself sweet physical release from the loneliness he felt.

Pepper could also never blend in and be just another member of the forest. He had tried once or twice while alone on patrol to spend a bit of time with wild animals again, but they all could smell him and knew that he was different. Not only that, but he could no longer understand the way they communicated. He didn't even remember how he had said his name as a ferret. The twitches of whiskers, the blinks, the wags of tails and other body language of the animals were lost to him. He didn't even know how it was that his mother had named him. The change that had occurred wasn't just to his body and mind. His soul itself had changed into something that would never be human and never be an animal. His feeling of living with a torn soul, out of place in every world he'd known, made him wish at times that he had never existed in any form.

Pepper wanted to grow small again for a while, and Coska gave him the thought that if he chewed on a small branch rather than a leaf, that he would shrink to his smaller size. Pepper noted this and relaxed a bit. He wanted to get inside the walls and find out what that scratching was. There were a few other things he'd like to take a look at as well. Being able to

236

become small was going to have certain advantages, he reckoned.

Pepper stood from his meditation and left the house for a jog, deciding that he would become small after the run. Gurril would want to know that Pepper had decided to shrink to a smaller size. Pepper wished he could run away, but knew that his fate lay in Hearthstone. His only friends belonged in Hearthstone, and his life would either end there soon or go on there for as long as destiny would allow. He jogged, breathing the morning air deeply and hoping that he at least wouldn't outlive Gurril. To lose the warrior was his greatest fear.

Gurril woke a few minutes later. The warrior walked to the kitchen and found a note from Pepper that said he had talked to Coska and was now out for a jog. Gurril growled. Ever since Snick had left, he hadn't slept well. Not getting the sleep he needed made him grumpy, and now something deep inside him had just broken loose. Gurril slammed the note down and marched over to Coska's courtyard.

He stared up at the tree. "So," he barked, frightening his cats, who climbed to higher branches in a scramble, "You talked with Pepper. How nice. You talk with Pepper a lot. You talk with Snick a lot. You talk to anybody who comes by, but *you never talk to me*!" Gurril punched the trunk of the tree, making his knuckles bloody. He looked down at his now damaged hand, and then at the undamaged bark. "Oh, so you're tougher than me now, too? Great. Always smarter, now bigger and tougher, and you won't say a word to me." Gurril paced back and forth before the tree, steaming. He turned back to the Coska tree. "Why can't you just be here for me? I mean here as a friend?" He shook his head, mumbling to himself, "Stupid tree." Gurril turned and walked back into the villa.

There was nothing the Coska tree could do. He looked down at Gurril and wept inside. Gurril had been and always would be his closest friend. Coska knew that he had to let Gurril live a life in which Coska was more of an idea than a being. He would let his friend vent when he needed to, but Coska hoped that soon Snick would return and that Gurril would see that she and Pepper were the friends he had to turn to when he was in pain, not the tree.

Snick stood over the bed where Atticus lay. The now faceless warrior was on his back, with a towel rolled up and snugged into the cavity that had been created when the Mer tore his face off. Two reeds that led to the man's air passage poked out of the central area of the towel. Snick wept lightly, knowing only by his rising and falling chest that the sole Flamingoan who had treated her as a proper human being lived. Snick brushed his thick white hair from his forehead, knowing she would never again see his brilliant green eyes.

Snick bent forward, and whispered into the open hole that had been Atticus's ear. "I can never come back, Atticus. I've been banished from Flamingo. But David and I have killed the Mer tribe. For all I know, they may never come back here. If you ever can, come back to Hearthstone and stay with my friends and me. Gurril, Pepper, and I will take care of you. You are the only person from this island who ever was fair to me, and I thank you for that."

Atticus reached and took her hand, squeezing it. She brought his hand to her lips, and kissed it gently. She whispered again to him. "Atticus, if they don't take proper care of you, send me a message somehow and I will find a way to have you brought to me. You saved the island, and you should be treated as a hero. Never let them shun you the way they've shunned me."

A Flamingoan warrior gently pulled on Snick's shoulder, and told her it was time to go. She nodded to the man, and said one last thing to Atticus. "The statue they built for the hawk should really be of you, Atticus. Goodbye."

Minutes later, she was on a boat, escorted by three warriors and with no luggage. Gregor had confiscated all of her belongings to keep her from mixing any potions, but allowed her to keep her small handbag. She had enough gold, silver, and copper to pick up a few supplies on the mainland and to get a coach back to Hearthstone.

The voyage to land was long, and when they finally arrived, it was past dark. The three warriors who escorted Snick left the boat when she did. The lead warrior was a stocky man whose eyes seemed eternally bloodshot.

He said to her firmly, "You can never come back. If you try, we'll kill you."

She nodded to him. "Yes. I know."

"You have money for a coach back to your new town?"

Snick nodded.

"Then buy your ticket and go."

With that, the three men walked from the dock to a hotel. Snick watched them go and left for the coachman's ticket counter. Above her in the night David circled, happy to be over land again.

3

The past few days, Pepper noticed that Gurril was in a more sullen mood than usual. Maybe he missed Snick a bit more than Pepper had originally thought, or maybe there was something else on his mind. Either way, Pepper needed the man to understand what he was about to do. They sat at the dinner table, eating lunch silently. Every now and then, Gurril might ask Pepper a question about how his training was going, but other than that, the warrior was quiet. Pepper began the conversation he wanted to have by going directly to the point of things.

"Gurril, I'm going to grow small later today so I can go into the walls. There's something bothering me about that scratching we keep hearing. Coska told me to check it out."

Gurril looked up at him and scowled. "You know what he told me?"

Pepper shook his head.

"Nothing, Pepper. He didn't tell me anything. The whole time he's been yacking it up with you, he never has said a word to me."

Quietly, Pepper said, "I'm sorry, Gurril. I'm sure he has a reason."

Gurril grunted in anger. "Yeah, just like he had a reason for sticking me with a seven-foot-tall circus freak. And by the way, if this supposed rat attack is coming, why in the world would you want to go crawling around in the walls? Afraid to fight? Just like when you should have killed that fisherman in the bar?"

"Because I didn't kill him, we've gotten fish three times a week for months now. Killing isn't always the right thing to do, Gurril."

"Right. But spending a few days examining the plumbing is always the answer. Go ahead and crawl in the walls... I don't care."

"Why are you so angry?"

Gurril slammed his fist on the table hard enough to make every piece of china, every glass, and every item of silverware jump. He shouted at Pepper.

"I'm angry because my best friend became a tree who's got something to say to everyone but me! I'm angry because he got replaced by a freak of nature! I'm angry because every time I start to think I want to spend my life with a woman she gets taken away! I'm angry because my life and my living are built on swinging a hammer at people's heads!"

Pepper looked across the table. The words had stung him. Gurril stared back, his eyes wide, wild, and red. Tears rolled down the man's cheeks. Gurril hunched over, gritting his teeth so hard that Pepper thought they might shatter. The ferret took a deep breath.

"Gurril, I'm the son of a tree who was your best friend. He made me this freak of nature. He has a plan for us both. Neither of us knows what that plan is, but he has one. You may feel like your best friend is gone, but I feel like *my* best friend is alone and angry right now. In a few minutes, I'm going to chew on a thin piece of branch and make myself small again. Once I go into the walls, I may not see you for a few days. If the attack happens, I'll get back to help you fight."

They continued to stare at each other. Talking had helped Pepper feel a bit better. He hoped that his friend would stop feeling this irrational anger toward him soon.

Pepper smiled. "Bet you three pike that I kill more rats than you do when they attack."

Gurril couldn't help it. Seeing that long face with those long, pointy teeth grin at him softened his anger every time, no matter how extreme. He offered a weak smile to Pepper and nodded.

"I need to work out, then rest. I haven't been sleeping well. Be careful in the walls."

Pepper watched as Gurril left the room and went to the courtyard where the two warriors trained.

Pepper finished his meal and went to Coska. He plucked the end of a small branch from the tree and looked at it with a sigh. He could hear Gurril in the other courtyard working out, probably doing pushups, the ferret thought.

He called out to his human friend, "Gurril, what do you think our odds are against an entire mischief of rats?"

From the other courtyard, he heard Gurril answer, "Fifty-fifty."

To himself, Pepper said, "Hmm. I thought they were a lot worse than that."

He stuck the branch in his mouth and chewed. The feeling of size change began in an instant, although it was much less painful than it had been before Coska gave him this new way of doing things. In a few minutes, he was his smaller version.

Gurril finished one hundred pushups and walked over to the Coska tree to apologize to Pepper for lashing out before. The ferret was gone. Gurril grunted to himself and went back to his workout.

4

The coach rocked back and forth as Snick rode, dreaming of her reunion with Gurril. She napped lightly, but kept seeing Atticus's mutilated face every time she closed her eyes. She knew somehow that leaving him in the condition he was in would haunt her. She hoped that someday she could see the man again but doubted it.

Her first day of travel she made it as far as a small town where she realized quickly she was nearly out of money. She sighed to herself at the thought of how quickly coins slipped through fingers. She let her disappointment blow away from her in the breeze and went into the woods to gather herbs to start making various powders and creams to sell. She would need to work fast in order to make enough money to pay for lodging during the rest of her trip. David hunted while she picked herbs, and by the time she retired to her room, she had four different potions in mind to create.

She mixed the potions, humming to herself while David sat on her window, eating a squirrel. She was still close enough to the sea that the breeze carried a bit of salt on it, and she smiled lightly, knowing that she would never have to see her cursed home again. She had felt this way the first time she left, and she supposed that if circumstances ever brought her back to Flamingo, leaving would be even easier now that she had confirmed that she was utterly cast out from the place. Then again, if she ever found herself in Flamingo once more, she'd probably be burned at the stake. The thought made her laugh, and she fancied herself a bit insane for that.

She turned to David and smiled wide. "My home is in Hearthstone, with you, Pepper, and my love, Gurril." The hawk chirped back at her, frustrated that she hadn't understood his message when he dropped the tiny rat into her lap in the middle of the ocean.

5

The space between the walls was thin, and partly out of spite (but mostly out of a need to entertain himself with a joke) Pepper *did* inspect the plumbing. It all looked good, and the ferret smiled as he felt the cold pipes behind the kitchen. There was a smell in his area that Pepper recognized, but couldn't remember from where. He sniffed, and followed the smell along the bottom of the wall to try to find its origin.

One smell led to others of the same type. It seemed to Pepper that there were animals in the walls. He followed the trails of scent as they converged, then dipped into a hole in the bottom of the wall. The hole led to the town's sewer. Here, everything widened, and the scents were masked by the flow of the town's waste. Pepper explored the area, noting that there seemed to be holes where small creatures (about the size of Pepper himself in this form) could crawl into the walls of every building in the town. Pepper crawled here and there up into other buildings. First the alehouse, then the elders' chamber, and finally the granary. The hole that led to the granary had some grain piled under it, and Pepper surmised that these tiny creatures, whatever they were, must be stealing the grain for food. He hoped to himself that they didn't carry any diseases.

He was working his way out of the hole when he saw a small shape pass under him, toward the direction Pepper had previously explored. He quickly shimmied down the hole and followed the animal as it ran up into the elders' chamber. Pepper followed as quietly as he could and watched the wee beast as it scrambled into the space between the walls, then pushed itself out of a hole and onto the floor of the chamber. Pepper watched from the hole as the tiny thing ran to the foot of Trina, then crawled up her leg.

It popped out at her collar, and Pepper could see its tiny tongue reach out and lick the old woman's lips. She cooed at the thing, and kissed back at it as it licked. Pepper was disgusted.

"My darling," Trina cooed, "Where have we been tonight?"

The animal squeaked into her ear, and Pepper heard her chuckle. The animal was about as long as Pepper was, but fatter and with shorter legs. Its teeth looked as if they were made for tearing into meat, but it didn't look ferocious at such a small size.

After the thing finished squeaking, and Trina finished chuckling and cooing, she said to it, "Now go be a good rat and check on the cannon for me."

Pepper gasped lightly at the word. *Rat!* How could it be? He hurried out of the hole and ran to a corner of the chamber while the rat climbed down Trina's body and then ran to the hole in the wall.

Trina turned toward Joseph, who sat near her. "Joseph, will you be spending dinner with Gurril again tonight?"

Joseph nodded. "Of course. Instead of sending him on a patrol away from our spies, like I've been doing, I plan on telling him that the rat attack is coming in three days. He'll plan on training hard all day today and hard again tonight and tomorrow, then lightly after that to rest and recover. We'll hit the town in the morning, when he's dog tired and his muscles are jelly from over-training."

"That will be enough to weaken him?"

Joseph chuckled. "My Dear, he's weak already. With Snick gone he hasn't been himself. The added stress of the coming attack will keep him up all night. His body will be so unrested, we might be able to take him down with only two or three full-sized rats."

"And when do we get to shed these skins? Being human feels... gross."

"Soon. Until that time, though, you are Trina, the elder."

"Yes, Joseph." With that Trina left the chamber and Joseph remained alone.

The old man seemed to nap, and Pepper left him to it. He had two things to do: first he had to get Gurril and warn him. He hoped that his friend would believe him about Trina and Joseph's betrayal. After that, he would go to the cannon and see why it was that Trina had sent the rat to check on it.

Pepper crawled into the wall, and curled up for a moment to gather himself. Joseph was not who he seemed. How could this be? And Trina... not really Trina. Not really a human. Pepper's head swooned. He had to get back to Gurril. Pepper turned and ran through the wall toward the house he shared with Gurril. As he made his way, a tiny set of eyes watched him. After the ferret passed, the eyes came out of the dark, and went through the hole in the wall to see Joseph.

The rat that had been transformed into Trina walked to the house she had been residing in since the rouse began. She entered and sat there in the kitchen, looking absently at the wall and remembering the taste of the old woman's flesh who used to live here. Billy, posing as Joseph, had all the power now. But soon, in the heat of the battle for Hearthstone, the rest of the rats would turn on him. She would see to that.

Pepper ran down into the sewer and then over to Gurril's house. The warrior had to still be working out; it had been just over an hour since Pepper had left him. He was about to scramble up the sewer wall and into the hole that would lead to Gurril's house when a small claw reached out and grabbed him. Pepper turned to see a small rat, about a foot long, holding him steady. The rat seemed to smile, and another rat scrambled from

244

a corner to join him. Pepper suddenly chilled, realizing how close to Coska's vision he was now.

6

Gurril sat in the alehouse, resting and drinking a tall glass of water infused with herbs when the door was flung open. It was Trina. Gurril had never seen the woman so distraught.

"Gurril," she said sternly, "You need to come to the chamber. Now!"

Seven rats carried Pepper, his front paws bound like a prisoner, and a length of bailing twine around his neck for a lead. They took him to the elders' chamber, jerking and pulling on his body as he struggled against them. Two of the rats poked sharp claws into his sides as they went, and finally, one drew just a bit of blood from his ribs. The rat sucked it off his fingertip the way a fat man would suck a bit of chicken grease.

Coska, in his courtyard, sensed all that was happening. He couldn't talk to Gurril, but he could try to send him a feeling. On the main street of the town, as Trina and Gurril walked silently together, a chill ran up the warrior's spine. He thought to himself, *Something is very wrong here tonight.*

The elders' chamber was dark, with the exception of a few torches. Pepper stood quietly as Joseph watched him.

"Gurril will be here soon," the old man said. "Whatever should I tell him?"

"What are you?" Pepper asked quietly. He noticed that the seven tiny rats who had escorted him had left for the shadows.

Joseph chuckled. "I'll tell you in hell. Just know that you being here tonight is a great help to me. I'd try to tempt you to join us, Pepper, but I know what you'd say. You're too loyal. Loyalty is an ugly trait, Pepper. It gets the weak killed by those who are smart enough to lure them to their death."

Pepper shook his head. "My mistake was being loyal to *you*. Gurril is loyal, and Gurril will save me."

"Hmm. I wonder."

Pepper stood in the chamber waiting for the fate he knew he would not escape, and Coska finally sensed Joseph's plan. The tree threw out his thoughts to Snick and David, who were

245

two days travel away. As her coach pulled away from the inn where she had taken a break to rest and mix potions, Snick captured the thought: *Either immediately come to Hearthstone ready to save Gurril, or stay away and let him die in battle.* Snick sat bolt upright, startling the other passengers. She needed to get to Gurril as soon as possible. She poked her head out the window to look to David. The hawk was already flying away from her, on a more direct path toward the town. She smiled and whispered to herself, "Good bird!"

Pepper watched as the chamber doors opened. He saw Gurril enter, tired and sweating. The man was escorted by Trina. "Gurril!" He called out.

Gurril looked to Pepper, standing there looking tiny in his bound and tethered state. He glared up to the elders, all present in their seats except for Trina, who was still standing next to him.

"What is this?" the warrior demanded. Trina left his side and walked to her seat as Joseph made a gesture to Gurril that was meant to calm him down.

"Gurril," Joseph began. "We're very sorry to have to do this to you. I know it's almost supper time, and you must have been busy training today."

"Why do you have a town warrior tied up like this?"

Pepper was about six feet from Gurril. He looked up to his friend and said, "We have to leave, Gurril. This is too much for us."

"That's enough," Joseph said from his seat. "Gurril, do you know what Pepper was doing today?"

Pepper said to Gurril, "Don't say anything!"

Gurril looked down to Pepper, then back up to Joseph. "He wanted to know what was scratching in the walls. He went to go see."

Joseph chuckled at Gurril, and shook his head. "No Gurril, he didn't. Our information has been telling us for months that there was a spy in Hearthstone. A spy who fed the rats information they needed for their attack."

Pepper shook his head and pleaded to Gurril, "Don't believe him!"

Gurril couldn't say anything to Pepper, but he didn't believe Joseph. Gurril would never have thought Pepper was capable of evil, and knew that somehow, someway, Joseph was setting the ferret up. But why?

"This spy," Joseph continued, "gave the rats information about the cannon, about our plans, and about the elders. He also gave them a lot of information about you, Gurril. They probably have plans and plans and plans to try to beat you."

Gurril acted incredulous. "Surely, you don't think that Pepper—"

"Yes! Pepper!" Joseph stood as he shouted this accusation.

In his courtyard, Coska began to gather all his power. To allow his friends to survive, he would need to perform magic that he didn't think was possible. The cats, sleeping in his branches, could feel a subtle vibration that stirred them. They looked at each other, then lay their heads back down. Perhaps it was just the wind.

The room stood silent as Trina and Roy stood and advanced toward Pepper. Gurril stammered out a "No!" as they advanced on his friend.

Pepper looked up at Gurril, tears filling his eyes. "Gurril, I wouldn't. I didn't."

Gurril looked back. "I know, Friend. Don't worry." He looked to Roy and Trina. "Do not take him! This is wrong!"

Trina only responded with a cold, "I'm sorry." It didn't sound sincere.

Pepper didn't have to tell Gurril that there was evil abound in the chamber. Gurril decided what must really be going on: Joseph was out to take the town by force. Roy grabbed the twine tied around Pepper's neck, and looked to Joseph.

Joseph looked down from his seat and demanded, "Hang the spy!"

Roy gripped the twine harder, then yanked upward on it, meaning to hang the ferret by using his hands as a gallows. Just at that moment, Pepper did an amazing thing: he disappeared.

The room was a collective gasp of breath. Gurril looked around. Roy's hand flung up at the absence of weight and he hit himself in the face. Trina turned to Gurril with a scolding look.

"What have you done!"

Gurril backed away, unable to speak.

Joseph stood from his chair. "Gurril! What sort of magic is this!"

"I… I don't know."

Joseph pointed down to the warrior. "Decide right now, Gurril! Whose side do you stand on? The magical friend to rats that betrayed you, or the elders who have given you your life?"

Gurril had to think fast. The wrong answer meant death. But giving the right answer meant playing along with the plan that Joseph had put into place, then trying to spring a stop to it at just the right moment.

Gurril licked his quivering lips, and answered, "My allegiance is to the town. I'll defend Hearthstone against rats, spies, or anyone else. What is our immediate danger of attack?"

Joseph smiled at him. "Do you believe that Pepper is a traitor?"

Gurril knew this to be the trick that it was. If he answered yes outright, then Joseph would know that the man was lying. But if he played his answer just right…

Gurril swallowed hard and thought for a moment. "I don't know. He's my friend, but he spent a lot of time alone. I have a hard time believing it, Joseph."

Joseph turned this answer over in his head. Was Gurril trying to play him? He thought the warrior probably was. But nothing he said had given him away yet. Joseph decided he would continue his plan as it was before the happy coincidence of finding Pepper sneaking through the walls.

"Gurril," Joseph began again after a short pause, "The rats are coming soon. I need you to train hard tonight. They'll be here in three days according to our spy. Without Pepper, you'll need to be ready to put a posse together, as well. I and the rest of the elders can begin work on rounding up other town members to fight with you. We'll meet in the morning at the cannon to review a plan of defense. Now go!"

Gurril bowed quickly to the elders, and left for his house. After he was gone, Joseph turned to Trina. "Where do you think the ferret went?"

She shook her head. "I don't know, but I'll bet the Coska tree had something to do with it."

"Agreed. After we take the town, we don't hesitate to chew down and kill the tree. In the meantime, round up as many hunters and fishers as you can to begin a search for Pepper. Anyone who finds him is to kill him for a reward. The rest of the mischief is gathering in the tunnels to become full-sized rats once more."

8

Pepper sat quietly in the dark. He had no idea where he was. Coska had no idea where he had sent Pepper in such a panicked blast of magic, and could not communicate with the ferret. Pepper moved his body a bit, and realized two things very quickly. First, he was back to his large size. Second, he was no longer tied up. The place he was in was completely and utterly dark. He sniffed the air, and all he could smell was the old scent of rat. Pepper felt around a bit and discovered that he was in a tunnel. He felt his way through, hoping he was moving in the direction that would lead him out.

Joseph stood in the center of a group of townsfolk just before sunset. A few of them held torches, a few more held various weapons.

"The rats," he intoned, "are coming. And they are coming with help of the giant ferret!"

The crowd murmured.

Joseph continued, "The elders are prepared to give anyone who captures the traitor Pepper five hundred gold pieces!"

A collective gasp ran through the crowd. Five hundred gold! Wealth beyond anyone's dreams!

Joseph yelled out to the crowd one final time to rally them, "Go find that ferret! He's responsible for the attack that is coming!"

The crowd broke apart and dispersed into the dusk as it fell around the town.

Joseph turned to Trina and said, "There won't be a living ferret within twenty miles of this town by tomorrow morning. And every person in this wretched village will have spent the night out hunting down Pepper. By the time we attack, they'll be just as worn out and unable to fight as Gurril will be."

Pepper felt around in the dark, and finally could see a sliver of light. He scrambled toward it, wanting to get out of whatever catacomb he was in. He emerged from the willow trees near goose hill. The sliver of light was the setting sun. Pepper brushed himself off and looked around to get his bearings. He began to hike to the top of the hill, but stopped when he heard a scurrying sound near him. Pepper turned, and saw a sea of the tiny rats had come out of nowhere to follow him. As he watched, they surrounded him. *So*, he thought, *this is how the vision comes true*. He tried to think of something clever to say that would insult a rat.

"Your mothers were cats! Now get your asses up here so I can kill you all!"

With that, the small rats advanced quickly and were on him. In a scream of pain and fright, Pepper was brought down to the ground by a thousand rats.

Gurril ate a loaf of bread and thought. He had at least to pretend to train tonight; Joseph would make sure to look in on him. If he didn't seem to be reacting correctly to Joseph's command, Joseph might turn on him. At the same time he was pretending to train hard, he would have to be careful to conserve as much energy as possible, in order to be capable of fighting whenever the attack really did happen. He wondered where Pepper had gone. He knew that Coska had to have been responsible. Gurril stood and took the remaining portion of the bread out to the tree with him.

The first thing he noticed was that both the cats had climbed down and were out of the tree (a rare thing lately). The next thing he saw was that a number of leaves had shaken out of the tree.

"Let me guess," he said to Coska, "You shook when you made Pepper disappear. That knocked off these leaves and scared the hell out of my cats. You never were crazy about

250

them, and now they spend nearly every hour of every day sleeping on you." Gurril grunted at the humor of this fact.

"I don't know what to do, Coska. Pepper is gone, Snick is gone, and I don't have any idea if there is one single person in this town that I can trust."

Gurril huffed out a sigh, then sat in front of the Coska tree, deciding to meditate for a bit. It always seemed to help Pepper figure things out.

9

David pumped his wings as hard as he could, racing toward Hearthstone. He knew that he had to help, even though it would be far more dangerous than his bombing runs against the Mer had been. David concentrated as hard as he could while streaking toward his home and sent a message out to Coska: I'm coming, and Snick isn't far behind me.

Snick mixed powders together wildly in the coach. Her fellow riders looked at her in amazement, afraid because by now they had all silently surmised that she must be a witch.

She finally finished mixing a dark green powder together, then knocked on the front of the coach, yelling to the driver, "I need a stop! Now!"

10

There was a knock at the door. Gurril stood from his meditation and went to answer. He was sure that Joseph or one of the other elders would be standing there, but to his surprise, it was the fisher that Pepper had spared in the bar.

The man smiled shyly at Gurril. "My name is Jones. You remember me, right? I'm the one who brings you and Pepper fish."

Gurril nodded and grunted a positive sound.

"Well, Gurril. Well, I just, um. Did you know that I haven't taken a drink since that night that Pepper had all rights to kill me?"

Gurril shook his head and grunted again, noticing that the man had put on healthy weight and had a more full color than he had that day in the bar months ago.

Jones proudly said to Gurril, "Not a drop. And I take it you've enjoyed the fresh fish?"

Gurril grunted once more and nodded.

"Good." The man smiled. "Joseph is claiming that Pepper is a spy for the rats. I don't believe him. Do you believe him, Gurril?"

Gurril shook his head and grunted out what sounded like a *no* answer.

"Good. Good. What should I do, Gurril? The entire town is out hunting Pepper."

Gurril thought for a second. "Hmm. Come in. You may be the only ally I'll have in this fight."

They stepped inside. Jones looked around the cottage in awe.

"You know, I've never been in here before. Just outside the front door to drop off fish. It's a nice place."

"Bathroom's down the hall. What type of fishing do you do?"

"I cast a hand net."

Gurril thought about this for a few seconds. "Okay. I need you to go get your hand net. Don't let anyone know what you're doing. Bring it back here. I've got a bit of training to do with you tonight."

Jones nodded, and ran out the door.

A few seconds later, there was another knock. Gurril opened the door, and saw Joseph standing there. Behind Joseph, townsfolk ran around wildly as a panic set in. Gurril grunted to Joseph, and stepped aside so the shaky old man could enter.

"Gurril," he began, "I'm so sorry about Pepper. When we caught him sneaking around in the walls earlier today, he was with some small rats."

"Small rats?"

"Yes. Apparently, there is a breed of small rats that help the larger ones. You haven't seen any evidence of large rats lately, have you?"

Gurril thought about this. It was true that he hadn't seen any sign of large rats.

"No," he answered, "I can't say that I have."

"And why do you think that is, Gurril?"

252

"Hmm. I guess that they must either have left to a rally point or are in hiding."

Joseph had made his way to the kitchen table and plopped down into the chair there, shaking as much as ever.

"Right, Gurril! Hiding. And do you know how they know where to hide from us?"

Gurril shook his head.

"I've been telling you and Pepper where to patrol. He's been feeding them information this whole time!"

Gurril sat across from Joseph and scratched at his chin. How could this be, that the things Joseph are saying blend so well with the reality that Gurril has been seeing lately? He knew that Pepper was not a spy. He knew that Joseph was a traitor. He just had to fit some missing pieces into the puzzle.

"Maybe," Gurril said, "It's been the small rats the whole time. Pepper hasn't been out of my sight very much. Not really."

"He's your friend, Gurril. I understand if you can't believe it. That's why I've assembled a posse and sent them out to find the ferret. That way, you don't have to do it."

Gurril sat quietly, hoping that Pepper could hide long enough for Gurril to come up with a plan to save him. Things were happening too fast, and Gurril was tired, confused, and afraid.

The front door flung open with a bang. It was Jones.

"Gurril, I've got my net, like you asked!" He looked over to Gurril and Joseph sitting together in the kitchen. Jones stammered, "Oh, uh… if you're busy, I can come back later."

Gurril saw the understanding in Joseph's eyes. The old man knew that Gurril had a plan for something. The warrior would have to cover his tracks, and fast.

"Jones," he said calmly, "I have the spear you wanted in back, in the courtyard."

He turned to Joseph, and said, "Jones is a friend of Pepper's, too. He can't bring himself to hunt the poor little guy. I agreed to give Jones a few lessons in spearing tonight while I train… So that he can do more of the fishing for the town in the next few days while everyone else is busy as a posse."

Jones stood in the living room, confused. "Huh?"

Gurril turned toward Jones and gave him a burning look. Jones immediately knew that his job was to shut up and just follow what Gurril said.

"Yeah. The courtyard," Jones said and trundled off to the back door of the house.

Joseph turned toward Gurril. "How big a fish is he expecting to catch? This doesn't seem to make much sense to me, Gurril."

The old man looked deep into Gurril. Joseph thought he was being lied to.

Gurril swallowed hard, then leaned to Joseph and spoke to him in a confidential tone. "The poor fisher, he's at his wit's end with worry for Pepper. I just wanted him to be distracted for a while. Besides, I always train better with company."

Joseph seemed to buy this, and nodded knowingly to Gurril. He spoke softly to the warrior, "You don't trust me anymore, do you?"

Gurril had to answer as honestly as he could to avoid letting the old man see through him completely. Also, a small bit of truth here would secure the old man's belief in Gurril's previous lies. "I don't know," he said.

Joseph measured Gurril carefully with his old, shaky eyes. "All right then, I guess I can't blame you. I'll be off with the other elders for the rest of the night, planning the best way for us to use the cannon against the rats."

With that, the old man was off. Gurril turned and went swiftly to the courtyard, where Jones waited.

"Jones," he commanded, "How much weight can that net take before it rips?"

Jones shrugged. "I don't know. Maybe a hundred pounds. Maybe only sixty. It isn't made for very big fish."

Gurril smiled, and said, "Good. Take your knife and begin cutting branches about the width of that spear. Don't cut any branches from the Coska tree, just those other trees there. Sharpen one end of each branch." Jones nodded, and did as he was told.

11

The night was leaping by. Rather than training, Gurril was fortifying his home. He knew that any good army would plan on attacking the strongest defensive points of a target first, which meant that he would probably be one of the first primary targets of the rats' campaign. As he boarded windows and helped Jones with his special project, Gurril wondered more about Joseph. Somehow, the old man was working against the town.

Gurril thought of the ferret and hoped to see his friend again. He understood in these black hours now what Pepper had meant to him. The ferret had been a bit of a pain, this was true, but he missed the animal's big, goofy smile, and the way he would swing tiny versions of his weapons around when he was sixteen inches tall. Gurril laughed to himself as he thought of Pepper complaining that the warrior grunted too much and that for a man who reads so much, he sure didn't have a very wide vocabulary.

From the living room, Jones heard the laughing and called over to Gurril. "Hey, what's so funny?"

"Nothing, Jones. Keep digging."

As Gurril checked over his work, counting ways in and out of the house, and envisioning good ways to defend himself and Jones from the initial onslaught, he thought about Snick. He hoped she was safe and far away from Hearthstone. This would be a long and bloody battle. It would begin with Gurril defending against the initial attack. That first wave of the attack would tell Gurril what he needed to know about the numbers and fighting style of his enemy to turn from a defensive posture to an offensive one. He had his weapons ready: five war hammers of various sizes, the bow staff and spears that Pepper had tried out and turned down, and Pepper's two-handed broad sword with the copper handle and red stone. He hefted the sword up once, and was struck by how strong the ferret must be: Gurril could hardly lift the weapon.

12

The small sub-mischief of rats that had eaten and then taken the forms of the elders lay in a huddle in the elders' chambers. They transformed to their rat selves at different rates, all of them wailing and crying with pain. Billy— once Joseph— having been the magic source for everyone's transformation, was finished first. He stretched out and stood in his rat form, enjoying the sight of pain before him.

He watched as the female rat that had eaten then transformed into Trina lay in pain. Her name was Snarl, and she was a powerful doe. She had been one of the mischief's leaders. Snarl lay, paralyzed by pain, almost completely in her rat form. Billy didn't know that this female had plotted and planned Billy's death to happen during the upcoming battle, but he loathed her incredibly even so. He watched her lay, breathing deep, trying to regain her strength and decided that he needed a bit of distraction before the fight. Billy crawled up to her, then mounted her. She tried to growl a warning at him, but her change from human to rat form had exhausted her. She had no choice but to lie there as Billy thrust into her hard and angrily, penetrating her so aggressively that she felt herself tear.

Before dawn, all the rats had transformed. They lay napping when the sun rose.

13

"Help me, Coska. I don't know what else to do."

Gurril leaned his body up against the tree, pushing his forehead against its smooth bark. He looked up at the branches. "I know you have a reason for your silence."

Above him, his cats (who had returned to the tree a few hours earlier) stirred, then climbed down and ran off, disappearing into a taller tree on the edge of the courtyard. A tear trickled down Gurril's cheek as a few flashes of Peter and Sheila passed through his mind.

"Why do I always think of them before a battle? I don't understand. Coska, I'm so tired."

He took in a deep breath and held it for a few seconds before letting it escape him. The fight would come soon now. Gurril could hear Jones in the kitchen, preparing a breakfast. In the east, the first lights of dawn peaked over the horizon. Soon, the day would warm. Joseph had said the attack would come in a few days. But Joseph was lying and Gurril could sense it. He

256

was prepared for an attack at any time. The weary warrior reminded himself that after breakfast, he and Jones would need to get rest.

Outside the cottage, the hum of activity around the town continued as people focused on trying to find Pepper, rather than trying to fortify their own homes. Gurril had considered trying to get everyone to change their focus, to begin readying the town, but he knew that it was too late for that. The people of the town would have to fight as best they could. It was close to a riot outside and if he tried to take their focus off searching for Pepper, Gurril was afraid they would turn on him. Not only that, but Joseph would know for certain that Gurril was working against him. The warrior had to let the town waste away its energy chasing something they would surely not find, rather than prepare for the coming attack. The warrior was convinced that Pepper was safe somewhere, that Coska hadn't led him into trouble.

14

It took all the power Coska could summon to make Pepper disappear. Coska's strongest magic lay in transforming beings. He had other limited abilities, but making a beast disappear and reappear somewhere else was far beyond what he could normally do. It was for this reason that Pepper ended up in the center of the mischief of rats that Billy had created the night he wandered into the middle of the funeral for the three rats that Gurril had killed. Billy had turned most of the large rats into small rats— and each large rat equated to about three dozen small rats. So it was that exactly one thousand small rats covered Pepper's body, which had transformed into its larger version when he was teleported by Coska.

The pain was an incredible sensation of penetration through every portion of Pepper's body. He reflexively reacted by screaming, but that only led to the rats chomping into his tongue and mouth. They meant to eat him alive, this much he knew. He thrashed as they bit down, tearing at them with his hands. As they bit his open mouth he chomped down on them, returning the favor of the bite, and spit out chunks of rats. Pepper rolled, killing more of them under his weight as the huddled mass of violence tumbled down the hillside to the cover of the willows below.

He had almost gained hope earlier, crawling around in the dark, that he could escape the night without the vision that Coska had shown him coming true. The vision was simple: Bitten by a thousand rats, Pepper would either die or live, depending on how soon after the attack he could get to someone and tell them about the vision.

15

Snick mixed vigorously in the now empty coach. She had chased the other passengers out on the last stop and convinced the coachman to drive his horses until they died of exhaustion— all with the aid of a potion she had mixed. It never occurred to her that this was the second time within two weeks that she had ordered horses run until they dropped dead.

David had been gone for hours, and the thick cream she mixed in the back of the coach stunk. It contained urine from the horses, and Snick couldn't help but hope that when Gurril saw her again he wouldn't immediately order her to bathe. That was, of course, assuming that Gurril was still alive when she got to Hearthstone.

16

The sun rose over the village. Gurril and Jones napped lightly, taking in what rest they could now that the cottage was fortified as much as possible. Gurril's cats, sensing the battle that approached, stayed hidden high in the trees around the courtyard. In the chamber of the elders, Snarl finally gained the power to stand. She took to her hind legs, hissed at Billy, and urinated onto the floor in front of him. On Goose Hill, Pepper crawled slowly away from the pile of a thousand dead rats that he had slaughtered in a hundred different ways. Their carcasses lay all around him, crushed, bitten in two, mutilated. As the seven foot tall ferret crawled, he left a trail of blood behind him. He had to get to Gurril soon and tell him of the vision, or his fate of death would be sealed. In the center of town, a mob of exhausted townspeople moved through the streets, beginning to

258

finally break up now that the double lunacy of two moons had faded, and the sun rose over them.

Gurril awoke, needing to use the bathroom. He walked from his bedroom to the toilet and relaxed as much as he could, letting the urine flow from him in a steady stream. He knew that soon an attack would come. He knew that Joseph was somehow behind it. He knew that this day was dire. Some would live; some would die. Battles were always like this, and the more Gurril fought them, the less he trembled over the thought of killing others. It had truly become his business. He dealt less and less in kind favors, but more and more in harsh blows of the war hammer.

Snarl, her pride and vagina both still stinging from Billy's earlier violation, hissed at him hatefully.

"When do we attack?" she asked with sparks of fury in her eyes. If Billy's rape had done nothing else, it had spurned her anger to the point where fresh blood would be even more of a pleasure to her than usual.

Billy smiled at her, not knowing that soon, as he was springing his trap on the town, she would spring her trap on him.

"The thousand small ones will converge to create another eighty rats of our normal size. They will be in town any time now. We'll wait another thirty minutes. If they aren't here by then, we'll attack without them. Their arrival to the battle will be a reinforcement; the nine of us should have no problem with the town."

In the field that marked the bottom of Goose Hill, Pepper continued to crawl, crying and quivering with fear and pain. The tears stained the fur near his eyes, and he felt embarrassed (even though he was alone) to cry like a child. He remembered his life before all of this. It was so simple to be a ferret in the field. There were no visions, no battles, and no training to kill. He had hunted, but that was a different type of killing. Hunting was a part of the natural order of things; it wasn't hate or war or battle. It was life playing out in nature.

He thought of his mother, and how he had gone one day to her burrow. She had just had another litter, and he wanted to see the kits. The burrow had been dug up; his mother and the new kits gone. There was a bit of bloody fur around and the smell of rats. He didn't know the rat that had done it and didn't care which rat it was. Ferrets could be prey just as easily as they could be hunters. To accept this fact was to understand one's place in nature. The more Pepper assumed a human form, the less natural this fact of life seemed to him. He knew this meant that his mind was tuned in to the human frequency of assuming a place above nature, separate from the world as it was created. He feared that someday he would see nature as a wild garden out his window, rather than the place from which he once carved out a place to live.

Gurril sat in front of Coska, meditating. He heard Jones wake up and call for him.

Gurril grunted and said, "In here. Come and meditate in front of Coska for a bit. It helps prepare for a long day."

The fisher came in and sat down, taking in a deep breath of the scent of Coska's leaves. They smelled bitter but also a bit like mint. The thick, waxy leaves hung on the tree and reached toward Jones like fingers from a baby who wants to be held. Jones, like most people in the town, had only heard of the Coska tree. To see it made him feel special, like a man who has travelled the universe to see a star ignite.

Jones's mind was usually not full of much. This morning as he meditated, it was brimming. He saw a million different points of light, like stars, and somehow knew that each was a vision of the future. He could see any vision he wanted, or he could simply look at the constellation behind his eyes and enjoy its beauty. Mentally, Jones cast out a net, gathering up a handful of the stars. A voice somewhere in his mind— he would have recognized it as Coska's, had he known the wizard— told him that if he tried to take in that many visions at once, it would drive him mad. Jones, being only a bit intelligent and not at all wise, decided it was best to only look at two of them.

Coska again warned him not to overdo it, saying, "These visions are for you, but only one at a time, Jones."

The fisher plucked two of the stars out of his net, and held them like eggs in each hand of his mind. Coska's words slipped away as he gazed at the two possibilities and wondered what lay inside of each of them. He looked down at each hand with one egg in it, and smashed the two eggs together to show the visions within. A light burst out of the eggs, blinding Jones.

He passed out on the floor, hearing the strange voice of Coska calling to him through the piercing light, "Tell Gurril! Tell him for the love of everything you hold dear!" The words, like the visions, were instantly forgotten by Jones.

There were nine rats in the elder's chambers. Seven of them had been posing as elders, one had been Joseph, and one of them had been living in the very rear of the elder's chambers, standing guard in case the humans found out Joseph/Billy's plan and came to attack the rats who had taken human forms. They snarled at each other, preparing themselves mentally for a long and hard battle. Eight of the rats hated the ninth. Eight of the rats would kill and eat the ninth. Only one of the rats knew how to activate the cannon that would explode and wipe out half the town. The eight had to wait for the ninth to wipe out the humans before making their move to kill him.

17

The horses pulled the coach ahead in a trance. They ran and ran, unable to stop or to even want to stop. The potion Snick mixed had been strong. Had an evil wizard mixed it, he would have enslaved a whole town. Had a general gotten it, his army would have fought until exhaustion killed more of them than the enemy did.

She mixed other potions, creams, and powders in the back of the rocking coach. Up front, the driver did little more than hold on for dear life. Snick mixed her magic in part to have an arsenal to use when she arrived in Hearthstone and in part so that she had something to do other than stare out the window and worry about Gurril and Pepper. She hoped that David would fly to them and be of help, and a tear slipped her eye as she wondered if it was going to be too late for her to share Coska's vision of her future with Gurril.

In the sky between her and Hearthstone, David worked his wings with speed, stopping for a few moments to dive onto and eat a squirrel. He relished the taste, but paused only long enough to eat the small animal and give his wings a rest.

18

Gurril and Jones sat on the roof of the house, a litter of weapons around them. They had climbed up Coska to get on the roof. Gurril felt oddly guilty about this, like he was somehow tromping on top of his friend. He smiled to himself, realizing that in fact he *had* been tromping on top of his friend.

Jones had been passed out for nearly an hour after smashing the dual visions in his mind, and was still trying to sort out everything he had seen and heard. He remembered that Coska had wanted him to tell Gurril something. Coska knew that he could only remind Jones of exactly what had happened, and if he pushed the man too far, Jones would simply pass out, and they would be starting at square one again.

Below, a familiar woman's voice rose to Gurril. "Gurril! You fool! What are you doing up there! Don't you have any brains?"

Gurril stepped to the roof edge and looked down to see his mother standing beneath him in day old clothes. Gurril thought to himself that those clothes must reek to high heaven after she'd been out all night in them.

"I've got a watch to keep, Mother. I don't think this is a safe place for you. Go home, sleep, and put on some clean clothes. If the rats attack—"

"That won't happen for another two days! You fool! You know, this is all your fault. You and that damned magician. If the two of you hadn't decided you needed a pet, the rats wouldn't have gotten their spy in the middle of our town. And to take him in like that! If your brother Angus hadn't disappeared, he would have set you straight by now."

Gurril decided he was tired of her already, and simply walked away from the roof's edge, sitting down beside Jones at the peak of the roof. Together, the two men looked out over the area they could see, readying themselves. Jones turned toward Gurril as the old woman continued squawking in the background.

"Do you really think it will happen today?"

Gurril grunted a questioning response. "I guess I don't know."

"Shouldn't we take more time to train? We hardly did anything last night."

Gurril shook his head. "Train hard when there is peace. Rest before a fight. You won't be sore, and you'll have more fuel to keep going."

Jones sighed, then pointed toward the river. "See there? Behind the ale house? That blue one is my boat. When this is done, maybe I'll take us all fishing for fun."

Gurril smiled at the man. "Fishing is a good way to live, isn't it?"

Jones nodded. "The best. I lost my way there for a bit, started thinking that whiskey was the best way to live. The day that Pepper could have killed me, I decided to never touch the stuff again."

"I'm glad you lived."

Jones laughed. "Me, too. I'm glad it wasn't you who I decided to get stupid around that day."

Gurril stopped laughing, realizing how hard this comment stung him. To the town, he was a killer. He simply replied, "Me, too."

In the trees behind the courtyard, a few birds sang their morning songs. Below, the town lay mostly silent, with the exception of an old woman who was trying as hard as possible to convince her son that he was an idiot. Eventually, she tired of it, and wandered to the ale house. Jones and Gurril enjoyed the silence.

Gurril turned once more to Jones after some time had passed. "Jones, Joseph is a traitor; I'm convinced of that."

Gurril had been wondering for some time whether or not to talk about this to Jones, but finally decided that he simply had to trust someone now that Pepper was gone. If Jones turned out to be in cahoots with Joseph, the harm was already done because the man knew Gurril's plan of defense.

"So am I. I always thought he was an odd old man, but accusing Pepper of being a spy... No way would Pepper help rats attack us."

Gurril nodded, happy to cover this ground again, knowing that he had more to figure out about the mystery of the old man.

"How much do you know about the cannon he was building?"

"Oh, lots! A good friend of mine, Jacob, is one of the iron workers. I don't think you've got anything to worry about with the cannon, Gurril. Jacob says it won't work."

"Really? That doesn't seem to fit. Why shouldn't I worry?"

"Like I said, it won't work. All the guys building it kind of laugh at the old man behind his back because of how foolish the whole idea is."

Gurril turned toward Jones. "I don't believe it. Why would the old man invest so much time and effort into convincing everyone the town needed it if it won't work?"

"Maybe he doesn't know that it won't work. Not all things an engineer designs work right, you know."

Gurril sighed. The old man had to have a reason for the cannon. Perhaps it was meant to fire onto the town, blowing holes through buildings. That didn't make sense to Gurril, though. An attacker would only try to take an entire town to get as many resources as possible. It was better to draw everyone out into a fight and then occupy the buildings later, or to go building by building and kill the town's inhabitants.

The warrior turned to the fisher once more. "Tell me *why* it won't work."

"Well, for two reasons. First, they never made the chunks of iron the thing was supposed to fire. Second, there's no way to aim the thing. It's just a long hunk of iron with that explosive stuff that Snick made stuffed into the closed end in the back."

"Where's the portion of the explosive stuff that didn't get put into the back of the cannon?"

"There was none left over. Joseph had them put all of it into the back of the cannon."

"All of it? Hmm. Snick said there was enough for five shots." Gurril turned and sat in silence, turning this fact over in his head. After a few minutes, he heard a thud on the roof behind him. Realizing that he hadn't been watching their rear, he sprung up and turned around quickly, ready to strike.

There in front of him stood David the hawk, looking up at Gurril. Jones looked incredulously at the bird, and asked, "Where'd he come from?"

Gurril clicked his tongue at the hawk, who hopped up onto the man's arm. "I think Coska called to him."

"The tree?"

"Mm hmm."

Jones looked down to the tree with wonder.

Gurril cooed a bit at David, then told the hawk, "David, I need you to find Pepper. Find Pepper, David, and lead him to me."

The hawk chirped back at Gurril, then flew off.

Jones, still sitting, looked to Gurril. "Do you really think he can find him?"

Gurril grunted happily. "I know he will. Stay here, I'm going to go down to the kitchen and get us some bread and jam for lunch. I'll be back in a minute."

Jones nodded to Gurril.

Moments later, as Jones sat alone on the roof, the door from the elders' chambers swung open hard enough to crash against the wall of the building. In the empty town, the sound echoed like the crack of a tree struck by lightning. Jones watched curiously. He counted one through nine as rats emptied from the building— he could only guess that they were rats, as he had never seen one for real before. The nine rats scattered around and into buildings near the chambers in groups of three. Jones bounced with nerves and excitement.

A few seconds later, Gurril was back to the roof.

"I thought I heard something," the warrior said as he walked to where Jones sat.

Jones turned, and Gurril saw the panicked look in his eyes. Jones pointed over his shoulder.

"Rats! Nine of them! Into buildings!"

Gurril set down the bread and jam, and watched.

Inside three homes, husbands tried to protect their wives and children. Babies wailed, dogs barked, and women cried out for help. Inside three homes, husbands were torn to shreds by sharp teeth covered in pink venom. Babies were eaten whole, dogs were ripped apart, and women clawed wide open. In minutes, the nine rats were out of the first three buildings, working their way to the next three. Gurril watched them move, seeing the blood stains on them, confirming that this was the attack. They hadn't attacked his home first, as he had anticipated, and he had to recalculate his battle plan. Rather than attack the strongest defensive point with their initial thrust, the rats were working around it, killing with ease while the town defender watched from his fortified structure.

Gurril calculated different moves quickly in his head. Jones was protesting what he saw as inaction, but Gurril didn't hear it; his hearing was tuned to listen for screams, banging doors, or any other sound of the battle. His eyes were focused on the three buildings the rats had entered. The first building was an apartment structure. The other two were homes with only one family in each. There were four apartments in the first building. Seven people lived there. He could hear their screams as he tried to determine what he should do. Finally, Jones's voice came through to him.

"- and they're just dying down there! We need to do something, Gurril!"

Gurril whirled toward Jones. "No. This is our strongest defensive point. If we get down from here, they'll have the two of us for a meal. We need to get them to want to come to us first, rather than work around us. Grab those spears."

Seconds later, three rats emptied out of a building. The lead rat walked on its hind legs and carried a man's head in its hands, sucking out the eyeballs. The beast dropped the eyeless head as the three rats ran on all fours to the next structure, and began pounding on the door. Gurril chucked a spear toward the group. He was never as good of a shot as Sheila— she would have speared one of them for sure, but he bounced the spear off the cobblestone street close enough to them that they took attention to him.

Gurril yelled to the rats, "Come and fight your fight with me! I'll kill every one of you!"

The rats stared back. Billy looked for a second to the head he had dropped on the cobblestones, and licked his chops. The blood tasted good— it tasted *right*. One of his companions, a young male, took two steps toward Gurril's house.

"No," Billy commanded him. "We take them later, after our reinforcements get here. The going is easier than we thought. He can't hurt us while we're down here and he's up there."

Gurril watched the conversation, but couldn't hear it. Jones gasped as the rats kicked in the door, and charged into the house. Three other rats left another house that had just been raided, and began kicking the door to the ale house. Behind them, the last set of three exited the apartments. One of them had a little girl's leg stuck between its teeth. A second rat pulled it out, and they squabbled briefly over the morsel before Snarl yanked it away and dropped it into her mouth.

"Okay," Gurril said sternly to Jones. "Here's what we do. You stay up here and call down to the courtyard every now and then, like you're telling me what they are doing. They'll think I'm back there working on something. Where I'll really be is working my way to them by circling through there." Gurril pointed to an alleyway near the buildings the rats would get to after their current position.

"You're going to fight them down there?" Jones asked.

Gurril grunted and nodded. "I'm going to start there and bring them up to the house. I'll climb up here and we'll fight them together from the roof."

Jones gulped down the fear that held him.

Coska, in his small courtyard, thought to himself that if he could talk to Gurril, he would approve the plan. It was a typical Gurril plan. He thought more like a general than a town warrior, and Coska admired that about him.

19

David circled the area around the town, widening his orbit with every completed loop. Finally, he found Pepper struggling to cross a small stream that would lead him into the part of town farthest away from the warriors' villa and behind the cannon. Now that he saw how injured the ferret was, David decided to do just the opposite of what Gurril had asked: he landed in front of Pepper to block him from entering the town. Pepper recognized the hawk at once. Huffing for breath, and shivering from the onset of shock, Pepper managed a smile.

"Hi, David. I guess someone sent you to find me, huh?"
The hawk chirped.

Pepper smiled back, and looked down at his bloody fur.
"Like my new coat? I thought red would be a nice change of
pace."

The hawk looked at the ferret, amazed that any creature
would make a joke at such a time. Pepper struggled to stand and
took one step forward. David lightly pecked his foot.

Pepper looked down at the hawk. "Ouch! You crazy
bird! Every inch of me is an open bite wound! Don't do that!"

He took another step forward, and the hawk pecked at
his other foot. "Ow! For the love of everything good, David!
Stop that!"

Pepper knelt down, too weak to walk on two feet. He
stuck out a hand to crawl forward, and the hawk pecked it.
Pepper pulled back his bloody hand (that looked only a bit like a
paw), and stared at the hawk.

"I need to stay put, don't I?"

The hawk screeched a loud call to the ferret. Finally!
All these animals with bigger brains, and finally, one got the
message. David, now satisfied that Pepper would stay safe, flew
off to join the fight in Hearthstone.

He glided high over the town. To the west, he could see
a dust trail from a coach. That was probably Snick, he guessed.
The hawk was a master of distance, and judged that she looked
to be about twenty-six miles away. In a little under an hour,
she'd arrive. David felt a mix of emotions at this fact. First, he
felt happy that he would see her again and was excited to land on
her shoulder and rub his head against her hair. Second, he felt
dread, not wanting his lady to be hurt by the rats.

David turned his attention again to the city below.
Gurril was working his way through the streets to circle behind
the rats and attack them from either the rear or their flank,
depending on where he encountered them. David decided to
glide overhead for a while, then shoot down to harass the rats
and distract them so that Gurril would have a bit more time to
get close enough to register a hit. David felt the excitement of
battle course through him as he saw that Gurril carried one
medium-sized war hammer in each hand.

Inside the ale house, Gurril's mother hid under the stairs. The door, which was being battered by rats, would give way soon. The brewmaster was in back, locked up in a closet, hoping to hide. Three men stood near the door with knives at the ready. The heavy wooden thing flew open with a crash, and three rats ran into the bar. The three men hadn't planned a coordinated effort. If they had, they might have taken out one rat with their knives. The way it was, two men went for the first rat through the door, and the third man went for the second rat. This resulted in two simultaneous fights that were a two-to-one match. One set of combatants consisted of two rats against one man. This half of the skirmish went very quickly. The larger of the two rats slipped around the man and stood behind him on his hind legs. The rat in front of the man stayed low on all fours. The man whirled around to face the larger rat, and the one behind him simply stood up, wrapped his arms around the man, and began gnawing on his head. The larger rat plucked the knife clumsily out of his hand, knocking it to the floor. Under the stairs, Gurril's mother stifled a scream. If she could stay quiet, perhaps she would remain hidden and safe.

The other two-to-one face-off in the skirmish was two men versus one rat. The two men took up positions at the rat's eleven o'clock and two o'clock orientation. The man on the rat's left came in first, and the rat turned his way. This allowed the other man to score one quick slash at the rat's right side. The knife moved quick down the rat's arm, cutting it only slightly though the thick fur that covered it. By the time this action was complete, the man who scored the cut saw that his friend's head had been ripped off by the rat's jaws, and the two rats who had just dispatched his other friend took this man from behind. He died with the pleasant thought that at least he had made one of the bastards bleed a bit.

In an apartment upstairs from the ale house, a boy heard the tussle below. He slipped from his window, and jumped to the yard below. The boy ran as fast as he could to the small building that housed the town's cannon. The building was next to the town bell, and the boy meant to reach it and warn Hearthstone of what was happening.

269

On the opposite side of the building, Gurril crept through the alley, waiting for a group of rats to emerge. His attack would have to be swift and punishing, then he would have to move as fast as his feet could take him to get back to the roof of his cottage. In front of him, three rats emerged from a house, covered in fresh blood. They didn't notice him at first, because Gurril was directly to their right rather than in front of them. One of the rats looked over and pointed.

"Him!" The rat shouted.

The other two turned, and the three rats stared at Gurril, who stared back silently. The rats began to growl, and one of them broke into a long hiss. Pink poison dripped off of its teeth. Gurril growled back, snarling like a dog. The rats began to walk forward, mirrored by Gurril, who advanced in small steps. He had to stay close to the alley.

David watched the standoff from above. He timed his dive perfectly, shooting his body downward like an arrow, as fast as gravity could pull him through the air. The shape of his body allowed the air to flow around him efficiently, and his altitude gave him incredible momentum and speed. When he hit the rat behind and to the left of the lead rat, he knocked the beast down to the ground. In a flash, David struck out his talons at the rat's eyes, then beat his wings for an escape. The loud *thud* caused the other two rats to turn and see what had happened. Gurril swung the hammer in his right hand upward hard, striking the lead rat in the back of the head. There was a horrible cracking sound, and the rat collapsed in a heap in front of him, his legs twitching as feces shot from the animal's convulsing body.

Gurril snarled at the last rat standing as it turned to face him. He issued a war cry that the six rats in other buildings could hear, and swung the hammer in his left hand at the standing rat. The rat reacted just fast enough to shimmy out of the way of a direct hit, and the blow glanced off its ribs. The rat swung out a claw a Gurril, but his reach was far less than Gurril's arm and hammer could reach. The claw swished through the air and was no threat to the warrior. Gurril turned and ran, hoping the rat would follow. If one would follow him, then the rest would, too. At least, that was the hope.

The rat watched Gurril run, not knowing what to do. The beast that had been attacked by the bird stood up. One of his eyes had been torn open, and lay bloody in its socket.

The injured rat growled, "Get him!"

The two took chase. As the next group of three exited the house they had just decimated, they saw one rat twitching, shitting himself, and bleeding in the street, with two more running after something down an alleyway. They immediately joined the chase.

Gurril huffed hard as he ran. The added weight of his two hammers slowed him down, but he had wanted to be doubly armed in case he had to stand and fight the entire gang of rats. His feet pounded the cobblestones as he sprinted by homes and businesses. Near the cannon, the town bell began to ring.

On the rooftop, Jones looked over the scene below. He had seen Gurril land the blow to the back of the first rat's head. It was a brilliant hit, and the rat lay twitching and convulsing. The three that had found the injured beast gave chase when they saw their two comrades running after Gurril. At least some of the rats would be heading this way, then. When the bell began ringing, Jones smiled. Now the town would know the attack was on, and they would come out armed. Mostly, it would be men with knives and pitchforks, but that was better than the town being picked off house by house. And there were only eight rats left. Surely the town could take eight rats.

Billy stood in the bar of the alehouse over the two dead men's bodies, sniffing the air.

"There's another human here," he said to the other rats with him.

They sniffed. It was the smell of an old woman, sweaty in clothes she had worn while trying to hunt down a ferret all night long. It took only moments for them to find her under the stairs. She never even had a chance to scream out any insults as they grabbed her and tore her limbs from the trunk of her body. It was over for her in seconds, and her dead eyes stared across the bar at two other sets of dead eyes.

Billy heard the town bell ring. He smiled, turning to the other rats with him.

"Once the town is gathered, I'll convince them to defend the cannon. I'll set it to explode while the entire town is gathered around it. I can slip out of the crowd and rejoin you. Go to Gurril's cottage now and try to chew down that damned Coska tree!"

The two rats nodded to Billy and exited out the door. Billy ran into the back room and sat behind some barrels to change back into his human form.

Chapter 8: Joseph, Revealed

1

Donatello Destone was no fool. His mother told him so often as a youngster, and not just to be nice the way some other mothers do. No, Donatello's mother was right on. The boy, then the man, was no fool. Because Donatello was no fool, there were two rules in life he always kept in the front of his mind: first, he always kept his head low and stayed out of the way; second, people were always going to be thirsty after a hard day (or night) of work.

So it was that Donatello found himself hiding in a closet in the alehouse. He had been preparing kegs for when everyone started waking up after their night out looking for a magical ferret. A snipe hunt, if you asked Donatello, but who would bother asking him? He was just a simple brewmaster.

He had been in the back of the ale house, the kegs he was filling almost ready to be plugged. There were three men, all fishers, and the town warrior's crazy mother, all having a drink of hard cider. Most of the people who rented rooms upstairs from the ale house were asleep, except for one apartment. They were a young couple with a four-month old baby. The husband and wife spent every afternoon shagging, and Donatello (being no fool), wondered how long it would be until the next baby was planted in the woman's belly.

There had been no real warning, and the only reason anyone knew what was coming was that one of the men happened to see through the window that six rats were walking the streets of the town. The old woman had hidden under the stairs. Donatello thought this was a good spot to hide but didn't want to be around the old lady. Mostly because she was crazy, but also because she reeked to high heaven. The woman hadn't bathed in days, and her clothes were sweat through from her wanderings around the previous night. He remembered asking her how the ferret hunt went. She had mumbled something about her son being a fool, a phrase Donatello was sure his own mother would never say or even think about him. So when the men locked the door, and the old woman hid, Donatello ran to the back. He had read once that rats can sniff out humans easily.

273

His clothes had been soaked in ale from filling and moving kegs, and Donatello, being no fool, decided to run to the back room and hide in a closet. His smell would blend with the smell of the kegs in back, and he thought that might be the thing that saved him.

Donatello listened to the fighting in the bar. He listened to one rat saying something but couldn't hear what it was. When the town bell rang, Donatello smiled to himself. Soon, the town would come out. Hearthstone versus six rats, unless there were more the men in the bar hadn't seen. Donatello calculated the odds in his head, and figured that the town would lose thirty or forty people, but would win in the end. Especially with Gurril fighting.

The silence in the bar told him that the rats had left. This meant that the wives, children, and shagging newlyweds upstairs were safe. He was tempted to leave the closet but thought to himself that in the spirit of keeping his head low, he should hide out another fifteen minutes. He sat in the closet quietly, looking out through the crack between the closet door and the wall. As he watched, a shadow fell into the room.

Donatello held a hand over his mouth and nose to mask the sound and smell of his breath. In his mind he kept telling himself, "You're no fool! You're no fool! You're no fool!" until he finally believed it. The shadow crept in and in, and then Donatello saw one furry foot. The foot advanced, and there was one furry leg, then another furry foot and furry leg. Donatello clenched his bladder and bowels against the exceedingly powerful urge to lose control of them. His body trembled, and an odd sensation of quivering ran through his ears as the fright of his situation filled him from bottom to top and back. He bit down on his tongue to keep his teeth from chattering.

He watched as the rat looked around the room, then collapsed in a heap on the floor. The rat groaned and twitched while its bones crackled and crunched. Urine ran out from between its legs as they shrunk and the fur fell out of them. Within minutes, what had been a rat lay still as a human form on the floor of the back room. From Donatello's point of view, all he could tell was that the human form had skinny white legs with bright blue veins running through them. An old man lay on the floor, unintentionally mooning Donatello.

The man stirred, then sat up. Donatello immediately recognized the face: It was Joseph! The old man stood shakily, then wandered out of the back room. Donatello, being no fool, decided to reset his fifteen minute hiding time. If he left his hiding place before the fighting was over, he'd send someone to get Gurril and tell the warrior about Joseph. In the meantime, he tried to focus on how he'd get ready for the thirsty people who would come to celebrate the town's victory in the ale house the next morning. Six rats… well, as far as he knew, it was six rats. It would be tough, but the town should win. Donatello relaxed a bit in the closet, wondering to himself if he could ride the entire attack out in this small space.

2

The house was just ahead, and Gurril could hear the rats behind him. He lowered his shoulder, and smashed through the front door, gingerly sidestepping around the middle of the living room floor, and running into Coska's courtyard. He jumped up onto Coska and scrambled up the tree to the roof, sensing the claws of a rat grabbing at the space he had filled just a half second previous.

As the rats chased Gurril in, the first rat saw him run around rather than through the middle of the room. The first rat did the same; it was only wise. The second rat in line (who was missing one eye, thanks to David) had missed this move, and ran through the center of the room. Gurril and Jones had built a trap there using Jones's net and the crude spears he had made from sharpened sticks.

The net held the floorboards up, but any weight beyond about sixty pounds would send an intruder crashing down into a pit, to be speared by the sharp ends of sticks that were mounted into the ground. The one-eyed rat fell through the hole and onto the sticks. He screamed first in surprise, then in pain. He twitched a few times, and was dead, three spikes having run completely through his body, and one having severed the jugular vein of his neck. Blood spurted in a high arc out of the pit and onto the floor in a thick stream as the rat's heart pounded its last beats. Now, there were seven rats left to fight.

The second group of rats, led by Snarl, bounded into the house and around the hole in the floor. A few seconds behind them were the two rats that had been in the ale house with Billy. The six live rats stood in the house, listening to the footsteps on the roof above them. One of them, a young male named Thorn, looked into the hole in the floor, and stared for a few seconds at the dead, one-eyed rat in the bottom. The pit was filling with blood as it drained from the skewered attacker.

Above them, Gurril and Jones stood near Coska, ready to swing swords and hammers down to any rats that tried to climb the tree. Rats were not good jumpers, and the only way up was going to be Coska. Gurril hated to put his friend in such a position, but it was the only way the warrior could think of to put himself in a defendable position. Behind him, the town gathered around the bell, their knives, pitch forks, and other assorted weapons at the ready.

The rats conferred inside the house, looking to Snarl for leadership. Gurril wondered why they weren't attacking him, when he finally saw the grand flaw in his plan. He rolled his eyes and hoped the rats wouldn't find this same flaw.

Six rats occupied the house, led by the large female, Snarl. Billy had told them their main mission was to kill the Coska tree. Snarl, however, had hatched a plan to kill Billy during the attack, and wanted to be sure every rat was with her. She turned toward her counterparts.

"Billy was right, we have to kill that tree. If we can chew it down, the warrior will have to jump from the roof to attack us. We can split up and have free reign over the town. When he jumps down, some of us will be waiting for him."

The other rats murmured agreements to this. She continued, "Once Billy comes back from activating the cannon, we'll kill him. The taste of his flesh will be a thrill!"

3

Overhead, David watched as Joseph exited the ale house. The hawk descended to the window the boy had left open when he escaped to ring the bell, and flew gingerly into the building.

276

He had to find a way to get a message to Gurril. Humans never seemed to understand David, and he wondered what he could do to tell the warrior that Joseph was a rat in human form. The hawk followed Billy's scent (not a natural way for him to hunt—David was sight-driven) into the back of the ale house, where the kegs were stored. He peered around the room eagerly, looking for a sign to give to Gurril.

Inside his closet, Donatello saw the hawk hop into the room. To the brew master, one hawk looked like any other, but this hawk seemed to be on a mission. He wondered if it was the bird that had belonged to Snick, and if this meant that she was back. He wondered these things to himself in his hiding place, as outside, the majority of the town gathered around the cannon and Joseph walked naked into one of the homes he had raided.

David observed the room. Through the crack between the closet door and the wall, he saw Donatello hiding. The bird hopped over to the door and tapped on it with his beak. Inside the closet, Donatello decided that the best thing to do was to try to give the bird what it was after so it would get the hell away from him, and he could go back to keeping his head low and his body hidden. He pulled the pad of paper and pencil that he took orders with out of his pocket, jotted down "Joseph = big fucking rat" and gave it to the bird. The hawk chirped two quick whistles at the man, then hopped out of the room.

David was amazed. A human had known exactly what to do. He decided there was hope for their species after all. He flew off with the note, heading for Gurril and happy that at least one human was no fool.

4

Joseph opened the closet door to the last house he had raided, and grabbed random clothes from it. He quickly and clumsily put the clothes on, then ran out the door toward the crowd gathering at the town bell. He approached them and tried to look frantic but in control.

The town, which had been on the verge of an all-out riot the night before, was now on the verge of an all-out panic. Few people seemed to notice that the old man's clothes were two sizes too large.

"People!" he shouted. "People! The other elders...
they've been eaten! The rats started their attack with us! Pepper
showed them a secret way in! We have to defend the cannon!
It's our only hope!"

People shouted agreements to this as Joseph made his
way through the crowd. He directed them left and right, until a
human ring four people thick was formed around the cannon.

"Yes!" he shouted as he began to smile, "Yes! Just like
that! Yes! Perfect!"

Behind him, the boy who had rung the bell rode up and
down on the bell rope, from almost ground level to over five feet
high, then back down again. The bell clanged loud and brassy.

5

Inside Gurril's house, the first rat approached Coska, and
began chewing gingerly at his bark, very near to the ground.
From above, Gurril shouted in anger. "Damn!" He turned to
Jones. "They know how to trap us. Maybe we can jump down."

"No," Jones responded, "I was thinking of that. They've
got sentries on each side of the house. If we jump down, they'll
be on us as soon as we land."

Gurril looked back down to the rat chewing at Coska.
The nasty animal's teeth were having trouble making it through
the smooth bark. Good.

Four rats stood sentry around the house, and a fifth
chewed at Coska. The final rat tore through the kitchen,
vandalizing the house. Gurril could hear the one in the kitchen,
breaking glasses, smashing dishes. He looked over their
weapons cache on the roof. They still had two of the practice
spears that Pepper had used to train with.

Gurril turned to Jones, "Hey! Hand me one of those."

He pointed to the spears. They were about three feet
long. It wouldn't be long enough to poke down at the rat trying
to chew through Coska's bark, and Gurril couldn't throw it down
through Coska's branches, so it would have to be used for one of
the sentries. If the sentries saw Gurril with the spear, they would
hide or run under the eaves of the house. Gurril mentally
marked where the sentry on the north side of the house stood,
then he got down on his belly. Jones quickly handed him the

278

spear. Gurril gathered his focus, then jumped to his feet as if he was coming out of a sprinter's crouch and threw to the mark where the rat had been standing. The rat simply watched it sail over his head, going high and long.

"Damn!" Gurril shouted, but before the word was out of his mouth, Jones had stuck the second spear into his hand. The rat was still turned to watch the first spear sail through the air, so Gurril quickly threw the second one. Now that he had a target that was in range and could see, he threw the spear true. The rat was just turning back to look at the roof when the spear hit the animal in the lower left abdominal area, impaling the rat's body. The rat looked up at Gurril with wide eyes, in disbelief that the spear had hit him. Gurril smiled, as the rat bled around the spear and slowly died before him.

The other five rats had no idea that a sentry had died. They continued their activities as before. Gurril and Jones waited to see if another sentry would come to replace the one they had killed.

6

Pepper woke up in the grass near the stream he had crossed. He had fallen asleep after David the hawk had told him to stay put. There was a patch of blood on the ground where he had lain, and he found it amazing that so much blood could come out of one animal. His muscles were stiff, and every single part of his body hurt. He wondered to himself if the tiny rats had poison in their teeth, as did the larger ones, and decided they probably didn't or he would be dead already.

Pepper shivered as he remembered being covered in biting rats and the feeling of the teeth and claws on his body. It was a horrible memory, and he decided instead to think of his friends, Snick and Gurril. Pepper passed out again, unable to move his sore, bloody body.

7

David the hawk circled the crowd of humans around the cannon, then circled over Gurril and Jones. He saw the spear fly over the rat's head and then the second spear take down the rat. David screeched out a battle cry when he saw the rat collapse and die. He thought about who should get the note, and decided to take it to the crowd of humans near the cannon; they were closest to Joseph and could do the most to stop him.

He turned back to the crowd, and swooped down low to survey the people for anyone he knew who might be of help. There were none that he could rely on. David pumped his wings and flew high to try to find Snick's coach again. He could see that it was just a few miles out of town now.

David flew toward the coach, deciding that Snick would have to be the one to deal with Joseph. He flew low over Gurril and Jones to greet them, and then was off to Snick.

8

"We have to jump down."

It was Jones who said this. Gurril looked at the man with surprise.

"Are you sure you want to do that, Jones? Down there you're an easy target."

Jones shrugged. "What else can we do?"

Gurril grunted and sat on the roof to think for a bit. "Jones, I've got a plan. I'm going to jump down from the north side of the roof. You go to the tree. Bring the bow staff. Remember how I showed you to use it last night?"

Jones nodded, picking up the bow staff. He went to the Coska tree while Gurril picked up Pepper's sword. The sentry on the west side of the house looked up at Gurril with the sword, then stepped over to alert the sentry on the north side and saw that he was dead. The rat looked up at Gurril and began shouting for the other rats. Gurril held the sword in both hands over his head, and threw it end-over-end toward the rat that was shouting. The hilt of the sword struck him in the chest, knocking him down. Gurril ran quickly to the edge of the roof, scooping up a medium and a small war hammer as he moved. He took a running jump, and as the two rats from inside the house exited, he flew over their heads and onto the street below, landing awkwardly and rolling as he smashed to earth. He felt both of his ankles twist and sprain and knew that he was going to be of seriously limited speed and mobility for the rest of the battle.

Gurril scrambled to his feet, and immediately felt intense pain shoot from his ankles. He knew that moving would give away his injury, so he stood his ground, and growled menacingly at the rats. The rat that had been knocked down to the ground by the sword stood up and joined his two companions. Gurril faced the three on with two badly sprained ankles, his small war hammer in his left hand, the medium hammer in his stronger right hand.

The other two sentries moved into position to stay directly below Jones. They had every confidence that the three other rats could take Gurril, and now their job became easier. The rat who gnawed at Coska's bark kept up his task, not noticing that Jones was slipping into the branches of the tree. Jones took up his position above the gnawing beast, and held the long bow staff in the firm grip of hands that had grown strong over years of grappling large fish in nets.

The three rats moved in a line toward Gurril. He would have to fight differently than usual, and his lack of mobility was going to make the battle between him and the rats a serious challenge. As they advanced, Gurril began swinging the small hammer in a wide circle over his head, building up momentum with the weapon. Gurril marked the first rat as a female with a dark brown stripe down the middle of her back; she advanced faster than the others, staying low to the ground. She watched the small war hammer swinging around in a circle, focused on any change in its path. This was exactly what Gurril wanted her to focus on.

9

One word kept creeping into Snick's head. *Ice.* Over and over again, the single word, sometimes coupled with the image of a frozen lake, came into her mind. Snick had never seen snow. She wasn't exactly sure what ice even was, but the mental image of a frozen lake helped her understand.

She so far had four types of mixes ready. The first was a combination of a healing cream and a bit of the coagulant she had used to save Atticus. The second was an anti-poison drink. Third was a thick cream that was extremely acidic, and could be whipped at an opponent's eyes. Finally, there was a strong poison. If she arrived in Hearthstone and found Gurril dead, she was determined to use the poison on herself. She had been forced away from her homeland for the second time; visions of her father being torn to bits by Mer as he drowned haunted her. If she found her love to be lost, she would have nothing left.

And now the vision of ice again. *Ice.* Even stronger now, *ICE!* She had no way to fight the word, the vision, or the urge. She knew it must be coming from Coska. She quickly determined that she would think of a way to mix up a powder to make ice. Then, thinking about Coska, she decided to also make up a batch of a sticky ointment that would heal damage to trees.

In his courtyard, Coska called out to Snick. He called out the word *ice* and showed her pictures of what it looked like. Coska wasn't even sure why he wanted her to make a potion to freeze things, but he knew it was important. The tree that had once been a magician tried to focus on the message, and to forgo the pain that he felt as sharp, gnawing teeth finally started to tear through his fleshy bark.

Snick looked over her ingredients. She needed to make ice. How? She started to mix a few things together, and as she added ingredients, a general idea of how to do it came to her. Within minutes, she was mixing the powder.

Above her, David pumped his wings. He knew he couldn't make the coach stop, and he would have to time his flight perfectly to swoop inside of it. He positioned himself behind the coach, then pushed forward with a strong stroke of his wings and dove.

Inside the coach, Snick was focused on her potion. When the hawk flew into the window, he was moving nearly twenty miles an hour faster than the coach. He was nothing more than a gray and brown streak across the air in front of her, thudding hard into the unoccupied seat directly in front of Snick's face. She screamed in surprise and jumped, barely holding onto the powder she was mixing to make ice. David had knocked himself a bit loopy and swayed on the seat for a few seconds, regaining his composure.

She cooed out to him, and the bird loved the sound. He shook his body a bit and looked up at her adoringly.   He held a small bit of paper in his claw, and he dropped it and hopped away, then looked from the note to Snick. She put down her half-mixed potion, then read the note that Donatello had written.

Her eyes grew large and her mouth dropped open. She held a hand over her open mouth, and tears welled up in her eyes. Joseph! They had trusted him so! Immediately, the whole story came to her. A rat had befriended the old man in the prison tower. What had the real Joseph said his friend's name was? Snick tried to remember but couldn't; she thought that it had sounded like a little boy's name. The rat must have used the real story of Joseph to work his way into Hearthstone— that's why the records in the elders' chambers had backed it up. There was a rat, or more likely a whole mischief of them, attacking the town while she rode back.

Snick turned to David. "Take this back to Gurril!"

She turned the note over and scribbled *On my way with potions. Snick.* onto the back of the paper. She handed the paper to David, then kissed his head gently.

"Oh, you're a good bird!" she told him.

David the hawk turned and hopped out the window, taking flight.

Snick surveyed her potions. All the finished recipes were in tightly sealed, small wooden casks. She had just gone back to mixing when all hell broke loose inside the coach.

10

Joseph surveyed the town's population standing in a circle around him. He already felt like a king. He wanted to be there for victory against Gurril but had decided that his servants from the mischief should do most of the work; Joseph now wanted glory more than blood. He would wait until the battle of the mischief against Gurril was almost done, then light the thin fuse that ran out of the cannon. The fuse would burn down slowly enough that Joseph could slip out of the crowd and into shelter. The blast would kill the bulk town's population, and wipe out over half the buildings of Hearthstone. What remained would be enough food and shelter for the mischief to guarantee that they would never have to be hungry or cold again.

He watched as a few blocks up the main avenue of the town, the standoff between the three rats and Gurril continued.

Joseph kept growing more impatient. Where were the reinforcements? The rest of the mischief was almost completely unneeded at this point, but it was entirely possible that Gurril could pull off some feat of strength to beat the rats that occupied his home.

Joseph nervously observed the standoff, and said "Calm, people. Calm. We need to wait for them to get ready to turn on us."

He said this mostly to calm his own nerves. He stood there, matches in hand, ready to light the fuse. Nothing could save the town now, he knew. It was only time that stood between him and the final victory. He envisioned a town full of rats, a mischief that held real supremacy, able to raise armies against men. The rat wearing the skin of a man grew more and more thirsty for glory and power.

11

Jones gripped the bow staff hard, while the sentries watched him in the tree. The sentry in the training courtyard was on the far side of Coska, but would be too far away to reach Jones, while the sentry on the other corner of the house was behind the courtyard wall, separated from the fisher.

Jones jabbed straight down with the staff, remembering Gurril's lesson: this weapon works best to jab with, don't swing it like a bat. Jabbing is a movement that takes very little time and is hard to block. Swinging takes more time, and if your enemy sees you swing, he sees how open your body is. He has more time to block your blow or to deliver one of his own.

The downward jab struck the rat gnawing on the Coska tree in the back of the head. The rat was annoyed, but not injured. He turned and looked at Jones, hissing. Jones froze with fear, and simply stared back at the rat. The rat turned his head, and went back to chewing at the tree's bark. Jones jabbed down again as hard as he could, this time knocking the rat's head to the floor, so that its teeth chomped together with a loud *clack!*

The rat decided he had enough. First, he had to chew through this damned hard bark. Now, there was some jerk over his head, whacking him with a stick. The rat shimmied out from the tree trunk as the man above him started climbing the tree to get back to the roof. The rat stood on his hind legs, and reached up, grabbing the man's lower foot, just as he was about to mount the roof.

Jones had thought his scramble would bring him to safety. He was almost all the way up onto the roof, and about to pull up his right foot when he felt the two large, clawed paws wrap around it.

To himself, to the unseen friend he had in Pepper, and to his dead parents, Jones said, "No. No, please."

But the spirits he called to were of no help. The rat tugged down hard, and Jones reached for a handhold as his body was yanked off the roof and into the tree below.

Jones tumbled down through branches, breaking a few of them, and knocking the thick, waxy leaves off of others. He landed on top of the rat's head, smashing his balls between his body and the rat's thick skull. A blinding light of pain shot through him, and he remembered a bit of something that Coska had shown him, just before pleading to him to tell Gurril what he had seen. The vision had been of three rats tearing out Jones's bowels.

Jones landed on the floor with a thud after bouncing off the rat's skull. He knew that he would die soon, and he knew that he would die screaming. He panicked, and tried to push himself away from the rat on the floor next to him. The beast was taller than him by a foot when it stood on its hind legs. It looked to him and lifted its lips in a sick cross between a smile and a snarl, pink venom dripping from its long, pointed teeth. A second rat ran in from the courtyard, and hissed at Jones. The third rat climbed over the courtyard wall, and came into the house through the back door.

Jones looked to his left at the hole in the floor and thought about rolling into it. He could defend himself from there. Just as he began his roll, the rat that had been chewing on the tree shot out one clawed paw into the fisher's stomach. The pain was immediate and like fire. The rat tore downward, opening Jones's body cavity the way a child tears open a paper candy wrapper.

Jones looked down at himself, seeing his guts revealed in front of him. He bled surprisingly little, and was fascinated by the way his bowels and stomach seemed to flex and curl. He lay back on the floor, unable to move himself with so many of his core muscles torn away, and watched up at the ceiling as the three rats converged over him, eating the organs of his digestive track while the man slowly died screaming in agony.

12

He didn't hear the scream from inside the house, but Gurril knew that Jones was dead when the three rats he held at bay were joined by three more, fresh blood dripping from their chops. It was now Gurril versus six rats, and Gurril could hobble, at best. He decided it was time to accept fate, that he would be the next human to go, and that the town was most likely lost.

He still swung the small war hammer over his head, while keeping the medium hammer held ready to strike.

The rats took up a circle around the warrior, and Snarl said to her companions, "One, two—"

There was another loud thump, similar to the one Gurril had heard earlier that day in the alley. David the hawk had decided to rejoin the battle.

The female stopped her count when she saw that the rat to her right had just been set upon by the damned hawk. The bird dove down, smashed into the rat's face, and had plucked out both of his eyes. The rat lay screaming in the street, rolling back and forth. David screeched with fury at the group of rats.

The smaller male rat to Snarl's left stood on its hind legs and looked up at the hawk as it flew away, and Gurril quickly lowered the arc of his small war hammer, bashing the smaller rat in the side of the neck. The rat fell to the ground, injured, but still able to fight. The four remaining rats advanced quickly toward Gurril, tackling him. He had the chance to score one blow to the female's stomach with his medium hammer, knocking out a sea of vomit from her as she came to tackle him. Gurril was covered with partially chewed, half digested body parts of dead town folk. Four rats covered him, snapping at his arms, legs, and body. He punched and kicked, rolling so that he was on top of one of the rats, using his small hammer's handle to choke the thing. Gurril was roughly pulled off the rat and dragged into the house.

13

The four horses had been run and run. They could only take so much. The coachman knew this, but the spell he was under made him forget to care about it. The horses knew this, but the spell they were under made them wish for death from exhaustion. The lead horse on the left side got his wish.

The animal's heart exploded in his chest, but his legs kept moving for a brief few seconds before the animal fell. As it fell, just a mile now outside of Hearthstone, the horse behind it tripped on it. The two horses on the other side were tied to these two, and they were pulled down as well. When the coach's front wheels hit the pile of horses, they instantly went from over thirty miles per hour to zero. The back of the coach, however, was a slave to physics and had to keep moving.

The first thing the coachman sensed after watching the horses pile up in front of him was being thrown forward. He flew from his seat onto the horses, smashing head-to-head into one of the poor beasts. The man's skull was crushed and his neck broken; he was dead in moments.

Inside the coach, Snick felt her world suddenly turn upside down. She was held in her seat by the centripetal force of the flipping vehicle and watched the landscape outside her window suddenly spin so that for a fleeting second the sky was below the ground. It was only as the coach was smashing top-first into the road in front of the pile of dead and dying horses that Snick was thrown from her seat.

Wooden casks of potions careened around the passenger compartment, and one of them smashed hard into the side of Snick's head. As she flew from her seat, she bounced off the walls of the coach's interior compartment, then was thrown out the side window. She skidded unconscious across the dirt road, finally rolling the last few feet as the destroyed coach came to rest another twenty feet away from her.

Her body, every inch of it, stung when she came to. Snick pushed herself up and out of the gravel, surveying the scene in front of her. Dead horses piled together with crying horses. The body of the coachman, his head caved in. Casks lying around the road side. Finally, the utterly destroyed coach, smashed to pieces near her.

She looked down at her body. She had changed into her traditional garb while on her home island, and was still wearing the small top and bottom which offered no protection from a crash on a gravel road. Blood oozed from her scraped off skin; most of her front side had been turned into a painful road rash when she skidded across the ground at high speed.

Snick walked to the casks, picking them up one by one. She had just packed the ice powder into a cask, but didn't know which was which. She would have to open them and look, then label them. She went to work quickly on this task, knowing that the last mile or so of her trip would be on foot. She looked down to her feet, wondering where her shoes had gone in the crash. She looked around for them as she picked up casks, but couldn't find them. They lay hidden under the bottom of the coach's remains.

14

There were now four rats around Gurril. They had thrown him onto his couch, and piled on top of him, holding him down. Gurril could hear David screeching outside. The hawk knew as well as Gurril did that it could not stage effective attacks inside the house. It would have to orbit the structure, waiting to pick off a rat if any tried to exit.

Gurril could see that Snarl was the group's leader. Her fur was now stained with vomit, and she breathed down on Gurril.

"Tell us where Pepper went!"

Gurril shook his head. "No. You'll know when he gets here, though."

He hoped the bluff would work. The rats were keeping him alive so that they could find the ferret. Gurril hoped that Pepper really was on his way. The ferret had been trained well and would even the fight.

Snarl curled back her teeth and hissed at him. "You can be bitten and tortured, Evil Man."

Gurril looked down at Jones's body on the floor before him. The man stared ahead with wide, dead eyes. He was whole down to his shoulders. Then, about where the top of his rib cage would have been, there was nothing but a mess of fleshy scraps and blood, with the man's spinal column still whole but visible. His body became whole again at his hips. Gurril swallowed hard, looking at the pale face of Jones, a snarl of pain imprinted on his dead lips.

He looked up at Snarl, and a vision of the various body parts she had vomited onto him flashed through his mind. A man's hand, a baby's arm, an unknown person's tongue.

He stared silently at her for a few moments, then simply said, "You'll know when he gets here."

She narrowed her eyes at him, then turned to the other rats. She had dealt with others such as this before. Mostly rats that had plotted against the mischief leaders, but also a human or two who had been plucked off the road while wandering from town to town. The only way to get the truth from him was to feign disbelief of his story. Her disinterest in him would make him think that whatever he knew they knew, and that the rats really didn't need his knowledge for anything but to confirm their intelligence. She looked to the rats beside her, and spoke quickly.

"He won't tell us anything we don't already know. Mook—"

Gurril saw a younger male rat perk up when she spoke this name to him.

"Go check on Billy. Give him the signal to start the cannon. We'll finish here, then meet up with Billy to give him what we planned."

A realization occurred to Gurril. When they spoke of Billy, they spoke of the cannon. Billy, Gurril realized, was Joseph, and Joseph *was a rat*.

15

Joseph watched Gurril's house with joy. They had gang-tackled the warrior, then dragged him into the house. Hopefully, they could figure out where Pepper was so that they would know whether or not he was a threat. The reinforcements still hadn't come, but Joseph did not grow concerned. Regardless of when the reinforcements arrived, it seemed the town was his.

He watched the house, noting that on the outside, one rat lay dead, and another was still writhing in the streets, blind. Mook, a young male, stepped out of the house, looked down at the crowd of people, and croaked out something that sounded like a cross between a howl and a roar.

Joseph smiled. The warrior's home was far enough away that the blast wouldn't kill the rats there. He turned to the cannon, ready to light its fuse. As he walked into the building, he felt a hard blow to the back of his head, knocking him to the ground. The old man stood up as the crowd around him gasped. He saw David the hawk flapping his wings and pulling himself high into the sky. The damned bird had pounded into him and torn a bit of his skull open. Behind Joseph, a man holding a pitchfork saw a scrap of paper on the ground. He picked it up. On one side, it said "On my way with potions. Snick." On the other side, in different handwriting, it said "Joseph = big fucking rat."

The man called to Joseph. "Hey, Joseph, where are the elders?"

The shaking old man with the now bleeding scalp stopped and turned to the man with a pitchfork. He licked his lips and said in a small voice, "They ate them."

He pointed up to Gurril's house.

The man tucked the note into his pocket, and put a questioning look on his face. "How did you get away, Joseph?"

Joseph grimaced. "Look, I can tell you all about it later. Now, we have to light the cannon!"

He turned back toward the small building that housed the weapon, and the man with a pitchfork put his hand on Joseph's shaky shoulders, holding him back. Joseph turned to face him again, and noticed that a few other townsfolk had gathered around this man who questioned him.

The man pointed his pitchfork at Joseph. "I think we need to know right now, Joseph."

The crowd watched as an amazing thing began to happen. The old man Joseph began to shake more and more, unable to hold his human form under the pain of his scalp wound and the stress of being interrogated while trying to focus on the battle. They heard crunching sounds as his teeth began growing long and his bones lengthened. The crowd backed away, watching a shaky old man turn into a rat.

16

Snick had gathered all of her casks and put them into a bag that she slung over her shoulder. She looked sadly to the dead coachman and four horses, two of which had died and two of which suffered from broken legs and other mortal injuries.

"I'm sorry," she said softly as a tear rolled down her cheek, creating one thin streak of clean skin. She turned and began jogging down the gravel road, the rocks of the surface biting into her feet unapologetically as she went.

She felt the bottom of her feet tear and had to grit her teeth hard against the pain. She turned to look behind her and saw a trail of bloody footprints. The urge to cry hit her hard, and she tried not to think about the small rocks that crammed their way into her flesh and the blood that marked her path.

A curve lay in front of her, and as she jogged, she looked over to the soft grass field beside her. She moved from the road to the grass and kept jogging, thankful for the relief the soft green blades gave to the soles of her feet. The only thing that kept her from breaking into a full run was knowing she would have to pace herself if she was going to make it without collapsing from exhaustion. Now that the grass cushioned her feet, the sting of long, deep scrapes over the rest of her skin set in. Every time she moved her body, her skin seemed to crack open, and the cool air stung her exposed flesh.

She followed the road, then saw if she turned to her right she could cut through the field, cross a small stream, and be to town quicker than the route the road took. She veered off, taking the cross-country route. The grass of the field felt even more kind beneath her feet than the grass near the road, and she was thankful that the pain she had felt in her feet at the beginning of her jog was over.

Near the stream, she saw what at first looked like a bale of cotton. She slowed, crossed the stream and realized that it was fur she was looking at, not cotton. The fur was not much more than a bloody lump, and she knew by its size that it had to be Pepper. The pain of her scraped skin, embedded with gravel and dirt, went away as soon as she saw the wounds on her friend.

The gigantic ferret lay still in front of her. At first, she took him to be dead, and was about to wail as her heart broke. As fresh tears began to follow the streambeds of her previous tears down her dusty, scraped face, she saw the ferret shift just a bit. He wasn't dead, she realized; he was just injured and had passed out from shock.

Quickly, she moved to him and knelt down at his side, shaking him gently. "Pepper, Pepper! It's me. It's Snick."

He opened his swollen eyes, and looked at her sweetly. He smiled. He took in one deep breath, and managed to say, "Hi, beautiful."

"Oh, Pepper! Let me help you. I've got a cream here that can heal you."

She dropped her bag and dug deep into one of her casks, pulling out a handful of cream and pushing it into the wounds that covered Pepper's body. The healing began immediately, and Pepper's eyes flew open.

"I have to share a vision!" he shouted to her. "Quickly! If I don't share it, I'll die."

Snick's eyes widened. "What is it Pepper?"

17

Gurril sat under a pile of rats, who held him down roughly. Mook, the young male, came back into the house and nodded to the female.

She turned to Gurril. "All right, Human." Although Snarl knew Gurril's name, she chose to insult him with this word, *human*. She spit the word at him, as if it was poison that might blind his eyes or burn his skin. "We want to know two things from you. Where did the tree send the ferret, and how do we kill the tree?"

Gurril shook his head and tried to bite the rats that held him down. Snarl laughed.

"We're supposed to bite you. I'll tell you what. I'll let you know what we're doing, and you can let us know what you and Pepper have planned. Maybe then we won't pull out your guts like we did to him." She motioned to Jones's corpse. "I don't like to keep you alive. So here's the other part of the bargain. Once you do tell us what you know, we'll make your death quick. I promise."

Gurril grunted anger and spat at the female rat. She laughed again.

"In a few minutes, the town will be destroyed. Everyone will be dead. There will be nothing to save. All right, now tell us where we can find the ferret and what your plan with him was. Then we can talk about that nasty tree over there."

18

Billy's transformation from Joseph was completed. He lay on a pile of shredded clothes in the center of the crowd, drawing in deep breaths as he fought the pain that had gripped him when he transformed. Somewhere unseen to the rat, a woman screamed. He heard her footfalls as she ran away. A small snarl of a smile passed Billy's lips as he thought of the woman being caught by the reinforcements (which surely had to be on the way soon) and eaten.

He rolled from his side to his stomach, the crowd gasping at every move. He struggled to stand, thankful that these village hicks were so in awe of him that not a single one had thought to stick a pitchfork or fillet knife into him.

They watched him gain his feet, standing on his hind legs so that he was taller than any of the crowd and kicking off the remnants of the cotton pants he had worn. He swept out a claw at the man who had questioned him earlier, knocking the pitchfork from the man's hands. Billy hissed as menacingly as he could at the crowd, and a few more people ran off in fear. Still, no one approached him. Billy growled, and the crowd backed away.

From his right, a man rushed at him with a knife used to skin deer. Billy whacked the man's hand away and chomped down on his shoulder, tearing the flesh open and injecting his venom into the man, who fell in a howl of pain and surprise. A few of the other people in the crowd, mostly men, but a few boys and women as well, began to encroach upon him. Most held small weapons like knives, but a few had pikes or pitchforks.

He quickly jabbed out a hand and plucked away a pitchfork from a strong young man, turning the tines toward the crowd, but fumbling a bit with the handle. He had grown used to human hands, and the adjustment back to paws was a bit awkward.

Two men rushed at him, and the crowd seemed to follow their lead. Billy dipped and rotated his body left, jamming the pitchfork into one of the men, while the other man swung wide with his fillet knife. Billy kicked up a back leg, tearing the man's legs open with his back claws. Blood poured from the attacker's femoral artery as he sunk to the ground. The man who had been impaled by the pitchfork fell to his back, the handle of the farm tool standing straight in the air like a bare flag pole.

Four more people piled on Billy now. He bit one in the head, tearing most of the flesh from the flabby man's face, and with one swipe of his claws, took out two other humans' throats. The fourth attacker, a young woman, managed to stab Billy in the upper right arm with a bread knife. It didn't do much real damage, but it did sting and annoy the rat.

A few more attackers stood near Billy, threatening him (ineffectively) with their pitchforks and knives. He counted them off as he stood his ground, growling and bleeding only slightly, while around him lay the bodies of six humans, dead or dying. Billy inventoried the weapons he faced; four pitchforks, one knife, and a club used for bludgeoning fish. Billy growled deep, knowing that he could easily kill every one of these people. The rest of the crowd either ran away or stood far off, gawking and ready to run. He counted one last attacker: a small boy with a short whip. Billy wondered where in the hell such a boy would get a whip, then refocused on his task at hand.

Billy lifted his right leg as if to take a short burst on foot that way, but dropped to his left side, using the fake-out move to roll over and take out two attackers' feet with his claws. He stayed low on all fours, as the other five attackers repositioned themselves. One of the two he had taken out was the knife holder, the other had a pitchfork. These weapons lay useless in the street as their previous, soon to be dead, owners rolled and crawled away from him.

Billy let the two escape, knowing he could blood trail them later. The young boy, now standing behind Billy, cracked his whip at the junction of Billy's tail and body. The snap hurt sharply, and Billy spun around to face the boy. The attacker with the club jumped onto Billy's back, bringing the bludgeon down with a hard *whack* on the top of Billy's head. The rat saw stars for a moment, then reached up and pulled the attacker off him, smashing the man head-first into the street. The man's neck cracked in a way that satisfied Billy, and the rat stood back onto his hind feet, directly on the dead man's chest. He leaned forward and roared at the boy with the whip, who cracked it again at Billy's open mouth. The sharp pain this time was a spot on his upper lip, just below his nose. It cut Billy's roar short, and the rat's eyes popped wide with surprise for an instant. He snarled at the boy, quietly growling. The boy backed off, past the range of the whip.

Billy turned away from the boy and saw that the three remaining pitchfork holders were running at him. He swiped two away with his front paws, but the third scored a blow, sinking the pitchfork deep into Billy's ribs under his right arm. The human tried to rip the pitchfork back out, but the tines were locked between the rat's ribs.

The two other men stood up and retrieved their weapons. Behind Billy, another crack of the whip zinged his left leg. Damn, but that hurt! Billy turned quickly around and hissed at the boy. The boy flung his whip again, and this time, Billy poked out a paw and the whip wrapped around his arm. He jerked the boy forward, meaning to bite his head off as the boy flew toward Billy's mouth.

Just before clamping down on the boy's skull, Billy felt two strong sensations. One was a deep striking pain in his back. The other was a cutting at his skull. The two men who had picked their pitchforks up both stabbed Billy from behind with them, and now three of the objects stuck out from his body. He reached wildly behind him as the boy who should have been headless by now took off running for home, trembling not with fear, but pride to be a hero for the day.

As he reached wildly, Billy looked up to the sky and saw the damned hawk, David, pushing his way into the blue

295

overhead. Billy roared at the hawk, still trying to grasp at the pitchforks that had impaled him from behind. As he roared, the two men who had stabbed him decided the boy was probably right at this point to run.

One man turned to the other and said quickly as he began taking flight, "Let Gurril finish him, we've done plenty!"

Billy turned a circle, looking around him. Every human was either dead at his feet or had run home in fear. He stopped turning, and decided that his companions would have to remove the pitchforks from his hide. Billy turned and walked into the small building that housed the cannon, looking like a cross between an overgrown child's stuffed toy and a pin cushion.

19

Gurril shook his head. "I don't know anything else. Just that we were supposed to meet by the docks if Pepper got caught. We were going to take a boat down the river and to the southern sea. From there, we'd go to Flamingo and meet up with Snick. Really. That's the whole plan."

He hoped the lie would work. The rats seemed to think about it, looking back and forth to each other.

Snarl grabbed two of the others and took them into the kitchen. Gurril heard them discussing things for a few seconds, and was amazed at how advanced the beasts were. They planned, they schemed, they knew that sometimes it was good to trust, and other times it was folly. Would they know he was lying?

The three rats that had been conferring came back into the living room. Snarl hissed at Gurril, and said, "You lie!" She turned to the others. "Hold him down, and we'll kill him slowly. I'm tired of him."

The gang of rats yanked Gurril to the floor, and one of the males urinated on him. Gurril, being a bit of an optimist, thought to himself that at least the vomit from the female was getting washed off. Every rat except Snarl held him down. She, being the group's obvious leader, stretched one single claw from her front left paw. She snarled at Gurril, growled deep in the back of her throat (a sound that conveyed the sensuous feeling this violence gave her), and poked the claw deep into Gurril's left bicep.

Gurril grunted and clenched his teeth against the pain. The female rat twisted her claw back and forth a bit, and Gurril flared his nostrils wide as more pain set in. She looked into his eyes, and for a moment he thought she would ask him more questions, give him more time to stall. Instead, she tore downward, ripping his left bicep open from near the shoulder all the way to the pit of his elbow. The flesh folded over on either side of the wound, and blood spurted out. Gurril looked down, and could see the muscle of his arm laid apart like two cuts of fresh red steak in a butcher shop window. He finally screamed in pain and fear. The female rat purred at the sound of Gurril's cries, the thick fur at the front of her neck vibrating in quick little pulses of passion as her claw penetrated deeper into his flesh.

20

Billy walked into the little building, the pitchforks protruding from him clunking on the door frame. He stumbled a bit, and stepped up to the cannon. The building was a small hut with walls that could be opened to large windows, so that the cannon would be inside the building, aiming at an enemy through a hole in the wall— or so he had told the town when he convinced them to build the weird weapon. Billy thanked his stars that he had inherited, absorbed, or otherwise gained such engineering knowledge from Seth when he ate the man's corpse.

The cannon was stuffed in the front of the barrel with a huge chunk of iron that was welded into the barrel, sealing it. Billy knew that doing this would capture the pressure of the explosive charge in the rear of the weapon, but he told the men who built it that this would only hold the chunk in place until the cannon was fired. With that chunk, the cannon became a pressure vessel, and Billy intended to make it explode.

A fuse ran from the rear of the cannon to the floor, where it coiled upon itself. The fuse was about six feet long. Billy had a hard time creating a fuse that would burn at an even rate, so he made the fuse far longer than needed in order to have enough time to escape the upcoming blast.

He reached for the box of matches that lay behind the cannon and sniffed the sulfur tip of one. It was a good smell, and Billy liked the idea of sulfur. It was poison, it burned, and it was in his fingertips. He stretched the fuse out long. It ran in a straight line almost to the door. It was a bit awkward to bend and move with the pitchforks skewering him, but Billy was able to fumble around enough to get the job done. When the fuse was stretched, he sighed, looking at the cannon with a sort of reverence. With all the townsfolk gone to their homes, far fewer would be killed in the blast, but at least none of them would be around to put out the fuse, either.

Billy struck the match against the handle of the pitchfork that stuck out from his right side, and touched the hot flame to the end of the fuse. He stepped back, turning to run to Gurril's house as he heard the fuse hiss. He bounced off the door frame again on his way out, the handles of the pitchforks wobbling to and fro. Billy looked forward to having the other rats pull the weapons out of his hide. He would bleed a bit, but none of the farmers' tools had done any serious damage. And they all stung far less than that damned whip. Billy promised himself again that he would chew the head off the boy who had cracked the stinging rope of leather at him.

He hustled himself up the street to Gurril's house, not seeing another soul as he went. From behind, he was struck once more by David the hawk, but Billy just stuck his head down and kept running on his back legs. Because of the pitchforks, he was unable to go to all fours, where his speed would have been better. Fresh blood ran from the back of his head as the hawk thumped at him again and again. Billy reached up for the infernal beast, but had no luck. The agile and quick bird easily dodged every swipe of a clawed paw, returning to attack the rat's head repeatedly.

Gurril lay on the floor, both biceps and the fronts of both thighs now laid open by Snarl's claws. He lay shaking in a pool of blood, looking from his own wounded body to the gutted corpse of Jones beside him. The female rat was about to start carving Gurril's face. The claw poked out and hovered above him, and she licked her lips, heaving heavy breaths as her eyes lit up with a new round of passion for this task.

The door burst open, and all the rats jumped up from Gurril and turned to face any attackers. Normally, this would have allowed Gurril to spring up and fight them, but with his muscles torn apart and in many places separated from his bone, the best he could do was force his mind to send unusable signals to his body, telling it to move but receiving no action in return.

The rats had turned to see Billy in the doorway, looking like some sort of rat-shaped cactus with three pitchforks sticking out of him. Two of the five started laughing, but stopped quickly when Billy snapped his jaws at them. Gurril couldn't recognize Billy; there was nothing about him that looked like Joseph. Billy saw Gurril down on the floor and turned to him. The other rats in the room parted as he addressed the warrior. He snarled a rat smile at Gurril.

"Do you know me, Gurril?" He started to feign shaking his body, and spoke in the voice of the old man. "I'm Joseph, the poor old man from prison." He went back to his normal stature, and kicked Gurril in the side with his back foot. "Ha! You fool! This town will die, because you were so damned trusting! You and your loyalty are the reason we will conquer the humans today! Your blind loyalty will be the reason the rats establish a foothold in Hearthstone and attack other humans village by village!" The rat turned his head high and howled.

Snarl approached him. "Billy, is the cannon activated?"

"Yes. I lit the fuse. It should go off any minute now. Half the town will be wiped out."

She snarled a smile at him. "Good." She stepped over to Billy, and wrapped her front paws around one of the pitchfork handles. "Does this hurt?"

"Yes. Take it out."

"Of course."

There was something in her voice that Gurril recognized. In an instant, he knew what it was: the blood passion she had been feeling as she tore his body to ribbons. The female rat lunged her body weight forward instead of back, sinking the pitchfork deeper into Billy instead of pulling it out. Billy screamed in pain, and looked at the female in disbelief. She snarled at him, growled, and repeated her motion. Inside of Billy's body, the tine penetrated his heart and lung. He felt his breath begin to escape him, and he was unable to take in another breath.

  Billy opened his mouth and reflexively tried gulping in air, but nothing was happening, other than him making a light "Hup!" sound every time his body tried to breath. His insides began to feel hot as the blood from his heart escaped into the rest of his body cavity. He felt heavy, and now began to cough out thick gobs of blood.

  Snarl knew Billy was dying, and she stepped away, watching him sink to the floor. As he fell, he lost his balance, and tipped into the hole that Gurril and Jones had used for a trap. Billy landed with a thud, breaking off one of the pitchfork handles. The pitchfork that had projected from the back of his head poked in deeper when Billy fell, penetrating into the portion of his brain that controlled his vision. From the bottom of the hole, the world turned a dull pink shade. Billy looked up, trying to remember why he had known he would see pink as his life ended. He turned his head and looked at the female, blood pouring like a river now from his mouth and nose. The hole in the floor filled with his blood and he died there, alone and trapped.

Chapter 9: Death from a Thousand Bites and Other Visions

1

Coska could see the hunk of iron as it flew through the air. In his vision, it was white hot, long, and thin. It whipped end-over-end through the air at Gurril as he choked a rat from behind, using the handle of a war hammer like a baton. Now, in real life and real time, Gurril lay on the floor of the house filleted like a trout. His arms and legs had been laid wide open, and blood poured from his wounds. Coska knew that Billy had lit the cannon, and now had to decide: Should he let his friend suffer, or talk to him and give him a bit of comfort, knowing the vision would happen not quite as Coska had seen it, but the chunk of iron would still kill Gurril quickly, putting him out of his misery.

Coska loved Gurril. He had loved him like a brother for a long time. Now he loved him like a son. Coska had learned a great many things as he became more of a tree and less of a man. There was a sort of harmony in the air and soil, and he absorbed it and let it nourish him. He supposed that it came from the same connection that allowed him to change animals from one form to another when he had been a human.

He saw things now not with eyes but with that harmony that flowed through him. He saw Pepper and Snick, but not where they were. He only saw that they were together, and that they might be able to help Gurril. He saw the young boy who had whipped Billy, but not what he looked like. He only saw the boy's fear finally flowing out of him as he cried in his mother's arms, learning the real price of being a hero is that the fear you should have felt in battle comes creeping up on you later, when you should feel safe.

Coska saw and felt these things. He saw and felt the rats, like black blots of cancer on flesh. One lay dying slowly in the street near the ale house, its brains leaking from the back of its head. One lay dying in the street outside this house. Two rats were dead inside the house, as well. One of them was Billy, dead in the hole that Jones had dug. Billy, who had fooled even Coska when he posed as Joseph. Billy, who had absorbed magical power from Coska's body the same way Pepper had.

301

The day that Coska's power had shot out of him in a great stream, the magician understood finally how powerful he really was. The stream of magic had been about half of what the young man had possessed. When it struck Pepper, it filled him as much as it could, and had to go to yet another source. It bounced, unseen, to the rat across the field. If Billy had absorbed enough power to turn himself into Joseph, to absorb wits from Seth, and to turn other rats into humans, then Pepper had to have absorbed power well beyond what he had shown. The ferret, Coska now realized, was either holding back or had no idea just how powerful he was.

Five rats now stood around Gurril. Coska decided that instead of guaranteeing his friend a swift death, instead of comforting him with his words and friendship, he would try to keep him alive (and yes, suffering) until Pepper and Snick could arrive to help him. He knew they would come, but did not know if they would make it in time. Even if they did make it into town before Gurril bled to death, they might arrive just in time to be blown to bits by the cannon. Coska turned his thoughts to the rats and began poking into their minds.

2

Pepper gulped down water from the stream, then sat up and looked to Snick. "Coska told me that I would suffer a death from a thousand bites."

"That's terrible!"

"Yeah, it was. I had to wait until I had been bitten, then I had to tell someone. I just assumed that I had to tell Gurril; I don't know why. But I think you'll do."

"I hope so," she said as she stroked the fur on the top of his head. Every move she made tore her scrapes open again, and she winced in pain. Pepper took another drink of water from the stream and looked at her scraped up body.

"What the hell happened to you? You look like my brother Remmy after he got covered in fleas. Except a lot prettier." He smiled his large toothy grin at Snick.

She laughed at him in spite of her pain, and said, "I was in a coach that crashed badly."

"Crashed badly. I think that may be putting it lightly."

302

"Maybe later I'll show it to you."

She tried to stand, and winced again at the pain of her body. She was beginning to stiffen up, her muscles and skin trying to make her rest so she could heal. She sat back down.

"I don't know if I can go on, Pepper."

"Of course you can! You've got the healing cream."

He reached toward the cask, and she pulled away from him.

"No!" she said sternly. "Gurril might need it!"

"I may be furry, but I'm not your dog. Don't tell me 'no' like that."

She returned this scolding with a shameful look.

Pepper continued. "Gurril *will* need us. *Both* of us. I need you to be in good working order, Snick. If he needs to be healed, we'll deal with it when we get there. In the meantime, we need to just get there."

She nodded, and slowly pushed the cask toward Pepper.

He scooped out a handful of the healing cream in his paw, smiled at Snick, and said, "Now, I finally get to rub you all over!"

Within minutes, she was peeling the flakes of dried blood off her skin while Pepper swung her pack of casks over his shoulder. There was still a bit of healing cream left, but not much. If Gurril was injured badly, she didn't know what she would do. Pepper turned to her. "Ready?" She nodded to him. "Then let's go. You set the pace, and I'll only run as fast as you."

"Shouldn't you go as fast as you can?"

They started off, and Pepper shook his head. "No. It will probably be best if we get there together. I may need you, and you may not want to walk into a battle alone behind me."

"I noticed you don't have any weapons."

"Nope. Left my sword with my wallet and house key back at Gurril's place. Guess I was just anxious to go to work this morning."

She giggled, then scolded him. "Quit making me laugh, it slows me down."

They jogged toward town silently for a bit. Pepper played out battle scenarios in his head, trying to figure out the

303

best way to approach the rats, and wondering how he would get his hands on a weapon. His broad sword would be best, but anything would do. Gurril had been careful to teach the ferret how to handle most weapons well. Pepper visualized the way Gurril had taught him. He thought about where to strike rats with different weapons and which hand-to-hand techniques would work best if there was a group of them in close quarters.

Snick thought of Gurril. She went over the ingredients to make more healing cream, remembering that everything she had besides the casks was smashed to bits with the coach. She would have to make some trips into the forest to gather what she needed if more healing cream was called for. Snick wondered about the town and if everyone was all right. She hoped that Coska had made it; the poor tree had no defenses.

After a bit of jogging, Pepper turned to Snick. "So, did Coska have any visions for you to share?"

She smiled at the thought of her vision, and hoped she could get to Gurril in time to tell him about it. "One. But I can't tell you. I can only tell Gurril."

"Can I listen when you tell him?"

"I think so." She smiled again as they ran toward town, her hawk, the cannon, a magic tree, and her love.

3

David spat a hunk of Billy's fur from his beak as he circled the town from high above. Small puffs of smoke came from the building where the big iron thing they called a "cannon" was. He could see Pepper and Snick about three quarters of a mile away, jogging toward town. He could no longer hear Gurril screaming in his cottage. The hawk took this sadly to mean that the warrior was dead. He changed direction and looked down on Coska, who stood safely in his courtyard. For some reason, the rats hadn't gone back to attacking the tree. David decided to investigate the cannon first, then fly out to greet Snick and Pepper as they worked their way across the fields and into town.

The hawk loved to dive (as all hawks do). He sped toward earth at extremely high speed, then threw out his wings and cupped the air beneath him. Had he been hunting a small

304

animal (or attacking a rat), he would have rammed directly into his target at around seventy miles per hour. The way it was, he touched down just inside the doorway to the cannon's house at slightly under five.

The hawk hopped around the floor, smelling the air as the fuse slowly burned. The thin, whitish twine of the fuse had grown wet with dew the previous morning and had been in the shadows until the attack. It still hadn't dried off, and burned slowly. Only about two feet of the fuse was gone. David noted this, and thought it would be best if he made sure to show the fuse to Pepper and Snick when they got to town. He flew up to the rear of the cannon, flitted his tail a bit, and dropped waste on the line of fuse. The hawk understood that the rat had lit this fire, and that wet things made fire slow or made it die. The hawk wanted to do anything that would counter whatever the rats did.

After his waste was emptied from his body, he noted that the fuse kept burning, but had indeed slowed down even more. He pumped his wings, and flew toward where he had seen Pepper and Snick running. He made the flight in quick time, swooping down over them to say hello. Snick smiled and waved, and Pepper hollered in joy. The hawk circled them once, then flew back to Gurril's house to check to see if the warrior really was dead.

4

The rats stopped attacking Gurril. There were no more claws pushed against his arms and legs, no more being held down; nothing. They simply stood there, staring at Coska. Gurril lay on the floor, unable to move. He felt warm blood flowing out of him and knew that the dizzy feeling he had was from that blood loss. If he didn't get help soon, his end was near.

Coska focused on the five rats. He sent them dazzling images of other worlds, visions of events the tree would know to happen in a million different planets and places. It was filling their minds up to the point where they could only stand and watch the many colors and sounds swirl by them. The five rats were locked in a daze, and Coska focused on keeping their minds trapped. He wouldn't be able to hold it for long, but he knew the others were now not far away.

David circled low and slow over the house, observing as much as he could. Everything was quiet. He decided to do a flyby below the roof level to look into the door of the house. Maybe he could see inside. As he cruised by, he peeked into the doorway and saw Gurril lying completely still, and the rats gathered in front of the Coska tree in the tiny courtyard. David took this to mean that the rats had finished off Gurril and were about to start chewing on Coska.

He pumped his wings and flew high, so that he could survey the entire scene. Pepper and Snick were still jogging toward town, closer but still not close enough. The puffs of smoke still rolled out of the small building housing the cannon. The population of the town lay dead in the streets, dead in their homes, or hiding away in locked rooms. He swooped downward, gliding into the courtyard and landing in the Coska tree. He peered at the rats, noticing that they stood with glazed, dumbfounded eyes. All five stared at Coska, their mouths agape. Even though each of them had all four paws planted on the floor, they looked as if they were ready to tip over.

David faced a choice, and he considered it long and with all the wisdom he could muster. He thought about attacking the rats, tearing out their eyes while they looked dazed at Coska. Or, he could fly past them and take a closer look at Gurril, to confirm whether or not the warrior was indeed dead. Coska knew the bird was considering these choices, but he could not break his concentration from the rats in order to communicate with David. Coska also knew that if the bird were to attack the rats, the violence and noise would break the spell he was holding over them.

5

Pepper and Snick jogged on, bringing the town closer with every stride. They could see the detail of buildings now, and Pepper pointed to the building that housed the cannon.

"Snick, it looks like there's no action in the streets, but a lot of dead bodies. All of the rats must be fighting Gurril in our house. One of us should go to the cannon to see if we can figure

306

out how Joseph was going to use it against us. The other of us should go to Gurril and help him fight."

She struggled to speak as she took heavy breaths to keep up her pace. "Yes. Wait... you knew about Joseph?" Big breath; lungs stinging.

"Yeah, he captured me before the battle even started. I'll tell you more later. I think he made the cannon to wipe out the town, not the rats."

She nodded, accepting this information as fitting with everything she had discovered on her journey. "You go to Gurril."

"Are you sure?" Pepper was having little trouble breathing; he was in better shape than Snick, and his body was built better for running.

"Yes," she huffed out. Her legs were on the verge of cramps. She took in another big breath as she went. "My potions..." she paused for a large, gasping breath, "are for healing and making ice." Another pause for another big breath, and Snick tasted a slight tinge of blood in the back of her mouth. "You fight."

"Ice?"

She nodded, not able to talk and breathe and jog at the same time any longer.

"Huh." They jogged on in silence a bit longer.

Pepper considered carrying Snick, but decided against it. He was already carrying her casks, and if he could keep her moving, they could keep up their current pace; carrying her would slow him down considerably. He had a million questions and (as usual) jokes about the situation, but he decided to stay silent. He could hear the way her breath rattled and knew she was pushing herself so hard that anything he said to break her stride, breathing pattern, or determination to keep going would cause her injury or collapse. She would need a lot of rest and attention after this day to avoid pneumonia.

They jogged on, and soon, they could see more details of the town. They would be arriving very close to the cannon. Pepper thought to himself that when they got there, he would find whatever weapons he could (he wished for, but did not expect to find, his sword), and head to Gurril's house. Pepper noted to himself that if he saw the hawk, and the bird was trying to lead him somewhere else, he'd follow David into battle.

The town looked empty. They could see a few dead figures lying in the streets here and there. Every home and building seemed closed and locked down. Windows were shuttered. People were too afraid, Snick realized, to even peek from their windows to see what was happening outside.

She knew Pepper saw the same thing when he told her, "They must be terrified, just waiting in their homes to be killed and eaten."

She nodded to him, and they ran on, leaving the wild field and coming now to the trimmed grass that marked the edge of Hearthstone. They slowed from a jog to a walk, and Snick put her hands on her hips, leaned forward, and vomited as she walked.

Pepper patted her on the back. "You did well to get here as fast as you did, Snick. Gurril is going to be proud of you when he hears the story."

She nodded, and kept stepping forward. Her breath rattled she tasted more blood. Her sides ached and cramped, and her bare feet throbbed. She had trouble standing up straight but motioned to Pepper to give her the pack with her small wooden casks in it. He obliged and within a few seconds, they arrived at the cannon.

The bodies on the street were a frightening sight to Snick. Pepper sighed, then saw a pitchfork lying on the cobblestones. He picked it up, quickly acquainting himself with the best way to wield it.

Snick walked into the building with the cannon, and managed enough extra breath to call out, "Pepper, come inside here!"

He trotted in quickly, pitchfork ready. He saw no rats, and immediately took notice of what Snick saw: the burning fuse. She pointed at it, tried to talk, but hacked out a few harsh coughs instead, doubling over and dry heaving. Pepper saw that about three feet of fuse remained, and he tried tugging it out of the end of the cannon. It didn't budge.

Snick, still doubled over, said to him, "My gel. It explodes with fire. The fuse…" She could say no more, and only pointed to the cannon as she hacked and coughed more.

6

David thought about the times when he hunted down prey. He knew when he was engaged in the hunt, he needed to focus. It made sense then, that Coska would need focus to keep these rats mentally busy (or stupefied, or whatever it was he was doing to them). He thought it was best then, to hop down and check on Gurril. He beat his wings twice, flying over the heads of the rats and landing near Gurril's head. The warrior turned his eyes to look at the bird. It hurt too badly to even *think* about turning his head, let alone actually performing the act.

David saw the man's eyes move. He was alive! By now, Pepper and Snick had to be close to if not already in town. He flew out the open door, and turned to head toward where he thought they would be. With just a few pumps of his wings, David landed just before the doorway. Pepper had just begun to chew at the fuse, trying to break through. He stopped after a few chomps, noting that all he had done was make his teeth sore.

David hopped in a few steps and chirped at them. They turned, and Snick smiled brightly.

"David!" she said with joy.

She was still breathing hard, but could now manage to say at least a few words without hacking and doubling over in pain. The hawk beat his wings once, landing on her shoulder and nuzzling his head to her cheek. He turned and looked to Pepper, then shrieked at the ferret. He flew from Snick's shoulder, and stopped on the street about ten feet outside the building.

Pepper turned to her. "He's leading me somewhere."

"How do I stop the cannon?"

"I don't know. I can't chew through it. Do you have anything sharp?"

"If you can't bite it, then it won't cut."

Behind them, David pierced the air with another shriek.

Pepper put his hands in the air in an *I don't know what to do* gesture, turned and ran toward the hawk, pitchfork at the

309

ready. As he ran, he cranked his head over his shoulder and yelled to her, "Try your potions!"

Gurril had seen the hawk hop up and examine him, then followed it with his eyes as best he could as it flew out of the house. He had no idea what the hawk was up to, but after watching how it had bravely attacked the rats earlier in the battle, he knew that having the hawk nearby was a good thing. He struggled and turned his head, watching as the rats stared at Coska. From behind them, he couldn't see that they were dazzled, and wondered what was going on.

The house was shrouded in the kind of dead silence that only a break in a battle can bring. Gurril's shallow breathing was the only sound breaking the current peace. After a day filled with noises of death and desperate fighting, he welcomed the sound of nothing but his own breath. The town outside was equally silent. All in all, Gurril thought if this was how he was to die, it was not the worst way to go. He hoped that he could get lucky and bleed to death before the rats turned around to face him again.

Pepper ran up the street, following David as the hawk flew ahead twenty feet, landed, and called. This went on, Pepper sprinting with the pitchfork, until the hawk landed just outside the house and hopped up onto something shiny on the street. Pepper surveyed the scene as he approached, then saw a glint of copper under the hawk's talons. The ferret's eyes widened as he realized that David stood upon the handle of his broadsword. Luck upon luck!

His pulse picked up at the sight of his beloved weapon, gifted to him by his best friend. He knew that in his palms the metal would feel warm from lying in the sun. Pepper, almost as dazzled by his sword as much as the rats were dazzled by Coska, absently dropped the pitchfork to the street, where it clanged uselessly. He bent and picked up the sword, relishing its weight. He had never felt such an attachment to an object before. He stroked the metal blade, and kissed it lightly, whispering "Thank you," to the hawk. David chirped back happily, then flew the final leg of their journey to the house. The red stone in the handle never seemed to gleam so brightly as Pepper squeezed the handle of the sword with his powerful hands. He breathed in deep through his nose, then out slowly through his mouth, an exercise Coska had taught him when he needed to calm himself.

Coska was exhausted. He couldn't hold the spell any longer, and the visions that dazzled the rats faded quickly. They all popped out of their haze at once, shaking their heads in a tired way. Snarl looked to her companions with tired eyes. She blinked hard twice, shaking the visions from her head for a final time.

A deep growl rattled in her throat, "Chew down that tree! He hypnotized us!" The other rats advanced on Coska, and she held one back, "Let's finish the warrior. I'm done playing with him!"

David stood on the street, watching Pepper stare at his sword as the warrior calmed himself and began to mentally prepare for battle. Inside the house, the rats stopped watching Coska and were moving again. The hawk squawked, and Pepper looked up from the sword. He held it in both hands the way a person might cling to a magic object gifted from unknown gods.

Coska felt mentally the way Snick had felt physically when she and Pepper had finally finished their run into town. Through his pain he registered that she was with the cannon, and he summoned the energy for one overriding signal to send to her. He concentrated and sent the signal to her in a blast of effort, while rats began to gnaw on the bark of his trunk.

Snick watched the fuse burn and dug through her casks. There had to be one in the pack that would help. With everything that had gone on during the day, she couldn't even remember the effect of the different mixes. Then, suddenly, one single and loud word screamed inside her head: *ICE!*

She grabbed her cask of ice powder and sprinkled it over the cannon. As soon as the two materials touched, a thin cracking noise occurred. She saw the iron of the cannon take on more of a shine then it previously had, and a thin layer of frost began to crawl across the cannon, creating a white film over the metal. It made light popping sounds as it moved, and beautiful, almost flower-like crystals appeared over the black iron surface. Snick realized that the metal would shatter into chunks of ice when it exploded. She was in a race against the fuse. Careful not to get any of the powder on her body, Snick continued

311

sprinkling the ice mix all over the cannon, freezing the beastly weapon until it stood completely frost-covered. About three inches of fuse remained, and Snick knew it was time to run.

She had been lucky to survive the first explosion, and that had been a far smaller amount of gel than was now packed into the back of the cannon. She turned and ran toward Gurril's house as fast as her cramped, burning legs could take her. Turning the cannon to ice would make it far less dangerous, but not harmless. Snick pictured huge chunks of ice flying through the air. The chunks would do much less damage than white-hot metal, but they would still be fatal if any struck her. She panicked as she ran.

Pepper was just about to enter the house when, behind him, Snick sprinted past the open door. Fear had taken hold of her, and she blindly ran as far away from the cannon as she could. Pepper barely heard the footsteps, his entire focus on the two rats about to eat Gurril. Snarl, the larger of the two rats, stuck out her tongue and ran it through a ghastly wound the man had on his right thigh. Even though his face was completely ashen and his body unable to move, the venom of her tongue being placed against his raw meat was enough to make him growl and grunt with pain. It was all the noise he could muster.

Pepper stepped into the door and the two rats near Gurril looked up at him. The ferret saw Gurril's eyes roll up to him, and the warrior seemed to have an odd look on his face. Pepper didn't understand what the look meant, but Gurril was trying to tell him: *Go away, stay safe, and don't sacrifice yourself for me; I'm already dead.*

Both rats rose to their hind legs, taking an intimidating stance against Pepper. They growled, and the ferret took in another deep breath, this one slightly shaky, to steady himself. He had never really fought a battle before, and fear filled him. He held his sword out before him and looked from rat to rat. They stepped forward, walking over Gurril. The living room was now the focus of another standoff.

The two rats came at Pepper together, and the ferret made a defensive swing of his sword, nicking Snarl over the ribs. She jumped back, and Pepper sidestepped the other rat. Now his back was to the hole in the living room floor. Pepper peeked over his back and saw Billy lying dead in the hole, skewered by pitchforks.

He turned back to the two rats and smiled. "Looks like he got his. Now who's next?"

The male rat charged Pepper again, and the ferret sidestepped him once more, driving the butt of his sword handle into the back of the beast's head. The rat fell forward to the floor near the edge of the hole, and Pepper spun around, kicking the rat in the side. He rolled down into the hole, landing safely on the bodies of his former mischief mates. Pepper moved away while the rat started to climb out. The three rats chewing through Coska's bark popped their heads up, and came into the living room to join the fray.

7

The three inches of fuse became two, then one. Finally, the ember that fizzed on the end of the tough rope of fuse disappeared inside of the cannon. For a brief second, smoke silently rolled out from the hole where the fuse had been.

Running as far as she could away from the cannon, Snick realized that she not only had passed Gurril's house, but was about to run into the edge of the river. She turned one corner and skidded to a halt. There in the street in front of her lay a rat with the back of its head caved in. It was face-down, and the thing's body still gently rose and fell with shallow breaths. All of a sudden, the world seemed to crack.

The gel exploded, and the ice/iron cannon shattered into a billion tiny pieces that shot off like cold little meteors. The blast wave of the explosion travelled through the ground just a bit faster than the sound wave travelled through the air. In Gurril's house, Pepper now faced four rats, with a fifth climbing from the hole in the floor. The blast wave hit the house hard enough to knock down Pepper and the four rats. Rat number five fell back into the hole.

The crack of the sound wave frightened Snick, and she screamed. The rat in front of her was as close to braindead as an animal could be. The stimulation of the sound wave, along with the shake that the blast wave provided, was more than his damaged brain could take. The last of the rat's systems shut down, and Snick watched as he unconsciously gurgled his last breath. She turned, and began walking quickly back toward the cannon. She had gotten far enough away so that she felt the blast as simply a loud cracking sound and rough shaking of the ground.

She rounded the corner she had taken and looked back over the village of Hearthstone. Where the cannon had been, there was now a crater about ten feet deep. Chunks of dirt and cobblestone were landing on streets and building tops in loud thunks. Snick ducked into the ale house, watching as debris rained down. After the bigger chunks, a steady rain of tiny iron particles, about the size of celery seeds, began. None of the other buildings were damaged, but every window in every structure in Hearthstone had shattered. The town was now littered with chunks of dirt, cobblestones, iron pellets, and glass. It was a grand mess, but Hearthstone still stood. Relieved, Snick left the ale house and began walking back toward Gurril's house, careful to watch her step to avoid cutting her feet on any debris.

Pepper scrambled to his feet as the rats— who had simply landed on all fours and immediately advanced toward the ferret when the concussion of the blast knocked them off their hind legs— snatched out clawed paws and snapped their teeth at him. He swung his sword in a short, downward arc, hacking the forepaw off one rat, who yowled in pain while blood shot out from the wound. The rats and Pepper scrambled more than fought, with a rat taking an occasional swipe at Pepper, and Pepper taking an occasional swipe back with his sword. Finally, the scramble ended with Pepper in a corner, four rats in front of him. They were joined by rat number five in short order.

Pepper's back was to the wall. He focused on the rats in front of him, and gripped the hilt of his sword, happy to have its long blade between him and his enemies. They charged in one large, fast, heaving wall at Pepper. He jabbed his sword straight out, poking one of the rats between the eyes with it. The beast's thick skull made the sword glance upward, and the rat backed out of the charge, yowling in pain. Pepper kicked out at another rat, who rolled to the side, knocking over the beast next to it. A quick swing of the sword caused the fourth rat to hesitate for just a second, but rat number five came up on Pepper's left side and sunk its teeth into his thigh.

Pepper's fur was still covered in dry blood from his experience with the mischief of one thousand smaller rats back at Goose Hill. Now fresh blood was added again to his matted mess of a coat. He drove the sword across his body and straight down into the ribs of the rat, running his blade completely though the animal. He felt the rat's jaws immediately relax as its eyes rolled back and it died. Thick blood poured from the wounds on either side of the animal's body as Pepper pulled his sword back out, dropping the rat to the floor.

The four remaining rats respaced themselves and faced Pepper again. There was a bit of space between each rat, and now Pepper saw something he hadn't seen before: the body of Jones, hollow from the shoulders to the hips, lying in a pile on the floor. He thought of how the man had brought him fish after Pepper spared his life. Pepper tried to push his thoughts of Jones to the back of his mind, focusing even more on the rats. In his heart, Pepper felt his emotions finally hollow away, leaving only the cold focus of battle.

8

Coska watched from the courtyard, his bark torn away completely around his trunk where the rats had chewed at him. He could feel that no more of his sap flowed through the area, and he realized that the rats had given him a death sentence by girdling his trunk. He already felt weaker, and wondered to himself how long it would be before the end would come.

Gurril lay on the floor, trying to look over to where the fight between Pepper and the rats took place, but he couldn't see it. Gurril hoped the ferret would remember everything he had been taught about fighting against a group. The warrior closed his eyes and focused on the lesson, knowing it would do no good for Pepper, but needing to keep his own mind busy.

They had been in the courtyard, training and talking. Pepper, at his sixteen-inch-tall stage, had just read a few chapters in various books offering advice about fighting against multiple attackers.

Pepper asked Gurril, "What would you say is the best way to face a group of enemies?"

Gurril grunted a thought and rubbed his chin. "Keep them in front of you. If they come at you singly, then it is just the same as fighting one-on-one. Stupid enemies fight this way. Smart enemies come at you all at once in charges. Fight each charge with quick blows, and wait for a kill shot. Have patience, and don't leave yourself open. Use quick, jabbing strikes. As you take out or injure the group members, it becomes a bit easier to handle each charge. After a couple of charges that result in a reduction of their numbers, most enemies will realize they can't get you that way. Hope that they become stupid and try to come at you individually rather than all at once. If not, just keep picking them off a little with each charge."

Gurril opened his eyes, and hoped again that Pepper would remember this lesson. He could hear the action behind him, but still couldn't turn his head and eyes enough to see a thing. The venom in his legs burned like fire, and Gurril knew his time was short.

9

Four rats glaring toward the ferret, one of them missing a right forepaw and another with a large gash between his eyes. Snarl, the big female leader, hissed and spit a bit of venom from her teeth at Pepper. He let it land on his blood-stained fur, and felt the burn of the previous attacker's venom running up the veins in his leg. They charged in another coordinated attack, and Pepper swung his sword across in a feint that caused two of the rats to stumble just enough for him to turn and face the other two as they came upon him. Snarl hit first, going for Pepper's left ribs, while the second rat curled behind the ferret and sunk its teeth into Pepper's shoulder and neck on his right side.

Pepper turned the blade first upward and then back, ramming it as hard as he could blindly behind him. The blade entered the rat who had bit his shoulder. It sunk in at the base of the beast's neck, and slid alongside its spine midway down the now squealing rat's back. Pepper turned his arms to rotate the blade upward, and the sword burst from the rat's back, sending a thick spray of blood shooting onto the wall behind the fight. As

316

the injured rat (Mr. One-Paw, Pepper noted) stumbled and fell into the hole, landing on top of the corpse of Billy, the other two rats jumped onto the giant, bleeding, fighting ferret and began to bite wildly at him.

Outside, Snick could hear fighting as she came closer to the house. Even though she was afraid, she felt an urge to try to help her friends. She knew they all had to be there. Pepper and Gurril (her boys, those boys she loved), Coska, and she could even see David standing outside the door, looking in at the ruckus she could only hear. She began running toward the house, not sure what she would do when she got there.

Inside, Pepper was covered again in biting, writhing rats. He couldn't score any hits at this range, and so he dropped his sword and began clawing and biting back at the rats. He sunk his teeth into one of them, and for the briefest moment became afraid that he would end up getting poisoned. That fear passed almost immediately as he realized that for the second time today, he was covered in rat bites. Only these rats were large and venomous. If he was going to be poisoned, the doom had already been set. Pepper was able to grab one biting head away from his body and punch at it with his balled-up fist. After four strong blows, the rat's eyes rolled back, and it slipped off of him, knocked out cold.

Snick entered the door at this point, dropping her bag full of casks on the floor in shock with the sight of Pepper fighting two rats. David the hawk was standing safely outside the door, but Snick did not order him in to fight. If she would have, the hawk would have obeyed. She knew the hawk was keen, and that if it could have helped Pepper, it would have joined the fight without an order. The action in the corner made her miss two things: first, the bleeding, filleted warrior she loved, lying on the floor in front of her; second, the gaping hole in the floor boards. Snick took two steps to jump onto the back of one of the rats biting Pepper, and noticed Gurril. She turned to stop and aid him, and promptly tumbled into the hole in the floor, landing on an injured and very angry one-pawed rat with his back torn open.

Gurril's vision began to double. He had seen Snick walk in, then gasp and disappear into the hole. He had no idea if the sharpened sticks were still there for her to fall onto. He didn't know that the pile of rats in the hole had made for a fall that had a surprisingly soft landing. He turned his eyes to the Coska tree, and wished he could tell the tree one more time before he died that he thought the former magician was the most incredible soul he'd ever met.

He hoped again that Snick wasn't hurt too badly when she fell into the hole. As much as he could move his mouth, he told her silently and without her there to hear, that he loved her. At that, Gurril closed his eyes and began letting himself fall into a pleasant feeling of sleep that he now understood to be death ushering itself upon him. He breathed quietly, finding a meditative state that not only took away his pain, but relaxed his calmed mind.

Pepper and two rats grappled and rolled around on the floor. At one point, Pepper was able to grab the front leg of one rat and use it as a shield against the other rat's chomping teeth. The rat bit deeply into the other, and the rat who had been bitten screamed blue murder. Pepper realized that the rat who had been bitten was a female. He had noted before that this same rat seemed to be the leader of the group. He wondered if he would ever learn exactly what role Joseph had played in this ruse.

In the hole, the injured rat was struggling to grab hold of Snick or to at least bite her. Pepper's sword tearing through the thing's back had sheered enough muscle in two that the damaged beast could only move its front legs in a limited range. Add to that the subtraction of a paw, and the rat was at a serious disadvantage. The rat knew this, and began to focus on trying to trip up Snick as she shimmied around him. She could quickly see that the rat was badly hurt, and she knew that if she could just hold out long enough, she might be able to live. She whistled a shrill pitch and kept dodging.

Outside the house, David heard the whistle and took one wing beat in. He dropped into the hole blindly, and quickly flapped out again as the rat inside with Snick almost grabbed him with its remaining, but limited, paw. David flew straight up, then dropped down on the rat's head. Snick could only see a scurrying of feathers and the desperate chomping of jaws. The rat's remaining paw clasped at the air, short of the hawk. When

David flapped his wings and exited the hole, he flew out the door again. Snick gasped at the horrible sight before her: David had torn out both of the rat's eyes, and it stared at the sky like a nightmare, blood oozing from its skull where just seconds before two black, hatred-filled orbs had been.

The beast turned its head and looked straight at Snick with its bloody sockets. It hissed blindly at her, and tried crawling toward her. She kicked out at it, knocking it to the side. Snick stood up and grabbed the floor boards, pulling herself out of the hole. As she scurried away from the rat, she heard its teeth clacking together behind her. She looked down into the hole at the rat as it chomped at the air around it, hoping for a bite of human flesh.

Pepper finally had a grab at the neck of each of the two rats he wrestled with, and he smashed their heads together as hard as he could. The poison from the bites was taking its effect on him now, and he moved slower than usual. Every nerve seemed to burn, and he could feel his internal organs spasm with pain. The two stunned rats both scrambled to their hind feet as Pepper picked up his sword once more.

Snick, seeing this, screamed "Hey!" to the smaller male rat on Pepper's right. Positions had been reversed, and now the rats had their backs to the wall, while Pepper and Snick stood facing the corner. The male rat turned its head and looked for the sound it had just heard, giving Pepper enough time to swing his sword in a fast arc, beheading the rat. Its body fell straight down like a sack of potatoes, claws and legs twitching. Blood pumped from the rat's neck for a few seconds, while Pepper and Snarl stared each other down. The rat that Pepper had knocked out with punches began coming to, and before the female could move to stop it from happening, Pepper drove the tip of his sword downward into the semi-conscious rat's chest.

He pulled the sword out with a smile. The female looked around her as the room grew quiet. The only sounds here now were the huffing and puffing of chests, and the chomping of the rat in the hole, who still desperately wanted to bite something. The bleeding finally took its toll, and with a huff, the rat in the hole dropped dead. Snarl knew she was beaten. She quietly prepared herself to be killed by the ferret when the oddest thing happened. The giant beast with a sword simply tipped over.

The poison had finally hit Pepper with its full strength. All his muscles seemed to give way at once, and the world spun as he fell to the ground, twitching slightly and searing with pain.

Snarl looked to Snick, and said in a matter-of-fact tone, "If you call your hawk in here, I'll kill it in front of you. If you don't call it in, I'll kill you and it will fly away from me where I can't reach it."

Snick stared back up at her in fear. Gurril was barely breathing and unconscious. Pepper was having a seizure on the floor in front of her, and the Coska tree was girdled. She stood facing the female rat.

With a shaky voice, full of fear and pain over the defeat she knew was imminent, Snick said, "No. You don't get to win." Tears rolled down her eyes.

The rat chuckled, still trying to catch its breath after the fight with Pepper. "You see, child, we have a whole mischief coming. They've been hidden in the walls of every building, and in tunnels at Goose Hill. Today, the rats conquer."

On the floor, Pepper's convulsing arm knocked over one of the casks Snick had brought with her. Another flop of his body covered his nose in the goop that ran out of the casks and onto the floor. Neither Snick nor the rat paid any attention to this. Snick swallowed hard and tried not to quake with fear as Snarl stepped toward her, walking on her hind legs and standing a full foot and a half taller than the woman. The rat grabbed the back of Snick's long, white hair and pulled it toward the floor so that Snick's face was forced upward. The two stared at each other for a few seconds.

The rat smiled. "Even for a human, you're a beauty. If you were a rat, you'd be weak. The males would rape you in great heaps. Maybe I'll save your corpse for them. They might like to try it on your dead, bloated— *guh!*"

Snick saw a look of surprise on the rat's face as its claw relaxed, letting go of her hair. Snick stepped back away from the beast, and watched as the tip of Pepper's sword pushed through its breast bone, then disappear back into Snarl's body. The giant female rat tipped forward, falling face down onto the floor before Snick's feet. Behind the rat was Pepper, still shaking a bit. He was breathing heavy and looked like he was in the greatest pain of his life. He fell back to the floor, and vomited as he rolled onto his side. His sword clanged on the floor next to him.

10

Snick scrambled over to her friend, looking back tentatively at her lover. "Pepper, how…"

He turned his head to her weakly, and smiled, using his long tongue to lick the tip of his nose. "One of your potions landed on me. Its either an antidote, or it has way too much caffeine to be healthy." He let his head thump back to the floor, and added, "Give it to Gurril. As much as you can cram in his mouth. It's the thick blue stuff there."

She scrambled back across the floor on her knees and with her left hand scooped up the thick blue anti-venom potion that had spilled on the floor. With her right hand, she forced Gurril's mouth open, and held it that way. She poured as much in as she could, then wiped the rest from her palm onto his lips. The potion slipped into the warrior's mouth and he coughed a bit, choking on it in his unconscious state.

Snick watched in suspense, and surveyed Gurril's horrible wounds. She didn't know if there would be enough healing potion for them. She would have to make more before his body healed itself very much, or he would not be helped by her concoction. Pepper crawled over to her, still weak. He tugged on her arm.

She turned to him. "Yes, Pepper? Are you feeling better."

The ferret slowly shook his head. He grit his teeth together and quietly said, "I think I need more."

She turned to the cask, and noted that it was empty. Snick pulled Pepper's head into her lap and pet back the hair on his face and head, rocking him gently.

"It's okay, Pepper." Now tears started streaming from her eyes, her breath hitching, "I can make more if you can just hold on for a bit."

321

She leaned down and kissed Pepper's forehead, then leaned over and kissed Gurril's forehead. The ferret's eyes rolled back and he passed out. Gurril's eyes slowly fluttered open, and he awoke.

He turned his eyes to her and, using all of his strength, whispered, "My love."

Outside, the first evening insects began to come out as the sun dipped a bit more than halfway below the horizon.

Snick let Pepper's head slip gently from her lap onto the floor. She smiled at Gurril, and said, "It's All right, Gurril. I can fix you. But only a little bit right now, okay?"

The warrior quietly grunted, and Snick slid the almost-empty cask of healing cream over to him. She turned the cask over above his right thigh, and the thick cream poured out into his wound there. The warrior bucked and grunted in pain. Had he been stronger, he would have screamed in pain and thrashed out. Snick pinched the two halves of muscle together, and Gurril grunted again in pain. She held his leg like this for a few moments, then let go. Although still covered in blood, the two chunks of muscle stayed together. The skin was even bound.

Snick stood, then ran out the door of the house. She screamed into the air toward the houses of the village, "People of Hearthstone! The rats are defeated! This is Snick, and I need your help to heal my boys Pepper and Gurril! Don't forget that I am magic, and I helped save this town! Come to Gurril's house now!"

She turned and re-entered the house, David the hawk hopping in behind her. She sat at Gurril's side again, and petted his hair back. Pepper was comatose and shaking, and Gurril was too weak to speak. Behind her, she heard a small, quiet whistle. She turned and saw David. The hawk hopped to her and rubbed its head against her thigh, showing her love by nuzzling her. She gently petted the hawk's soft head.

"David, I need you to get me a few things. Can you do that?"

The hawk hopped back and stood at attention for her. She smiled, and began giving him her shopping list of herbs, frog eyes, and other ingredients. He flew off in a rush, and now

322

Snick could hear a sound that gave her real hope: the slamming of doors as people left their homes.

11

She waited in the darkness as the first stars poked out to peer down on Hearthstone. It would be a cool night after the long, hot day. Snick hoped for a breeze as she sat alone, waiting. Not even David had returned yet. Snick was happy that Pepper had told her about his run-in with the rest of the mischief. Had she not known those rats were dead in a pile right now, she would have panicked. As it was, she kept herself busy checking on Gurril and Pepper and putting a thick coat of bark-repair potion on Coska's trunk where he had been gnawed at by the rats.

It was nearly morning before David showed up, his talons full of the things she had asked for. She began mixing as the hawk took rest in the Coska tree. As she mixed up another batch of antidote for Pepper, she hummed to herself. She only felt comfort in being near all her friends and caring for them. Just before dawn, both of Gurril's cats appeared from the courtyard, strolling in as they sniffed the air. They cautiously approached Gurril (who had long ago fallen back asleep), sniffed him a bit, then curled up on his chest. They lay there together purring, as residents of Hearthstone began arriving at the door with the various ingredients Snick had asked them to go into the woods to gather for her.

By noon of the day after battle, she was pouring antidote into Pepper's mouth. The unconscious ferret didn't choke the way Gurril had, and this worried Snick. She turned to mixing the healing cream for Gurril. The scene around her was an incredible mix of peace and death. Coska, soaking up the light of the noonday sun, with a sleeping hawk in his branches. Purring cats asleep on Gurril. Jones, dead and torn to shreds, surrounded by the warriors he helped save. Flowers littered the floor around Pepper and Gurril. The villagers had brought them along with the supplies Snick had asked for from the forests and fields surrounding the town.

Gurril woke up again near suppertime. He grunted and smacked his lips, and Snick smiled as his previously immobile

323

right leg slowly bent and straightened a few times. She sat next to Gurril and kissed him gently on the lips.

"Shh," she told him, "You're still bleeding a bit. I need to heal you more."

He cleared his throat weakly and tried to mouth some words, but Snick placed her fingertips over his lips.

She shook her head lightly, and said, "No talking. You're too weak right now. I have a healing cream almost ready for you." She kissed him again, and went back to mixing her healing cream.

It was nightfall on the day after the battle. Gurril had turned a very alarming shade of gray, and Snick placed a small chunk of bread in his mouth.

"Chew on this while I heal you, love."

He did as he was told, and as he chewed, he felt the incredible pain of his body sewing itself back together with incredible speed. His mind reeled at how much it must have hurt Pepper to go through his size changes. He grunted, swallowed the bread, and passed out again from pain. Snick watched and held his damaged body together long enough for it to heal. By the time she was finished, Gurril was back together in one solid piece. Now he just needed a lot of nourishment to replace the blood he had lost. Snick said a silent thank-you prayer to every star in the night sky that none of Gurril's wounds had severed an artery.

She used the rest of the healing cream on Pepper's various wounds, and was surprised when the ferret's eyes popped open.

"Ouch!" he griped loudly.

Snick jumped and yipped in surprise. "Pepper! You're all right!"

She scooped her hands around his back and squeezed him as hard as she could, crying with joy. In the courtyard behind them, the Coska tree shivered just a bit with joy, its bark regrowing fast under a gooey mix Snick had coated over the damage the rats had done.

12

That last night of healing was also a night of celebration for Hearthstone. The townsfolk helped move Pepper and Gurril to their beds. When Pepper was helped up, he looked down at the corpse of his friend Jones, who lay dead on the floor. The ferret sobbed, dropping his head in sadness as he gingerly walked with a helper under each arm from the living area to his bedroom.

Gurril was next and had to be carried with a stretcher. Cami took his vital signs, and gave Snick instructions for caring for him until he was stronger. That night as she lay next to him, they spoke softly of future plans.

As the universe turned above them, Snick told Gurril, "I have a vision to share with you. Coska gave it to me a long time ago now."

"Are you sure you should tell me?" His voice wasn't much more than a whisper, still.

"Positive. He told me that if I tell you about the vision it will come true, and that if I don't tell you about it, it won't. I want it— I *need* it to come true, Gurril."

"What is it?"

"You and I will marry, and we'll have three children." She smiled at him, joyful tears pooling in her eyes. He smiled back brightly. They kissed and made more plans for the future.

Chapter 10: The Offer

1

Pepper, Gurril, and Snick meditated under the shade of the Coska tree. A warm breeze blew through the grassy park that had once been the site of the Hearthstone town warrior's home. In the days after the events the people of the town had taken to calling "The Rat War", the house where the day had been won was torn down. It didn't feel right to anyone that it should be repaired and lived in again; such a thing could cause a haunting.

The park was meant to be a memorial site for those who had died. Buried under the grass of the park were the human victims. The dead rats had been chopped to bits and burned over a fire of coal and oak. Pepper had led the townsfolk to the piles of small rats he had killed, and they were summarily soaked in kerosene and burned as well. Shortly after, volunteers began razing Goose Hill.

The air in Hearthstone smelled of the freshly cut stalks of stonecorn and wheat in the fields around the town. Near the river, fishing boats bobbed and the alehouse brewed beer and served it to fishers, farmers, and hunters. David the hawk rustled restlessly in a branch of the Coska tree, looking down at his mistress. A new feeling stirred inside of him, and he yearned for wild freedom, even though he loved Snick. The bird did not know what it was he yearned for, but he found himself leaving for lonely night flights more and more often. Gurril's two cats rested on their usual branch, asleep in a pocket of warm sunlight.

A robed figure approached the three meditating friends. Snick popped her eyes open and looked up to see the great wizard, Martin.

She smiled up to him, and said "Coska told me you'd be coming."

The wizard smiled back down at the beautiful young woman who looked up at him, while her two companions opened their eyes to see who it was that she spoke to. Gurril immediately began to rise, and Martin gestured for him to remain seated.

327

"Sit, Gurril, sit. I came as soon as I could after word reached Girand of your war against the rats." He reached out and gripped a branch of the Coska tree. "So, this is the young wizard who impressed me so by turning a hawk— that very one, if I recall correctly—into a dove." Martin turned to address the tree directly. "You, Coska, are the most powerful wizard this land has ever seen. I knew it that Beating Day when you became a defender of this town."

Martin sighed, and gripped the branch harder. It was a kind, almost reverent gesture, and Gurril thought that the wizard looked as if he was shaking the hand of some type of immortal being.

Martin turned to the group. "You must be Pepper. My goodness! I've heard tales of you, and I wanted to come meet you myself."

Pepper, in his over seven-foot-tall state, smiled up at the man. "It's a pleasure. Gurril has told me of your kindness and great power. It is a great honor to meet you, Sir."

Martin smiled broadly back at Pepper. "The honor is mine. I was busy with some important things, and couldn't get away as soon as I would have liked. There'll be other visitors like me, Pepper, but we can talk about that later."

He looked to Snick once more. "The tales of your beauty can't even begin to describe you. When the messenger told me about you, I thought he had exaggerated. I see now that exaggeration was not even possible. You are a dream, Young Lady."

Martin turned once more to the tree, and looked at David. "This hawk fought bravely, too. He needs to fly free now, though. He's of breeding age, and must be set wild." The wizard closed his eyes for a bit.

In David's mind, the realization of breeding suddenly and forcefully fell upon him. He shook his feathers and looked to the woman who had been his mistress. He loved her, and promised his heart that if he lived beyond breeding age, he would come to her again. Snick recognized that David was looking at her as a mistress for the last time. Tears welled up in her eyes as the hawk hopped out of the tree and nuzzled her knee one last time while she sat cross-legged on the grass. In a rush

328

of wind, the hawk's wings pushed him up and away from her, into the wild beyond the town.

Gurril looked to the ferret on his left, the woman on his right, then to the tree before him. It was easy for him to feel left out, and the warrior began to wonder if Martin would start telling his cats how terrific they were, as well. Martin chuckled, and looked Gurril in the face. In that instant, a certain knowledge came over Gurril; this wizard before him could read thoughts.

"Gurril," he began, "We, the four of us that is, need to talk. I have some business to attend to around the town, first. Can we meet for dinner at your temporary housing?"

Gurril looked back up at Martin. "Yes, of course. We are staying in two apartments above the ale house."

Pepper chimed in once more. "Mine has more room. Just come up the stairs and look for the red door."

Martin nodded, smiled at the group, and walked away.

2

On the island of Flamingo, Atticus lay in a bed. He was cared for by three nurses who took shifts changing his linens and pouring a finely blended liquid diet of fruits and mashed fish down a tube that led to his stomach. They rarely looked at the gaping hole that had once been his face.

He had no jaw bone, no eyes, no nose, and no ears. He was hollow from his forehead and cheek bones down, and woke every morning to searing pain. Atticus wished over and over for death or comfort, knowing he was doomed to neither. He lay there, being fed but wasting away, unable to do much besides sit up. The world was a place no longer of senses to the man; the only real perceptions he had were of pain or hunger.

A boat, large and with a small crew of sailors from the Loath region, bobbed next to the king's hut. Inside the hut, Gregor sat on his driftwood throne, facing a tall thin man of about sixty. While this would be young for any Flamingo resident, this was old to most other humans, and Gregor always thought it odd that mainlanders had such a short lifespan. The thin man, who was old but not quite elderly yet, had short light brown hair and piercing blue eyes. His teeth were spectacularly white, and he wore loose blue robes that looked to have been made of felt.

Gregor stared at the man, thinking. The hut was crowded with Gregor's guards, sailors, and this tall man who called himself Lucian.

Gregor huffed. "He is our warrior. A hero to us. How do we know you will treat him as you say you will?"

Lucian smiled at the king, and clapped his hands together twice. "A gift, to show you that my efforts are only for good."

He held his right palm out in front of him, and the skin on the palm began to boil. A large green topaz erupted from Lucian's palm, along with five gold pieces that tumbled to the floor.

Gregor looked to the floor, then back up to Lucian. "This *is* for the best, isn't it. You've presented yourself as a kind man, Lucian. I believe you will take care of Atticus as you say, and that he will be happier at the warrior retirement village." He sighed, actually more of a huff again, and scratched the back of his head. "Two hundred more gold pieces, ten more topaz of that size, and his nurses go with him. That's my final offer."

Lucian smiled, and bowed slightly to the king. "As you wish. And you have my word that he will be treated almost as if he were a king. No more pain, no more suffering."

Gregor narrowed his eyes. "Lucian, I don't trust wizards. If you experiment on him…"

"I won't dream of it, Sire."

Lucian turned to his crew of men. As with all the people of their region, they were covered in light brown coarse hair and stood only about four feet tall.

"Load Atticus onto our boat, and make for the shore just west of Pathnore."

The Loathian captain clicked his heals together and said, "Yes, Lucian. I'll also make arrangements so that his nurses will have a cabin."

Lucian bowed his head to the short, hairy man who ran the affairs of Lucian's boat, saying, "Thank you, Danforth."

Donatello Destone, being no fool, had delivered two bottles of his best wine to Pepper's apartment free of charge as soon as he heard that the wizard Martin was going to be dining with the town defenders. Business was good, and there had been a lot of visitors to the town, wanting to see where the War of the Rats had taken place. Donatello had put up a few plaques around the ale house, outlining the action that had taken place there. The wood floors had dark stains where death had been dealt. The villagers mostly ignored them, and the visitors relished them. Around the town, shops were popping up to serve those who came to see the town that had defeated a mischief of rats in a great battle.

So far three new town elders had been chosen by vote. They would confer with each other for a few days, then choose four more elders to join them. The old law had always been to replace elders this way if all seven died; power in the population to vote for all seven was limited to stop an overzealous political process from taking shape. Martin had spent the day meeting with the three new elders, and when he arrived at the ale house, he said not a word to anyone, moving straight up the stairs to the red door at the end of the hallway. His robes trailed in flutters behind him. Those who noticed the robes and their unnatural movements thought the long cape-like fabric seemed to linger behind the wizard a bit, perhaps to watch for any followers. But then, robes could never think for themselves to do such a thing, could they?

He motioned to the door, and it opened itself onto a surprised group of warriors who had been expecting a knock. Martin smiled as he strolled in, and his robe flowed out to the door and pushed it closed. He seated himself at the small table Pepper had arranged for the dinner. The table was set with a plate on each side, and the group sat down together.

Martin took in a deep whiff of the dinner that had been waiting for him. "Mmmmmm! Pike! And hot rolls! Tell me, Gurril, what kind of wine have you chosen for us this evening?"

Gurril unfolded his napkin, and said, "Afton. A sweet white."

"Good! Good! Tell me, Gurril, do you, Snick, and Pepper have interest in working for me rather than a town that is becoming a tourist trap?"

The wizard asked this in a nonchalant manner, but Gurril was taken aback by the question anyway.

"Working for you? Why would you need us?"

Martin nodded as he cut away a portion of fish and set it on his plate. He looked to the group sitting around him.

"What I tell you now must stay secret. If you try to tell anyone, I'll know. Do any of you doubt that?"

They all shook their heads and murmured "No".

When Martin was satisfied, he said in the same matter-of-fact tone he had used with Gurril, "I've been tasked by the Coska tree with raising a small army to fight a legion of undead. If the towns and villages knew this, they would think that I meant to become a tyrant, using the Coska tree as a logic shield. Gurril, I need a military leader to plan battles and train warriors. Pepper, I need you, too. You have many talents yet to discover about yourself. And Snick," he said turning to her and smiling, "I need someone who can make healing potions and other magical concoctions." They all stared at him incredulously while he buttered a hot roll and took a bite from it. While chewing, he added, "Oh, and we'll be starting an academy for young magic-makers. Coska has already agreed to be the headmaster."

In the night air outside the ale house, Hearthstone sat at peace. The bread continued to bake in ovens, the fish and game continued to thrive in the hills and fields, and in the snowy lands of Garthore, an army of undead gathered.

Acknowledgements

As an independent author, I have certain advantages and disadvantages that authors who are aligned with a publisher do not have. One of the advantages I have is the ability to hand-pick a team of people to provide input and necessary aid. I have been fortunate to find people who understand my creative goals and are willing to help me achieve them.

First, to my family for their love and kindness.

This book would be a lot more difficult for you to decipher without the wonderful proofreading of Diane Wells. I am by nature spelunking-impaired (damn you, auto-correct!) and my grammar ain't always so good. Her help in this area is invaluable and she is appreciated not just by me but by everyone who reads this book.

The cover art for this book was created by JD Ryan. He has done a wonderful job bringing the feel of the book out in art, and I know that many of you reading this picked it up because of his creative interpretation of my request to create something "simple, that reflects the literary value of the story and is reminiscent of two of my favorite book covers—*To Kill a Mockingbird*, and *The Great Gatsby*." I have always been most fond of cover art that follows the basic tenet of keeping things simple and related to the idea of the story, and I think that he has done a great job.

Finally, I have to give credit to my wife Melissa, who read through the first draft of this novel and started her notes with advice to describe Gurril's war hammer in more detail, so it didn't sound like I was using it as a penis metaphor (it was really good advice; if you could see the first draft, you'd be giggling right now). Her insight and input, especially into the mysteries of the female mind, has been incredibly helpful.